# BETWEEN
# THE LINES

# BETWEEN THE LINES

*a novel*

## ERIN KLINGLER

Covenant Communications, Inc.

Cover images: *Golden Gate Bridge-Night* © md8speed, *Agent* © duncan1890 courtesy iStockphoto.

Cover design copyrighted 2010 by Covenant Communications, Inc.

Published by Covenant Communications, Inc.
American Fork, Utah

Printed in the United States of America
First Printing: May 2010

17 16 15 14 13 12 11 10      10 9 8 7 6 5 4 3 2 1

ISBN 10: 1-59811-766-1
ISBN 13: 978-59811-766-0

For my dear friend CC. Your help with the first incarnation of this story caused it to be something very special and dear to my heart, and for that I am eternally grateful. I can only hope to someday be as talented a writer as you.

# Acknowledgments

Many thanks to:

Noelle Perner, my editor extraordinaire. Words cannot express how much I appreciate your tireless efforts to make this novel the best it could be. I couldn't have gotten here without you.

Cindy Bezas, Carole Thayne, and Julie Bellon, for reading this in its various stages of completion and offering suggestions and such valuable insights. You made this so much better!

BJ Rowley, my fellow LDStorymaker and "official" San Francisco consultant. Thanks for answering my Bay Area questions and making sure I got it right.

Suzanne Reese, for passing along the hilarious, true-life cooking disaster that I use later in this story. To save her reputation, however, I should point out that the mistake wasn't her own doing!

My fellow LDStorymakers, who are the best friends and cheerleaders anybody could have. Thank you so much for your help, words of encouragement, and all that you teach me. I love you guys! And special thanks to Annette Lyon, my LDStorymaker grammar guru. I was happy to give you a reason to break out your beloved OED.

My husband and children, who accept me for the hopeless romantic that I am, and put up with freezer dinners and crazy bursts of inspiration that send me running for my computer during the months when I'm writing. Thanks for understanding that, to me, books (both writing and reading) are like having air to breathe. I love you!

My dear friend Barb Knutson. How I didn't bore you to tears during the hours we spent discussing this story, I'll never know, but I love you for putting up with me. I consider your friendship one of the biggest treasures in my life.

My favorite librarians, Mandy Bush and Christine Wilson. I love seeing you when I go in to pick up the stacks of books I always reserve. Those books are my motivation and inspiration, not to mention my escape—but so are you! Thanks for your cheerful chatter and your interest in what I'm writing. What would I do without you?

And last but certainly not least, to the young women in my ward. You amaze and inspire me every week as I watch you become the incredible women you are becoming. Thanks for continually asking me about this book and motivating me with your interest. You're wonderful, and I love you!

# Prologue

The front door was ajar. Bryce's hand stilled, his key poised in front of the lock. *Someone's been in my house.*

His heart thundered in his ears, silencing the sound of crickets and the rumbling of nighttime traffic down the street. He glanced around, searching the late-night darkness. Nothing appeared out of the ordinary. The windows of the neighboring townhouses were dark, which was to be expected at this hour—Bryce's swing shift at the precinct had just ended, and it was after one in the morning.

Bryce turned his attention back to the door. Studying it more closely, he saw that the wood around the dead bolt was intact. No signs of forced entry.

His confidence in his initial assessment wavered. Maybe he was jumping to conclusions. He'd been preoccupied lately. How many times had he locked his keys in his car over the last two months? It was possible that he'd simply forgotten to lock the door or even pull it firmly closed. That door did require quite a tug to get it to latch, after all.

But as Bryce lifted his hand to push open the door, he again hesitated. *Maybe I should call for backup.* As quickly as the thought came, though, he pushed it aside. If he called for backup and it turned out that he'd only forgotten to lock his front door, the guys at the precinct would never let him live it down. *No, I'll check things out first. If anything seems unusual inside, I'll come right back out and call for backup.*

Bryce's leg suddenly itched under his ankle holster, as if reminding him that he had his off-duty gun. With a slow, wary motion, he leaned down, unsnapped the gun, and slipped it from the holster in one deft movement. Having the gun in his hand gave him more confidence. He took a deep breath and inched the door open.

The hinges creaked, and Bryce cringed and waited. If there *was* someone in the house, he'd just alerted whoever it was to his presence.

Holding his breath, he took a cautious step inside. He strained to hear the sound of anything amiss. All was quiet. The only sound was the soft ticking of the clock in the entryway.

Bryce could feel the adrenaline pumping through his veins as he took a step toward the living room. A floorboard creaked slightly above him, and he jerked his head toward the ceiling. He stared and listened and waited, but no other sound came. *It's an old home,* he reminded himself. *Things creak all the time.*

Still, he curled his fingers more tightly around the gun before moving silently into the living room. What he saw froze him in place. The room was in shambles. The drawers from the computer desk had been pulled out and dumped; the shelves of the entertainment center had been cleared, the contents scattered across the floor; the couch cushions and throw pillows had been pitched halfway across the room.

Stunned, Bryce lowered his gun slightly and stared at the mess. It took him a moment to regain the presence of mind to pull out his cell phone and press the speed dial button for the precinct dispatcher. As he held the phone to his ear, his thoughts whirled in confusion. *Who did this?*

His gut told him this wasn't a burglary. The television and stereo equipment—easily the most valuable things in his small townhouse—hadn't been touched. Nor had his computer. But upon further scrutiny, he saw that his computer CDs and backup disks had been strewn about, many of the cases lying open and empty. It appeared that whoever had done this had been looking for something.

*Looking for something specific.*

Bryce's blood ran cold.

*They know.*

His heart pounded in his chest, and he took a step backward. The DA's office. The senator. The tip from the anonymous source. The cover-up he'd discovered. They were onto him.

A sound to his left caused Bryce to whirl. An unmasked man in dark clothes stood at the bottom of the stairs—only feet away. In his hand, the dull black finish of the Glock seemed to absorb the moonlight streaming in through the kitchen window. The silencer on the gun told Bryce that this guy was here for one reason, as did the fact that he wasn't wearing a mask. The man wasn't worried about being identified.

Bryce stared into the man's cold, gray eyes, and a bead of sweat broke out on his forehead. His fingers tightened instinctively around his weapon. He saw the man's eyes flicker to the movement, then shift back to Bryce's anxious gaze.

A twitch at the corner of the intruder's mouth became a half smile, half snarl. He wasn't the least bit concerned about Bryce's gun, which wasn't trained on a target. That meant he knew the statistics. Three-quarters of a second—that's how long it took the human body to react. Even if Bryce's gun were trained on him, the intruder could bury a hollow-point round in Bryce's chest before Bryce had time to react to the shot. He had the upper hand, and he knew it. Even if the police dispatcher answered Bryce's call right now, there would be no stopping what was about to happen.

Frozen with dread and disbelief, Bryce watched as the man's finger twitched against the trigger. Standing there, staring down the barrel of the Glock, Bryce realized that trying to defend himself would be useless. It was over.

In the next instant, a blinding light accompanied the explosive sound of the bullet being fired from the gun.

# CHAPTER 1

*Several hours earlier . . .*

With weary fingers, Sydney typed the final words of her story and sent the file to Carl Calhoun, her editor in chief. Then she leaned back in her chair and sighed in relief.

She was done. The realization left her elated—and exhausted. She'd been working so hard and for so long on this investigation. Now that all the evidence had been gathered, every source had been checked out, and every fact had been documented, she felt too tired to even move from her chair. But she also felt an incredible sense of exhilaration, knowing that between her exposé in yesterday's paper and the follow-up article she'd just finished for tomorrow morning's edition, heads were going to roll.

Carl had been concerned when she'd gone to him a month earlier, asking to be put on the story. Without hard evidence, a story implicating several high-profile businessmen and city officials could cause the *San Francisco Chronicle* a world of trouble. But even he hadn't been able to find fault with the tirelessly obtained evidence she'd presented, which backed up what was turning out to be one of the most incredible exposés the newspaper had ever printed. The articles also presented prosecutors with enough evidence to make the necessary indictments. It was investigative journalism at its best.

*Dang, I'm good!* Sydney congratulated herself, a confident smile crossing her face. In the few years she'd been a reporter, she'd built a name for herself by writing stories that exposed everything from money-laundering schemes to gun-running operations. She had dealt devastating blows to several local crime lords, thereby helping clean up her corner of the world. If something was hidden, she would find it. Everyone knew she was the best.

Lately, though, being the best at her job didn't seem to be enough. She had the persistent, nagging feeling that something was missing from her life. Something . . .

"Sydney! Where's your follow-up article?"

The voice jerked Sydney back to the present. She turned to see a familiar scowl on her editor in chief's stern, dark face as he stormed about the newsroom making sure everyone was going to meet the evening deadline.

"It's done," she called back. "I just sent it to you."

He nodded with satisfaction, but his mouth maintained its firm line. "Great. Now get out of here. Go home and get some sleep. That's an order."

Sydney let a weary smile slip out, and she pushed her chair back from her desk. "No arguments from me. G'night, Chief."

"'Night, Sydney." This time his voice was a little less gruff. He turned and headed back down the row of desks to hassle other reporters about their deadlines.

Sydney shut down her computer then stood and collected her attaché and jacket. She had just turned to leave when she remembered her cell phone. It had been on her desk earlier.

She looked at the mess on her desk in dismay. Her desk always resembled a battlefield after she had devoted several days to a big story, but this was ridiculous. Unkempt piles of research sat everywhere, and her stacked IN and OUT boxes were nowhere to be seen amidst the clutter. A decidedly browning plant sat in one corner, with only the tops of the wilting leaves visible to pronounce its unhappy state. More than one fast-food wrapper peeked up from the sea of paperwork, reminding her that it had been several days since she'd eaten a decent meal. And if anyone needed further proof of how hard she'd worked this week, the now-empty small glass canister that was usually filled with peanut M&Ms was evidence that she had been suppressing stress with chocolate.

Sydney made a face. Had she really eaten two pounds of M&Ms this week? She must have. Nobody else in the newsroom was brave enough to try to take any. A colleague had once joked that she was like a pit bull guarding its bone when it came to her M&Ms.

With a defeated sigh, she set her attaché back down and started to collect the food wrappers. She was too tired to tackle the rest of the mess tonight, but at least she could throw those away before a science experiment began to develop on her work space over the weekend. The excavation of a small Chinese takeout box unearthed her cell phone. She slid it into her coat pocket, then turned back to her tidying. With the last of the food wrappers deposited in her garbage can, she decided to call it a night.

Just as she was settling the strap of her attaché onto her shoulder, her desk phone rang. She stared at it for a moment, contemplating whether or not to answer. It had been a long day, and there was nothing she wanted more than to go home and unwind. In the end, her curiosity won out. She picked up the phone and put it to her ear. "Sydney Hallam."

There was a long pause on the other end of the line. Then a man spoke, his voice wary. "Ms. Hallam?"

"Yes?"

Another pause. "What's your policy about keeping sources confidential?"

Sydney lowered herself into her chair, her curiosity piqued. "I never reveal a source, Mr. . . . ?"

"Davies," the man answered after a moment. He took a long breath, then went on. "I overheard a conversation that indicated that some high-ranking officials were involved in something illegal. If I pass along the information, can you promise to keep me anonymous?"

She scrambled to dig out a pen and notepad from her desk drawer. "Of course. Nobody will ever know where I got the information. What do you have?"

"Not on the phone. I want to meet."

She nodded. "When and where?"

There was a brief silence on his end, as if he were considering. "Tomorrow morning, say seven o'clock? At the eastern entrance to Golden Gate Park at Haight Street."

Sydney scribbled down the information. "That works for me. How will I know who you are?"

"I know who you are, Ms. Hallam. I'll find you." And with that, the line went dead.

A shiver ran up her spine as she hung up the phone. The guy had sounded scared, which probably meant that whatever he'd overheard was big. And there was nothing Sydney loved more than a scandal.

She tore the paper off the notepad and slipped it into her jacket pocket. Then she grabbed her things and headed out into the autumn night. She hurried to the parking garage across the street, but as she rounded the corner and approached her silver sedan, her steps slowed out of habit. It was a fact that her investigative reporting made more enemies than friends. This exposé would probably make her more of a target than ever. She knew there were risks in her line of work, but, strangely enough, that's what made her feel alive. It was an adrenaline rush, and it was addictive.

With a critical eye, Sydney glanced over her car for any signs of tampering. When nothing appeared out of the ordinary, she hit the UNLOCK button on the remote, climbed in, and started the engine. She headed for home through San Francisco's Friday night traffic, expertly negotiating the steep hills, hairpin turns, and one-way streets that made up the city she loved. A short time later she pulled into her apartment building's underground parking garage and then rode the elevator up to her fifth-floor apartment.

When the elevator chimed and the door slid open, Sydney stepped out and crossed the hall to her apartment. She was just inserting her key into the lock when the door to the next apartment opened a few inches. A head with a bright blue, clear plastic cap covering a dozen or more hot pink rollers poked through the crack.

Sydney raised her eyebrows at her elderly neighbor. "Hello, Agnes. Nice hairdo."

Agnes snorted in response and stepped the rest of the way out of her apartment. She was dressed in a wild, floral-print robe and bright pink slippers that almost matched the color of her hair rollers. In her arms she held a tiny white poodle with little red bows secured above each ear. "Don't get smart with me, young lady," Agnes scolded, yet an unmistakable note of affection contradicted her words. "You're looking rather tired and run-down, if you ask me. What have I told you about working too hard?"

Sydney smiled and repeated the words Agnes had told her many times before: "That I'm going to grow old before my time and end up an old maid." Then she glanced pointedly at the little dog her neighbor was holding, and her voice took on a light, teasing tone. "Like you, perhaps? Living alone with only a dog for a roommate?"

Agnes's eyebrows furrowed. "Never you mind about that. This isn't about me, this is about you. You need to have a little fun once in a while, instead of working at that newspaper all hours of the day and night."

Sydney stepped away from her door and closed the distance between herself and her neighbor, then reached out to rub the dog's ears. The dog responded by pressing its head into Sydney's hand, enjoying the attention. "Princess sure is sweet," Sydney said.

"To you." Agnes smiled. "She takes her time warming up to people, but once she does she's sweet to them. In the meantime, strangers better watch their ankles."

Sydney laughed and gave Princess one more pat. Then she let her hand fall back to her side and took another look at her neighbor's curler-clad hair. "Got a hot date tonight, Agnes?"

"One never knows." Agnes flashed a cryptic smile. "Just because I'm old doesn't mean I can't have a life. And that holds true for you, too, dear. Are you going out tonight? It *is* Friday."

Sydney felt a pang of sadness, but she pushed it aside and shook her head. "Not tonight. I think I'll curl up with some ice cream and a good book. I'm tired."

Agnes made a tsk-tsk sound and shook her head reprovingly. "You're young and beautiful, Sydney. You probably have a dozen dashing young men eager to take you out. You should take one of them up on his offer."

"Maybe sometime." Sydney shrugged. "None of them interest me, I guess."

"Interest, schminterest. I'm not saying you have to marry one of them. Just go out! Having a life outside of that newspaper would do you some good."

"I know. It's just . . . Maybe I'm looking for something that doesn't exist." She paused a moment, afraid of moving into territory that was better left unexplored. In an attempt to lighten the mood, she grinned and met Agnes's gaze. "I guess I'm waiting for that knight in shining armor to sweep me off my feet, just like you are."

Agnes laughed. "I always knew there was a hopeless romantic in you beneath that hard-nosed reporter act you put on." She reached out to pat Sydney's arm. "Can I convince you to come with me to church this Sunday?"

Sydney hesitated. Church attendance had been a touchy subject with her during the last several years. But Agnes had been assigned to be her visiting teacher when Sydney moved in, and she'd never stopped working to get Sydney to go to church with her. Once in a while Sydney would go, but more often than not, she found herself declining Agnes's invitation, just as she did now.

"I'm sorry, Agnes. I can't go this week. One of my friends from work had surgery yesterday, and a bunch of us are helping her this weekend by running errands and stuff. I said I'd help her with some dusting and vacuuming on Sunday morning. Maybe next week."

Agnes frowned, but she nodded. "I'll hold you to that, you know. At least read the Relief Society lesson. I'm going to ask you what it's about, so you'd better study up."

Sydney laughed. "Deal."

Agnes said good night and went back into her apartment, her dog still cradled in her arms.

Sydney smiled. Despite their age difference, she thought of Agnes as a good friend, and in many ways as the mother she didn't have. Turning back to her own apartment, she unlocked her door and went inside. She dropped her keys and attaché on the credenza beside the door, slipped out of her jacket, and kicked off her shoes. Then she crossed the darkened living room to the floor-to-ceiling windows at the far end that overlooked the bustling city.

For several minutes she stood at the window, staring out at the flickering lights below. It was a beautiful sight, one she never tired of. It had soothed her many a time after a long, stressful day of work. But tonight, even the spectacular view of the city couldn't soothe the nagging sensation rising within her that something was off-kilter.

*It's the after-story blues,* she reasoned. *I always feel like this after a big story breaks. All those weeks of tracking down leads and digging up dirt—it's only natural that I'd feel a sense of letdown.*

Somehow, though, she couldn't quite convince herself that this was the only reason she felt the way she did. She felt restless. Discontented. Despite everything she had going for her, she felt strangely empty.

Her gaze shifted, and she caught the reflection of her face in the glass. Agnes was right. She did look tired. The lines around her eyes suggested a need for a good night's sleep—or two or three—and her hair was mussed from a long, hard day. She lifted her hand to smooth the stray strands of shoulder-length brown hair back into place as she tried to analyze her emotions. She had a good career, a decent apartment in a safe part of town, and a life that was her own. She could come and go as she pleased.

*Then why am I not happy? What is it that I think I'm missing in my life?*

A low growl from her stomach interrupted her musings. She made her way toward the kitchen to see what leftovers might be in her fridge, but as she passed the sliding glass door, the moonlight spilling across the balcony beckoned her. She slid the door open and stepped out.

The cement was cool beneath her bare feet as she walked to the edge and rested her forearms on the wrought-iron railing. She stood there a moment, looking out over the city lights, then closed her eyes and drew in a long, deep breath of the cool night air.

Sydney loved nighttime. She'd always felt that there was something soothing about the night—the inky black sky sprinkled with stars, the cool breeze that tickled her face, the feeling of oneness with the universe. It was a feeling she had only at night, when the darkness seemed to ease her repressed heartache and mask the cares of the world behind the veil of moonlight. It quieted her doubts and fears and freed her mind. She'd done some of her best brainstorming on this patio, curled up in a blanket with her laptop in the cushioned chaise.

The breeze picked up, causing an unexpected chill to run down her back. She stared out over the horizon. Something felt different . . . something she couldn't quite put her finger on. In some strange, eerie way, it felt like there was change looming on the horizon.

She wondered fleetingly if the strange sensations she felt had anything to do with the unusual phone conversation she'd had earlier with her anxious new source. He knew something—something big enough to scare him. Sydney often had sources approach her wanting to remain anonymous. Not many of them seemed to fear for their lives, however. This was going to be big. She could feel it. Maybe the change she felt coming had something to do with this Mr. Davies.

She shivered and wrapped her arms around herself. It was getting late. With one last, lingering look at the stars overhead, she turned and went inside, sliding the door shut behind her.

\* \* \*

The next morning, anticipation of her meeting with the mysterious Mr. Davies woke Sydney even before her alarm clock went off. She dressed and did her hair and makeup, then went into the kitchen for breakfast. She opened the cupboard but spotted only one nearly empty box of cereal inside.

*I've got to go grocery shopping.* She grimaced at the thought. Reaching for the last clean bowl, she shot a look of disdain at the pile of dirty dishes in the sink. *And do the dishes.*

She emptied the last of the cereal into her bowl, poured the last of the milk over it, and ate it hurriedly, standing at the counter. Then she set her bowl in the sink, grabbed her jacket and purse, and headed out. It was a beautiful day, with only a hint of fog for a change and a bright blue sky that was textured with a scattering of clouds. She drove to Golden Gate Park with the windows down, enjoying the crisp morning breeze blowing in off the ocean.

When she neared Haight Street, she steered into the first open parking spot she saw and hurried to the park entrance. She glanced at her watch. 6:52. She was a few minutes early. But early was better. It didn't give nervous sources time to reconsider.

She sat on the low wall near the stone columns to watch the other early risers enjoying the September morning. Some people whizzed past on roller blades while others jogged, their iPods isolating them from those around them. The park was always a busy place, with an average of 75,000 visitors a weekend. Sydney knew that this was the reason her source had chosen to meet her here on a Saturday morning. It was a good place to fade into the crowd.

Long minutes passed, and Sydney grew more anxious. She glanced down at her watch. 7:01. Then 7:10. Then 7:15. Where was he?

Deciding to call her voice mail at the *Chronicle* to see if Mr. Davies had left her a message saying he'd be late, she pulled out her cell phone. But when she got through, the automated recording told her she had no new messages.

With a sigh, she ended the call and dropped her phone back into her purse. She was just going to have to be patient. It was a big city. People got stuck in traffic every day. He was probably just running late.

But by 7:45, she realized she was going to have to face facts. Mr. Davies wasn't coming.

With one last, wistful look around, she headed for her car. She could only hope she hadn't missed out on something big.

# CHAPTER 2

"That would be great. When would be a good time for me to get that from you?" Justin Micklesen secured the phone between his ear and shoulder as he listened carefully and scribbled down the information.

Out of the corner of his eye, Justin saw someone approaching. He looked up to see Brad Nelson, his friend and coworker, standing beside him and tapping his watch impatiently.

Justin held up a finger and turned his attention back to the caller. "Uh-huh," he said into the phone, his hand moving once more across his notepad. "Okay. Yep, I've got it. Perfect. I'll see you this afternoon then. Thanks."

Justin hung up the phone and tossed his pen onto his desk, then leaned back in his chair so he could better see Brad. "Another warehouse was hit over the weekend. Sounds like the same guys."

"Same MO?"

"Yeah. The police still don't have many leads, but I do." A satisfied smile spread across Justin's face.

Brad's eyebrows lifted. "You do?"

"I interviewed one of the security guards at the warehouse this morning. He thinks he recognizes one of the men from the security tapes. I've been checking with the other warehouses to see if I can get copies of their security tapes to show this guard. Maybe he can identify the same guy in the other break-ins."

Brad chuckled and shook his head. "It would be just like you to break this thing wide open before the police do."

"Yeah, well . . ." Justin pushed a hand through his sandy blond hair. "It's still early yet. We'll have to wait and see what happens."

"My money's on you, Mr. Investigative Reporter. So, are we still on for racquetball? If we're not there soon, they're going to give our court reservation away."

Justin stood and quickly began gathering his notes. "Yeah, sorry, I didn't realize it was lunchtime already. Let me put this stuff away and I'll be ready. Can we take your car?"

Brad gave him an accusing look. "Let me guess. You rode your motorcycle today."

"You got it." Justin flashed him a grin. "There won't be many more good motorcycle days this year, so I have to take advantage of the nice weather while I still can."

"You're going to get killed on that thing in this city's traffic. Do you know how many motorcycle casualties there have been in Utah this year alone?"

"You're just jealous and you know it," Justin teased. "If Christie didn't keep feeding you these stories about motorcycle accidents, you'd be trying to convince her that you need one too."

A short time later, both men were dressed in gym clothes and standing on the gleaming hardwood floor of the racquetball court. Justin tossed Brad the ball and gave him a broad smile. "Best two out of three. Loser buys lunch," he challenged.

Brad caught the ball and pointed at Justin with his racquet. "You're on."

Their game began, and both men became intent on the blue ball bouncing off the walls around them. When they took a break two games later, they were both breathing heavily, wet with perspiration, and tied at one game apiece.

"I have a feeling I'm going to be eating and you're going to be paying," Justin taunted as he wiped his face with a towel.

Brad took a long drink from his water bottle. "Don't get so cocky. This third game is mine."

"Dream on."

They fell silent as they caught their breaths. Just as he was about to suggest they start their third game, a motion outside the back glass wall caught Justin's attention. He looked over to see two women in their early twenties pausing behind the racquetball court on their way to the workout center. They smiled and waved flirtatiously when they caught his eye.

Brad leaned over to him, a grin tugging at the corners of his mouth. "Looks like they're checking you out."

Justin ran his fingers through his damp hair and glanced down selfconsciously at his baggy shorts and sweaty T-shirt. He knew he didn't exactly look like heartthrob material at the moment.

Brad gave him a nudge with his elbow. "Maybe you should ask them for their numbers."

"No way." Justin shook his head. "What could we possibly have in common?"

"You'd find out if you had anything in common by *talking* to them," Brad said, speaking slowly and emphasizing the words as if he were speaking to a young child. Then he chuckled and shook his head. "Man, sometimes you are so clueless. It's no wonder you're almost thirty and still single."

"Twenty-six is *not* almost thirty," Justin said.

"Whatever. I'm just saying, you never go out. You've gone on, what, two dates in the last six months?"

Justin's lips stretched into a firm line. It was one date, actually, but he wasn't about to admit that. "What's your point?"

"My point is, you're missing out on the finer things of life by not finding someone and settling down. Marrying Christie was the best thing I ever did. And being a dad is pretty great, too."

Justin smiled at that. Brad's eighteen-month-old daughter was, he agreed, adorable. Watching her toddle after her daddy and look up at him with worshiping eyes made Justin want to be a dad too. But the reality of his situation was, he didn't want to settle for somebody he just liked. He wanted to meet a woman he could love with all his heart, a woman he wanted to spend eternity with. And that just hadn't happened yet.

He shrugged at Brad and took a quick drink of water. "When I find somebody I really like, I'll go out with her. Until then . . ."

Brad gave him a look of frustration as he downed the rest of his water. "Okay, but don't say I didn't try."

They set their things outside the door of the court and went inside again. Brad picked up the racquetball and tossed it to Justin with an evil glint in his eyes. "Let's say we up the stakes on this next game," he said with a note of challenge.

"Yeah? What did you have in mind?"

"If I win, my wife gets to set you up with this cute single girl from our stake. Christie thinks you two would be perfect together."

Justin grimaced. "I'll tell you what. You win this game, and I'll go out with Christie's friend. But if *I* win, no more bugging me about dating or trying to set me up. Deal?"

"Deal."

With renewed determination, Justin moved up to the service line with the ball in hand. This was one game he had to win. Glancing behind him to make sure Brad was ready, he crouched low and served the ball.

\* \* \*

Justin walked into the *Salt Lake Tribune*'s newsroom forty-five minutes later, freshly showered and feeling victorious. Brad had not only bought him lunch, he'd also grudgingly agreed to leave him alone about his love life. Justin suspected his muscles would be aching the next day due to the extra effort it had taken to win, but he knew it would be worth it.

"Justin! Good, you're back."

He turned to see his managing editor approaching. There was determination in the man's short-legged stride, and a hint of worry replaced the usual smile in his bright blue eyes. "Hey, Mike," Justin answered. "What's up?"

"They've just called a press conference to address Senator Longhurst's alleged campaign finance violations. Can you get over there to cover it?"

Justin gave him a look of surprise. "Sure, but isn't Ted supposed to be on the political beat?"

His boss nodded and pushed a hand through his short hair that, these days, was more gray than brown. "Ted's daughter's sick, so he left early. I was hoping you'd cover for him."

"Yeah, no problem."

Mike looked relieved and reached over with a thick, burly hand to thump Justin's arm gratefully. "Thanks, Justin. I appreciate it. By the way, how's your dad?"

Justin smiled. Not only was Mike Kuhn his boss, but the man served as bishop in his parents' ward. Justin had wondered if it was this connection that had given him an edge over the competition when he'd applied for the job at the *Salt Lake Tribune* a few years earlier, but Mike had assured him that even if he hadn't known him personally and known him to be a hard worker, Justin's writing and reporting skills alone had put him head and shoulders above the other applicants. Justin was now enjoying a lot of success in the business, and he held Mike, as his mentor, personally responsible for that success.

"He's doing much better," Justin told his boss. "The doctor said the pneumonia is clearing up and he'll be back on his feet in no time."

"That's great to hear." The crinkle lines around Mike's blue eyes reappeared, and he gave a throaty chuckle. "I'm sure your mom will be glad to get him out from underfoot."

Justin grinned. "You know my mom. She's always going. Staying at home to take care of him has given her a serious case of cabin fever."

"I bet." Mike started to turn away, then paused and turned back, his face thoughtful. "Do me a favor. Record the press conference, will you? I want to hear the whole thing myself. I don't trust Senator Longhurst. If anything sounds fishy in his statements, I might have you do a little extra digging."

"You got it."

As Mike hurried away, Justin gathered his things and made sure to grab his palm-sized digital recorder. Mike had been a great reporter in the years before he became the managing editor at the paper, and his instincts were solid. If he suspected something was going on with the senator, there was probably a reason.

Justin got to the press conference a little early and sat near the front, where he had a better chance of getting a clear recording. Senator Longhurst wasn't present, but a spokesman read a statement that categorically denied any wrongdoing by Longhurst or his administration. When it came to answering questions regarding specific allegations, though, the spokesman was less than clear in his responses. Justin took notes and circled the issues he wanted to bring to Mike's attention. His instincts told him Mike was right—something just didn't add up.

On his way back to the *Tribune,* Justin stopped to pick up copies of the security tapes from two of the warehouses that had been robbed recently. He hoped that maybe now he'd be able to make some headway in that investigation.

When he got back to work, he pulled out his notes from the press conference and had just sat down to go over them when his phone rang. Picking it up, he said, "Justin Micklesen."

"Justin, it's me."

The emotional tone in his mother's voice caught his attention. "Mom? What's wrong?"

"Oh, honey, I'm sorry to be delivering news like this to you at work," she began, sympathy heavy in her voice. "But I got a phone call from Bryce's father in California a little while ago."

Justin stiffened in his chair at the mention of the name. Bryce had been his best friend growing up, and even after Bryce's family had moved to California at the beginning of their senior year, they'd stayed close. They'd roomed together their freshman year at BYU before leaving on their missions and again after they returned, even though Bryce had transferred to UVU to enroll in their criminal justice program. It wasn't until Bryce had graduated and moved back to California to take a job on the police force and be near his family that their contact had become a little more sporadic.

Clutching the phone tighter to his ear, Justin asked, "What happened?"

There was a brief pause. "Honey, Bryce has been killed."

The air rushed out of Justin's lungs. "What?" he managed in a shocked whisper.

"His father said it was a break-in. Bryce got home late from work on Friday night and surprised an armed burglar."

Squeezing his eyes shut, Justin leaned forward and dropped his head into his free hand. "No," he said in an agonized whisper.

His mother fell silent as he tried to process the news. At last she went on. "Bryce's father said his funeral will be in California in two days—on Wednesday. I thought you'd want to know."

Justin let out a long, shuddering sigh and leaned back in his chair. "Yeah, I want to go. Did he give you the details?"

"Yes, I have them here. Your dad and I would love to go with you to support you and pay our last respects to Bryce, but with your dad recovering . . ."

"I know, Mom," Justin reassured her. "Don't worry about it."

She gave him the funeral details, which he wrote down. After hanging up, Justin stared at the notepad until the writing blurred through his tears as the awful reality began to sink in.

Bryce was dead.

Getting through the rest of the afternoon proved to be a challenge, but somehow Justin managed. He rode his motorcycle home after work in a daze, and when he pulled up in front of his townhouse, he found himself wondering how exactly he'd gotten there. He parked his bike, got the mail, and went inside.

Still feeling numb, he set his motorcycle helmet and keys next to the door, then tossed the mail onto the coffee table as he walked through the living room to the kitchen. Looking in the fridge, he decided on the leftover lasagna.

In an attempt to distract himself from his grief, he turned on the TV and channel surfed until he came across a local news station talking about the press conference he'd attended earlier that day. He ate as he watched. The newscaster passed along the statements made by Longhurst's spokesman, and then the screen flashed to a shot of Senator Longhurst coming out of the building later in the day, smiling confidently and waving to the gathered press.

Justin had seen the man many times before, but now he took a minute to really study him. The senator was a well-built, good-looking man in his mid-forties with the polish of a suave diplomat and a commanding presence that was clearly meant to intimidate. The man also prided himself on his athleticism, and there were just as many photos of him running marathons or scaling the face of some mountain as there were of him doing his job as an elected official. This fact seemed to endear him to the press and his constituents. His ability to win over a crowd was evident as the camera showed him interacting with the people milling around him. The senator's wife was with him, and while she stood poised and smiling at his side, it was clear she wasn't as comfortable under the media's scrutiny as her husband was. She had been a professor of ancient civilizations before her husband turned his attention to politics, and she still maintained a lecturing schedule. They made an intriguing couple, which also helped Senator Longhurst's popularity amongst his constituents.

The bottom line was, the multi-millionaire–corporate-businessman-turned-savvy-politician was a media darling, and he knew it. Something in the man's confidence yelled *untouchable*.

The gears in Justin's mind started to turn, giving him a momentary reprieve from his grief. Like his editor, he sensed there was something more to this man—something that lay buried deep beneath the clean-cut, well-groomed façade.

*If only I can dig deep enough to find out what it is . . .*

Shaking his head in frustration, Justin took a long drink of water. When he set his glass down on the coffee table, the mail he'd tossed there earlier caught his eye. He reached for it and sorted through the envelopes. *Junk, junk, bill, junk . . .*

He was about to toss the stack aside when a long, white envelope with a familiar scrawl caught his eye. His heart started to pound. It was Bryce's handwriting. Judging from the postmark, the letter had been mailed the day Bryce had been killed. .

With shaking fingers, he opened the envelope and pulled out the contents. A newspaper clipping fell to the ground, but he ignored it for the moment as Bryce's firm, neat penmanship leaped off the page.

> *Justin,*
>
> *I'm sorry I haven't been better at keeping in touch. I know snail-mail is a little archaic, but I have something I need to tell you that is probably safer said this way. I still love it here in San Francisco, but lately things at work have seemed a little . . . off. Weird things have been happening—like investigation reports being waylaid, witnesses changing their stories . . . Even aspects of a crime ring investigation we've been working on seem to have been swept under the rug. After a report on a case I'd handed in to the chief of police mysteriously disappeared twice, I decided to personally walk a copy into the district*

*attorney's office the other day. That's when I overheard the district attorney talking to somebody. He and some other man were talking about a payoff for a job and about recovering some shipment from Customs lockup. Most of what they said was too quiet for me to hear, but I did hear something about a company called Marengo, and I heard them mention Senator Longhurst a couple of times. I don't know what he would have to do with anything out here, but the mention of his name suggests he's involved.*

*Justin, I don't know who to trust in the police department anymore, and with your senator being mentioned, I hoped you could help me figure out what's going on. You're the best investigative reporter I know. If anyone can get to the bottom of this, you can.*

*The problem is, I'm worried about having the wrong people figure out that we're looking into things. That's why I'm writing to you snail-mail instead of just calling or sending an email— I'm sure you know this, but criminals hack phone lines and email accounts all the time. So be careful how you go about investigating this, and don't call me or email me with any important information—wait for me to contact you. I haven't figured out yet how I'm going to do that, but I know we need to be really careful on this.*

*In the meantime, I'm planning to meet with a local reporter named Sydney Hallam to see if she can help me do some digging around here. She was behind the investigation into the crime ring I mentioned and had a big part in blowing the case wide open for us. I'm pretty sure I can trust her, but to cover all my bases, I'm passing this information along to you, too.*

*Thanks, buddy. I promise I'll call you soon—not to talk about any of this over the phone, but to catch up on what's been going on in your life.*

*Your friend,*
*Bryce*

Justin finished reading the letter just before the tears started spilling down his cheeks. To hear his friend's "voice" speak to him, so real and alive, made his heart ache even more. Bryce had had no way of knowing he would be dead so soon after writing this letter.

Brushing away the tears with the back of his hand, Justin set the letter down and reached for the newspaper clipping at his feet. When he picked it up, he realized it was actually two articles folded together. The headlines jumped up at him: "Drugs, Stolen Shipments Found in Local Warehouse" and "Warehouse Fire, Arson Suspected." Both had been written by Sydney Hallam of the *San Francisco Chronicle,* the reporter Bryce had mentioned.

He read the articles and had to admit he was impressed. This Sydney Hallam was a no-holds-barred, gutsy journalist who obviously got to the bottom of whatever she investigated. He understood why Bryce had wanted to meet with her. He sensed that she took a great deal of pride in her work, which spoke volumes about her character. At least, it did to him.

Justin's throat tightened. Bryce had been such a good person. He'd sincerely cared about people, and he was kind and generous. He had chosen a career in law enforcement because he believed he could make a difference. It would be tragic if he'd been killed for trying to do just that.

In one fluid motion Justin was off the couch. He snatched his keys and helmet from beside the door and hurried outside. Moments later he was speeding away in the waning light of dusk. Without making a conscious decision to do so, he headed up into his favorite canyon, speeding through the turns at a velocity he rarely attempted.

When he reached his favorite lookout point, he pulled into the dirt lot and turned off his motorcycle. The engine noise gave way to an abrupt silence. Justin ripped off his helmet and sat still as tears coursed down his cheeks.

*Why Bryce?*

Justin looked out over the millions of lights beginning to twinkle throughout the city and its surrounding areas. He often came up here when he was troubled or had a bad day. He loved the peace that the lights brought and the feel of the wind on his face as he rode up the canyon road. It was the one comfort he could rely on to make him feel better. But tonight it didn't.

He didn't know how long he sat there, staring out over the city and thinking, but it was dark and a brisk breeze was beginning to blow through the canyon when he finally decided to go home. As he slipped his helmet back on and tightened the strap under his chin, determination started to crowd out his sorrow.

Bryce had stumbled across something that he thought needed to be investigated, and that's just what Justin was going to do. Investigate. If there was a connection between Bryce's death and the unsettling information he had disclosed in his letter, Justin would find out what it was. With a quick flick of his wrist on the key, the motorcycle's engine roared to life. Feeling a renewed sense of purpose, Justin headed for home.

\* \* \*

Mike Kuhn looked up at the sound of the light knock on his office door first thing Tuesday morning.

"Mike, can I talk to you for a minute?"

The editor nodded and waved Justin in. "What's up?"

Justin walked to the chair in front of the desk and sat down. "I got word yesterday that a close friend of mine was killed in San Francisco, and I can't help wondering if there was more to it than just him walking in on a burglar like the police reports claim."

Mike's face creased into a concerned frown. "Justin, I'm so sorry. Is there anything I can do?"

"As a matter of fact, there is something. Remember when we talked yesterday about the press conference, and you said you didn't trust Senator Longhurst?"

"Sure, I remember. What does this have to do with Senator Longhurst?"

"I'm not sure yet, but . . . Well, here. Read this." Justin handed him Bryce's letter.

Mike's brows knit together in concentration as he read the letter. When he finished, a myriad of emotions played across his face. "So this friend of yours didn't know how the senator might be involved?"

Justin shook his head. "It doesn't sound like it. But according to the postmark on the envelope, Bryce was killed the night after he sent this. My instincts tell me that's too big a coincidence—there's got to be a connection. And if Longhurst really is involved in something he's willing to kill somebody over, it needs to be investigated."

Mike nodded in agreement. "What do you need from me?"

"A few days in San Francisco. I was going to take some personal leave to go to Bryce's funeral tomorrow morning, but if I could work it out with you to stay there an extra day or two, I might just get some leads into that big story you want—the one that proves Longhurst is involved in something illegal."

"I agree it would be a big story, but can you handle this?" He eyed Justin, and the expression on his face conveyed a mixture of sympathy and concern. "Your friend was murdered. It's impossible to stay objective under those circumstances."

Justin considered his boss's words. "I admit it'll be hard, but I'd like to try. Besides, one visit to the Bay Area isn't going to break a story like this—

I'd just be doing preliminary stuff. I thought I'd ask around a little, talk to the reporter Bryce mentioned. Maybe she knows something."

"Maybe. Just be careful not to step on anyone's toes. If she thinks you're there to rip her story away from her, she could get territorial and give you nothing."

"Good point. I'll be careful about that."

Mike sat back in his chair and nodded. "Okay, go ahead and do it. If you pick up some leads, I should be able to convince management to let you travel a bit to pursue this officially."

"Thanks, Mike." Justin stood up and had turned to leave when his editor's voice stopped him.

"Do you know where you're going to stay?"

He turned back around and shrugged. "I'll just find a hotel, I guess. I haven't thought that far yet."

"I'll tell you what. Hotels can get pretty expensive. My brother has a condo in San Francisco that he only uses a couple of times a month when he has business in the city. He's overseas for the next couple of months, though, and I know where he keeps his extra key. I'll get in touch with him and see if he minds having you stay at his place while you're there. It'll save on hotel bills."

"That'd be great. Thanks."

"Just be careful, okay? It sounds like you could be going after some big fish. I wouldn't want to have to explain to your mom why I let you endanger your life." His eyes crinkled into a smile.

Justin chuckled. "I'll be careful. And thanks."

"Just bring me back something good."

As Justin left Mike's office, he hoped that was just what he'd do.

# CHAPTER 3

"Sydney Hallam, will you come up here, please?"

Sydney stepped out of line and walked toward her sensei, grinning when her classmates began clapping and whistling in a show of support. She stopped in front of the sensei and gave the customary bow, and he bowed in return.

He spoke again, his voice carrying through the dojo. "Tonight Sydney has proved herself worthy of advancing to the level of brown belt." He handed her the coveted belt, and they exchanged bows once more. He smiled, then leaned forward so she could hear him above the applause. "Well done, Sydney."

"Thank you," she replied, her grin widening even further. She returned to her place in line, and her friend Jennifer, who was standing beside her, reached over to give her a quick hug.

"Congratulations, Sydney," Jennifer whispered in her ear.

"You, too." Sydney nodded at the brown belt Jennifer held in her own hands. "We've both worked hard to get these."

"You're not kidding." Jennifer made a face. "Tonight my sparring opponent got me in the hip. I'm going to have an ugly bruise tomorrow."

Sydney grimaced in sympathy, then turned her attention back to the sensei as the ceremony continued and other belts were awarded. When the ceremony finished, the class dispersed, and Sydney and Jennifer walked to the corner of the room to retrieve their things.

As Jennifer passed in front of the mirror, she let out a sound of dismay and stopped to run her fingers through her layered, chin-length auburn hair in an attempt to restore her short, spiky hairstyle. With her large, dark eyes and smaller mouth, she resembled an anime-inspired pixie.

"Why didn't you tell me I looked like this?" Jennifer accused.

"Are you kidding? Only you could go through a brown-belt test and look so good. It's not fair." Sydney dragged Jennifer away from the mirror and pulled her down onto the bench by their stuff.

Jennifer pulled her gym bag out from under the bench and began to rummage through it. Sydney smiled when she noted the design on her friend's bag. Brown with pink butterflies. It was Jennifer to a T.

"New bag?" Sydney asked.

"Oh, yes!" She lifted it onto her lap to show it off. "I found it on clearance at the mall. Isn't it fabulous?"

Sydney's grin widened as she leaned over to put on her tennis shoes. "You and your butterfly obsession. I'm just waiting for you to show up at work and announce you've painted your apartment in some kind of butterfly motif." She looked up at her friend just in time to see Jennifer's eyes widen with inspiration. Sydney jerked upright and pointed a reprimanding finger at her friend. "Don't. Even. Think about it."

"Yeah," Jennifer murmured in disappointment. "I doubt my landlord would let me, anyway." She set her gym bag back down on the floor and pulled out her shoes. "I don't know about you, but I'm going to take a long, hot bath when I get back to my apartment."

"I probably will too," Sydney said. "My sparring partner wasn't as vicious as yours, but I worked so hard on my *katas* this week that my whole body is achy."

"By the way, I meant to tell you. That was a great story," Jennifer said. "You really rocked the media this weekend with that crime ring exposé."

Sydney and Jennifer had worked together in the city section for the last two years and had become fast friends when they learned how much they had in common, including being involved in Shotokan. "Thanks," Sydney said, giving her friend a gracious smile. "Carl went out of his way to compliment me on it. Can you believe it?"

"Of course I believe it. You can do no wrong in Carl's eyes."

"You're kidding, right?" Sydney made a scoffing noise. "I'm in his doghouse more than the rest of the newsroom staff combined."

"Maybe, but to write the hard-nosed investigative pieces you do, you're bound to appear on his radar more often. Sometimes I wonder what it would be like to attract that kind of attention from him."

"Believe me, you don't want to. When he yells, he gets this look in his eyes that's downright scary. Besides, Carl loves your writing. I overheard him saying he was planning on submitting your piece on the homeless shelters to the awards committee this year."

Jennifer looked up, her eyes hopeful. "He said that?"

"Yeah. The things I write may draw a lot of attention, but I don't have the beautiful, emotion-evoking style you do. I envy that about your writing."

Jennifer's expression melted into one of appreciation. "Thanks, Sydney. That's so nice of you to say."

"I'm not being nice; I'm being honest." Sydney finished tying her shoelaces and stood up. "Speaking of work, Carl had me put together another follow-up on the exposé for tomorrow morning's edition. You'll have to tell me what you think. I told him we didn't have enough new information to run it, but he wanted me to do it anyway. I hope it doesn't sound soft."

"Knowing you, it'll be great. Don't be so hard on yourself."

"What are you working on now?" Sydney asked, changing the subject. "Anything exciting?"

Jennifer frowned. "I was trying to get an interview with Stephen Dover for an article I'm writing about one of his newest companies' recent successes, but his press secretary hasn't returned any of my calls."

"Yeah, well, *everybody* wants an interview with Dover," Sydney sympathized. "I suppose he can pick and choose who he wants to give interviews to."

"True. But he's such a great story—a young, good-looking billionaire business mogul with a rags-to-riches story, not to mention being the country's most eligible bachelor. Did you see his latest interview in *Forbes*? It said that his last merger earned him millions when the stocks went public."

"As if he needed the money. And yes, I knew about that merger. He merged with the company I was investigating for insurance fraud and sacked the staff. There went my story."

"That stinks. Anyway, I just wish I could get him to return my calls."

"Well, if it helps, yours aren't the only calls being ignored. I tried to contact him for an interview too. I'm sure both our names are on a long list of interview requests that are being ignored."

They left the dojo and walked out into the late-summer evening. "Do you want to do lunch tomorrow?" Sydney asked. "There's that new sandwich shop down the street from the *Chronicle* that's supposed to be good."

"That sounds great. I'll see you then."

\* \* \*

"No, you've got to get Hastings' signature by tonight," Senator Longhurst insisted, reaching for the suit jacket he'd draped over the arm of the Italian leather couch in his office. "I have to file that paperwork with the committee tomorrow."

His aide nodded and scribbled the information in his notebook. "And if he says he's too busy?"

The senator's expression hardened. "Then you get down there and tell him you're not leaving until he signs. He's had the paperwork long enough. I need it now."

Longhurst slipped his arms through the sleeves of his tailored suit jacket and reached for the briefcase his aide held out to him. Without another word, he hurried out of his office and down the hall.

As he approached the reception area, the receptionist called out to him. "Senator, you have an urgent call on line two."

He slowed but didn't stop. "Who is it?"

"It's Carlos Rojas."

His forward progress halted. "Rojas?" When the receptionist nodded, he continued on past her. "Tell him to meet me at the gym. I'm on my way there now."

Longhurst was on the third mile of his treadmill warm-up when Rojas opened the glass doors of the expansive training room and stepped inside.

"Carlos." Longhurst greeted him from across the room without breaking stride. He waved him over, feeling confident about doing business in his private training area. "I didn't expect to hear from you so soon. I take it this means you have good news about the dig?"

The Colombian man's bronze-toned face creased as he smiled and nodded. "I do." He crossed the large room, navigating through the maze of state-of-the-art weight and cardio equipment. When he stopped beside the treadmill, he held up a manila envelope. "Your wife was right. The ancient city is still there, but as we suspected when we started the dig seven months ago, little is intact. It has taken us months to unearth some of the more important artifacts—including the pieces you were hoping for."

Longhurst hit the button on the treadmill's console and the belt groaned to a halt. "You found them?"

Rojas handed him the envelope. Longhurst took it with eager hands and pulled out the glossy 8 x 10s. His excitement grew as he flipped through the series of photographs taken of the centuries-old Mayan artifacts. It was just as he'd hoped.

"Excellent. The buyers I have lined up will be ecstatic. Where are the pieces now?"

"I arranged for them to disappear before they could be catalogued. They're safe."

"Any problems with the Colombian government?"

"No." Rojas shook his head. "Perez paid off the right people. And the workers at the dig site know when to keep their mouths shut."

A satisfied smile slid across Longhurst's face. "Thank you, Carlos. I'll have the money wired into your account first thing tomorrow. Keep me apprised of what else you dig up. I'd like a little something to give my wife as a gift."

Rojas chuckled. "Too bad you can't tell her where it came from."

"True. But if she knew anything about this, we'd be out of business. She'd see this as a historical find of utmost importance and would want everything preserved in a museum. Me, I recognize the importance of a dollar. But still, I should thank her even if she doesn't know why. Without her connections in the archaeological community, I would never have learned just how much money I could make selling these pieces."

"Good point. Before you get back to your workout, though, there is one other thing I needed to talk with you about." From the leather folder tucked under his arm, Rojas produced a series of photos. "You told me to have our boys keep an eye on that *Chronicle* reporter, Hallam, when she started getting close to your seaboard business. Apparently she's still nosing around, asking questions about that warehouse fire on the docks. This is what our guys sent over."

Longhurst glanced through the surveillance photos taken of Sydney Hallam speaking to one of the detectives investigating the warehouse fire— the fire that had been a successful demonstration of what happened when defiance surfaced in the ranks. As a result, he had once again secured the dock owners' loyalty to his operation.

"I didn't think she'd give up on the warehouse fire incident easily," he said.

Rojas's eyebrows rose. "Why do you say that?"

"I know her type. She's young; she's hungry. She's out to prove herself to the world, and she loves nothing more than shaking things up with a good exposé." He continued to look through the photos. "What about that cop the security cameras caught eavesdropping at the DA's office?"

"Smith took care of him before he could go to anybody with whatever he overheard. He'd picked up a copy of the lockup surveillance tape at the DA's office, but a thorough search of his house and his desk at work came up clean. Griffin took care of the original, so there's no evidence tying him and Douglas to the recovery of our goods. They just finished with the distribution, by the way. We made a nice profit."

The satisfied smile pulled at one corner of Longhurst's mouth. "As expected. Having Griffin as DA has proven beneficial."

"It has. The problem, however, is that we're going to have to rework our shipping routes. Hallam's exposé caused us a lot of problems with that part of our operation. Two of our companies came under investigation, and we had to do some damage control. We were able to take the heat off Douglas with that company merger, but he still has to maintain a low profile."

Longhurst lifted one sandy eyebrow. "He's still heading up my next projects, isn't he? Including overseeing these artifacts to the gallery?"

"He is. The pieces will be arriving by boat in a couple of weeks."

"Make sure Douglas oversees the shipment personally. The sales of this one will fund several of my upcoming ventures."

"I'll see to it."

The senator handed the surveillance photos back to Rojas, then punched the button to restart the treadmill. "Arrange to have our trucking company move the goods from our new dock locations to our San Francisco warehouses and out of state from there for distribution. The rest of the operation should be business as usual."

"And the reporter? What do you want us to do about her?"

Longhurst's strides lengthened as the belt beneath his feet gained speed. "I wouldn't be surprised if she still has something big in the works. If she does, I need to know if it involves any of my operations."

"Our men are on it," Rojas assured him.

"Not good enough." He shook his head as he ran. "We need more than an inside informant. We need somebody to talk to her one-on-one, find out what she's working on. A social situation when her guard is down would do nicely."

"I assume you have somebody in mind?" Rojas cocked an eyebrow at him.

Longhurst flashed his colleague a confident smile. "I know just the man for the job."

When the senator punched a couple more buttons on the console, the whine of the machine increased along with the speed it produced. "How many miles today, Robert?" Rojas asked conversationally as he started to back away.

"Nineteen. I have a marathon next weekend, and I plan on breaking the record."

"As I'm sure you will." Rojas gave him a nod. "I'll send word when the shipment's on its way."

"Thank you, Carlos."

After Rojas had exited the room, Longhurst shuffled through the pictures once more as he ran. He shook his head, marveling at the treasures that had sat beneath the earth's surface for so many hundreds of years. It was too bad his wife couldn't know about this. She'd be over the moon.

He smiled. His wife deserved something nice for unknowingly helping him with this deal, which would amount to millions when all was said and done.

Sliding the photographs back into the envelope, he turned his attention back to his run.

\* \* \*

Sydney walked into the newsroom the next morning with a spring in her step, still on an emotional high from her Shotokan class the night before. When she reached her desk, she sat down and pulled her flash drive out of her attaché. She'd been so wired last night that she'd ended up working on a couple new story ideas from home. She plugged the flash drive into her computer and started transferring the files.

While she waited, she took a moment to admire her clean desk. It had taken her a good part of the morning the day before to finally find the top of her desk, and she'd even remembered to bring another super-sized bag of peanut M&Ms to refill the glass canister next to her monitor. The colored candies now filled the jar clear to the top. All was right with her world.

Deciding to check her voice mail before she got working, she reached for the phone on her desk. The first message was from Nancy down in research, saying she'd finished fact-checking one of Sydney's articles. When she skipped to the next message, an unfamiliar woman's voice sounded in her ear.

"Ms. Hallam, this is Deirdre Long, Stephen Dover's personal assistant. Mr. Dover has learned that your name is on his list of requested interviews, and he is hoping you might have time to do a dinner interview with him sometime in the next couple of days. Please give me a call back and let me know when you're available."

Sydney sat, frozen, with the phone still pressed to her ear. Stephen Dover wanted to do a *dinner* interview with her? Her conversation with Jennifer last night had confirmed how hard it was to get a call back from his people. For good reason, his attention was in high demand by the media and members of the business world alike. *Not to mention being in high demand because he's such an eligible bachelor,* a little voice inside her head chimed in.

She smiled and shook her head. No, he was too old for her—about ten years her senior. Even so, she couldn't help feeling flattered that he'd picked her off the long list of people clamoring for interviews.

Stirring herself to action, she replayed the message, this time writing down the phone number. Then she dialed.

"Mr. Dover's offices," a female voice answered. "May I help you?"

"Hello," Sydney said, trying to sound professional in spite of the butter-flies in her stomach. "Is Deirdre Long available?"

"This is Deirdre Long. What can I do for you?"

"This is Sydney Hallam—"

"Oh, yes, Ms. Hallam," the woman cut in. "Let me put you through to Mr. Dover. He's expecting your call."

There were a couple of clicks on the line, and Sydney's throat seized up. She was actually being put through to Mr. Dover? She'd expected to schedule something with Deirdre, not talk to Mr. Dover directly. But it was only moments before his smooth, cultured voice came across the line.

"Ms. Hallam, how kind of you to return my call."

Sydney shook herself out of her momentary state of shock and cleared her throat. "Mr. Dover, it's a pleasure to talk with you. I was a little surprised to receive a message from your personal assistant. I'm sure you have a long list of interview requests."

The smile in Mr. Dover's voice was evident. "That I do. I saw your name on the list, however, and—I have to admit, I'm such an admirer of your work—I decided I didn't want to pass up the opportunity. Would your schedule allow for a dinner appointment this week?"

"I think so," she answered, trying not to sound too eager. "Is there an evening that works best for you?"

"How about tonight? We could go to The Dining Room at the Ritz-Carlton. The chef there is one of the most renowned in the world, not to mention a personal friend of mine. We could have a wonderful meal while we talked. What do you think?"

A shocked but delighted grin crossed Sydney's face. Dinner at a five-star restaurant with Stephen Dover? And the meal prepared by a world-renowned chef, no less. *Such a tough decision,* she thought.

"Actually, tonight would be great," she said. "I'll look forward to it."

"As will I. I'll come around for you at seven."

She gave him her address, then hung up and stared at the phone for several minutes. She was having dinner with Stephen Dover. At the Ritz-Carlton.

*Unbelievable.*

She replayed every word of their conversation, stopping to dwell on the fact that he'd said he was a fan of her writing. A fan? She had to admit she was flattered. Most "fans" who contacted her were usually more interested in delivering death threats. This was a nice switch. But was Stephen Dover's being a fan reason enough for him to single her out for a private dinner interview?

The investigative reporter in her told her to be cautious. If there was one lesson she had learned in this business, it was that not everything was as it appeared to be. Even so, nothing was going to stop her from taking advantage of the opportunity to interview one of the most intriguing men in the country.

With a smile on her face, Sydney went in search of Jennifer. She just had to hear this.

# CHAPTER 4

Justin walked across the parking lot toward his rental car on Wednesday morning as he left the LDS church building where Bryce's funeral had been held. If he hadn't just sat through his best friend's funeral, he would have enjoyed the beautiful California weather. Instead, all he could think about was the fact that Bryce was dead.

A familiar thickness welled up in his throat. It was so unfair. Bryce had always been so easygoing and so willing to help others. And he'd been compassionate and fair in all his dealings. He'd been a good man and a good friend. Justin was going to miss him dearly.

He'd almost reached his car when he heard somebody calling his name. He turned to see a short, stocky man who looked to be in his mid-forties walking toward him, wearing a dark suit and tie. Curious, Justin waited for him.

"I'm sorry. I tried to catch you inside before you left," the man said, his voice a deep baritone. "I was talking with Bryce's father, and he told me who you were. My name's Roger Calloway. I worked with Bryce at the police department."

Justin shook Roger's extended hand. "It's good to meet you, Roger. Did you know Bryce well?"

Roger nodded. "Pretty well. We were partnered together for a while before I took a job as a detective in our same precinct. He was a good guy." He studied Justin for a moment, then continued. "Bryce's dad said you were a reporter. What paper do you work for?"

"A paper in Utah, actually. The *Salt Lake Tribune*."

Roger looked disappointed. "I thought maybe you worked for one of the local papers. I was hoping you'd be doing a story on the circumstances surrounding Bryce's death."

"Oh?" Justin prompted.

"The official report says he surprised a burglar, but I don't buy it. If it was a simple burglary attempt, why was his place such a mess? I was one of the first officers on the scene, and I'll tell you, someone had been looking for something. Drawers were dumped out all over the floor, the closets gutted . . . but not a single piece of electronics had been touched—and Bryce had some nice stuff." He shook his head. "He didn't surprise a burglar. He surprised somebody looking for something."

Justin nodded slowly. "What do you think they were looking for?"

"I don't know," Roger answered. "A bunch of us suspect we have some corruption in the department, and last week Bryce told me he'd overheard something that might prove it. Maybe whoever he overheard that day found out he'd been listening and thought he had evidence."

Justin was glad he wasn't the only one who'd come to that conclusion. "That would explain the ransacked apartment," he replied, his tone grim.

"Yeah, it would."

Roger reached for his wallet and pulled out a card. "Here's my number at the police station. If you ever need to, you can reach me there."

Justin pulled out a business card of his own and handed it to Roger. "The same goes for you. If you come across anything, let me know."

After Justin climbed into his car, he sat for a moment, mulling over their conversation. Roger's suspicions confirmed his own—and his volunteering of information suggested to Justin that he was not part of the corruption in the police department.

Reaching into the back seat, Justin retrieved the paper on which he'd written the phone number for the *San Francisco Chronicle*. There was another person he had to talk to—somebody he hoped could give him some answers.

* * *

"Sydney!"

Hearing her name, Sydney looked up to see Carl approaching. "Yes?"

"Remember that investigation you were doing into the missing evidence linked to the district attorney's office?"

She frowned. "More like *allegedly* linked to the district attorney's office. There's such a conflict in paperwork that it's impossible to prove their office had that security surveillance tape in the first place."

"Well, then, I think this is your lucky day. I just got off the phone with a buddy of mine. He told me he knows somebody inside the district attorney's office who might be willing to talk. The guy's name is Hyo Park, and he's one of the county detectives. I want you to drop everything and get over to meet this guy in half an hour."

"Okay. Where?"

Carl relayed the arrangements, then said, "I know that doesn't give you much time, but it's the only time he'd agree to a meeting. My friend says Park's a little squirrely about dealing with the press, so do what you can to keep from making him antsy. I don't have to tell you how important this is. An inside source isn't easy to come by."

"You got it, chief." Sydney gathered her things and headed out of the newsroom.

On her way out, she called Jennifer on her cell. "Hey," she said when Jennifer answered, "I'm sorry, but I'm going to have to skip our lunch today. Carl's sending me to interview a source."

"No problem," Jennifer replied. "Did you find those notes for me on the restoration of that old theater downtown?"

"Oh, yeah, yeah. They're in the notebook in my top drawer. Grab it and I'll talk to you about it when I get back. I should be back by two."

"Perfect. Thanks, Syd!"

Sydney hung up and dropped her phone into her purse as she hurried out of the building and across the street to the parking garage. When she drove down to street level and saw the bumper-to-bumper vehicles, though, she groaned. It was almost lunchtime, and the traffic was horrendous.

As she stopped for her third red light in as many blocks, she shot a glance at the clock on her dashboard. How did Carl possibly think she could make her meeting in such a short time in this kind of traffic?

The light turned green, then red again before she even got to the intersection. Leaning to her left, she tried to see what was causing the holdup. A flash of orange caught her attention. *Great.* A construction crew was working on the street up ahead.

"You've got to be kidding me," she groaned. She looked around and caught sight of a street sign to her right. A sudden burst of inspiration hit her. If she took several side streets, she could bypass the construction and the lunchtime traffic and maybe, just maybe, make it on time.

With a harried glance to her right, she saw a small opening in traffic and whipped the wheel to the right to pull into the turning lane. Horns blared, but she ignored them and sped around the corner. When road daylight opened up in front of her, she punched her foot down on the gas pedal, sped to the end of the street, and turned onto yet another side street.

The area she'd detoured through wasn't the most desirable part of town, but her doors were locked, and she knew she'd be safe enough. Besides, she was almost there. She glanced at her clock. Ten minutes left. She could make it! Her heart pounding, she eased the pedal down a little more to speed down the street. The road curved to the right, and her car hugged the corner as she turned—directly into more stopped traffic. She gasped and slammed on her brakes, narrowly missing the bumper of the car in front of her.

"I can't believe this!" she exclaimed, stretching up in her seat to see what was going on. A short distance up the road, she could see red-and-blue flashing lights. *Terrific.*

Starting to feel panicked, she whipped her head around to see if she could back up and take another route to bypass the accident. No such luck. Cars had pulled in behind her, and she was stuck. Traffic was packed in a solid block, and nobody was moving.

With a defeated moan, she slumped in her seat and looked at the time again. Her ten minutes had ticked down to eight.

*What now?*

Her gaze drifted to the street sign on the corner up ahead. The café where she was to meet her source was only a few blocks away, yet there was no way she would make it on time in this kind of traffic. She could *walk* faster than the traffic was moving.

A new idea surfaced. *Why* couldn't *I walk? Or run, even?*

She looked around and surveyed the industrial area. There were a couple of empty parking spots along the street in front of the machine shop to her right. She couldn't imagine that the shop owners would notice if she used one of the spots for an hour or so.

Hope surged through her as she cranked her steering wheel to the right and managed to squeeze her car out of line. Then she whipped into the parking spot, thankful to find a space that was unmetered for once. Although, she realized, it was probably unmetered because no one would elect to park in this seedy part of town if they had a choice.

She climbed out of her car and made it a point to activate the alarm system before heading down the street at a fast walk. An alley appeared on her left, and she decided to take it. It would cut a minute—maybe even two or three—off her time. And right now, every minute counted.

Moving at a brisk walk, she reached the end of the alley and turned into the next one, knowing it led to the street she needed. She glanced at her watch. Only six minutes remained, but she was almost there.

She'd just turned the corner into the next alley when a hand came out of nowhere and grabbed her arm in a vise-like grip. Too surprised to scream, Sydney felt herself being shoved back against the brick wall of the building.

She looked up at the culprit now standing a few feet in front of her—a scruffy man who looked desperate enough to try anything to get some money.

He pulled out a long pocketknife and waved it menacingly toward her. "Give me your purse," he growled.

Managing to recover from her surprise, Sydney pulled herself up to her full five feet, nine inches and stared back at the man, unblinking. Adrenaline rushed through her as she forced herself to remember everything she knew about defending herself against a mugger: *Maintain eye contact. Go for the groin. Don't just hand the attacker your purse; throw it away from you and run the other direction.* But how could she throw her purse and run the other direction if she was backed up against a wall and the attacker was just feet away waving a knife at her? She knew she couldn't outrun this guy in the heels she was wearing. She had to get that knife away from him, or she'd never get away.

Still staring the man down, she kept her voice steady and said clearly, "I don't think so."

The man's face contorted in anger. "Give it to me now, or I'm going to cut that pretty face of yours. Get it?"

Sydney tensed, and anger flared up inside of her. Her Shotokan training was about to be put to the test. With a swift, trained movement, she kicked the knife out of her attacker's hand, sending it skittering down the alley floor. The man glanced back at his knife now lying several feet away, but Sydney didn't wait for him to regroup. She drew her leg back and swung it forward into his groin. When he doubled over in agony, she quickly kneed him in the face, then swept his legs out from under him with a well-placed kick to the back of his legs. He went down in a crumpled, moaning heap, and Sydney immediately took off running toward the end of the alley, kicking the knife further from the would-be mugger on her way.

Only when she had reached the safety of the busy street beyond did she dare to look back. When she saw no movement, she allowed herself a moment to catch her breath and try to slow her racing heart. Then a smile slowly lifted the corners of her lips. It felt good to be able to take care of herself in the city. She really did deserve the brown belt she'd been awarded yesterday.

But a glance down at her watch started her heart pounding again. She was four minutes late! She clutched her purse and ran the remaining three blocks to the café.

Out of breath and disheveled, she finally made it. She scanned the outside tables, her gaze falling on the one in the back corner, where she was supposed to meet her source. It was empty.

"No!" she panted. But after talking with the waiter at the café entrance, her fears were confirmed. Her contact had come several minutes early but had left promptly at one minute after their scheduled meeting time.

* * *

When Sydney got back to work, she stomped into the newsroom and over to her desk, where she dropped her bag onto the floor in an unceremonious heap. Spotting a message next to her keyboard, she picked it up and recognized Jennifer's flowery handwriting. The message said that a source named Justin Micklesen was coming in to meet with her at three.

Her bad mood eased slightly. Another source. She didn't know what information he might have, but at this point, she'd take anything.

Just then she looked up to see Jennifer approaching. Her friend's initial smile faded as she took in Sydney's rumpled appearance.

"Sydney, what happened? You're kind of a mess."

"Gee, thanks," Sydney drawled. "I ran into some difficulties trying to get through lunchtime traffic to meet a source Carl found—but I ended up missing him anyway."

Jennifer gave her an apologetic look, then gestured to the paper in Sydney's hand. "I see you got my message. He called when I was at your desk getting those notes. He said he's only in town for a couple of days and needs to talk to you about a story. If three o'clock doesn't work, his cell number is there."

"No, three should be fine, thanks," Sydney said. She blew out a breath. "I guess I need to go tell Carl that I missed the meeting. He's not going to be happy."

"I bet." Jennifer's tone was sympathetic. "Let me know how it goes."

Sydney nodded, and Jennifer headed back to her own desk. Sydney made a quick stop in the restroom to fix her hair and makeup, then forced herself to walk to Carl's office.

When Carl saw her in the doorway, he waved toward the chair in front of his desk. He tossed his pen down onto the stack of papers before him and leaned back in his chair, his expression eager. "So? How'd it go?"

Sydney sighed as she dropped into the chair. "I got there four minutes late, and Park was gone."

"What?" Carl sat upright in his chair and fixed her with a glare. "Sydney, I put you on this because I thought I could count on you. Do you have any idea how big this story could be? How much is riding on having a reliable source to break the story?"

"Of course I do!" she said, refusing to be intimidated by her editor's lecture. "Remember, *I* was the one who pursued the alleged corruption scandal in the first place. It's just that I got stuck in lunch-hour traffic, and then there was this guy in the alley—"

"I don't want to hear it," Carl cut her off. "All the excuses in the world won't put that headline on our front page. What if he decides to take his story to another paper?"

Sydney shook her head. "He won't. I won't let him. I'm going to get hold of him and convince him to reschedule. I've already worked my tail off on this, and I'm not about to let somebody scoop me. I'll get you this story. I promise you that."

The angry look in Carl's eyes softened. "Okay, you're off the hook for now, but you'd better not let me down."

She flashed him a confident—and relieved—smile. "I won't."

# CHAPTER 5

Justin walked into the *Chronicle*'s busy newsroom and stepped out of the way when an overeager copy boy barreled past him. He smiled. The bustling newsroom and the people working in it didn't seem much different from his newsroom back home.

He'd only gone a few steps when a young man dressed in jeans and a T-shirt appeared at his side. "Can I help you with something?"

Guessing him to be an intern or a staff gofer, Justin nodded. "I'm looking for Sydney Hallam. Could you tell me where I can find her?"

The young man smiled cordially and gestured toward the far end of the newsroom. "She's over there. Come on, I'll walk you over." He led the way and turned back to talk to Justin as they walked. "I'm Derek, by the way. Is Sydney expecting you?"

"Sort of. I have an appointment with her in half an hour, but I was nearby and thought maybe I could catch her a little early."

"No problem. I'll introduce you, and you can see if she has time to see you now."

They approached a large office, and through the open door Justin caught a glimpse of a dark-skinned man sitting behind a desk—the editor in chief, he assumed. He could hear the man arguing with somebody. A moment later he heard a woman's voice arguing back. He couldn't see her over the series of file cabinets near the office door, nor could he make out the words that were exchanged, but he guessed the two must be on pretty solid ground to be arguing back and forth so freely.

When Derek stopped directly in front of the large office window and Justin saw who the editor was talking to, his heart lurched. Sitting in the leather chair in front of the editor's desk was a beautiful, slender woman about his age, with a light, creamy complexion and rich brown hair that hung in layers to just below her shoulders. For a moment, she turned her face toward the newsroom, and he saw that long, thick eyelashes framed beautiful brown eyes that seemed to miss nothing.

Feeling a little breathless, Justin leaned over to Derek and asked in a whisper, "Who is that with your editor?"

Derek flashed him a broad, knowing grin. "That, my friend, is Sydney Hallam."

"*That's* Sydney Hallam?" Shocked, Justin looked back at the woman in the office. He didn't know what he'd expected, but he certainly hadn't expected Sydney Hallam to look like this. After reading the articles Bryce had mailed him, and noting her strong, edgy writing style, he'd pictured her as older and somewhat tough, hardened by years of investigative reporting. The young woman he was staring at was . . . not. And with eyes trained from years of looking for girls to date at BYU, he noted that her left ring finger was conspicuously bare.

His first instinct was to wonder what she'd say if he asked her out. But with that thought came several harsh realizations. One: he was only in town for a couple of days. Two: what were the chances that someone who looked like that wasn't already in a relationship? And last, but most important: the chances that she was LDS were almost nil.

His feelings of infatuation for the stunning brunette deflated with the rapidness of a spiked tire. It wasn't even remotely feasible. Besides, Bryce was counting on him to get to the bottom of things—things that had possibly gotten him killed. This woman could very well be the key. Justin was here to work. And only work.

Derek stepped forward into the office doorway, and the editor stopped talking and looked up. "What is it, Derek?"

"I'm sorry to interrupt, but Sydney's appointment is here a little early."

Sydney's head jerked up, and her eyes met Justin's. For a second Justin forgot to speak. Then, realizing everybody was watching him, he cleared his throat. "Sorry, I *am* a bit early. If I'm interrupting something, I can wait . . ."

"No, no, we're finished." Sydney jumped to her feet and shot a glance at her editor. "Aren't we, Chief?"

The editor sighed in resignation. "I guess we are." But before she could disappear out the door, he called after her, "Don't forget what I said. I don't want to lose that story!"

Sydney muttered something unintelligible as she hurried from the office toward Justin. "Thanks, Derek," she said, giving the *Chronicle* staffer a smile.

"No problem," Derek replied and then went back to whatever it was he'd been doing before Justin showed up.

Justin would have thanked him for his help, but he was too preoccupied at the moment. Up close, Sydney Hallam was even more beautiful, he realized, but she also had a slightly intimidating air about her. She walked with a confidence that spoke volumes about how she'd gotten to where she was in her career. She was good, and she knew it.

"I'm Sydney Hallam," she said, extending her hand when she stopped in front of Justin. "You must be my three o'clock."

He reached for her hand and was pleasantly surprised by her solid grip. "Justin Micklesen. I apologize again for showing up early, but I was driving around the area and decided to come in on the off chance you were free."

She nodded. "I understand you wanted to talk to me about a story?"

Seeing the spark of interest in her eyes, Justin hesitated. He wished he'd planned out how he was going to explain to her that he was also a reporter and wanted to work on a story that was obviously in her jurisdiction. Mike had warned him to tread carefully, and he knew it was sound advice. If somebody were to show up in his newsroom in Salt Lake City acting like they were moving in on one of his stories, he'd tell them to take a hike. He had to think of a way to convince this woman he wasn't a threat. Bryce was counting on him.

Trying not to waver beneath the intensity of Sydney's gaze, he cleared his throat and asked, "Is there somewhere we can talk?"

\* \* \*

Sydney studied the man standing before her, wondering at the hint of intensity and sadness in his intriguing green eyes. Whatever emotions lurked there, they were close to the surface, and that surprised her. Not many guys her age let their emotions show so plainly. But then, it was clear that this man wasn't like the other guys she knew.

It wasn't just that he was attractive in an all-American kind of way. There was simply something about him that made her heart beat a little faster—especially now, as his eyes met hers with an intensity that made her a little breathless. In fact, his eyes were one of his best features, she decided. Not that the rest of him wasn't equally as impressive. While he wasn't overly tall—just over six feet, she guessed—his broad shoulders and muscular build added to his stature. His strong jaw and thick, sandy blond hair gave him a handsome, boy-next-door look that appealed to her. He was nicely dressed in a tailored gray suit, and his crisp, white shirt was a stark contrast to his tanned skin that suggested time spent outdoors.

As he stood there, steadily meeting her gaze, she suddenly realized he was waiting for her to answer. "Oh! I'm sorry," she said, jumping to attention as color flooded her cheeks. "Let's go to my desk. We can talk a little more privately there."

She led him across the newsroom and gestured to the empty chair beside her desk. "So. What can I do for you?"

He sat, then seemed to consider his next words. Finally he leaned forward in his seat, rested his forearms on his knees, and regarded her with a solemn and anxious expression.

"I'm going to be up front with you," he began. "I'm a journalist for the *Salt Lake Tribune,* and I flew in from Utah last night for my best friend's funeral this morning."

"I'm sorry," she sympathized, now understanding the raw emotions on his face, as well as his choice of clothing.

"Thank you." He dropped his gaze to his clasped hands for a moment. When he looked back up, his eyes held a hint of anger. "What makes it even tougher is that I think foul play was involved."

Sydney's forehead creased into a frown. "Why do you say that?"

"Two days ago, I got a letter in the mail from my friend. It had been sent just before he was killed. He was on the San Francisco police force, and the letter said he'd overheard a conversation that seemed to indicate a high level of corruption within the SFPD. He didn't know who to trust, so he contacted me. I spoke with one of his old partners at the funeral this morning, and he has the same suspicions—that Bryce was murdered by somebody to keep him quiet."

"I'm so sorry," she said, feeling compelled to soothe the pain she saw in his eyes. After a moment, she asked, "I don't mean to sound unfeeling, but . . . what do you want from me? Did you want me to write a story about it?"

"Actually, I was kind of hoping you could help me with something else. Some of the things that Bryce overheard . . . They seemed to indicate that my state senator could be involved, which is why Bryce contacted me about it. Bryce mentioned you in the letter, too. That's why I'm here."

Sydney's eyebrows flew up her forehead. "Me? He thought *I* was involved?"

"No, no, not at all," Justin hurried to clarify. "He said he didn't feel safe going to his superiors because he didn't know how far up the corruption went, so he contacted me . . . and he said he was planning on contacting you. That's one of the reasons I'm here. I wanted to find out if he ever did."

"I don't think so," she answered, trying to remember a contact sharing any information about a Utah senator. She came up blank. "I'm sorry, but it doesn't ring any bells. You said this friend of yours worked for the SFPD, right?" When Justin nodded, she went on. "I've talked with a lot of police officers over the years. I wouldn't remember them all. What was his name?"

"Bryce Davies."

As soon as the name was out of his mouth, Sydney felt the color drain from her face.

# CHAPTER 6

Davies. That couldn't be a coincidence. It had to be the same man Sydney had attempted to meet with in Golden Gate Park. He'd been murdered?

Justin leaned forward, studying her intently. "What is it? You're remembering something, aren't you?"

She nodded. "Davies is a common last name, but I did have a Mr. Davies call me on Friday evening asking if I could meet with him the next morning. He said he'd overheard something about high-ranking officials involved in something illegal, but he wouldn't say more over the phone. When I went to meet him the next day, he never showed up."

Justin's expression became pained again. "That's because he was killed Friday night." He went on to tell her what he knew, and Sydney could tell it was still hard for him to talk about. He also told her about his conversation with Roger Calloway after the funeral.

"Did Roger mention if there's an ongoing investigation into Bryce's death?" Sydney asked.

"I don't think there is. Roger said he was hoping I'd look into things since I'm a reporter and Bryce's friend."

Sydney thought for a moment. "What else did Bryce say in his letter? Anything that would indicate who might have been after him? Maybe he had suspicions about somebody in particular?"

"No, he just said that he'd overheard the district attorney talking to somebody. The DA mentioned my senator's name, plus something about a payoff and a shipment in Customs lockup. What I'm wondering is, what payoff were they talking about? And what was the shipment in the lockup?"

"Hmm," Sydney murmured, thinking. "I wonder if they were talking about the artifacts."

"Artifacts?"

"A couple of weeks ago, Customs was tipped off that some Mayan artifacts that had been stolen from an archaeological dig in Guatemala were arriving in the area by boat. Customs intercepted the boat and found the artifacts, plus an assortment of antiques and wares, some of which had also been reported as stolen from museums and private collections in various parts of South America. A few days later, however, the artifacts and other items went missing from the Customs lockup."

"Does anybody know what happened to them?"

Sydney shook her head. "It was one of my colleagues that followed the investigation. The word on the street is that the stuff was shipped out of state and sold on the black market, and that the board members of the corporation that owns the shipping company got a good-sized cut of the profit."

"A payoff for their part in the smuggling of the goods?"

"That's the rumor."

"Does your colleague have any leads?"

"A few, but I don't think the investigation's going very far."

Justin was quiet for a minute as he digested the information. "But what does my senator have to do with this?" he mused. "Or the district attorney?"

Sydney snorted. "I can offer a guess on that last one. There are a lot of us who think our district attorney is dirty. We just haven't been able to prove it. If something fishy is going on, I wouldn't be surprised to hear that Griffin's involved."

"Hmm," Justin murmured. "Right now I think we've got more questions than answers."

"You're right. We do." After a moment, she asked, "So what is it you want from me?"

A look of apprehension crossed Justin's face, and he shifted anxiously in his seat. "Well, I kind of have a favor to ask."

"What do you need?"

"I know this is your turf, and I don't want you to feel like I'm encroaching, but I could really use your help investigating this. I got my editor's sign-off to poke around while I'm down here to try to find out how my senator might be involved and see if I can learn more about what's going on with some of the other things Bryce mentioned in his letter. But I don't have any contacts here, so I can't do it alone. I'm only going to be here for a couple of days, and I'm not expecting to blow this whole thing open in that short a time. I just need to find something to show my editor that it's worth pursuing."

His eyes were pleading when they met hers. "Is there any way I could talk you into a joint investigation? You're already familiar with some of the matters Bryce mentioned, like the Customs lockup and the suspicions about your district attorney. Maybe we could tie all this together and bring these people to justice. It sounded like Bryce trusted you enough to approach you with what he overheard. I'm just asking you to follow this through with me."

Sydney leaned back in her chair as she mulled over his request. She didn't like partnering with people. The times she'd done so had been disastrous. She knew she wasn't the easiest person to work with. She tackled her investigations with ferocity and determination, and that kind of intensity often sent partners running for the door. If Justin was serious about getting to the bottom of this, though, maybe he'd stick it out. She hoped he would. If a senator really was involved, this story could be huge. What did she have to lose?

She arched a questioning brow at him. "Joint bylines? My name first?"

He broke out into a full, heart-stopping grin that lit up his entire face and produced a hint of a dimple in each cheek. Sydney felt a little weak in the knees under the intensity of that smile.

"Of course," he assured her. "It is your city, after all."

Trying to ignore the fluttering in her heart, she swallowed and managed to sound somewhat normal when she spoke. "Then you've got yourself a deal."

"Great!" He leaned forward, his face eager. "Where do we start?"

She gave him a look of challenge. This was where the big dogs got separated from the pups in their profession. "How are you at research?"

He met her challenging gaze with a determined stare of his own. "I can hold my own."

"Yeah, well, we'll see about that." She gave him a dubious look as she reached for a notebook and pen. "Let's start with everything Bryce told you he overheard."

Justin jumped right in. "Bryce mentioned hearing the name of a corporation, but it's a little unusual. I can't remember it offhand. I left the letter in my car. I'll get it later so you can read it."

"Good," she said. "In the meantime . . ." Her voice trailed off as she stood and looked out over the bustling newsroom. She raised her arm to get a colleague's attention. "Derek!"

The young man hurried over. "What's up?"

"Can you pull everything you can find on Utah senator Robert Longhurst? We'll need background info, business holdings, financial records—the works."

"You got it," Derek said before hurrying off.

Sydney turned back to Justin. "It could take a while to get all that research. Is there anything you need to do for a couple of hours? You could check back with me later."

"I didn't have anything planned." He checked his watch. "I suppose I could grab a bite to eat. I ate breakfast pretty early and haven't had anything since."

"I haven't had lunch yet, either," she realized, paying attention to the sudden rumbling of her stomach.

Justin's eyes lit up. "So why don't we grab some lunch? We can eat while you read the letter."

"That sounds good. How do you feel about Thai food? There's a great Thai place not far from here that serves the most incredible lahb gai."

Justin raised one eyebrow in question. "What's lahb gai?"

She grinned. "It's a spicy chicken salad. Trust me, it's to die for."

"I'm game."

When they got outside, Justin retrieved the letter from his rental car, and they took Sydney's car to the restaurant. The place wasn't crowded, so they opted for a booth away from the other diners so they could talk more freely.

While they waited for their orders, Sydney sat back and started to read. After a minute her eyes went wide. "Justin, this mentions Marengo, Inc."

He nodded. "Yeah, that's the name of the corporation I couldn't remember. So?"

"Marengo is one of the companies that reported shipments missing in my crime ring investigation. During my research, I gathered information on a couple of high-profile businessmen who appeared to be laundering money. I managed to follow some leads and a money trail, and I discovered they were trafficking drugs through a shipping company in San Francisco. When I tipped off the police and they ransacked the warehouse, I did a little snooping and found evidence that the men behind the shipping company had not only been smuggling drugs but had also been stealing goods from inbound and outbound freighters and selling them."

"On the black market?"

"You got it. The people at the shipping company were obviously good at covering their tracks, and they never stole enough at one time to send up red flags—it was only a carton or two here and there. It was enough to make me suspicious, though, which is why I ended up doing some research on the missing items. I turned over what I'd found to a detective I know on the force, and they managed to track down some of the items."

Justin's curiosity grew. "What kinds of goods went missing?"

"Antiques, mostly. But there were also computer components, high tech gadgetries—anything that could bring a price. On a hunch, I started piecing together a list of everything that was stolen. This is where it gets interesting.

You'd think that once a company started having bad luck with a shipping company not getting them their stuff, they'd change shipping companies, right?"

Justin nodded, but Sydney shook her head, her eyes bright. "Not the case. In fact, one company in particular had more items go missing than any of the others, and the dollar amount listed on the claim forms filed with insurance companies grossed almost three million dollars."

Justin's eyebrows shot up. "Three million dollars!"

"Yes. And guess who that company was?" She paused for dramatic effect. "Marengo, Inc."

Justin stared at her for a long moment, trying to digest the information. "That doesn't make any sense. You'd think the owners of the company would care enough about getting their things that they'd switch shipping companies with those kinds of losses."

"You'd think so," Sydney agreed, "which is what made me suspicious. And get this. One of those stolen antiques—a vase—made headlines in France a short time ago for selling at an auction for nearly half a million dollars."

"Maybe the company recovered it and sold it at the auction."

Sydney shook her head. "That's just it. When the authorities questioned the people at Marengo about it, they claimed their vase had never been recovered and that the vase sold at the auction wasn't the same one. But I did a little digging, and guess what I found? The day after the auction, a tidy sum was deposited into Marengo's account by guess who? The person who sold the vase at the auction."

"Very fishy. Any luck finding out who's running Marengo, Inc.?"

Sydney sighed and leaned back against the booth, crossing her arms. "Word on the street was that the owner of the company is some high-profile businessman who has his hands in some pretty questionable enterprises, but I could never find out who he was. And I was never able to prove that Marengo was in on the sales with the shipping company, either."

"Are you still researching the story?"

"Afraid not." Sydney frowned. "My editor axed the story because I was at a dead end. It killed me to let it go. I was sure the people behind Marengo were tied to the shipping company, the smuggled drugs, and the high-profile businessmen that my crime ring exposé took down. I just couldn't prove any of it."

She looked down at the letter in her hand. "If the name Marengo keeps coming up like this, I'd be willing to bet there's a reason for it."

"I agree. We need to do some more digging into this corporation. There's got to be a connection to Senator Longhurst if Bryce overheard the two mentioned in the same conversation."

"Yeah, that's too much of a coincidence. I'll tell you one thing, though—we're not going to get to the bottom of this in a couple of days." She looked frustrated for a moment, but then her countenance brightened. "Hey, here's a thought. We should both keep researching, and we can keep in touch with what we turn up. Maybe together we can blow this thing wide open."

# CHAPTER 7

*Maybe together we can blow this thing wide open.* While Sydney texted someone at her office, Justin replayed Sydney's words in his head, and a slow smile worked its way across his face. *Together.* That meant keeping in touch. The idea definitely appealed to him. Even after spending such a short amount of time with Sydney, he realized that he was more attracted to her than any girl he'd ever met. She was dynamic. She thought well on her feet, was clever and intelligent, and knew just how to approach an investigation. He was already intrigued by her and wanted to get to know her better. Staying in touch after he returned to Utah sounded perfect.

But then reality brought him back to earth with a thump. So they kept in touch. They got to know each other. Maybe they even got close. But what then? Long-distance relationships rarely worked out. And what about religion? Dating someone not of his faith would only complicate his life. The voice of reason sounded clearly in his head, but his heart wasn't falling into line.

"Here you go, sir." A heavily accented voice at his elbow drew him out of his thoughts. He looked up to see the waitress standing beside their table, setting dishes of food before them. After making sure they didn't need anything else, she left them to their lunch.

The tantalizing smell of chicken, onions, and spices wafted from his plate, and Justin breathed deeply. "Man, this smells great."

Sydney grinned as she scooped some of the salad onto her fork. "Try it. It tastes even better than it smells."

Justin put a forkful into his mouth and sighed as the flavors blended and invaded his senses. He couldn't remember the last time he'd had a dish this good. When he saw Sydney watching him, waiting for his response, he nodded in genuine appreciation. "You're right," he managed after swallowing. "This is incredible."

"Told you," Sydney said, a pleased smile on her face.

"What's in this? I taste the onions and mint, but there's something in here that I can't quite place." He put another forkful into his mouth and looked thoughtful. "Maybe a touch of chili powder?"

Sydney stared at him, clearly impressed. "You sound like quite the cook. I'm surprised."

"Surprised that I cook?" He looked up from his salad and arched an eyebrow at her. "Sure, I cook. Even bachelors have to eat, right?"

Sydney laughed. "I guess so. So, how did you learn to cook?"

"My older sister is a cooking fanatic," Justin explained. "She studied at a culinary institute and did a culinary internship in Italy. When she came back to the States, she was a chef in a five-star Italian restaurant on the east coast before she had kids. She still experiments with new recipes and has taught me a lot."

It wasn't long before they were both stuffed, even though neither of them had finished their large salads.

"There's still a little left," Justin said, peering at her plate. "Do you want to take it home with you? You wouldn't have to cook tonight."

Sydney laughed. "Cook? You're kidding, right? I eat out. It's a lot easier than trying to cook and setting my kitchen on fire. I have the fire department on speed dial."

Justin laughed. "You can't be that bad."

"Believe me, I am. Anyway, I won't need anything tonight. I have a dinner appointment."

An unexpected stab of jealousy shot through him. Dinner appointment? That sounded suspiciously like another way of saying "date." Did she have a boyfriend? Somebody special she was seeing? His hopes plummeted. It made all the sense in the world. Somebody like Sydney would certainly have a boyfriend.

Gathering the nerve to ask, he did his best to sound casual. "You've got a date? Anyone special?"

She shook her head. "It's an interview, actually. With Stephen Dover, of Dover Enterprises?" She voiced it as a question, obviously asking if he knew who she was referring to.

Unfortunately, Justin did. Everybody knew who Stephen Dover was. Justin had seen televised interviews of Dover, and there was just something about the man he didn't like. Maybe it was how he seemed to talk down to people rather than *with* them. So much of a journalist's success in this profession came from the ability to read between the lines, to discover the hidden truths about people. By scrutinizing Dover's print interviews, Justin had come to the conclusion that the billionaire didn't care so much about the people he helped as he did about the recognition a cause brought him. That told Justin everything he needed to know about the man.

"That's—that's great," he said when he realized Sydney was watching him curiously.

"I see it as an opportunity," she admitted. "I put in a call to his scheduling assistant last week, but I didn't really think I'd hear back. *Everybody* wants to interview Mr. Dover right now. But his assistant called back and set up an exclusive interview with him over a private dinner at The Dining Room at the Ritz-Carlton."

Justin knew he should have felt better, knowing it was an interview, but the words *Ritz-Carlton* kept rolling around in his head. How strictly business could it be if the dinner interview was at a five-star restaurant?

"I see," he replied. He tried to muster up some enthusiasm and stamp down his irrational feelings of jealousy.

"I take it you don't like him."

Justin looked up. He caught her studying him intently, analyzing his reaction. "Not really, but then I've never met him personally. Don't let my opinion ruin your date."

A smile quirked at the corners of her mouth. "It's not a date. It's an opportunity to have a nice dinner *and* get an exclusive with one of the richest and most powerful men in the country. It could mean big things for my career."

Justin lifted his eyebrows in disbelief. "He's often referred to as one of the country's most eligible bachelors. You're not the slightest bit interested in him?"

Sydney leaned back in her seat and lifted one shoulder in a half shrug. "I don't know. Sure, he's good-looking, but from everything I've heard about him, he's into high-class events, public appearances, and hobnobbing with the rich and famous. While I'm incredibly flattered that he would contact me about a dinner interview, he's really not my type."

Justin felt an unreasonable flash of hope. "So, what *is* your type?"

"I guess I'm more of a pizza-and-a-movie kind of girl."

*Dang.* Justin suppressed a sigh. That wasn't what he needed to hear. A night in with pizza and a movie was his favorite indulgence too. Here he was trying to distance himself from her, but instead he kept corralling himself into learning things about her that made her even more attractive.

"Back to what you said earlier," Sydney began, "why don't you like Stephen Dover? I'm curious."

"It's nothing I can put my finger on. There's just something about him that makes me wonder if he's not what he appears to be."

"Hmm," she murmured. "You think he's hiding something?"

"Could be. I've been around this business long enough to know that men like that don't usually get where they are by playing nice."

"Good point."

Just then, Sydney's cell phone rang. She pulled it from her purse and glanced at the caller ID. "Sorry, it's work. I should probably get this." She flipped the phone open and pressed it to her ear. "Hello? . . . Yeah, Derek, what's up?" She listened for a minute, then said, "Thanks, I'm on my way."

She hung up and turned to Justin. "There's been a break-in at one of the labs in the city, and the guy locked several employees in a security vault before taking off with some high-tech equipment. My boss wants me to get over there."

Justin tried to ignore his sudden flash of disappointment. "I understand." He signaled for the waitress, and she was at their table a moment later with the bill in hand.

Before Sydney could reach for the bill, Justin picked it up and pulled out his wallet. "My treat," he said with a smile, then proceeded to ignore Sydney's protests over the matter.

Once the bill was paid, they headed out of the restaurant. There was an awkward moment as they climbed into the car and Sydney slid her key into the ignition. "Thanks for lunch," she said, looking suddenly shy and vulnerable.

Justin felt a little tongue-tied himself. "You're welcome."

Sydney started the car, but she sat for a moment, appearing to ponder something.

"What's the matter?" Justin asked.

She gave him a sheepish smile. "I'm trying to figure out what to do with you. Your car's at the *Chronicle* in one direction, but the lab is in the other."

An idea formed in Justin's mind. "How long will your on-site interviews take you?" At her confused look, he hurried on. "If it's not long, what would you say to letting me tag along with you on your story? When you're done, I could ride back with you to the *Chronicle* and pick my car up then."

Sydney's eyes brightened, and he dared to hope that it meant she was enjoying his company as much as he was hers. "I wouldn't mind you tagging along, but I'd hate for you to get bored."

He shook his head. "It's nothing I haven't done before."

"All right then." She gave him an eager smile. "Let's go."

# CHAPTER 8

Justin arrived back at his borrowed condo early that evening, feeling surprisingly good considering the day had started off with Bryce's funeral. The reason for his mood had only one explanation—Sydney.

He smiled. Sydney had worried that he'd be bored tagging along with her on her assignment, but in truth, he'd loved watching her work. She'd walked right through the boisterous crowd of reporters all vying for the story and managed to be one of the few to get statements from the people involved. She was fearless and confident, so unlike any girl he'd ever met. She was definitely something special, and the time they had spent together that day had only furthered this belief.

Glancing up at the clock in the front room, he noted it was after five. Right now Sydney was getting ready to have dinner with Stephen Dover.

Justin frowned as an unsettling emotion weighed him down.

*There's no reason to feel jealous,* he told himself. *She said herself that this was business, and that Dover isn't her type. Besides, why do you care who she has dinner with? It shouldn't make any difference to you.*

But if that were true, why couldn't he shake this feeling?

Deciding to take his mind off Sydney's dinner date, Justin went into the bedroom to change out of the suit he'd been wearing all day. He put on jeans and a T-shirt, grabbed his cell phone, and retrieved Roger Calloway's business card from his wallet. He might be in an unfamiliar city without all of Sydney's resources, but he did have a source of his own in Bryce's old partner. With any luck, Roger would still be at the precinct.

As luck would have it, he was. He answered Justin's call warmly, and when Justin told him he was looking into Bryce's death, Roger was eager to help. He answered Justin's questions about the cases Bryce had been working on prior to his death. Justin jotted the information down, along with the names of the detectives in charge of each case.

"Is there anything else I can do to help?" Roger asked when Justin finished writing down the information.

"Nothing I can think of right now," Justin said. "But if you think of anything else that might help, could you call me? If you can't reach me on my cell, you can also call Sydney Hallam. She's a reporter with the *Chronicle*. She and I are working together on this. Do you know who she is?"

"Not personally, but I read her stuff. She's good."

Justin smiled. "Yes, she is. If anybody can help us get to the bottom of this, it's her. Let me give you her number."

After doing so, he thanked Roger and hung up. With a sigh, he leaned back on the couch and stared down at his notes. It wasn't a lot to go on, but it did give him and Sydney a jumping-off point. With some digging, perhaps they could find out which case it was that Bryce was working on that had prompted him to fill out a new report and walk it into the DA's office. Maybe this would turn up something significant. Maybe it wouldn't. But it was something.

Feeling satisfied that he'd made some strides today, Justin tossed his notebook onto the coffee table, swung his feet up onto the couch, and reached for the remote control. He turned on the television and tried not to look at the clock on the far wall. It would only remind him that it was going to be a long evening with thoughts of a certain beautiful brunette stuck in his head.

* * *

Sydney looked around the limo in which she was riding. It boasted black leather seats, a high-resolution television and expensive stereo system, and darkly tinted windows that blocked the view of outside observers. When Stephen Dover had said he would come by for her, she'd assumed the vehicle would be nice—maybe a Lexus or some other luxury car. A limousine had not been in the running.

*If he's trying to impress me, it's working.*

She looked over at the tall, handsome man sitting across from her, his thick, dark hair cropped short in a fashionable style, and his shockingly blue eyes standing out against his tanned face. He was impeccably dressed in a black tailored suit that she was sure cost more than she made in a year. He looked every bit the billionaire that he was, yet he'd done nothing but put her at ease since the moment he'd picked her up at her apartment.

Stephen, as he insisted on being called, had been charming and funny during their drive to the restaurant, even sharing an amusing story about a golf game gone awry in his latest attempt to divert himself from work—something he apparently didn't do well. His likable nature put her at ease, and she soon found herself relaxing and enjoying herself as they wound through the streets of San Francisco toward their destination.

Unexpectedly, Sydney wondered what Justin might say about all this. The thought made her smile. When she'd mentioned her dinner appointment with Stephen Dover earlier that day, she could have sworn Justin had been jealous. She'd been amused by that, especially since they hardly knew each other. But if he had been jealous, wouldn't that mean he was interested in her? She shook her head. It was probably just her wishful thinking. She didn't know Justin very well, but he didn't seem the type to fall for a girl he'd just met.

While Stephen apologetically took a business call, Sydney thought back to the raw emotions on Justin's face when they'd talked of his friend's death. It was obvious he felt things deeply and was very thoughtful and caring. He was also very easy to be with.

She'd enjoyed spending time with him that afternoon when he'd tagged along to the labs where the break-in had occurred. She'd expected him to be bored, but the light in his eyes and his interested expression had told her he was enjoying himself. He'd listened intently to the officers responding to her questions, and he'd even asked a couple of perceptive questions that she hadn't thought to ask. He was obviously good at his job, but was also clearly respectful of her skills, which Sydney found refreshing. Most men she'd worked with were either turned off by her take-charge attitude or felt threatened by her. To her satisfaction, Justin didn't appear to be either.

The limousine slowed, bringing Sydney's attention back to her surroundings. They had turned off the street and were pulling up to the beautiful and historic Ritz-Carlton. She'd always admired the elegant neoclassical architecture of the building, with its stately exterior columns. The behemoth was a city landmark, located in the heart of Nob Hill and within walking distance of Union Square, Fisherman's Wharf, and the Financial District. Perched on a hill, it provided breathtaking views of the city that stretched out around it.

"You look impressed."

Stephen's voice dragged her attention away from the famous hotel, and she looked over to see him smiling at her. Sydney nodded and returned his smile. "I am. But that was your intention, wasn't it?"

Stephen laughed, a charming sound that suggested appreciation of her candor. "Nothing gets past you. Yes, I'm trying to impress you. What interviewee wouldn't try? You hold my fate in your hands with that article you'll be writing about me."

Their limo driver slowed, and a valet hurried to their car to open the door. Stephen alighted first, then turned and offered Sydney his elbow in a very gentleman-like fashion. Unable to help feeling flattered, she slipped her hand into the crook of his elbow and allowed him to lead her inside.

When they stepped through the front doors, it was all she could do to keep her mouth from falling open. *Spectacular* was the best word she had to describe the interior, with its rich, plush carpeting, crystal wall sconces and chandeliers, and tables elegantly draped in white linen tablecloths with crystal glasses and gleaming silverware that sparkled in the soft light.

As soon as they were seated, a waiter appeared to take their orders. The rest of the evening passed in a happy blur as Sydney enjoyed an incredible gourmet meal, beautiful surroundings, and good company. Stephen was well educated and a great conversationalist. They talked about books, politics, current events, and how many of today's events related to the events of world history—one of his passions, she learned. Sydney had always enjoyed world history, but Stephen's knowledge of historical events, places, and the lessons learned from each was truly remarkable.

She jotted down notes in the notebook she'd brought, writing the answers to her questions about his new business ventures. He dodged questions about his personal life, but Sydney felt confident she had enough information to write a good article. It wouldn't be Pulitzer material, but it would make her editor happy.

When they were done with their meal, Stephen talked her into dessert, assuring her that the raspberry mille-feuille—basically layers of pastry, fruit, and cream—was not to be missed.

As they waited for the dessert to be brought to them, Stephen leaned back in his chair and smiled. "I'm afraid we've spent most of the meal talking about me and my passions. I think the time might have been better spent talking about you."

The corners of Sydney's mouth curved upward. "There's not much to tell. I spend most of my time working."

"Surely there's more to you than work. From talking to you, I can tell you're well-versed in politics, history, and a myriad of other subjects. You must have outside interests that led to your exposure to such things? Involving yourself in political groups or art circles, perhaps?"

"Nothing as exciting as that." Sydney smiled. "I've always loved learning, and I took a wide range of classes in college when I majored in journalism. Since then, though, my life's pretty much been about work. I love to read whenever I get the chance, but my schedule allows little time for it. I've had to work nonstop since graduating just to get where I am."

"Well, I'd say that hard work paid off. Your last piece, the exposé you wrote on the crime ring, was impressive. Are you currently working on something equally as exciting?"

A warning touched Sydney's thoughts, urging her to be cautious. "Nothing of that magnitude," she said vaguely. "I have one story I'm working on that has been on-again and off-again, but I think I finally have a source that will get things going again. I can't do anything else with this story until I have inside information, so we'll see how it goes."

Clearly intrigued, Stephen leaned forward, resting his forearms on the edge of the table and clasping his hands. His eyes were intent upon hers. "You've piqued my interest. What is it you're looking to find?"

Trying to play it cool, she lifted her glass to her lips and gave him a coy smile. "I won't know until I find it, will I?"

Stephen didn't move, nor did the intensity of his gaze waver for several moments. It made her feel as if he were assessing an opponent, searching for a weakness that would give him the upper hand. Then he blinked, and it was as if that simple movement restored his previous mood. His body relaxed, and that charming, debonair smile flashed across his face.

"Well, whatever it is you're working on," he said, lifting his glass to salute her, "I'm sure you'll find a way to accomplish it."

She felt her own body relax, and she managed to return his smile. "Thank you. I'd like to think so. Truth be known, I've always been rather ambitious."

"As have I." He paused for a moment, then asked, "Are you familiar with the painting *Bonaparte Crossing the Alps at Grand-Saint-Bernard*?" When she nodded, he went on. "I have it in my study. It's the most famous depiction of Napoléon's career. His strategy in that Italian campaign was instrumental in securing his victory."

"You know a lot about Napoléon," Sydney replied. "I take it you're a fan?"

His eyes glowed as he quoted, "'Ambition is never content, even on the summit of greatness.'" When Sydney looked at him with interest, he explained with a smile, "Napoléon said that. I've always taken it to heart and lived my life accordingly. It helped me to get where I am today."

"Interesting. Do you mind if I quote you on that?"

"By all means," he said as she reached for her pen and notebook and began scribbling across the page. When she finished, he held up his glass. "Here's to ambition."

* * *

Longhurst snapped his cell phone shut, ending his call, and set it down on the end table beside him. Pressing himself deeper into the Italian leather armchair situated in front of the fire, he stared at the dancing flames as he pondered the phone call he'd just had.

Apparently, Ms. Hallam had a few tricks up her sleeve.

His thoughts were interrupted when his assistant came into the study. "Did we manage to learn anything from that reporter tonight?"

Longhurst shook his head. "Not enough."

"Does she know anything?"

"If she does, she's hiding it well." His hands tightened on the arms of the chair. After several moments, Longhurst pushed himself out of the chair. "Continue to have her followed," he said, and with that, he hurried from the room.

# CHAPTER 9

"Sydney, what have you done to follow up with Park, the county investigator at the DA's office?"

Carl had all but swooped down on her the next morning the moment she set foot in the newsroom. "I'm on it," she promised as her editor fell into step beside her. "I called the DA's office right after I finished up with the story about the break-in at the lab. Park wasn't in, but his receptionist told me that the best time to reach him is after lunch. I'm going to track him down this afternoon. In the meantime, I got an exclusive interview with Stephen Dover last night. I'm about to type up that copy."

That seemed to appease Carl. "Nice job, Syd. But don't think this gets you completely out of my doghouse for missing Park yesterday. I want you hounding that man until he talks."

When Sydney assured him she would, he left her to her work, and she continued on to her desk. Her steps slowed, however, as she neared her desk.

*What in the world . . . ?*

Sitting next to her computer was the biggest, most gorgeous bouquet of flowers she'd ever seen.

*Who would send me flowers?*

Curious, she reached for the small, white envelope tucked inside the bouquet.

> *Sydney,*
> *Just wanted to thank you again for a wonderful evening. It was a pleasure to finally meet you. I hope we can do it again soon.*
> *More a fan than ever,*
> *Stephen*

She smiled at his thoughtfulness. But as she lifted a hand to touch a delicate, striped orchid nestled in among the arrangement, she realized that a small part of her felt disappointed at seeing Dover's name at the bottom of the card. With a frown, she asked herself, *Who were you hoping they were from?*

"Oh. My. Gosh."

Sydney turned to see Jennifer approaching, her friend's eyes wide as she stared in shock at the huge bouquet. Sydney smiled at Jennifer's appearance. She had spiked her short, reddish hair and wore glittery butterfly earrings that dangled almost to her chin. On anybody else, they would have looked gaudy, but on Jennifer they were adorable.

"Who sent you those? They're amazing!" Jennifer gushed, looking through the bouquet for the telltale card.

Sydney held up the note and waved it at her friend. "Stephen Dover. Can you believe it?"

"Oh, I am *so* jealous!" Jennifer plopped down in the chair beside her desk. "Tell me all about it. Every detail."

Sydney laughed and proceeded to tell Jennifer all about the evening— the limo, the fancy restaurant, the incredible gourmet meal, and Dover's irresistible charm.

Jennifer propped her elbow on the corner of the desk, dropped her chin into her palm, and sighed dreamily. "I can't believe how lucky you are, getting handpicked to interview him, taken to a five-star restaurant, and wined and dined."

"I didn't have wine. I had an Italian soda."

Jennifer dismissed this comment with a flick of her hand. "Doesn't matter. The principle is the same. Did he ask you out again?"

"It wasn't a date. It was an interview. Remember?"

"But it could *lead* to more," Jennifer insisted.

Sydney shook her head. "I don't think so. Besides, even if he called and asked me to do something, I don't think I'd accept. I'm just not interested in him romantically."

Jennifer looked disappointed. "No sparks?"

"No sparks."

"That's too bad." Jennifer sighed. "I keep hoping you'll meet Prince Charming and ride off into the sunset. You deserve a prince."

Sydney laughed. "That'd be nice, except I stopped believing in fairy tales a long time ago. The reality is, I've got Stephen's interview to write up for Carl, plus a ton of research to do on that senator I'm investigating. Work. Now that's reality."

"Yeah. Bummer." Jennifer stood. "Well, I'm off to do that reality-work thing, too. Talk to you later."

As she headed back to her own desk, she passed Derek, who carried a large stack of papers. He dropped them onto Sydney's desk with a thump and grinned.

"Everything you've ever wanted to know about Senator Robert Longhurst," he said. "This should keep you busy for a while."

"Thanks, Derek." When he hurried off, she pulled her notebook out of her attaché and turned to her notes from the dinner interview with Stephen the night before. As much as she wanted to look through the Longhurst research, she had to complete the interview article first.

When she was finally finished, Sydney picked up the first page from the pile Derek had brought her and started to read. Two hours later, she was so engrossed in the research that she didn't hear the sound of approaching footsteps. It wasn't until she heard the sound of a man clearing his throat that she looked up and saw Justin standing beside her desk.

Instead of the suit he'd worn the day before, he was wearing jeans, a white T-shirt that brought out his tanned complexion and sandy blond hair, and a brown leather jacket that accentuated his rugged good looks. The only thing missing was his heart-stopping smile. He stared at the large bouquet of flowers on her desk, his expression decidedly jealous.

"How was your date?" he asked dryly.

"Hello to you too," Sydney answered with a smile. Realizing that he was jealous made her heart flutter. It seemed he was interested after all. "My 'date' was fine, thanks. Stephen is a fascinating man. We had a lot to talk about."

"Hmm," Justin answered noncommittally.

Realizing he wasn't going to give anything further away, Sydney changed the subject. "So what did you do last night?"

He held up a leather portfolio. "I managed to get hold of Bryce's old partner Roger Calloway last night. I got a list of the cases Bryce had been working on before he died. I thought it could possibly give us some clues as to what might have gotten him killed."

"Good thinking," Sydney said. "Anything that jumps out at you?"

He shook his head and sat down in the empty chair beside her desk. "Not really. But then, you'd be more familiar with the cases than I would." He looked at the research cluttering the desk. "I'd set this down so you could look through my notes, but it doesn't look like there's any room."

Sydney laughed. "No kidding." She gestured to the stacks of papers on the desk in front of her. "This is everything Derek could find on your senator. And these," she said, picking up several sets of stapled pages, highlighted and dog-eared, proving that she'd been hard at work for a while, "are most of the businesses he owns. His corporate empire is impressive, to say the least. Some of this you probably already know, but here's what I learned. Most of these places were owned by his father, Robert Longhurst Sr., who had his hands in everything from alternative-power research to scientific labs and deep-space research. When he died, he left his entire fortune and corporate empire to his only son, Robert Jr. However, Robert Jr. was more interested in politics, and sold off many of the companies, some of which, interestingly enough, are co-owned by Stephen Dover."

Justin's eyebrows darted upward. "Seriously?"

Sydney nodded, and her voice grew more enthusiastic as she continued. "It seems Longhurst Sr. and Stephen Dover had been in business together for years and had several lucrative business dealings between them. From what I gather, Dover was the son of a friend of Longhurst's, and he took Dover under his wing and helped him get his start in the business world. The rest of Dover's rise to wealth and power is, as they say, history. That's where Longhurst Jr. comes in."

She handed Justin a highlighted sheet. "As you can see from this, Dover was one of the biggest contributors to Longhurst Jr.'s senate campaign."

"So they know each other," Justin observed.

"Pretty well, judging from his sale of the co-owned companies back to Dover. They still share ownership of several major corporations." Sydney tapped her pen on a smaller stack of papers near her keyboard. "What I find even more interesting is that Longhurst's voting record is questionable, at best. He doesn't seem to understand 'conflict of interest.' He's voted for and been an integral part of pushing through legislation that gives business owners a lot of leniency in business laws and tax breaks. I'm sure his and Dover's companies have made millions, thanks to his involvement in politics."

"Looks like Stephen Dover bought himself a senator," Justin muttered.

Sydney nodded. "Very likely. I got curious and tried to connect Dover to the things we're investigating to see if he might be involved, but other than the fact that he and Longhurst share common business interests, there isn't anything connecting him to the illegal activity. Dover's a dead end."

"Well, Longhurst owns hundreds of companies and has connections to powerful businessmen all over the world. Just because we're investigating him doesn't mean everybody else he deals with is involved."

"True."

"What I want to know is, what does all this have to do with what Bryce overheard?"

"I wondered that, too, until I found this." She handed him another set of pages. "I was grasping at straws, really, trying to make some connections, when I came across a list of the members on Longhurst's political team. Longhurst's principal advisor's son was the Customs officer involved in the investigation of the confiscated shipment—including the Mayan artifacts."

"Did the police question him?"

"Thoroughly. They suspected he had something to do with it, but they never found any proof." She thought for a moment. "Customs wouldn't have had any control over the crime ring investigation as a whole, but having someone on the inside would have been instrumental in getting those artifacts and other goods out of the lockup. Maybe the district attorney was involved in finding out who was in charge of the lockup and gaining access to it."

Justin shook his head in amazement. "And you learned all this just this morning? How long have you been here?"

Grateful that he recognized the amount of work she'd done, she gave him a weary smile. "A long time."

He looked back down at the papers strewn across her desk and let out a long breath. "It's a great start, but do we have anything concrete to link the stolen goods to Longhurst? Or to the DA?"

Sydney shook her head. "Not yet."

"What about Marengo? Have you made any connections to them?"

"Okay, I haven't been here *that* long," Sydney said, laughing. "I can only research so many things at once."

"Well, I'm here now. How can I help?"

Sydney's heart warmed at his eagerness to help. The crestfallen expression he had worn earlier was gone, and in its place was the smile that made her heart unexpectedly twist in her chest.

"I have an idea," Sydney said. "I have a good friend at the SFPD—Detective Richardson. He worked on that series of shipments where the goods went missing, so we ended up doing a lot of the same research. He might be able to help. Let me give him a call."

Sydney picked up her phone and dialed, and soon she was talking to the detective. When she hung up, she smiled at Justin. "We're in luck. He says he has a meeting in an hour, but if we hurry over, he can see us."

"Great, let's go."

# CHAPTER 10

Justin followed Sydney into the police department and down the hall to Detective Richardson's office. When she knocked, a deep voice bellowed, "Come in!"

Sydney opened the door, and Justin spotted a huge bear of a man sitting behind the desk. He looked to be in his early fifties and had salt-and-pepper hair and a neatly trimmed mustache. His aura radiated confidence, and his expression meant business, but when he looked up from his paperwork and spotted Sydney, his eyes crinkled into a smile that made him look gentler somehow. It was easy to see that he had a soft spot for Sydney.

"Sydney," he rumbled, getting to his feet. "Come on in."

If the man had been intimidating sitting behind his desk, Justin decided he was infinitely more daunting standing up. He stood a good six inches taller than Justin's six feet, and his broad shoulders and thick chest made the space behind the desk seem small. The white dress shirt that was tucked into his pants showed him to be carrying quite a few extra pounds in the midsection, but Justin suspected that in the man's younger years, he would have been a force to be reckoned with on a ball field.

"Hey, Paul," Sydney greeted him with a warm smile. Then she introduced Justin, and the detective reached a thick arm and beefy hand across his desk to give Justin a crushing handshake.

"Have a seat," he said, motioning them to the chairs in front of his desk. "What can I do for you today, Sydney? You said something about that shipping theft we investigated a few months ago?"

Sydney explained the situation, and he listened intently, nodding every now and then and asking the occasional question. "So, what we're looking for is more information on Marengo," Sydney told him. "Has your investigation turned up anything that might be helpful?"

Detective Richardson leaned back in his chair and scrubbed a hand over his face. "There might be, but nothing leaps to mind. Maybe something in there is more important than we thought, though. How about I do some looking and get back to you?"

Sydney beamed. "That would be great."

"Just remember our deal," he said, his tone playfully stern. "If I share information, you come back to me with anything significant."

"Of course. Thanks, Paul."

As soon as they had left Detective Richardson's office, Justin voiced the question that had been on his mind since meeting the detective. "So what's Paul's story? The guy is *huge*."

Sydney laughed. "He used to play linebacker for the 49ers until he blew out his knee. It killed his football career, but he'd always been interested in law enforcement, so that's how he ended up here. The first time I met him, I was ready to turn tail and hide, but when I got to know him, I learned he was a pretty gentle guy with a big heart. We don't tell the bad guys that, though. He says he prefers to look intimidating in this line of work."

"I can imagine. So where to now?"

\* \* \*

Sydney mulled over Justin's question as they headed for the parking lot. "Let's head back to the *Chronicle* and go through some of that research on Longhurst. You said you could hold your own at researching." She gave him a teasing look of challenge. "Let's see how good you really are."

Justin laughed. "Throwing down the gauntlet, are you? Bring it on, Hallam."

They started to step off the curb into the parking lot, but a sudden eerie, prickling sensation jerked Sydney to a halt. Her smile faded as a chill coursed through her, causing the hairs on her arms to stand on end.

She shivered. The feeling was undeniable.

They were being watched.

Glancing back at the police station, she studied the people coming, going, and milling about. Nobody seemed to be looking their way, but still the feeling persisted.

"Are you okay?"

Justin's voice roused her, and she turned to see concern written across his face.

"Yeah, I'm fine." She gave Justin a smile she was sure looked as shaky as she felt. He surprised her by reaching for her arm and giving it a reassuring squeeze. The warmth of his hand sent a little tingle up her arm, and she felt somewhat soothed by its warmth.

She looked around for any signs of somebody watching her as they walked, but by the time they reached the car, the unsettling feeling was gone. If her intuition had been right, whoever had been watching them wasn't anymore.

As she slipped into the driver's seat, she took a deep, steadying breath and forced her mind back to the task at hand. Research. Longhurst. She had work to do.

She and Justin were back at the *Chronicle* a short time later, ready to dive in. But before they had reached her desk, Derek intercepted them and handed Sydney several sheets of paper. "This fax came for you a few minutes ago."

Sydney flipped through the pages. "That was fast," she murmured as she read through some of the information.

"What is it?" Justin asked.

"It's from Detective Richardson. They're shipping manifests from the trucking company I was investigating before I hit some dead ends. Maybe these will give us some new leads. There's also some other miscellaneous information that could be helpful."

"Wow, he really came through."

She grinned. "Told you. We've worked together on a lot of the same things over the years. I'm sure he's so willing to help because he wants to get to the bottom of this as much as I do."

Knowing she had a willing research partner, Sydney had Justin help carry their research into an unused conference room, and they spread everything out across the long table in the center of the room. Time flew by as they tried to connect the elements in Bryce's letter, but it was becoming increasingly obvious that this mystery wasn't one that would be quickly solved.

Sydney dug out her old research on Marengo, and together they pored over that information as well. A few interesting pieces of information turned up as they did. Sydney already knew that the people behind Marengo had their hands in several lucrative affairs, but she hadn't been aware of the connections that turned up between several of the company's board members.

Several of the board members' names showed up as owners on seemingly non-related companies that didn't appear to do much of anything. After doing some more research on those corporations, she began to suspect they were shell companies. When she reported her findings to Justin, he listened with interest.

"If all these possible shell companies are, in fact, subsidiaries of Marengo, Inc.," Justin said, "I can't help wondering if they're using Marengo to launder profits from other smaller corporations. Or maybe because the companies are small, they get some kind of tax break or government grants that a bigger company would never get. There are a lot of possibilities. I'm having a tough time following the paper trail, though, so it could take us a while to connect them all."

"I wouldn't rule any of it out," Sydney said. "Have you been able to tie the smaller companies to a bigger corporation?"

"Several. But for all I know, those could be shell companies too. Do you think they're connected to the shipping company in San Francisco?"

"I have no idea," she admitted. "Whoever is behind this has obviously covered his or her tracks well. I wonder how deep it all goes? I mean, to pull off this kind of scam, you'd have to have a lot of people on the inside— people at the insurance company, black marketeers, the people shipping them the goods . . ."

Justin frowned and pulled a blank sheet of paper from his portfolio. He set it down on the table and absently folded it. "I'm beginning to think it's not just a case of somebody wanting to collect the insurance money. If what you're thinking is right, there's the possibility of money laundering, smuggling, and more. This story isn't just big. It's *huge*. We could work on this thing forever and never know the full scope of it."

"That's not necessarily true," Sydney said, feeling a little distracted as she watched him fold the paper in a second direction. *What is he doing?* Trying to keep her mind on what she'd been saying, she went on. "Look how much we've tracked down in just a few short hours this morning. The key to getting a good lead is simply knowing where to look."

He looked up from his folding and lifted an eyebrow. "Which is . . . ?"

She let out a long breath and deliberated for a moment. Then she leaned forward and reached for a stack of papers on her right. "I say we look more into these board members. I think it's the only way to follow a paper trail back to whoever's ultimately involved. We already suspect that the board members are involved. Take the confiscated shipment that disappeared from the Custom's office, for instance. Rumor was that they got their share of the profits made from the sales for orchestrating this whole thing."

"Okay. Let's start there." He folded the entire sheet lengthwise twice and then turned down a couple of short corners.

Sydney gave him a look of exasperation. "What on earth are you doing?"

Justin looked up in surprise. When he saw her looking from him to the paper in his hands, he flashed her one of his trademark smiles. He held up his project for her inspection. "Paper airplane. It helps me think."

She laughed. "You're kidding, right?"

"Nope. Doing something with my hands frees my mind and lets me think." He gave her a look of challenge and held out a sheet of paper. "Care to try?"

After a moment's hesitation, she reached for the paper. Justin walked her through the steps, but it took Sydney three attempts to get the various angles correct, and by then she was growing frustrated.

"How can this possibly be relaxing?" she growled as she unfolded her third attempted airplane to try yet again.

Justin laughed and got up from his chair, then hurried around to her side of the table. "Okay, wait!" he told her, still laughing as she attempted the fold once more but only succeeded in crinkling the paper. "You're going to rip it and then it won't fly."

"Who cares if it's ripped?" she argued as he moved to stand behind her.

"The plane cares," he teased, still grinning at her pitiful attempts. "All airplanes—paper or not—still have to adhere to the three basic forces of aerodynamics: thrust, drag, and lift. And if there's a hole it in, it's not going to fly."

Sydney muttered something unintelligible under her breath, but Justin ignored her grumbling. He reached around her from behind and gently moved her fingers aside to refold the nose of the plane for her. "See, this is where you're struggling. The tip of the triangle shouldn't go all the way to the top. Does that make more sense?"

Sydney suddenly wasn't sure she could make sense of anything. With Justin's chest pressed against her back, and the way his breath moved across her ear and cheek as he talked, it was all she could do to hear the words he was speaking, let alone understand them.

She watched his hands—strong, capable, and gentle—turn down the corners of the airplane, and when his arm brushed against hers, a warm, jittery sensation started in her stomach and warmed her body as it worked its way up to her heart.

"There," he said a moment later, straightening up and smiling down at her. "Now it should fly. Let's see how it does."

Trying to calm her pounding heart, she picked up the airplane and sent it airborne. She watched in excitement as it sailed across the room smoothly, turned, then drifted gently into the corner.

A childlike giggle erupted from her mouth before she could suppress it. "That was awesome!"

Justin laughed, a low, rumbling sound that warmed her inside and out. She looked up at him and their eyes met. For a moment, the world around them faded away, and Sydney began to wonder . . .

A new voice entered the conversation. "Am I interrupting?"

# CHAPTER 11

Sydney looked up to see Jennifer leaning in through the open conference room door.

"Hey, Jennifer," Sydney said, forcing what she hoped was a casual smile to her face. "What's up?"

"I'm just returning the notebook I borrowed from you the other day." She walked in to hand it to Sydney. "Thanks. Your notes really helped with my story."

"No problem." Sydney took the notebook and caught the curious look Jennifer directed at Justin. When Justin gave her a pointed look, she started. "Oh, I'm sorry. Jennifer, this is Justin. Justin, Jennifer. Justin is the one you talked with on my phone yesterday."

A look of understanding settled across Jennifer's face. "Oh! It's good to meet you, Justin." She glanced at the conference table scattered with research. An amused smile touched Jennifer's face. "Are you two working together?"

Before Sydney could answer, Derek appeared in the doorway. "Sydney. There you are. I have another stack of research for you, but I left it on your desk when I couldn't find you. Do you want me to bring it in?"

"I'll go get it," Justin volunteered. "I need to stretch my legs anyway."

"Thanks," Sydney called after him as he headed out of the room.

The second he was through the door, Jennifer whirled on Sydney. "Talk very quickly. What's going on between you and Mr. Drop-Dead Gorgeous?" She jabbed a thumb over her shoulder in the direction Justin had gone. "Are you actually working with him? He doesn't work here, does he? I would have noticed somebody who looked like that!"

Sydney laughed. "Jen, take a breath. He's from Utah, actually, and works for the *Salt Lake Tribune*. It's a long story how he came to be here, but the bottom line is he came to me with the beginnings of a big story, and we're investigating it while he's in town."

"And?" Jennifer's eyes danced with excitement. "Did you feel them?"

Sydney gave her a look of confusion. "Feel what?"

"Oh, come on, Syd!" Jennifer threw her hands up in the air. "The sparks! Don't tell me you didn't feel them. There were some serious ones flying between the two of you when I walked in. And don't you dare try to deny it."

Sydney rolled her eyes. "We've only known each other twenty-four hours. Besides, he's leaving to go back to Utah on Saturday. You're jumping to all the wrong conclusions."

Just then Justin walked back into the room with the research from Sydney's desk and smiled at them. Apparently that disarming smile had the same effect on Jennifer as it did on her, because Jennifer turned and gave her a look that said Sydney was crazy if she didn't go for him.

"It's not like that," Sydney whispered as Jennifer started to turn away.

"If you say so," Jennifer sing-songed under her breath, cutting off just before Justin got within hearing distance.

Justin walked around to his side of the table and sat down with the new research. "Derek found some more details about Longhurst's businesses."

Jennifer cleared her throat. "Well, if you two will excuse me, I've got some work to do. I'll see you later, Sydney."

"Bye," Sydney responded, ignoring the knowing look her friend sent her way.

"Nice to meet you," Justin called after her. When she was gone, he turned back to Sydney. "She seems nice."

"She is," she agreed. "We've been friends for a long time." Then, changing the subject, she set down the papers in her hand and nodded at the research strewn along his side of the table. "So, what paperwork do you have over there on the board members?"

Justin let out a little groan of protest. "You're relentless. My eyes are starting to cross from all this reading, and my stomach is rumbling so loudly that somebody could hear it clear across the bay. Why don't we break for lunch?"

Sydney's stomach had been growling for a while now too, so she was all too happy to comply. "Good idea. Let's go."

Justin's look of surprise melted into another of his wide grins. "Well, that was easier than I expected. Lead the way."

As they left the building, Sydney asked, "What are you in the mood for?"

"It's a beautiful day," he answered, looking up at the clear blue sky. "Why don't we grab sandwiches and eat outside?"

"Sounds great. There's a sandwich place just down the street."

A short time later, Sydney and Justin had sandwiches and drinks and were headed for a nearby park. The beautiful late summer day had brought out the lunch crowd in droves, and every bench was being used. They walked to an unoccupied spot on the lawn, and Sydney watched with a smile as Justin slipped out of his leather jacket and laid it, lining down, on the grass for her to sit on.

*Such a gentleman,* she thought as she settled down onto the soft, brown fabric. She kicked off her shoes and pulled her stockinged feet up underneath her as she sat. Justin lifted his eyebrows in amusement.

"Offering your leather jacket as a picnic blanket was such a noble gesture that I didn't want to ruin your jacket by putting my shoes on it," she said by way of explanation.

He smiled. "It'll be fine, don't worry."

As he reached for the bag of sandwiches, Sydney couldn't help admiring the powerful muscles in his arms that showed plainly beneath the short sleeves of his T-shirt, or the way the cotton fabric stretched across his broad chest and shoulders as he moved. It was obvious he was involved in some sort of athletics, or at least spent a lot of time working out.

They fell into a comfortable silence as they unwrapped their sandwiches and began to eat. Their quiet was interrupted by a loud rumbling, and Sydney looked over her shoulder to see three leather-clad bikers on Harleys passing by.

She shook her head. "I'll never understand that obsession."

"What? Motorcycles?"

"Yeah. Why would anybody want to do anything so dangerous? Do you know how many people are killed every year on motorcycles?"

Justin chuckled. "You sound like my friend Brad. He works in the advertising department at the *Tribune,* and he's always rattling off stats like that. I'm pretty sure his wife feeds them to him to keep him from buying a bike of his own. Have you ever ridden one?"

"A motorcycle?" Sydney made a face. "Not on your life."

"I think you might change your mind if you took a ride." His expression grew more animated as he talked. "There's nothing as liberating as riding a motorcycle and feeling the wind whipping past you. Really, there's no feeling like it."

Sydney frowned. "Let me guess. You have one."

"As a matter of fact, I do."

She shook her head and took another bite of her sandwich. "Just don't expect me to be impressed by your hog."

He laughed. "I don't have a hog. I have a Yamaha street bike. It's not top-of-the-line, but I love getting out and taking long rides on the weekends. As a matter of fact, I took a trip this summer with a group of guys—"

"Stop!" Sydney held up a hand, halting him mid-sentence. "I don't want to hear about some cross-country trip you took with your biker buddies. It would spoil my image of you, and I wouldn't get any of the lingo anyway."

Justin grinned. "Fair enough."

Their conversation dropped off, and Sydney took a drink of her bottled water. "Mmm, this is nice," she murmured as she stretched out her legs and leaned back on her hands, tipping her face up to the sunshine. "I don't usually find time to stop and enjoy a beautiful day like this."

"Everyone should take a minute to stop and enjoy the day, especially a day as nice as this one." Justin finished his sandwich and looked at the business people around him, many of them talking on cell phones and conducting business while eating. "Maybe the world would be a less stressful place if everyone learned to slow down and enjoy life's simple pleasures once in a while."

Sydney's eyes held a teasing glint as she met his gaze. "I didn't know you were a philosopher."

Justin grinned sheepishly. "Sometimes."

"Well, I, for one, feel invigorated by work."

"I do too, but don't you ever feel like taking time off? Leaving work behind and doing something different for a change?"

"Not really." Sydney finished her sandwich, then crumpled her empty wrapper into a ball and tried to toss it into the nearby garbage can. She missed, and it bounced off the can and rolled back toward them.

Justin laughed as he reached for the wrapper and tossed it into the garbage for her. "I don't think the NBA will be pounding down your door any time soon."

She threw a handful of grass at him. "Watch it, buster."

He continued with what he'd been saying. "You don't ever feel the need to get away? To quit working for a while?"

"Nope. I can count on one hand the number of times I've thought about taking a vacation—and I wouldn't need any fingers to count the number of times I've actually taken one." She smiled wryly. "Seriously, though, work is what I do. It's all I really know."

"Don't you have friends you do things with?" Justin asked. "What about Jennifer?"

"Yeah, Jennifer and I do quite a bit together. And there's Agnes."

"Agnes? Who's that? A relative?"

Sydney chuckled. "No, though I suppose we both think of her as a surrogate something. Agnes Gerard is my neighbor. She's seventy-four going on twenty, and I've known her since I moved into my apartment building several years ago. She's quite a character."

"Sounds like you're close."

"We are. But what about you?" she asked, changing the subject. "Do you have a lot of friends you do things with?"

"A few." Justin brushed a few stray crumbs from his slacks. "It's hard, though, because most of my friends are married and have families. When they have free time, they usually spend it with their wives and kids."

Sydney studied him for a moment. Not for the first time, she found herself wondering if he was Mormon. She couldn't bring herself to ask him outright, because then he'd ask the obvious question back . . . and she didn't know what she'd say. "What about your family?" she asked instead, wondering if that subject would give her more clues. "Do they live in Utah too?"

"They do, as a matter of fact. My parents were thrilled when I got my job at the *Tribune* because it meant I wouldn't be moving away. Plus, most of my brothers and sisters still live in the area, so I get to see them a lot. We're really close."

Sydney's smile slipped a bit, and she averted her gaze to fiddle with a long blade of grass. "I think that's great. You're really lucky."

They were quiet for a moment. Then Justin pressed on. "What about you? Are you close to your family?"

Sydney kept her gaze on the grass between her fingers. Her "safe" question had led their conversation down another path she didn't want to take—this one infinitely worse than a discussion of her activity in the Church.

"I was," she said at last. "My mom, dad, and younger sister were killed in a car accident when I was fifteen."

# CHAPTER 12

For a moment, neither of them spoke. Sydney looked up and met Justin's pained expression with her own carefully guarded one.

Justin's voice was sincere and full of compassion when he whispered, "I'm so sorry."

Sydney lifted one shoulder in a shrug. "It's okay, really. It happened a long time ago."

"Do you have any other brothers or sisters? Or were they your only family?"

"No, it was just the four of us. They were all I had."

Justin didn't say anything right away, and Sydney concentrated on the sound of the afternoon breeze rustling the leaves of the nearby trees. When Justin spoke again, his voice was soft and gentle. "That must have been so hard. What did you do? Who took care of you?"

Sydney took a deep breath. "My great aunt was the only family member I had on this side of the country, so she took me in for a couple of years, but she wasn't in the best of health. When her doctors recommended she be placed in a full-time health care facility, I went out on my own for most of my senior year."

She paused to pull up a few blades of grass, then rolled them absently between her fingers. "I bounced around a bit, staying with different friends for short periods of time while I worked a couple of jobs—one in the evenings and another on the weekends. It was tough, but I refused to let my schoolwork slip, because I knew I'd never be able to pay for college if I didn't get some good scholarships. I had a lot of sleepless nights staying up late to finish my homework." She smiled, but there was little humor in it. "It paid off, though, and I got several scholarships. Between those and the money I saved while working, I was able to put myself through college."

"I don't mean to be nosy, but didn't you have an inheritance, or get anything from your parents' life insurance policies?"

"That would have been nice, but the ironic thing is, as smart as my parents were, they were never very practical. My dad was a software developer with his own software company, and my mom was in real estate. They made a decent living, but they put most of their earnings into my dad's company. The company was struggling, so there wasn't much left to inherit. To make matters worse, their life insurance policies lapsed several months before the accident." She shook her head. "No, I was pretty much on my own."

Justin sat, stunned, for several moments. "Wow," he said at last. "I hope this doesn't sound trite, but I'm impressed with what you've managed to accomplish. I don't think there are many people who would have made it through what you have."

"Oh, I don't know about that," Sydney answered, downplaying his compliment. "Besides, people don't choose the trials that come their way. You simply do your best to play the hand you've been dealt."

"True enough. How you came through it, though, says a lot about the kind of person you are. I'd say it proves you're a fighter."

This time, a genuine smile—albeit a small one—broke through. "There you go, philosophizing again."

Justin smiled back. "Sorry. I believe that, though." Then his smile faded, and his voice was hushed, almost reverent, when he continued. "Do you miss them?"

"Sometimes more than others," she admitted, trying to keep her tone light even as she fought to hide the deep well of emotion the topic brought up. "Especially my sister. Kate and I always had a lot of fun together. She was only fourteen months younger than me, and both of my parents worked so much that we spent a lot of time entertaining ourselves."

"What about your parents?" Justin asked. "Were you as close to them as you were to Kate?"

"Not as much. Like I said, they weren't home very much, but we did love each other." She smiled as a memory surfaced. "We used to take these really great family trips every summer. In fact, the last trip we took together as a family was to Utah to visit some of my dad's relatives. We were only there for two days, but we had so much fun. We went to Lake Powell, and to a really great amusement park . . ."

"Lagoon," Justin filled in, a flash of recognition in his eyes.

Sydney grinned. "Yeah, that's it. Have you been there?"

"Many times."

She nodded. "Well, Kate and I headed out on our own for much of the day, and we had such a blast . . ." At the sudden thickness of her throat, Sydney let her voice trail off, and she cleared her throat.

In an effort to hide the tears springing into her eyes, she turned to watch a squirrel a short distance away, its tail twitching nervously as it moved in quick stops and starts across the manicured lawn.

Justin seemed to sense she wasn't ready to continue, so he waited patiently in silence. His gaze moved to the squirrel she seemed so intent upon. When it finally reached a tree and scurried up the rough bark, Sydney spoke again, her voice wistful and full of longing.

"Anyway, as families sometimes are, they were kind of a pain, but . . . well . . ." She trailed off again as her voice caught, and she shrugged. "I loved them."

"I can tell," Justin said softly.

He reached out to set his hand on top of hers and rubbed his thumb lightly across her knuckles, sending a wave of warmth coursing through her veins. Somehow it felt very right to have his hand there.

When Justin spoke again, his tone was gentle. "Sometimes I forget how lucky I am to have parents and brothers and sisters who are still very much a part of my life. It makes me feel almost guilty to have what you don't."

Sydney's stomach twisted at his words, and she silently scolded herself for getting emotional. "I'm sorry. I didn't mean to make you feel guilty." She rallied her emotions and put on a smile. "To be honest, I don't have it all that bad. It's not like I don't have anybody. I have Jennifer. And I have Agnes. She's been kind of a second mother to me. She's my best cheer-leader." Sydney's voice was upbeat as she tried to brighten the solemn mood that had fallen over their conversation.

But Justin didn't smile. His eyes seemed to be staring into the depths of her soul just as they had the first time she'd met him. She found herself squirming under the intensity of his gaze.

"Do you always do that?" he asked seriously.

She frowned. "Do what?"

"Try to pretend something doesn't upset you?"

His eyes were searching, and Sydney felt the wall around her tender emotions start to crumble. She looked away. "It doesn't do any good to dwell on the past. I chose a career that I'm good at and enjoy, so I focus on that."

"I'm not saying you don't enjoy what you're doing," Justin clarified. "Or that you aren't good at it. I'm just saying that you don't have to pretend it doesn't hurt to think about your past. There's a world full of people out there, Sydney . . . many of whom are eager to listen and understand. It's not a crime to let them in—to admit you're hurting."

Sydney's pent-up emotions finally found their release in the form of anger. "Don't try to tell me how I should deal with things, okay? I'm doing just fine!" She scrambled to her feet and refused to look at Justin as he got up beside her. She grabbed her shoes and jammed her feet into them. Then she bent over to snatch Justin's leather jacket off the ground at the same time he bent over to pick it up, and their heads clunked together.

"Ow!" Sydney protested, putting a hand to her head and rubbing the tender spot. She straightened up and glared at Justin as he straightened up beside her.

"Sorry," he mumbled, a flash of red creeping across his cheeks. He reached for the jacket clutched in her hand. As he did, their hands brushed. A jolt of electricity passed between them, and they both pulled back, startled.

Sydney looked up, and their gazes met. She stared into Justin's beautiful green eyes and found herself transfixed by the gentleness she saw there. She was aware of Justin lifting a hand to her face, but she felt unable to move, unable to breathe, as the world around her faded into a misty haze. The only thing that remained in focus was the man standing before her.

At the feel of Justin's hand on her cheek, she closed her eyes, savoring the sensation of his thumb stroking her cheek. When she opened them again, she found Justin's gaze still upon her, an intensity in his eyes that hadn't been there before.

"I'm sorry," he whispered, his words so quiet they were almost lost on the breeze. "I didn't mean to upset you. I just meant . . . well, I know it might sound strange, since we just met yesterday, but . . . I do care. If you ever want to talk, I'm here. Okay?"

Sydney nodded wordlessly. He was right; it did sound strange to have a virtual stranger tell you he cared . . . that he wanted to listen. But something about Justin saying it just felt right.

Slowly, Justin closed the distance between them and pulled Sydney into a gentle hug. Her breath caught in her throat. Something about Justin's proximity encased her heart in warmth, and she felt vulnerable. But at the same time she felt safer than she had in a long time. She closed her eyes and breathed in the moment.

*BZZZZZZZ!*

Justin jumped back, and Sydney looked around, startled. Then Justin glanced down at her purse, and she realized her cell phone was vibrating. Muttering under her breath, she pulled her cell phone from her purse and flipped it open. "Yes?" she grumbled into it.

She recognized Derek's voice as he quickly told her that Carl needed her to head out to a press conference that had just been called downtown. She groaned inwardly. One day she would tell Derek that he had the world's worst timing.

"I'm on my way," she said, then ended the call and turned back to Justin. "That was Derek. I need to get downtown for a press conference."

Justin nodded and bent over to pick up the bag their sandwiches had come in. As he did, Sydney took a couple of steps away to try to reclaim her emotions. She wrapped her arms around herself in an attempt to ward off a sudden shiver. *What just happened?* she asked herself, feeling flustered.

Justin returned to her side after disposing of their garbage, and wordlessly they began walking back to the car. They were only a few feet from it when Justin's hand on her arm stopped her.

"Sydney."

His soft voice compelled her to look up. With a wary expression, she met his gaze. Uncertainty was etched clearly on his face. He cleared his throat and spoke again; this time his voice was firm yet sincere.

"I meant what I said back there. If you ever need to talk . . ."

She forced a smile she didn't feel. "Thanks, Justin. For now, though, let's just head back. It sounds like I have work to do."

# CHAPTER 13

Justin climbed into his car across the street from the *Chronicle* after Sydney left for her press conference. He hadn't bothered to ask if he could tag along this time. He sensed that she needed her space.

After their hug in the park, he could practically see the protective wall going back up around Sydney's tender emotions, and he didn't want to push her farther away. He'd given her his cell phone number, and she'd agreed to call in a couple of hours when she was finished so they could meet again and resume their research. He knew that would have to be good enough.

His mind drifted back to their conversation in the park. His heart ached as he thought about her losing her entire family at once. He could tell she'd been deeply affected by their deaths, though he guessed she'd never admit just how much. But the knowledge that she'd grown up virtually alone gave him new insight into her character. Yes, she was tough and stubborn, and she was reluctant to let him get too close, but he now understood that she acted that way because she'd had to carve out a place for herself in the world alone. Being alone was clearly something she was used to.

He shook his head, marveling that she'd come through the experience as well as she had. She was an amazing woman. Yet, at the same time, he worried over this realization. Every piece of insight made him more captivated by her. But he would be flying home soon. They'd likely be in touch in the coming weeks over details of their investigation, but he knew he was already in danger of losing his heart to her. With a heavy sigh, Justin pulled up in front of the condo and went inside. He was definitely going to need some time to regroup before he saw her again.

\* \* \*

Not quite two hours later, Justin was back in his car driving to Sydney's apartment. She had called and asked if he could meet her there instead of at the *Chronicle* because the conference room was being used, and her desk wasn't big enough to spread out all their research. He told her he didn't mind, and he didn't. In fact, he was eager to see where she lived and what her apartment was like. It would help him fit one more piece into the puzzle that was Sydney Hallam.

The directions she gave him were easy to follow, and soon he was turning into Sydney's underground parking garage. He parked his car, then took the elevator to the fifth floor. When the doors slid open and he stepped out into the small foyer, he took in the neutral carpeting, the warm tan wall paint, and the bright white chair rail that ran about chest height along the walls.

*Nice,* he thought as he scanned the apartment doors for Sydney's apartment number. He didn't have to look long. Her apartment was the first one on the left. He crossed the foyer and stopped in front of her door.

Just as he lifted his hand to knock, the apartment door next to Sydney's flew open, making him jump. He looked over to see an elderly woman standing in the doorway, her short but thick silvery hair curled around her face.

"Can I help you with something, young man?" she asked, her tone suspicious.

Feeling very much like he had in third grade when he'd been caught snooping in the school's janitor closet during lunch, he froze in his tracks. "Um, I'm here to see Sydney. I'm a friend—"

He was saved from saying anything further when Sydney's door opened and she emerged from her apartment, smiling at him. When Justin's eyes darted back to the woman, Sydney's gaze followed his. She gave her neighbor a reassuring smile.

"It's okay, Agnes. This is Justin. He's my . . ." She paused, then turned back to Justin, her smile turning mischievous as she met his gaze. ". . . good friend," she finished.

Upon hearing the elderly woman's name, Justin put two and two together. He relaxed as he understood that the elderly woman was only being protective of her "adopted" daughter.

Agnes snorted. "Good friend, huh? What does that mean?"

Sydney rolled her eyes playfully, then turned back to Justin. "You'll have to forgive Agnes. She seems to think everyone who comes to see me requires the third degree."

"Hmmph," Agnes sputtered, but Justin suspected she wasn't as put off by Sydney's good-natured teasing as she sounded.

He opened his mouth to reassure the woman that his intentions with Sydney were honorable, but just then a small white dog barreled out of

Agnes's apartment into the hallway, barking viciously. The next thing he knew, the dog was lunging for his ankle. He jerked his leg out of the way, but the sudden motion only sent the poodle into a barking frenzy.

"Princess!" Sydney exclaimed, looking at the dog in dismay. "What's gotten into you? Agnes!"

Agnes bent over to pick up the dog and gave it a couple of reassuring strokes. "Princess is protective, that's all," she said in defense of her dog. "Just like I am." She took a step closer to Justin, the dog still growling in her hands. Her eyebrows drew together as she scrutinized him. "What exactly are your intentions with Sydney, young man?"

To Justin's immense relief, Sydney came to his rescue.

"Oh, Agnes, leave the poor guy alone." Sydney grabbed Justin's hand, sending a series of sparks shooting up his arm, and turned back to her apartment. "See you later, Agnes."

Justin followed Sydney into her apartment, and he heaved a sigh of relief when she shut the door. "Whew," he breathed. "That's some neighbor you have there. She's certainly watching out for you."

Sydney smiled. "Yeah, well, I've known Agnes a long time. Naturally, she's protective."

"And what's with that dog of hers? I nearly had teeth marks on my ankle."

Sydney laughed as she led the way into her living room. "Well, like Agnes said, Princess is protective of me too. But don't worry about Agnes. Her bark is worse than her bite. It's actually kind of nice, knowing I have somebody looking out for me. Without her, I would have been terribly lonely."

The unspoken "since my parents and sister were killed" hovered in the air, and Justin decided to change the subject.

Looking around Sydney's apartment, he took in the high ceilings and comfortable furnishings. What impressed him the most, though, was the large bank of floor-to-ceiling windows at the far end of the living room that offered a spectacular view of the city.

He let out a low whistle. "Nice place," he said. "Your view is incredible."

"Thanks. It's not as fancy as some of the other buildings in town, but I love it." She smiled. "So. Are you ready to get back into research mode?"

"Definitely."

"Make yourself at home. I'll get the research I brought home, and we can spread out in here."

When she headed for her bag on the credenza, Justin sauntered over toward the large windows. The computer desk and overstuffed armchair were situated near the window, placed to enjoy the view. He smiled. It was clear Sydney enjoyed the sight of the city stretched out below her.

He moved to the armchair and noticed an end table with a lamp and several books sitting beside it. He ambled closer to see what she'd been reading, and when he did, a little gasp escaped his lips. On the end table sat a leather-bound quad and a Relief Society manual.

His heart somersaulted in his chest. As he looked closer, he saw her name inscribed in gold lettering along the lower right corner of the scriptures.

His heart pounding, he turned to face her, his voice a shocked whisper. "You're LDS?"

A slight flush crept across her face, and she nodded. "You are too?" When he could only nod in response, she gave him a sheepish smile. "I wondered if you were, being from Salt Lake City and all, but I guess you never know."

"That's great!" Justin's words came out with casual enthusiasm, but inside he felt like jumping for joy. He felt an enormous sense of relief, knowing that this new piece of all-important information created one less major obstacle. It gave him the possibility of developing something more with this beautiful, spirited woman to whom he was quickly growing attached.

"Are you hungry?" Sydney asked, changing the subject. "I know it's a little early for dinner, but I'm starving. Want anything?"

"Thanks, but I grabbed something a little while ago." He glanced down at the smudge of grease on the inside of one wrist. "Though, since you're being so hospitable . . . Would you mind if I used your bathroom? I fueled up on the way over here, and now my hands smell like gas."

She gestured down the hall. "Go right ahead. First door on the left. I'm going to see what leftovers I have in the fridge. Are you sure you don't want anything?"

He shook his head. "No thanks, I'm fine."

"Okay, then. When you're done, come on into the kitchen. I can at least get you something to drink."

\* \* \*

Sydney escaped into the kitchen and opened the fridge, grateful for the cool air wafting out that cooled her warm cheeks. What was it about this man that made her insides dance and flutter?

She searched the fridge's meager contents for something she could warm up for a quick dinner and spotted a plate of chicken drumsticks Agnes had brought over the day before. She stuck them in the microwave, turned the knob, then punched the START button. With dinner on its way, she turned and surveyed the kitchen.

She grimaced. It had been a few days since she'd cleaned up. The sink held several dirty glasses, plates, utensils, and even a couple of cereal bowls with rings of congealing milk in the bottom. Making a face, she ran hot water into them, then grabbed the garbage can from the corner and swept the empty takeout cartons near the stove into it with a swipe of her arm.

She heard the bathroom faucet turn off and knew she'd better hurry. She grabbed the sponge next to the faucet and began scrubbing furiously at the bowls in the sink. When she heard Justin coming through the living room, she slowed her movements to a more normal pace.

"Do you mind if I keep you company while you eat? Or would you rather I keep researching?" Justin asked from the doorway.

Just then the sound of something exploding in the microwave made them both jump. Their gazes flew to the appliance, and Justin rushed over to open the microwave door. Sydney followed him. She grimaced as she peered around him to see little bits of exploded chicken clinging to the insides of the microwave.

Justin chuckled as he took the plate of what remained of the chicken out of the microwave and set it on the counter. "You really *are* a disaster in the kitchen. You've only been in here five minutes, and already you've blown up your dinner."

Sydney shrugged and gave him a sheepish smile. "I warned you."

"Well, I'm sorry to say, but your chicken looks pretty hopeless." He picked up the plate of sorry-looking chicken and set it in the sink. "Let's see what else we can find you to eat." He walked over to her fridge and opened the door. When he looked inside, his eyes widened in disbelief. "How do you stay alive? There isn't even enough in here for a decent snack."

He then moved on to the cupboards, opening and closing each door in search of ingredients and making disapproving noises at the meager contents.

Sydney watched him from her perch on a barstool at the island in the center of her kitchen, feeling a little like a scolded child. How did she explain that her meals usually consisted of frozen pizzas, takeout, and microwave dinners? Since she'd been eating alone basically from the time she was fifteen, she'd never seen the value of spending time preparing something fancy when she knew she'd be just as happy with a sandwich or bowl of cereal.

When Justin had finished taking inventory of her kitchen, he shook his head in disapproval. "There isn't enough here to make anything," he scolded. "But you're totally set as far as M&Ms go." He gestured to the glass canister with its gleaming stainless steel lid sitting on the counter beneath the corner cupboard. "What's up with that?"

Sydney looked over at her stash and shrugged. "I love peanut M&Ms," was all she offered by way of explanation.

"More than real food?" he teased. He shook his head, then pointed a commanding finger at her. "Wait here. I'm going to go save the day."

# CHAPTER 14

Sydney watched, her mouth open in an unspoken question, as Justin grabbed his keys and headed out of the apartment.

*Oookay,* she thought, lifting her eyebrows in amusement as the door shut behind him. Where was he going?

Fifteen minutes later he was back, and she hurried to let him in before Agnes—and Princess—reappeared. "Hey," she greeted him with a smile, noting the large bag in his arms. She took it from him eagerly. "I see you took pity on me. What exotic takeout location did you find so quickly?" She reached into the bag and pulled out a can of cream of mushroom soup. She looked at it blankly. "What is this?"

Chuckling, Justin took the bag back from her and carried it into the kitchen. "The exotic location I found is called a grocery store. You should visit it one of these days. It's just down on the corner. They have all these different kinds of foods and spices. It's pretty cool."

"Ha ha, very funny," she said dryly as she followed him into the kitchen. "I know what a grocery store is. But where's that great takeout I thought you were going to get?"

"Not in this bag." He set the bag on the kitchen island and started pulling out items. "Tonight we're having a casserole, and you're going to help make it."

She gave him an incredulous stare. "You're kidding."

He shook his head and smiled. "Nope. Now come over here, and I'll show you a really simple recipe."

Justin pulled out several cans, a package of hamburger, a bag of noodles, a block of cheese, and a glass casserole dish. Then he talked her through preparing the meal, adding the ingredients into a small casserole dish, and sliding it into the hot oven. Thirty minutes later, he pulled the bubbling dish out of the oven and set it on the stove with a flourish.

"Voila. Instant dinner."

Sydney had to admit, she was impressed. He hadn't even worked from a recipe card or a cookbook. "How did you know what ingredients to put in? I never would have been able pull something like this together."

He shrugged as he took two plates out of the cupboard and set them on the counter next to the casserole dish. "It just takes practice. The more you cook, the easier it is to know what will work and what won't." He dished them each up a hearty serving, and they sat down next to each other at the island.

"This is really good," Sydney said with appreciation around the hot bite in her mouth.

"It's nothing fancy, but it's better than mutilated chicken."

Sydney blushed. "I'm still embarrassed about that. The last thing I wanted to do was make you cook for me."

"Hey, I enjoyed cooking for you," he said, his tone sincere. "I enjoy cooking, period. My mom made it a point to make sure all of us boys were capable in the kitchen."

When they were finished with dinner, Justin stood up and took his plate to the sink. "Where do you keep your dish towels? I'll help with the dishes."

"Justin, you made dinner. I don't expect you to clean up, too."

He grinned. "Hey, I wouldn't ever want to hear you say I didn't pull my weight around the house."

"Well, when you put it that way . . ."

They talked and laughed as they did dishes, and Sydney couldn't remember the last time she enjoyed a household chore. It wasn't long before the dishes were washed and dried. While Justin put the utensils in the drawer, Sydney put away the mixing bowls they'd used to combine the ingredients. She'd just stood on her tiptoes to put the last bowl up onto one of the higher shelves in the cabinet when she heard Justin gasp.

"Sydney, what happened?"

Startled, she glanced over at Justin to see him staring at her stomach. Her gaze lowered to see what he was looking at, and she saw that her stretching motion had caused her shirt to lift up, exposing her stomach. In plain sight was the long, harsh scar running from just above her belly button up towards her ribs, where it disappeared beneath her shirt. A few other smaller scars ran at various angles on either side of it.

She quickly dropped her arms and tugged her shirt down self-consciously over her stomach. "Oh, um, nothing," she stammered. "It's nothing, really."

Justin opened his mouth to press for information, but then apparently thought better of it. Sydney breathed a sigh of relief when he let the subject drop.

"Well, that's finished," she said, looking around her clean kitchen. "Thanks for your help."

"No problem."

"If you feel up to it, we can get going on some of that research."

Justin clapped his hands together once and smiled. "I'm up for it. Let's get going."

They went into the living room, and Justin helped Sydney spread out their notes on the living room floor, coffee table, and every other available surface they could find. For the next two hours, they continued their research on the board members, noting which corporations each was linked to. Sydney tried to follow the paper trail to tie those corporations to parent companies, but it was a tedious process, and it didn't net them many results.

Feeling like they were hitting a dead end, they turned their attention back to Senator Longhurst and pored through his corporate information, hoping to find some connection that could further implicate him in the web of activity they were researching. Upon inspection of a list of his businesses and holdings, one business seemed to stand out.

"Look at this," Sydney exclaimed, holding out a page of the business's financial records for Justin to see. "One of Longhurst's biggest companies is called Sandstone Enterprises. It's a conglomerate that deals with a bunch of different kinds of businesses—power and phone companies, a few retail chains, some scientific research labs. There's one business in particular that stands out, though—Premiere Enterprises. According to this, it's a public relations firm in Nevada, but what PR firm pulls in these kinds of profits after only two years in business?"

Justin took the paper and read through the information. "That is suspicious," he agreed. "Are there any indications that it belongs to a parent company?"

Sydney shook her head. "It doesn't say on this paperwork, but we could try to find out. With these kinds of annual profits, it raises suspicions as to Premiere's legitimacy. It could be a shell company, used to launder profits from other businesses."

"It's possible. Let's ask Derek in the morning to pull up everything he can find on Premiere Enterprises. We can start there tomorrow."

"Good idea."

"I hope this pans out," Justin said with a sigh. "We've got so much research that it feels like we're running in circles. If we could get just one solid lead, something I could bring back to my editor to show him what we're onto, I can guarantee he'd officially put me on this story. But until then . . ."

Their conversation drifted off, and the room was quiet for a minute. Then Sydney got to her feet. "I need a break. Want a snack?"

"Yeah, like what, exactly?" he teased. "Your cabinets are bare."

Sydney returned a minute later with the large canister of peanut M&Ms tucked under one arm. She walked over to Justin, set the jar down on the couch beside him, then sat down on the other side of it. She popped off the lid and lifted an eyebrow at him. "You were saying?"

He chuckled and shook his head. "I stand corrected."

They each took a handful of candies and relaxed back on the couch. "So, tell me," Sydney began as she crunched her M&Ms. "What do you do when you're not working?"

That got Justin talking. It wasn't long before Sydney had a mental tally sheet of Justin's likes and dislikes. He loved sports but didn't necessarily enjoy watching them on TV. He played racquetball and went running with his friend Brad from work (apparently the same Brad who was always telling him how dangerous motorcycles were). His mother was an interior designer, his father worked in international law, and he loved his traditional Sunday night dinners with his large family. But he hated formal events like company Christmas parties, wasn't a fan of seafood, and had a pet peeve about people not returning things they borrowed.

She wanted to learn more, but Justin said it was only fair that he get to ask a few questions of his own. She was grateful when he seemed to understand that she didn't want to talk about her family, but he seemed to consider everything else fair game. And unlike her own questions to him, his were creative. He wanted to know if she'd ever been sent to the principal's office (she hadn't), if she'd ever accepted a dare (yes, by going skydiving when she turned eighteen), and if she'd ever gotten in trouble with the law (sort of, when she and some friends were caught toilet papering a teacher's house and the officer stuck around to watch them clean the whole mess up). She also told him about her brown belt in Shotokan, her love of reading, and her guilty pleasure of watching the history channel. (She was relieved when he didn't laugh.) She admitted to refusing to spend money on seemingly frivolous things like manicures, and she despised laziness.

As they continued to talk, Sydney marveled that she'd known Justin for such a short time. He was so easy to be around and talk with that it felt like she'd known him forever. The realization that he would be leaving soon affected her more than she'd expected.

When the grandfather clock in the living room chimed nine, Justin stretched and stood up. "It's getting late. I guess we should call it a night."

Sydney's disappointment at the announcement was eased when she realized Justin didn't sound like he wanted their evening to end either. She stood up beside him and comically stepped over a series of piles at her feet.

Justin laughed. "Let me help you pick all this up."

They gathered all the research, and soon everything was stacked neatly on the coffee table. When they were done, Sydney walked Justin to the door.

"So, what's on the agenda for tomorrow?" she asked. "Are you planning on helping me do research at the *Chronicle*?"

Justin stopped at the door and turned to give her a smile. "Of course. Do you want to meet somewhere for breakfast before we head in?"

Sydney's heart skipped out an erratic rhythm. "I'd love to."

The air became electric as their eyes met and held, and Sydney wondered for a brief second if he was going to kiss her. She was startled to realize that she actually wanted him to. But instead he flashed her another smile and put a gentle hand on her shoulder in farewell.

"Good night," he said softly. "See you in the morning."

\* \* \*

Longhurst looked up from his Blackberry as the car slowed. The dark, looming shapes of corrugated metal warehouses appeared outside his window through the dense fog settling in over the docks. "Number nine," he instructed his driver.

With a nod, the driver slowed and took the first left between the rows of warehouses. The single bulbs hanging in rusty metal fixtures above the warehouse doors did little to break through the darkness and guide them down the dirt road toward the docks.

When they pulled to a stop outside the second-to-last warehouse on the row, a bulky figure stepped out of the shadows, opened the back door of the car, and slid into the back seat.

"Douglas." Longhurst smiled in greeting. "It's been a while."

"It has. I didn't even realize you were in town until you phoned last night. What can I do for you? I've got the last-minute plans for your shipment to oversee."

"That's what I wanted to talk to you about. Is everything ready?"

"Yes. The goods are on board, and the ship will be arriving at dawn. We won't have any trouble this time. The right people have been paid off, and everything's going according to plan. Don't worry."

"I never worry. That's what I pay you the big bucks to do."

"Of course." Douglas chuckled. "Speaking of payment, I told our men we'd run it through the usual channels."

"Then we're set."

"We are." Douglas reached for the door handle. "I'll call you when the deal's done." And with that, he pushed the door open and stepped out into the night, disappearing quickly into the dense fog and shadows along the dock.

# CHAPTER 15

Sydney had just finished applying her makeup in the bathroom the next morning when her cell phone rang. She hurried into the bedroom to grab it off her nightstand where it had been charging. "Hello?"

"Hey, Sydney, it's Justin."

The sound of his deep voice sent a rush of warmth through her body. "Hi. How'd you get my number?"

"You called me yesterday afternoon from your cell to ask if I could meet you at your apartment, remember?"

"Oh, yeah. I forgot about that. So, what's up?"

"I hope you don't mind, but Bryce's father called me last night right after I left your place. He wanted to get together before I leave town tomorrow so he invited me over this morning. The down side is, I won't be able to meet you for breakfast. I'm sorry. I was really looking forward to it."

The fact that he sounded so disappointed made her feel better. "I understand. Maybe we can take a rain check on breakfast and do dinner instead?" She knew her voice sounded hopeful, and she waited eagerly for his response.

"That would be great," he said, his tone enthusiastic. "Let's plan on it. I'll meet up with you at the *Chronicle* early this afternoon, and we can decide where and when to go."

After they'd said their good-byes, Sydney finished getting ready for work, then took a little extra time driving to the *Chronicle*. A thick blanket of fog had settled in over the city, making visibility poor. The tension she would have normally felt from the drive was overwritten by her state of euphoria at the thought of her plans with Justin that night. They'd eaten quick lunches together, but something about the idea of an actual date made her stomach dance with anticipation.

When Sydney got into the newsroom, she tracked Derek down and asked him to get her everything he could find on Premiere Enterprises, the public relations company she and Justin had stumbled across the night before. She worked on other tasks until Derek arrived at her desk later that morning with the research she wanted.

As she read through it, she highlighted and cross-referenced several sections that caught her attention, but one name in particular jumped out at her as she was nearing the last of the research.

"I know this name," she muttered, sitting more upright in her chair. "How do I know this guy?"

After thinking for a minute, she picked up some of the research she and Justin had been going through last night. She riffled through it, looking for the piece of information that loomed just out of memory's reach.

Suddenly her hand stilled. As she read the information again, a slow, victorious smile worked its way across her face. This discovery was just what they'd been looking for.

* * *

When Justin finally walked into the newsroom just after two o'clock, Sydney gave him a bright smile and waved him over to her desk. He crossed the newsroom in long strides and took the empty seat beside her. He returned her smile, but she noticed that it didn't quite reach his eyes.

She reached out to give his forearm a sympathetic squeeze. "How'd it go?"

"It was hard," he admitted. "Bryce and I were inseparable growing up, and we spent a lot of time at each other's houses. His parents felt like mine, and mine like his. It's tough to see his dad going through this."

"I'm sorry." Her tone was wrapped in gentle sympathy.

"Thanks." He placed his hand over hers for a moment, then visibly rallied. "So. It looks like you're hard at it. Tell me you found something interesting so I can get my mind on something else."

"As a matter of fact, I did," she said, understanding his need to get immersed in work. "You're not going to believe this. Take a look."

He took it and read the information. "It looks like Premiere Enterprises is a subsidiary of Higher Plains Industries." He looked back up at her and shrugged. "So?"

"So," she echoed, her voice growing more animated as she reached for another paper from her desk and handed it to him, "according to this, Higher Plains Industries is a subsidiary of Marengo, Inc."

"Isn't Higher Plains Industries one we fingered as a shell company owned by Longhurst?"

"Yes," she exclaimed, her eyes bright, "and if Higher Plains is a shell company . . ."

". . . then maybe Premiere Enterprises is too," he finished for her.

"And Higher Plains Industries ties Longhurst to Marengo! Justin, do you realize what we have here?" Sydney asked excitedly. "This story has the makings of an exposé on a crime ring even bigger than the one I just nailed. Who knows who else is behind this if we're already drawing connections to a United States senator!"

Justin's excitement rivaled Sydney's. "This is great! I can go back to my editor with something concrete, and he'll officially put me on the story. We don't have enough hard facts to go public with this yet, and it may be a while before we do, but I can tell we're onto something huge. Can you imagine where all this could lead?"

"I know," she agreed. "I love this part of a story, when it's new and the possibilities are endless."

He laughed. "Spoken like a true workaholic."

"Speaking of that . . ." She set the papers back on her desk and regarded Justin with a mischievous smile. "I've decided that you're right. It wouldn't kill me to take a little time off once in a while. How would you feel about joining me for a little fun this afternoon?"

Justin looked at her with interest. "What did you have in mind?"

"How about doing something touristy?" she suggested. "You got here three days ago, and I bet you haven't seen a single San Francisco landmark."

That made him smile. "You're right. Seeing the sights sounds like a great idea. I'd hate to leave tomorrow morning without seeing more of the city."

She felt a rush of disappointment at the reminder that he'd be leaving the next day. Being with Justin already seemed so natural that she couldn't imagine not seeing him every day.

Pushing those thoughts aside, Sydney went to Carl's office to turn in the short article she'd been assigned that day, then told him she was going to leave a couple hours early. Carl seemed surprised, but he didn't object.

Sydney and Justin went to their respective homes to change, then met back up at Sydney's apartment a short time later. Sydney couldn't help noticing how great Justin looked. He was wearing nice jeans, a thin, green, crewneck sweater that brought out the green in his eyes, and his brown leather jacket. Her heart tapped out a nervous rhythm, and it was all she could do to concentrate on navigating the busy Friday traffic as they made their way into the heart of the city.

"Are there any places in particular you'd like to see?" Sydney asked.

Justin thought for a moment. "I've always heard about the cable cars. I'd love to see those," he admitted. "And maybe one of the piers? Which one is the most visited?"

"Pier 39," she said without hesitation. "It's one of my favorite places, actually. And Telegraph Hill is close by, so we could see Coit Tower and the Transamerica Pyramid. We'd be able to see the Golden Gate Bridge from there, too. And we just have to drive down Lombard Street!" she rushed on, her voice gaining enthusiasm. "Those are San Francisco landmarks that I couldn't possibly let you go home without seeing. And afterward we should take a cable car downtown. You'll love it."

Justin laughed at the excitement in her voice, which seemed to grow with each landmark she mentioned. "Okay, let's do it all," he said. "I'm game for anything, so lead on."

\* \* \*

As they drove, Justin relaxed in the passenger seat, content to listen as Sydney pointed out landmarks and filled him in on some of the city's best attractions. She suggested they grab a bite to eat at one of the many exotic restaurants in the city and asked him about his food preferences, explaining that the city was well known for its restaurants and its variety of foods— Thai, Greek, Chinese, Cambodian. The list went on, but they finally decided to visit a Chinatown restaurant that Sydney recommended.

When they reached the eight-block area in the middle of downtown San Francisco that made up Chinatown, Sydney explained that Chinatown was the most visited attraction in the city. Justin could see why. The place was incredible. Chinatown's entrance was marked by a stunning, ornate pagoda-topped gate, with carvings of dragons and fish sitting atop the green tiled structure and stone lions flanking its base. Justin was so impressed that he asked another tourist if he would take a picture of him and Sydney in front of one of the stone lions with the small digital camera he had thought to bring along.

Afterwards they headed to Stockton Street a couple of streets over, and Justin could see why Sydney had brought him there. Colorful shop fronts covered with paper lanterns lined the streets, and everywhere you looked there were outdoor produce stands, herb and medicinal shops, and touristy shops selling everything from antiques to Chinese silk fabrics and kimonos. The sounds of haggling and shouts in the foreign language filled the air, and the colorful displays and cultural ambience created an atmosphere that was energizing.

Sydney told him that the little alleyways held some of the best surprises, and she led him down one of them. When they stopped at a little hole-in-the-wall restaurant, Justin knew he must have looked skeptical, because Sydney laughed.

"I promise, you'll love it," she reassured him, grabbing his hand and leading him inside. "It looks bad, but the food is incredible."

The place didn't look any better on the inside, but Justin soon learned that first impressions were deceptive. Sydney was right—the food was incredible.

When their meal was finished, they left Chinatown to continue their exploration of the city. They drove around for a while, and Justin found himself holding his breath on several occasions as they navigated the hilly streets. Signs dotted the curbs, warning drivers who were parking cars to "curb your wheels" to prevent runaways down the steep inclines. He shook his head in amazement as he watched Sydney use her left foot on the brake and her right on the gas almost simultaneously. He smiled and shook his head again in disbelief, wondering how anybody would be able to drive with a standard transmission in the city.

Sydney's enthusiasm at playing tour guide grew as they traversed Russian Hill and started down Lombard Street. The one-block section of Lombard Street they were approaching, she explained, was famously called "the crookedest, most winding street in the world," a design born out of necessity since the grade was so steep that it was too difficult for most vehicles to handle. When they reached it, Justin took one look at the line of cars creeping back and forth down the hillside below them and decided that the street certainly lived up to its reputation.

The brick-paved block of Lombard Street, with its unique design of scenic, flower-landscaped switchbacks along the steep grade and grand Victorian homes on either side of the street, wasn't the only thing that fascinated Justin, though. The route also gave them a breathtaking view of the bay in the distance, the water turned brilliant shades of orange and yellow by the setting sun. As they made their descent, Sydney pointed out Telegraph Hill in the distance with the tall Coit Tower sitting atop it, and the stately Golden Gate Bridge beyond.

From there they continued on to Telegraph Hill, which boasted further impressive views of the bay and the famous island prison Alcatraz in one direction, and the famous San Francisco cityscape in the other. As dusk continued to fall and the city lights flickered to life, Justin wasn't sure which view he loved more. Sydney pointed out the Transamerica Pyramid, the most recognizable skyscraper in the skyline, its lit spire a beacon against the darkening sky.

Afterward, they headed over to Fisherman's Wharf and Pier 39. As they walked along the wood decking, Justin reached for Sydney's hand. It seemed the most natural thing in the world to entwine his fingers through hers. A tingle moved all the way up his arm, and when he met her gaze, he could tell she'd felt the same thing.

A beautiful, shy smile touched her lips, and he felt his heart catch. What was it about this woman that had him falling so hard and so fast? He couldn't say. All he knew was that being with her felt so right.

They strolled down the bustling pier, occasionally stopping in one of the many stores lining the wooden walkway. When the faint sound of organ music drifted across the night to them, Sydney flashed him a mischievous grin and tugged on his hand.

"Hurry up! You've got to see this," she said, pulling him faster down the pier.

Justin laughed and followed along. Soon the sound of music became louder until finally the source stood before them.

Justin's jaw dropped. "Oh, wow."

# CHAPTER 16

Sydney felt a sense of pride as Justin stared up at the beautiful double-decker carousel, the sound of merry organ music filling the night air. His expression was one of awe and delight as hundreds of twinkling lights created trails of color as the painted horses flashed past on their gold, jewel-adorned posts.

"Isn't it incredible?" she asked. "It was handcrafted in Italy. And look at the paintings up there." She pointed up at the intricate, hand-painted depictions around the top of the carousel that showed many of San Francisco's landmarks, including the Golden Gate Bridge, Coit Tower, Chinatown, Lombard Street, and Alcatraz.

They stood staring at the spinning carousel for several minutes, smiling at the kids whizzing past on the horses and chariots. "I have a lot of good memories of this place," Sydney said, almost to herself. "Every time my family came here, my sister and I would have a ride. I love it."

When Justin's hand tightened around hers, she looked up to find him watching her with understanding in his eyes. He lifted a hand to brush a blowing strand of hair off her face, and his touch did startling things to her heart.

The bell on the carousel pealed to signal the end of the ride, and the moment was broken. Justin's disarming smile returned, and he took a half step back without releasing her hand. "So what's next?" he asked.

Sydney forced a breath of air into her lungs to help clear her head. "There's one more thing you need to see here."

Justin seemed happy to follow her lead, so she led him to the edge of the pier where dozens of sea lions lounged about on log rafts just off the dock. Sydney and Justin leaned on the pier railing and watched the animals for a while, laughing at the sound of the sea lions' barking filling the air. Justin took a few pictures, then they moved on.

The next thing they did was board a traditional cable car. Justin decided he wanted to be daring and ride on one of the running boards. Sydney thought he looked like a little kid at Christmas as they stood on the edge of the cable car, clinging to the poles and watching the city fly by on their exhilarating ride downtown. They got off at Union Square, where a bustling shopping district attracted tourists and residents alike.

"This place is amazing," Justin said in awe as he took in the sights of the bustling city. "I can see why you love it here."

The daylight was gone, but the night was barely noticeable through the blaze of lights gleaming down from streetlights and buildings throughout the city. The energy and pulse of the city seemed to be a living, breathing being.

"It's never boring, that's for sure," Sydney answered with a pleased smile.

When they'd both had their fill of San Francisco's downtown shops and sights, they took another cable car and climbed off a few short blocks away from where they'd parked. A breeze had picked up, and Sydney pulled the sleeves of her sweater down further over her wrists.

"Are you cold?" Justin asked as they stopped on a street corner to wait for the pedestrian light signal to turn green.

"A little," she admitted. "The city always gets chilly at night with the cool air coming in off the bay, but it's chillier than usual tonight."

"Here." He slipped out of his leather jacket and held it out for her. "Put this on."

Sydney hesitated, then slipped her arms into the sleeves. She could feel his body warmth radiating from the jacket's lining, and she smiled up at him gratefully. "Thanks."

"You're welcome."

Sydney started to button up the jacket in an effort to retain the comforting warmth, but just then the light turned green. She giggled as Justin grabbed her hand and pulled her after him at a jog as they hurried across the street. They didn't slow until they were several yards past the corner and found a store's darkened doorway that sheltered them from the breeze for a moment.

Sydney was a little breathless from the jog in the cold night air and took advantage of the break to finish buttoning up the jacket. Her fingers, stiff from the cold, fumbled at the task.

Justin's hands were suddenly taking hers, stilling their movements. Butterflies exploded in her stomach when she looked up and saw the intensity in his gaze as he stared down at her. He moved closer, and the noise of the city streets faded until the only sound Sydney could hear was the sound of her heart hammering in her chest.

His fingers brushed along her cheekbone, and the simple contact sent a jolt through her. The air seemed to crackle with electricity as Justin closed the remaining distance between them and lowered his face to hers.

As his lips touched hers, she realized she'd been unprepared for the strength of emotions that flooded through her at his touch. She'd been kissed before, but this was vastly different. The connection she felt with this man as his lips moved gently over hers sent such warmth through her chest that the walls she'd built around her heart long ago threatened to melt away. The sensation both thrilled and frightened her.

When they pulled apart, Justin let out a low sigh and gave her a crooked half smile. "I've wanted to do that since the first time I saw you."

Sydney had to remind herself to breathe. Before she could gather her wits back together to reply, the sounds of talking and laughter pulled them back to the present.

Justin took Sydney's hand, and the easy camaraderie they'd shared returned as they walked the rest of the way to the car. On the drive back, they talked and laughed about the things they'd seen in the city, and before long they were pulling up in front of Justin's condo.

"Tonight was amazing, Sydney," Justin said, reaching once more for her hand. "I enjoyed spending the evening with you."

She gave him a soft smile. "I enjoyed spending it with you, too."

Their eyes met and held, and then Justin leaned across and kissed her gently for the second time that evening.

When their kiss ended, he gave her an endearing grin. "Better be careful," he teased. "I could get used to doing that."

She giggled softly. "Me too." But then the reality of the situation sank in, and she realized this man would be flying back to Utah the very next morning. She cleared her throat quietly and asked, "What time does your plane leave in the morning?"

"Eleven," he answered, his expression becoming more solemn. He started to say something, hesitated, then apparently decided to go on. "If you don't want to, you can say so and it won't hurt my feelings, but . . . do you want to drive to the airport with me in the morning?"

Sydney smiled at the vulnerability in his eyes. "I'd love to."

They talked about what time they should meet up, then Justin flashed her his megawatt smile that nearly turned her insides to Jell-O as he reached for the door handle. "Good night, Sydney." And with that, he opened the door and stepped out.

He lifted his hand in a little wave as she pulled away, and Sydney fought to keep from looking in the rearview mirror while she merged with traffic.

For the first time in a very long time, she felt alive. And not just the I-nailed-a-big-story kind of alive. No, this time it was her heart that felt alive. And it felt wonderful.

# CHAPTER 17

Justin dried the last of his dinner dishes and put them away. He glanced around the clean kitchen and sighed. There was nothing left for him to do. In an attempt to keep his mind off Sydney, he'd cleaned every last speck of his place since arriving back in Salt Lake City earlier that day. But it hadn't worked.

His mind kept replaying the scene in the airport. Before heading through the security checkpoints, he had asked the question that had been on his mind since shortly after meeting Sydney. The conversation still stuck out in his mind.

*"Can I call you?"*

*One side of Sydney's mouth quirked up. "Of course you can call me. How else are we going to keep up with the story?"*

*At that, Justin panicked. Had he read more into this than there was? Had she no interest in him, personally? What if he'd just imagined her having feelings for him? Either way, he had to know. Now. Before he got on the plane and contemplated a possible future with her.*

*He cleared his throat and cast about for his courage. "Um, true, but I wasn't just talking about the story."*

*The look of realization on Sydney's face made him want to wilt with relief. She looked surprised, then delighted. A shy smile lit up her face as she said, "I'd love for you to call me."*

And then there had been their good-bye kiss. He'd kissed a few women before, but this . . . It had been spectacular. The only thing he could have wanted more from her was . . . well, more.

The last three days had been filled with such highs and lows. Bryce's funeral had been hard, but meeting Sydney and getting to know her had been incredible. There were times when he felt guilty for leaving San Francisco feeling so exhilarated when he knew he should be mourning the death of one of his best friends. The only thing that kept him from dwelling on that was that he knew Bryce would have wanted him to go on with his life, and he knew his friend would have been thrilled for him about a budding relationship with a woman like Sydney.

He let out a growl of irritation. *Is this all you're capable of doing today?* he asked himself. *Thinking of Sydney?*

Deciding that he needed to do something that didn't involve thinking about her, he walked into his room to get his scriptures and Sunday School lesson manual. He had a group of sixteen-year-olds to teach the next day. Hopefully the distraction of working on his lesson would do the trick. Being away from her was hard enough. Thinking of her constantly was only going to make things worse.

\* \* \*

On Monday morning Justin headed straight for his editor's office. He knocked on the door and stuck his head into the office to see his boss already hard at work. "Mike, do you have a minute?"

"You're back," Mike said with a smile as he waved him in. Then his expression softened into a look of sympathy. "How are you holding up after your friend's funeral?"

"I'm okay," Justin answered truthfully. "It was hard, but I'm moving on." He held up the papers in his hand. "Do you have a few minutes? I wanted to show you what we found."

Mike's eyebrows rose. "We?"

"That reporter from the *San Francisco Chronicle,* Sydney Hallam," he explained, the mere mention of Sydney's name causing his heartbeat to accelerate. "She agreed to work with me on this, and I spent most of my time there researching. You won't believe what we found."

Justin went through the notes and research he and Sydney had gathered, showing Mike the connections they'd made and the suspicious activity that included Longhurst.

"It looks like you're onto something big here," Mike said when he finished. "I'd like to say that it comes as a shock that Senator Longhurst could be involved in something like this, but it doesn't. I've never had a good feeling about him." He frowned and shook his head. "Okay, you're officially on this story. What's your next move?"

Encouraged by his editor's approval, Justin said, "I'll keep digging. I thought I'd spend the week going over this research to see if we've missed anything, and I'll see if our research department can pull up anything new."

Mike leaned back in his chair and laced his fingers behind his head. "What about this reporter from the *Chronicle*? Does she want in on the story?"

Justin chuckled. "More than anything. We agreed to work on this together, so we'll keep in touch through email and faxes." He couldn't help smiling as he remembered Sydney's enthusiasm for the story. "I wish you could meet her, Mike. You'd probably offer her a job on the spot. She's amazing. With her help, this story's going to be huge."

"The way you're talking about her makes it sound like there's more going on here than just investigating a story." Mike tilted his head slightly and regarded Justin with renewed interest, a curious glint in his eyes. "Is there?"

Justin felt his cheeks redden at Mike's correct assessment, though he knew he shouldn't be surprised; Mike was a news man and had great instincts. Justin considered not answering, but he knew that Mike was a good enough friend of the family that he'd only keep pestering him for the information.

"Maybe," Justin said after weighing his answer. Then he pointed a finger at his now-grinning editor as he backed out of the office. "But don't get any ideas. Just because she's single and LDS doesn't mean things will automatically work out. San Francisco is over seven hundred miles away."

"Long-distance relationships aren't as difficult as they used to be, you know," he heard his editor calling good-naturedly after him. "There's email, text messages, phone calls . . ."

Justin laughed and shook his head as Mike's voice faded into the background. He had only taken a couple more steps when Brad fell into step beside him.

"Welcome back," Brad said. "I'm sorry about your friend."

"Thanks." Justin noticed that the sentiment was becoming easier to accept. "Have I missed anything around here?"

Brad shook his head. "Not much, but I think I have. What was this I overheard Mike saying about long-distance relationships?"

Justin grinned as he reached his desk and set his research down. "Are you going to give me a hard time too?"

If possible, the look of curiosity on Brad's face grew. "About what?"

Justin lowered himself into his chair. "If you must know, I met somebody."

Brad's eyebrows darted upwards as a pleased smile crossed his face. "Are you serious? That's great!"

Justin let out a breath and rubbed a hand along the back of his neck. "Well, we'll see. She's pretty incredible, and for some strange reason she seems to like me—which actually doesn't speak well for her." He gave a chuckle and shook his head, but he sobered a moment later. "It won't be easy trying to build something living so far apart, but I want to try."

Brad clapped him on the shoulder. "I think that's great, man. Christie will love this."

"I don't mind if you tell Christie, but don't tell anybody else, okay?" He gave Brad a pleading look. "I'd rather not have the whole world know."

"Only Christie," Brad promised. "Any chance I'll get to meet her soon?"

"I hope so, because that would mean she was here." Justin grinned. "Can't say I'd object to that."

They talked for another few minutes, then Brad left to get back to work. Justin did the same. Not only did he want to go through the research he'd brought home with him, but he needed to follow up on the warehouse break-ins he'd been investigating before leaving for San Francisco.

Deciding the warehouse investigation should be his first priority, he pulled out his notebook and thumbed through his pages of notes. He found the phone number of the security guard to whom he wanted to show a copy of the security footage from the other warehouses. He hoped the guard would still recognize the thief on the tape, even though it had now been over a week since the last break-in.

Eager to get to the bottom of the crimes, he picked up the phone and dialed.

# CHAPTER 18

"What do you mean he just left?" Sydney complained to the receptionist on the other end of the line. "Fifteen minutes ago you told me he wasn't in yet. How can he come in and leave in fifteen minutes?" She breathed out a frustrated sigh. "Never mind. Did he say when he'd be back?"

When the receptionist suggested she try back shortly before noon, Sydney muttered a halfhearted thank-you and then hung up with a growl.

"Uh-oh. Sounds like you really need this."

Sydney looked up to see Jennifer holding two tall Starbucks cups. When Jennifer held one out to her, Sydney took it and asked in surprise, "What's this?"

"Hot caramel apple cider." Jennifer perched on the corner of Sydney's desk with her own cup in hand. "I know you don't drink coffee, so I ordered something else really heavenly for you while I was doing a Starbucks run. I figured you'd need it."

Sydney looked at her in confusion. "Why?"

Jennifer gave her a look of sympathy. "Justin flew back to Utah on Saturday, didn't he? I thought that right about now you could use a little pick-me-up."

The beginnings of a smile touched Sydney's lips. "When have you ever known me to be depressed about a guy?"

Jennifer stared unseeingly across the room for a few moments while she considered. Then she shrugged and smiled. "Well, never, I guess, but Justin really seemed to make an impression on you. And don't deny it," she said, cutting Sydney off when she opened her mouth to do just that. "Let's look at the facts."

Jennifer set her cup on the desk, freeing her hands. "First of all, he's drop-dead gorgeous—there's no disputing that," she began with a devilish grin, ticking off her first point on a perfectly manicured pink fingernail with a delicate silver butterfly affixed to the nail bed. Then she ticked off her next point on her second finger. "He held his own with you during research. *Nobody* does that. Usually you run them off in a couple of hours."

Sydney conceded the fact with a grimace, and Jennifer went on, touching a third finger.

"I also saw him hold the newsroom door open for you, which is bonus points by itself. I mean, who has those kinds of manners anymore?" Jennifer put a dreamy expression on her face and heaved a dramatic sigh. "And then there were the sparks!" She ticked the last qualifier off on another finger. "That alone clinches it!"

Sydney laughed. "Yes, but you seem to have forgotten about the little fact that Utah is two states away."

Jennifer waved off her concern with a flip of her hand. "Who cares these days? It's the twenty-first century. We have technology. Heck, I talked to my mom in Virginia last night on my computer's video phone. And we have all kinds of high-tech things—cell phones, email, even a really cool thing called an airplane."

Sydney laughed. "You know, I think I've heard of it."

"Then use one, for cryin' out loud." Jennifer shot her a teasing smile as she picked her coffee back up and wrapped her long, manicured fingers around its warmth.

Sydney lifted a shoulder. "We'll see how it goes. Before I jump on an airplane, I think I'll try the cell phone and email thing. You know—make sure we still like each other in a few weeks." Sydney brought her cup to her mouth and sipped, then closed her eyes in blissful appreciation. "Mmm."

Jennifer beamed. "Isn't it to die for?"

Sydney let the smooth, hot liquid blaze a comforting path down her throat. "Just what I needed."

"Sounds like it." Jennifer gestured to her phone. "Who were you talking to when I walked over?"

"*Not* talking to is more like it." She sighed. "Remember that source in the DA's office that I was supposed to meet but didn't get to in time? Well, I've been trying to call him for days but he's ducking me."

"That's never stopped you before. Forget the phone and just go over there. Camp out at his office, and as soon as he arrives, convince him to talk."

"I think I'm going to have to."

"Uh-oh." Jennifer clutched her cup and slid off the desk. "Here comes Carl. I guess I'd better get to work." She gave Sydney a parting smile. "See you later."

"Thanks for the cider," Sydney called as she retreated.

Deciding it was time for her to get to work as well, Sydney got up from her chair and slid her arm through the shoulder strap of her attaché just as Carl reached her desk.

"What are you working on this morning?" he asked.

She pulled a notebook from her desk drawer. "I'm heading over to the DA's office to talk with Hyo Park."

Carl's expression lit up. "That's great! What did he say when you talked to him? Does he know if the DA's involved with the missing evidence?"

She felt a tug of conscience at letting Carl assume she'd already managed to talk to the county investigator, but what good would it do to correct him? While it was true she didn't have an appointment with Park and doubted the man would even be there this morning, he had to show up at his office sometime today, didn't he? And when he did, she'd corner him and convince him to tell her what he was originally going to tell her at that first meeting. So what was the harm in letting Carl think she had this in hand? She would soon, anyway.

"That's what I'm going to find out," she said vaguely. "Well, I'm off. I'll let you know as soon as we have anything concrete." Before Carl could question her further, she picked up her cup of cider and headed out of the newsroom.

The crisp morning air cleared her head as she drove to the DA's office, and by the time she walked into the reception area, she felt more like the tenacious investigative reporter she needed to be to get this job done.

The thirty-something receptionist tried to covertly swipe a bottle of nail polish under the counter as Sydney walked up to the reception desk. Annoyance at the interruption was heavy in her voice as she drawled, "Can I help you?"

"I'm here to see Mr. Park."

"He's out on an appointment," the woman said as she glanced down, obviously wondering if her stealthy motion had smudged any of her newly painted nails. "He's not due back for at least another hour."

Sydney gave her a tight-lipped smile. "I'll wait." Then she turned on her heel and strode toward one of the chairs near the reception desk that gave her a good view of the front doors.

"But—"

Sydney sat down, dropped her bag at her feet, and fixed the receptionist with a look of challenge. It was clear the woman was unhappy at the idea of long-term company in the waiting area, but she took one look at the determined look on Sydney's face and backed down.

"Fine," she said with a defeated sigh, then discreetly returned to her task of painting her nails.

Feeling victorious, Sydney settled back in her chair to wait.

# CHAPTER 19

Sydney worked on the city council piece Carl had assigned her while she waited for Hyo Park. It didn't require much concentration, so she managed to work and still keep an eye on everyone who came and went through the doors. About an hour into her wait, a Korean man coming in through the door caught her attention.

Sydney hadn't met Hyo Park before, but a colleague had given her his description: five-nine, mid-forties, short black hair spiked up in the front, and athletic build. The guy fit the description. He also wore a gray suit and carried a briefcase. The guy obviously worked here. It had to be him.

Sydney shoved her notebook back into her bag and stood up. "Mr. Park?"

The man stopped and glanced at her. "Yes, may I help you?" he asked with the hint of an accent.

She picked up the bag at her feet and crossed the reception area toward him. As she neared, a look of uneasy recognition flashed in his eyes.

"Mr. Park, I'm—"

"I know who you are, Ms. Hallam," he cut in, his voice quiet. He shot the receptionist a wary glance, but the woman wasn't paying any attention to them. His gaze moved back to Sydney, and he shifted from one foot to the other. "Look, I can't talk to you—"

"Please, Mr. Park," Sydney jumped in, keeping her voice low. "I just need a few minutes of your time. I've been calling your office, leaving you messages . . . I really want to get to the bottom of what's going on, and I can't do that without your help."

She stared at him, waiting, hoping. The instant she saw him start to waver, she pounced. "We can talk wherever you'd feel most comfortable. Your office? Mine?"

His gaze swept the room, noting the people coming and going around them. Then his gaze fell on hers once more. "I've got a few minutes before my next appointment. Let's take a walk."

Sydney wanted to pump her fist or do an end-zone dance, but she managed to give Park an accommodating smile and follow him sedately out of the building.

"I'm sorry I missed meeting you at the café last week," Sydney began when they were a distance from the building and nobody was around to overhear their conversation. "I was told you had some information that would help me find out what's going on."

"What exactly do you think is going on, Ms. Hallam?" Park asked, his expression guarded.

"It's no secret that the DA's office has come under fire recently for the sloppy way cases are being mishandled, reports and evidence going missing, and cases being dismissed on technicalities. Nobody's been able to prove that the DA's directly involved, but I suspect he's at the heart of it. And I heard something recently that only strengthens my suspicions."

Interest flashed in Park's eyes. "What did you hear?"

Sydney considered for a moment, working her bottom lip between her teeth. She didn't want to give too much away, but she needed him to know how serious the allegations could be. Deciding that she had to gain trust by giving it, she went on. "A couple of weeks ago, an officer with the SFPD overheard a conversation between the DA and another man, suggesting he was deeply involved in some sort of criminal activity. The officer told a friend what he'd overheard, but a few days later the officer was killed. Shot in his home."

Park paled. "By whom?"

"That's what I'm trying to find out." Sydney let out a long breath. "The official story is that he surprised a burglar, but a friend of his on the force said the home had been ransacked but nothing stolen, as if somebody had been looking for something. This officer suspected there was some corruption going on in the PD, as well as in the DA's office. He said reports had gone missing, certain investigations were being swept under the rug . . ."

She took a moment to let the information sink in, watching as Mr. Park stared off into the distance. "Mr. Park, please," she began. "You're a county investigator. Surely you know something—have seen something."

He turned to her then, his expression anxious. "What you say is true. I have seen things that have made me suspicious. The DA is not the same man he was when he appointed me."

Sydney tried not to appear too eager for fear it would scare the man off. "What do you mean?"

Mr. Park sighed. It was a deep, heavy sigh that told her this burden had been weighing on him for a long time. "I've been an associate of Ken

Griffin's for a long time, long before he considered running for district attorney. He was always ambitious, and I felt confident he would do a good job in this office. But over the past year or so he's been . . . different. Cold. With an agenda that's as much a mystery to me as it is to everyone else. He's sloppy and careless, and he refuses to go by the book. I was working with him on a case recently, and he mismanaged some crucial evidence that left the judge no choice but to dismiss the case. It seemed almost deliberate. When I confronted him, we argued, and he threatened to fire me."

His voice was growing angry, and he stopped to compose himself. "I don't know what he's involved in, but maybe it would be better if I made a job change. I see things going downhill, and I don't want any part of it."

"What about the most recent missing piece of evidence—the security tape that would have shown who it was that broke into the lockup and stole that shipment of items confiscated by Customs?" Sydney asked. "Do you know anything about that?"

Park nodded, his lips tightening into a firm line. "It's nothing I can implicate Griffin with, but I was here working late on a case the night it disappeared. I was heading down to the evidence room to check on something when I surprised Griffin coming out of the evidence lockup. He seemed nervous, agitated, but I didn't think much of it at the time. He's been like that a lot recently. But the next day, we discovered that the security tape was missing."

"And you think Griffin took it."

"Yes—though I can't figure out why, unless he was deliberately trying to get rid of that piece of evidence. We hadn't even had time to analyze it yet. It was going to need to be cleaned up a bit, so the computer forensics lab was going to take a crack at it. Turns out they never got the chance. We made a backup copy for the police, but we haven't been able to track it down."

Sydney's heart skipped a beat. "There's a copy of the tape?"

"Somewhere. An officer came by for it the day we logged the security footage into evidence."

"What's his name? Do you remember?"

"Not offhand, but I'm sure I have that information in my notes in my office. I can call you with it this afternoon."

"Would you, please?" She reached into her attaché, pulled out a business card, and handed it to him. "My cell number's on there, too."

Just as Park took the card, an uneasy feeling settled around her. It was a prickling, burning sensation on her neck that made her turn and glance around. It was the same sensation she'd felt when she and Justin had been coming out of the police station—the sense that somebody was watching.

"Are you all right, Ms. Hallam?"

Sydney turned back to see Mr. Park looking at her, his brow furrowed in concern. She quickly pasted a smile on her face. "I'm fine," she insisted, then nodded at her business card in his hand. "Please call me with that officer's name, and I'll do what I can to track down the copy of that tape for you. In return, would you be willing to compile a list of cases you feel like Griffin has mismanaged? Maybe that will help me with my investigation as well."

"Sounds like a fair exchange," Park said with a nod, his tone warmer than when they'd started their conversation.

Sydney thanked him and headed for her car. As she walked, she continued to survey her surroundings. She no longer felt eyes on her as she had a few minutes before, but it didn't keep her from wondering. This made twice now in a matter of days. Was there really someone tailing her? Or was this just a matter of an overactive imagination?

Deciding that all she could do was stay alert and cautious, she got into her car and headed back to work. Back at the *Chronicle,* she finished up the city council piece for Carl, then did some more research on Longhurst. Something had to turn up sooner or later. A paper trail. A connection. Something.

And that's just what happened later that afternoon, when Hyo Park called with the name of the officer who'd picked up the copy of the security footage.

It had been Bryce Davies.

# CHAPTER 20

Sydney pushed open the door to her apartment that evening and glanced at her watch. Doing some quick math, she calculated it was almost seven o'clock in Utah. Would Justin be home if she called? Ever since talking to Hyo Park that afternoon, all she could think about was calling Justin to tell him what she'd learned.

Dropping her things on the couch, she wandered into the kitchen and grabbed a handful of peanut M&Ms, then walked back into the living room and sat in the armchair near her picture windows. Pulling her cell phone from her pocket, she dialed Justin's number. She waited anxiously as the phone rang once, twice, then three times. Discouraged, she was about to hang up when Justin's voice came across the line.

"Hello?"

Sydney's breath caught in her throat at the sound of his voice. "Justin? It's me, Sydney."

"Sydney!" His tone reflected both his surprise and delight at hearing her voice. "How are you?"

"I'm good," she said. "I hope I'm not interrupting anything. If I am, I can call back later—"

"No, you're fine," Justin hurried to say, sounding unwilling to let her go. "You have great timing, actually. I just finished running some errands. I'm thrilled you called."

Her heart warmed at the sincerity in his voice. Did he have any idea what simply hearing his voice did to her? Pulling her feet up underneath her, she settled deeper into the corner of the armchair. "How are things?"

"Good. Busy. Frustrating." He laughed. "All three, believe it or not. How's that for an honest answer?"

She laughed along with him. "Sounds like your day's been as interesting as mine."

"Interesting, huh?" It was obvious from his tone that his curiosity was piqued. "Tell me."

Knowing she had an attentive audience, she told him about her meeting with Park. She filled him in on the changes Park had noticed in the DA, and how he'd caught Griffin coming out of the evidence room the night before the security footage had turned up missing. She also told him that Bryce was the officer who had picked up a copy of the footage.

Justin was quiet for a minute as he let the news sink in. "That could explain why his apartment was ransacked. Do you think whoever broke in found it?"

"I don't know," she said, understanding that it was still hard for him to talk about anything concerning his friend's death. "He could have had it at work. Or he could have given it to somebody. Park said they were going to need to have the footage cleaned up and digitally enhanced. I'm going to call around the computer forensics labs and see if Bryce gave it to anybody."

"That's a good idea. Whatever's on that tape is obviously important. It could very well have gotten Bryce killed."

Sydney's heart twisted at the sadness she could hear in Justin's voice. "I'm sorry," was all she could say.

He let out a deep sigh, as if purging the emotion the subject had caused. "Thanks. All we can do is move forward, though. Can I make any of the calls to the labs for you?"

"Sure. I'll put together a list of labs and we'll split them up." She changed the subject. "What did you work on today? Anything interesting?"

Justin seemed grateful to talk about something else. "Before I left for San Francisco, I was investigating a string of warehouse burglaries. One of the security guards at the warehouse thought he recognized one of the thieves on the surveillance tape. I managed to get copies of the tapes from the other warehouses to show to this guard to see if he could ID the guy in the other burglaries. When I tried to get in touch with him today, though, he was gone. His boss said he just didn't show up for work last week. I checked with his landlord, but he said the guy just up and left last week, no explanation, no forwarding address. And nobody else I talked to at the warehouse is talking. I tried to get some information, but the crew seemed scared."

"Of what?"

"I don't know. Maybe something happened to this guy and they know about it. The security guard had told me he'd heard some grumbling among the receiving crew lately. Some had said they weren't getting their fair share and were going to demand more from their boss."

Sydney frowned. "What do you mean, demand more? Aren't they paid an hourly wage?"

"Yes, but apparently they were getting bonuses for handling certain shipments. Nobody will say what was in those shipments, though."

"That's weird," she said. "What kind of shipping does this company handle?"

"They're pretty diversified. They handle everything from deliveries to retail chains to more sensitive jobs like transporting gems to jewelry stores and artwork to museums. Their main warehouse is here in Salt Lake City, but they have a string of warehouses throughout the valley. From what I can tell, the trucks coming into the area stop at the main warehouse here in Salt Lake and are unloaded. Then the items are put on other trucks and moved out to the other warehouses for distribution."

"And did this receiving crew work at the main warehouse?"

"Yes, which put them in the perfect position to see what was coming in and where everything was going. If they were disgruntled, they could have broken into the warehouses to get what they wanted and then sold that stuff on the black market."

"What kind of things were stolen?"

"The police aren't releasing inventory lists, so all I know is that the thieves broke in and stole large quantities of certain shipments. As it is, the company seems to want to keep this quiet. But why? And what's with the bonuses for the receiving crew? It all seems a little suspicious."

Sydney adjusted her position in the chair and smoothed her hand along the soft leather under her palm. "I agree. Just out of curiosity, what's the name of the company?"

"West Coast Shipping. Ever heard of it?"

Sydney's hand stilled. "Justin, West Coast Shipping is a subsidiary of Sandstone Enterprises, Longhurst's biggest company."

Justin gasped. "Are you serious? How did I miss that?"

"Well, unless you were deliberately trying to follow a paper trail to learn its corporate details, you wouldn't have known. I only know because I've been through the research with Longhurst's holdings about a zillion times."

"Okay, now I'm even more suspicious about this whole warehouse thing," Justin ground out. "What is it about that man that keeps him popping up in our investigation?"

"It definitely means something," Sydney agreed. "Do you think you can get a shipping manifest that would tell us where those stolen shipments originated and a list of dates the shipments arrived? Maybe try to find a correlation with the dates the shipments were stolen?"

"I can sure try."

Sydney shifted in her chair and stared out the picture windows at the darkening San Francisco skyline. She could just see the top of the Transamerica Pyramid from where she sat. The view reminded her of the tour she'd taken Justin on and the amazing time they'd had together.

"I wish you were still here," she said with a touch of wistfulness, surprising herself with her boldness. "Right now I'm staring out my windows at the city lights and thinking about our trip around the city."

His laughter was a low rumble. "I'm just glad your brakes didn't go out on Lombard Street."

"That would have been a sight, wouldn't it?" She laughed along with him. "I can just see it now—pedestrians running and screaming, my car in a twisted heap of metal at the bottom of the hill . . ."

He laughed again, and their conversation became casual and lighthearted. They talked for over an hour about everything and nothing, and Sydney couldn't remember the last time she'd enjoyed a phone conversation so much.

When Sydney heard her stomach growl, she decided it was time to hang up. "I guess I should go," she said regretfully. "I've got to grab something to eat. I'm starving. I only had time for a bagel at lunch. Oh, and the handful of peanut M&Ms I grabbed before calling you."

"You and the dratted jar of M&Ms," he muttered, but she could picture him grinning and shaking his head as he said it. "What are you going to eat for dinner? Your couch?" he teased. "I'm willing to bet you haven't gone grocery shopping since I left on Saturday."

She felt her cheeks grow warm. "As embarrassed as I am to admit it, you're right. I guess I'll just have a bowl of cereal or something."

"Sydney," he scolded. "You've got to have something better for dinner than that."

"Oh, yeah? What are *you* going to eat, Mr. Bachelor?" she challenged.

"For your information, I've got a small roast that's been simmering all day in the Crock-Pot. I was just about to eat when you called."

"Oh." She felt sufficiently humbled. Her mouth watered at the thought of roast for dinner instead of a bowl of cereal. "You're just rubbing it in, aren't you?"

His deep laughter rumbled across the line once more. "You bet. Maybe it will make you actually go out and get that shopping done."

Just then a knock sounded on her apartment door. "Somebody's at my door, so I guess I should go."

"Okay," he said, sounding as disappointed as she felt to have their conversation come to an end. "But email me the numbers for those computer forensics labs, and I'll help you call around about that security camera footage. And I'll see what I can do to get you the shipping manifests from the warehouse here."

"Sounds good." Sydney stood up and headed for her door. "I'll talk to you later."

"Oh, and Sydney?"

She paused. "Yes?"

"Thanks for calling. I loved talking to you tonight."

Sydney wanted to melt through the floor. "I did too."

They said good-bye, and Sydney practically floated the rest of the way to the door. When she pulled it open, Agnes was standing there smiling at her.

"Sydney, dear, I just dropped by to drag you over to my place for dinner," she informed her in a no-nonsense tone. "I'm sure you were planning something horribly unhealthy like a frozen pizza."

Sydney had to grin. Agnes knew her too well. "I was thinking of having a bowl of cereal, but you were close. What's for dinner?"

"Lamb chops, if you can believe it. I got a great price on them at the market last week so I splurged. It's not a meal for one, however. You have to enjoy it with me."

Sydney's mouth watered for the second time that evening. "Sounds fabulous, Agnes. Let me just change out of my work clothes, and I'll be right over."

When Agnes left, Sydney went into her room to change, but she couldn't help texting Justin: *Agnes just invited me 2 dinner. Having lamb chops. That trumps roast! :)*

She changed into a T-shirt and her favorite jeans that were so worn they were tissue soft. Just as she was pulling on socks, her cell phone's text alert sounded. She reached for it and laughed at the message on the screen: *LOL. Glad you're having something besides cereal. Thank Agnes 4 me 4 taking care of you!*

Sydney reread the message several times, feeling happy and a little dazed. Thank Agnes for taking care of her? That one line sent little tendrils of happiness through her. It meant he cared. Cared enough that he wanted her taken care of.

She left her apartment feeling as if she could fly.

# CHAPTER 21

Sydney sat with her elbow propped up on her desk and her chin in her hand, staring at her monitor. She sighed. She was tired. She'd spent the last two days juggling several different things, including trying—unsuccessfully—to track down Bryce's copy of the security footage. As far as she knew, Justin hadn't had any luck either with calling his half of the list of the computer forensics companies she'd emailed him. Now she was finishing up an article about the arrival of a foreign diplomat—an assignment she considered dry and completely beneath her. It was her third time reading through her article as she searched for something—anything—that could spice it up, but she was drawing a blank.

A sudden commotion in the newsroom drew her attention. When she looked up, her eyes widened in surprise. Strolling down the aisle toward her in all his glory, wearing a navy blue tailored suit, silk tie, and devastating smile, was Stephen Dover.

Before she could gather her wits about her, he stopped beside her desk. "Sydney," he said in that smooth, cultured voice. "I was hoping you'd be here."

Feeling daunted by his presence, she got to her feet. "Stephen. How nice to see you again. I never got a chance to thank you for the flowers. They were beautiful."

"Not as beautiful as you looked Wednesday night." His tone was low, warm, and sincere. "Thanks for having dinner with me."

She smiled up at him. "Thanks for agreeing to do the interview."

Seemingly oblivious to the eyes of every person in the newsroom on him, he smoothed a hand down his tie and said, "I was in the neighborhood and thought I'd stop by to see if you had a few minutes for lunch. Are you free?"

Sydney stared at him, dumbfounded. He wanted to take her to lunch? She glanced around the newsroom, aware of the curious whispers and admiring stares she was getting from the other women nearby.

"What did you have in mind?" she asked, self-consciously glancing down at her dark slacks and simple white blouse. "I'm not exactly dressed for a fancy restaurant."

He clapped his hand over his heart and acted pained by her comment. "You think I only patronize establishments that require formal attire? Do you think I'm that much of a snob? Sydney, I'm hurt."

Sydney's eyes widened in mortification. "Oh, I didn't mean—"

Stephen laughed. "I'm only teasing. But seriously, we don't have to go somewhere fancy. This time I'll let you pick the place. Anywhere." He hesitated and made a wry face. "Well, almost anywhere. You mention McDonald's and I'm out of here. A man does have his limits."

Feeling herself relax under his lighthearted banter, she caved. "Okay, you win," she said. "Lunch. But somewhere other than McDonald's." She thought for a minute. Then a mischievous smile crossed her face. "How do you feel about Chinese? I know this great out-of-the-way place . . ."

"Great!" His delight at her acceptance was evident on his face. "My driver is waiting across the street. He can take us anywhere we want." Then he leaned closer and lowered his voice, as if he was finally aware that they were the center of attention. "I'm sorry to just show up without calling. Like I said, I was in the area and had this impulse to see you."

Trying to act nonchalant, she smiled and pulled her purse out of her desk drawer, looping the strap over her shoulder. "It's not a problem. I'm glad you stopped by."

He flattered her with another charming smile and gestured toward the newsroom doors. "Lead on, Ms. Hallam."

\* \* \*

Sydney strolled into the newsroom a little over an hour later, her mind still on her unexpected lunch date. Stephen had claimed he wasn't a snob, so she had decided to put his claim to the test and had taken him to the same hole-in-the-wall restaurant in Chinatown she'd taken Justin to the week before. Dover had surprised her by admitting it wasn't the first time he'd eaten there.

They'd enjoyed their meal and had had stimulating conversation on a myriad of topics, but in spite of the fact that Stephen was a great conversationalist and a charming, handsome man, she simply didn't feel the same connection she did with Justin. So, while she had thoroughly enjoyed herself at lunch—and it seemed he had, too—she simply didn't see a future for them.

Jennifer seemed to magically appear at her side as she turned down the aisle leading to her desk. "So?" Jennifer's eager voice sounded in her ear. "How did it go?"

Sydney opened her mouth to reply, but Jennifer rushed on. "Lunch with Dover. I can't believe it! The newsroom is abuzz with gossip. Sydney's gallant prince, swooping into the newsroom to sweep her off her feet. It's so romantic!"

Sydney laughed. "Okay, first of all, he's not some prince sweeping me off my feet. And secondly, there's no romance! Can't a man ask a woman to have lunch with him without it being about romance?"

"With Stephen Dover? Billionaire and arguably America's most eligible bachelor? Hardly." Jennifer snorted. "He already gave you an interview. You honestly think anyone's going to believe he was here to talk about a follow-up or something business related? Nope, there's only one reason he'd be here, and everyone in the newsroom knows it—he's interested in you."

Sydney rolled her eyes and continued on to her desk with Jennifer nipping at her heels like an eager puppy. "Nobody in the newsroom is thinking that."

But a quick glance around at her colleagues told Sydney otherwise. Their curious gazes followed her as she walked past, and she barely contained the urge to check to make sure she didn't have food in her teeth. Was this what being with Stephen was like? Everyone watching your every move with a rather disturbing expression of awe and admiration?

Probably.

Jennifer was right—there was no doubt that she was the highlight of the day's gossip mill. Stephen had seen to that.

She reached her desk, dropped her purse in her bottom desk drawer, and sat down in her chair. Jennifer sat down in the other chair and looked at her expectantly.

"What?" Sydney asked as she reached for her pile of research sitting next to her monitor.

Jennifer gave her a look of exasperation. "Details! You haven't given me any details!"

Sydney smiled. Giving a casual lift of her shoulders, she said, "I had a great time. He was charming, funny, and a great conversationalist. But like I told you before, there just aren't any sparks between us. Besides, have you ever thought what it must be like to live in his world? To be in the public eye and have the media hounding you day and night? To deal with paparazzi and constant demands for your attention? To be the object of gossip? I wouldn't want to be a part of that."

Jennifer's expression sobered. "Yeah, I guess that's true. Having a relationship with somebody in the limelight wouldn't be all fun."

"Exactly. I'm flattered by Stephen's attention, but we live in different worlds. Besides, I'm already interested in somebody else."

The smile flitted back across Jennifer's face. "Oh, yeah. Justin. I forgot about that for a minute there."

Sydney laughed. "The blinding light of Stephen's fame and fortune could definitely cause that. Justin may seem like small potatoes compared to Stephen, but he and I just seem to fit."

"So if Stephen asked you out again, you wouldn't go?"

Sydney shook her head. "No, I don't think so. Even if I didn't think I had something good going with Justin, Stephen and I are worlds apart, you know?"

"Yeah, I know." Jennifer gave her a disappointed sigh and dropped her chin into her hand. "Still, it was nice to think about—a prince on a white horse galloping in to sweep you off your feet and ride off with you to his castle."

"You," Sydney said with a smile as she pointed an accusing finger at her friend, "have been watching too many Disney princess movies."

Jennifer grimaced. "I think you're right."

Just then the phone on Sydney's desk jingled. Grateful for the interruption, she picked it up and leaned back in her chair. "Sydney Hallam."

"Go check the fax machine." Justin's excited voice came over the line without so much as a hello. "There should be a bunch of stuff on it I just sent."

Sydney looked up and met Jennifer's interested gaze. She smiled as she pointed comically at the phone and mouthed to her friend, "It's Justin!"

Jennifer grinned back and stood up from her chair. "I'll talk to you later," she stage-whispered before heading back to her own desk.

Sydney turned her attention back to her phone call. Her smile broadened as much from the sound of Justin's boyish enthusiasm as from the pleasure of hearing from him. "Why?" she asked him. "What did you find?"

"Just go get the papers. I'll wait."

She laughed softly as she put him on hold and pushed her chair back from her desk, then walked over to the fax machine and retrieved the dozen or so pages sitting there. She thumbed through them briefly on her way back to her desk. When she was seated once again, she picked up the phone.

"Okay," she said to Justin. "I have them in front of me. What am I looking at?"

"The shipping manifests we wanted to see for West Coast Shipping. They list where the targeted shipments originated and when they arrived in the warehouses in Utah. If you'll look at the dates, two of the shipments that arrived in Salt Lake City left San Francisco the day after the lockup was broken into."

"I doubt that's a coincidence," Sydney murmured as she thumbed through the pages. "I wish there was a way to find out what was stolen."

"Even if we managed to get an inventory list, I doubt it would do us any good. If the people at the shipping company were moving something illegal, they wouldn't inventory it on a police report."

"True." Sydney dropped the pages onto her desk and leaned back in her chair. "I learned something rather interesting today too as I was digging a little deeper into West Coast Shipping's background. Turns out they're based in southern California, and they have a fleet of trucks that deliver goods across the country, but they also have boats that run shipping routes from other countries into the U.S.

"But what really caught my interest," she went on, "is that I found records of dozens of shipments coming in from Colombia and a few other South American countries to an art gallery here in the Bay Area. So I called a contact of mine who's a high-profile art dealer in San Francisco, and he said he's never heard of the gallery. Out of curiosity, I drove by when I went out to run an errand. Get this: it's just an old building in a crummy part of town."

"That's weird. Could you have misread the address?"

She shook her head. "It was the address listed on the shipping manifests. I suppose the gallery could have their goods shipped there and then taken to the real art gallery for display. But if that's the case, why hasn't my art dealer contact ever heard of them?"

"Good point. You know, it's interesting that you mention Colombia," Justin said, and she could hear the shuffle of papers across the phone line. "When I was doing some more research on Longhurst, I came across a list of donations he's made to charities and other organizations over the past couple of years. I've been able to validate all the organizations listed for the past two years . . . except one. The Colombian New Council."

Sydney frowned. "What's that? I've never heard of it."

"I hadn't either. I did a little research and learned that the Colombian New Council is a charity organization in the southern part of Colombia. They supposedly help fund schools and orphanages, but when I dug deeper, it looks like this 'New Council' has ties through its organizers to a band of rebels involved in some bad stuff."

"And by 'bad stuff,' you mean—"

"Gun running, drugs, kidnapping . . . Last year this rebel group held a couple of high-profile British businessmen hostage until a large ransom was paid for their release. They're also suspected of breaking into a hotel safe and stealing hundreds of thousands of dollars from visiting diplomats."

"Thugs for hire," Sydney murmured.

"You got it."

"Why on earth would Senator Longhurst support a charity that's linked to rebel mercenaries? It seems like political suicide."

"Beats me," Justin said. "I know this isn't what we set out to investigate, and on the surface it doesn't look like it has anything to do with the shipping company and Marengo leads we've been pursuing, but maybe this will help us tie some things together."

"I agree."

"When I called a couple of my contacts and asked about this Colombian New Council, I learned there was a big drug bust at the border several months ago, and several of the smugglers arrested appeared to have ties to the organization. My source didn't know anything more than that, but he pointed me to the DEA office. I know an agent there who consulted on the case, so I called him, and he agreed to meet with me."

"That's great," Sydney said. "But how did you swing that? Those agents at the DEA don't just offer to meet with the press."

"I just let him know that we've stumbled onto a potential crime-ring organization that links back to a Colombian group they've been investigating. He jumped at the chance to learn more."

"You," Sydney declared, "are a genius."

Justin laughed. "I'm so glad you think so. Anyway, I'd better go. I'm meeting with Agent Ramus in an hour, and I have some things to wrap up before I leave."

"Okay. Let me know what he says. Oh, and thanks for faxing the manifests to me. I'll go over them and see if anything else hits me."

"That's why I sent them. If anybody can make a diamond out of coal, it's you."

Sydney smiled, flattered by his confidence in her. "If you're trying to butter me up, it's working."

"Good." He chuckled. "Listen, I'll call you later. Are you going to be home tonight?"

"Later tonight I will be. I'm going over to Agnes's after work. I asked her yesterday if she could teach me to cook a simple dinner, so we're making a chicken-something casserole. I guess you inspired me."

There was a moment of what Sydney interpreted as stunned silence. Then Justin seemed to regroup. "Wow. Sorry, I'm just a little shocked," he admitted with a sheepish laugh. "I didn't think my effort to teach you a simple casserole would make an impact. I'm glad it did, though. I think that's awesome, Sydney. Really. Good for you."

"Yeah, well, I'm still putting the fire department on speed dial for now," she said. "I'm sure it will be interesting. For Agnes," she hurried to add. "She'll probably laugh herself silly."

"She wouldn't dare. She cares about you too much. At least I can count on her to get one good meal into you today."

"Hey, I had lunch," she protested. "A nice one. And not just a bagel at my desk, I'll have you know."

"Oh?" he asked, curiosity evident in his voice. "With Jennifer?"

Sydney opened her mouth to reply, then froze. What had she done? With a feeling of dread, she realized she'd just painted herself into a corner. Everybody knew you didn't tell the guy you liked that you'd just been out with someone else.

Groaning inwardly, Sydney dropped her head into her hand. *Nice going, Sydney.*

"Sydney?" Justin's voice came across the line. "Are you still there?"

She sighed and let her hand fall back into her lap. "Yes, I'm still here." She tried to sound nonchalant as she explained, "Oh, Stephen Dover just dropped in and took me out to lunch. He said he was in the area."

There was an uncomfortable silence. Then, "You went to lunch with Dover? Sounds . . . interesting." Justin's attempt to sound supportive fell well short of the mark. If anything, he sounded jealous.

Sydney regretted ever opening her big mouth. "It was nothing, really. He's great to talk to, but he's not my type. We're too different. Not to mention the fact that he's way too old for me."

"You don't care that he's one of the richest men in the country and could probably buy you some private island in the Caribbean?"

She gave a little laugh. "Nope. Money is nothing. I bet he doesn't even know how to fold a decent paper airplane."

Justin's warm chuckle told her she'd managed to ease his insecurity, and she breathed a sigh of relief. "Well, I should probably go," she said. "Carl's going to have my head if I don't get my article to him in the next half hour."

"Okay, I'll let you get back to work." Justin's voice held the familiar warmth that made her feel safe and comfortable. "I'll call you later tonight."

She felt the tense muscles in her shoulders start to relax. "I can't wait. And thanks for faxing the research. I really appreciate it."

"You're welcome." His tone was sincere. "I'll talk to you in a while."

\* \* \*

Justin hung up the phone and stared at it for a long minute. What on earth had gotten into him? The second he'd heard Dover had taken her out to lunch, a surge of jealousy had flooded through him. What was it about this woman that made him feel that way?

He thought back to the remorse that had been evident in her voice when she'd realized she'd let the news slip about her lunch with Dover. She'd been worried she'd hurt him, that much was obvious. She cared about him. He would do well to remember that—and not act like the jealous boyfriend.

He leaned forward and picked up the 5 x 7 framed photograph he'd brought to work just that morning—the one the accommodating fellow tourist had taken of him and Sydney standing in front of the stone lion at Chinatown's entrance.

He'd taken a lot of pictures on his trip, and many that included Sydney during the evening she'd shown him San Francisco, but this one was his favorite. They were standing close, shoulders touching, grinning at the camera, looking happy and relaxed. She was stunning when she smiled like that.

The carefree expression she wore in the photo was one he hadn't seen much during the time he'd spent with her. She poured so much of herself into her work that her expression was usually businesslike and carefully schooled, her emotions closely guarded. But in this photo, she looked bright, happy, and alive. It was an expression he hoped to see far more of in the future. She'd had a hard life, but underneath that tough façade he knew there was a woman who had a tender heart, who wanted to love and be loved. And more than anything, he wanted to be the man that she loved.

Justin was jerked out of his reverie by the picture being pulled from his hands. He looked up to see Brad studying it.

Brad whistled. "Pretty. Is this the girl you met in San Francisco?"

Knowing he was cornered, Justin nodded. "Her name's Sydney. She's a reporter for the *Chronicle*."

Brad chuckled and handed the picture back to him. "You're a goner, my friend. I walked up to your desk to see if you wanted to play some racquetball tomorrow, but you were off in your own little world, staring at that picture with a ridiculous grin on your face. So what's the deal with you two?"

Justin stood up and gathered the things he needed to take to his interview with Agent Ramus. "It's only been a few days since I left California," he said dryly. "It's not like I'm rushing out to the jewelry store."

"Yet." Brad gave him a crooked smile and quirked an eyebrow. "I hate to say it, but you're pretty transparent. You look just like I did when I met Christie." He chuckled and slapped Justin on the back. "Welcome to the club, my friend. I predict you'll be in that jewelry store by Christmas."

Justin laughed and shook his head. "We'll see. Racquetball tomorrow sounds good, by the way," he said, changing the subject. "Right now I'm off to an interview, so I'll see you later."

Before Brad could interrogate him further, he hurried out of the newsroom.

* * *

Agent Ramus was a tall, thin man in his mid-forties with short-cropped brown hair and silver wire-rimmed glasses. *The image of efficiency,* Justin thought as he was shown into the man's neat, organized office.

"So," Agent Ramus said after offering Justin a seat and then settling into his own chair behind his desk. "What's this investigation you're working on?"

"A colleague and I have been investigating a crime ring, and we've made some connections to a group in Colombia. Do you remember that drug bust at the border, where huge shipments of drugs were intercepted?" When Ramus nodded, Justin went on. "Has anything new turned up on that?"

"As a matter of fact, yes. It's no secret that we've managed to track the laundered money involved in that investigation to a Colombian militia group fronted by a man named Alvaro Perez."

"Perez?" Justin thought for a moment. "I don't think I've ever heard of him."

"Probably because you're not in drug enforcement. Everybody in this line of work has heard of him. Many of the shipments of drugs we've tracked over the years have been traced back to him. We just can't seem to get our hands on him."

"This militia group you tracked the laundered money to," Justin asked, "do they have a name?"

Ramus looked apologetic. "You know I can't comment on that, since it's an ongoing investigation."

"I understand." Justin thought for a moment, then approached from a different direction. "One of my contacts told me that several of the men arrested in that particular drug bust had ties to the organization that popped up in our investigation recently."

"Oh? What organization is that?"

"Something called the Colombian New Council."

The flash of recognition in Agent Ramus's eyes told Justin he'd hit the mark. "How's your investigation tied to them?"

"One of the men we're investigating has been a major contributor to the organization. I've learned that the organization is connected to a Colombian rebel group known for drug running, so let's just say that I don't think the charity is completely aboveboard. If we can track down some more connections to this New Council, we have a good shot at nailing the men behind the crime ring my partner and I are investigating."

Ramus leaned back in his chair and seemed to ponder this information for a minute. "It sounds like you've come across some leads that could put away the men we're both after. I'd love nothing more than to see those men rot in jail." He glanced at his watch. "I'm on my way to another appointment, but if you call me early next week, I'll see if I can clear a block of time for you. I'd love to learn what you and your partner have found. Maybe we can help each other."

Justin wanted to cheer. Any lead was worth pursuing at this point. He stood up and shook Ramus's hand. "Thank you. I'll be in touch."

# CHAPTER 22

"We'll let that chicken cool before we chop it," Agnes said as she pulled a glass pan from the cupboard. "After it's chopped, we'll put it in here and add our other ingredients."

All Sydney had to do was look at the various cans and spices set out on the counter waiting to be added to the "simple" meal Agnes was teaching her to make, and she wanted to run for the security of Pizza Hut. The recipe card before her seemed to be written in a foreign language.

Her panic must have shown, because Agnes patted her arm kindly. "Don't fret, dear. I promise it's not as complicated as it looks. Why don't we sit and visit for a minute while that chicken cools? We can talk about something other than cooking."

"Thank you," Sydney breathed as she followed Agnes to the table in the adjoining dining area. "I feel completely overwhelmed."

"You won't feel that way for long," Agnes said, her tone reassuring. "Once you learn a few simple things, you'll see it's not that difficult." They sat down next to each other at the table, and Agnes changed the subject. "Oh, I almost forgot. Don't make any plans for Sunday."

Sydney lifted her eyebrows at her in surprise. "Why not?"

"Because I'm taking you to church with me." Her no-nonsense tone left no room for argument. "We have a new Relief Society president, and she's asked me about you every week this month. She told me it was my duty as your visiting teacher to get you to church. I told her I would."

"Don't I get any say in the matter?"

"No, dear, you don't. She's right, you know. With your family gone, somebody's got to make sure you keep going to church. And that somebody is me."

The reminder of what she'd lost caused Sydney's heart to ache. Her family had been very active in their ward before the accident. Her father had served as ward clerk and her mother as a counselor in the Primary presidency. But after their deaths, her church attendance had fallen by the wayside as she'd struggled to maintain grades, work, and care for her aunt. And after her aunt's death . . . well, it had just been easier to stay away.

She'd tried a couple of times to go to church, but it had been too painful to sit in a sacrament meeting by herself when families were all around her, reminding her of what she'd lost. So she'd slipped into inactivity, with the exception of attending general conference broadcasts or the occasional Sunday meeting with Agnes. She still had a testimony, and she continued to feed it through studying the scriptures, reading Church magazines, and talking with Agnes about the Relief Society lessons. She'd tried a singles ward, but she hadn't felt any more at home there than in a congregation full of families. She had thought she'd go back eventually but hadn't found the nerve.

But apparently Agnes was putting her foot down. Sydney sighed. "All right, Agnes, I'll go."

Agnes's face creased with sympathy as she reached over to pat Sydney's hand. "I know it's hard, sweetie, but your parents would be so pleased to see you going. And you won't be alone, remember. I'll be with you. Us single women have to stick together, you know." She winked, making Sydney smile.

"Speaking of which," Agnes went on, her expression becoming mischievous, "what's going on with this young man I met in the hall last week? Justin, was it? He seemed like such a nice young man. How did you meet him?"

Feeling an enormous sense of relief at the subject change, Sydney relaxed in her chair and let a smile slide across her face. "This was your plan all along, wasn't it? To lure me into your apartment with the promise of edible food and then try to worm details out of me about the cute guy you tried to frighten away outside my apartment. Your attempts didn't work, by the way."

Agnes laughed. "I'm glad to hear it. That's the first test a suitor of yours must pass with me, you know. If he likes you enough to hold his ground under one of my interrogations, he must be okay. So are you going to tell me about him or not?"

Sydney grinned at her neighbor's antics and took a minute to collect her thoughts. "Well, let's see. I met him just last week, and we spent about four days together. We worked a lot together while he was in town, but we did some other things that gave us a chance to get to know each other. I gave him a tour of the city, for example."

She went on to tell her neighbor about how they met, what Justin had been in town for, and the investigation they were continuing to work on together.

"There's just something about him, you know?" Sydney finished, running a hand through her hair and flipping it back over her shoulder. "We had a great time when he was here, and we've talked on the phone almost every day since he left. Even though I've only known him a few days, I feel like I've known him forever. We've gotten pretty close in a short amount of time. There's just a kind of chemistry between us that I've never felt with anyone before." She glanced up at Agnes. "Is that weird?"

"Not at all," Agnes said with an understanding smile.

"The funny thing is, I went on a dinner interview last week with Stephen Dover. You know who he is, right?"

"Of course I do. Who doesn't?"

Sydney smiled. "How true. Anyway, he dropped into the *Chronicle* today and asked me if I'd go out to lunch with him."

Agnes's eyes widened. "Did you go?"

"Yes, and it was nice, but I'm just not attracted to him," she admitted. "Jennifer said he had to be interested in me if he was dropping by to whisk me off to lunch, but I don't know. Even if he is . . ."

Agnes arched her eyebrows up knowingly. "He's not Justin?"

"Exactly!" Sydney answered. "Justin and I just clicked. He's the one I want to see again."

"Oh, Sydney, I'm happy for you." Agnes leaned forward and reached out to cover one of Sydney's hands with her own. "It's nice to see you opening yourself up to somebody like this. I was beginning to wonder if it would ever happen."

Sydney felt a blush rising to her cheeks. "Well, I don't know for sure what's going to happen. Justin and I have only known each other a week, remember."

"But you really like him." Agnes lifted one craggy eyebrow in anticipation of her answer.

She gave Agnes a sheepish smile. "Yes, I really like him. But he's in Utah and I'm here. How are we supposed to make a relationship work with all those miles between us?"

"You talk," Agnes stated simply. "You call. You email. You talk through that newfangled texting thing you're always talking about. You find ways to develop what you have. It's not impossible, you know." She gave the younger woman a mischievous smile. "And better yet . . . you visit."

"How am I supposed to do that?" Sydney asked with a shrug. "I have a job, you know."

Agnes rolled her eyes. "Good grief, girl. Don't you even know what a vacation is? Buy a plane ticket and go out there sometime soon."

"My editor would probably fall off his chair if I asked for vacation time." Sydney thought about that for a minute as she fiddled with the fork next to her empty plate. "I guess I could, but I'm not sure Justin and I are to that stage yet. I'll keep that in mind for a little further down the road if things keep building between us, though."

"You do that," Agnes said. Then she stood up and waved for Sydney to follow her. "I bet that chicken's cooled by now. Let's chop it up and get this casserole put together."

* * *

Sydney kept Agnes's advice in the back of her mind over the next few weeks as her relationship with Justin fell into a comfortable routine. They took turns calling each other in the evenings, and they often exchanged text messages and emails during the day. With every conversation they shared, Sydney could feel something growing between them, something strong and solid.

Sydney felt so positive about their budding relationship that she gracefully declined when Stephen Dover called her at work a week after their impromptu lunch date to ask if she'd like to attend a play with him. She tried to let him down easy, explaining that she was seeing somebody. Stephen had been understanding, though he'd sounded disappointed. Even so, she was relieved to know he wouldn't pursue her further.

Sydney and Justin got to know each other well over the course of their daily talks, and she often marveled at how accomplished they had become at sensing each others' moods by listening for the tones and inflections in each others' voices. Justin seemed to be able to sense when she was in a bad mood, no matter how hard she tried to hide it, and he knew just how to tease her out of it. He also seemed to know when she just needed a sounding board for something that had happened during the day. In return, she learned to pick up on the times when Justin wasn't his usual cheery, glass-is-half-full self. When he continued prodding for information about her day without sharing anything about his, she knew it meant he'd had a bad day but didn't want to talk about it. In those cases, she learned he could be cheered up by a humorous story about something that Agnes or Jennifer had done.

They continued to work on their joint investigation, as well, researching and following leads, but they still didn't have anything concrete to indicate who was behind Marengo, or what criminal activity Longhurst or even the San Francisco district attorney were involved in. They hadn't had any luck in tracking down the copy of the security footage Bryce had supposedly had in his possession, either. But they continued to investigate, turning up little pieces of information that they hoped would soon lead to a break in the story.

Other things in Sydney's life also fell into new routines. When she went to church with Agnes that first Sunday, she was pleasantly surprised to get a warm welcome. The new Relief Society presidency bent over backward to make her feel like a valued part of the ward, and within two weeks she'd been issued a calling to be on the enrichment committee. She surprised herself by accepting, and Agnes was thrilled when Sydney started going to church with her every week. It also became part of their Sunday routine to go back to Agnes's apartment after church for Sunday dinner.

Sydney's world suddenly seemed to be a brighter place, and she was happier, more full of hope. She couldn't help marveling at the changes that were taking place in her life, and that happiness she felt started to reflect in her attitude.

Jennifer often commented on her annoyingly good mood at work and teased her that falling in love was making her soft. Sydney would laugh at the accusation, but she couldn't deny it. She felt different. Ever since Justin had come into her life, everything had changed for the better.

As her relationship with Justin continued to blossom, Sydney felt both exhilarated and scared. Was this what falling in love felt like? Like losing a piece of yourself, but also gaining something that made you stronger in return? Sydney voiced her concerns to Agnes one Sunday as they drove home from church together, and Agnes gave her an understanding smile.

"Falling in love is an amazing thing and a true gift," she said. "It makes you a better person, a stronger person, because when you fall in love, you're stronger together than you are alone. You should treasure that, not be afraid of it."

"But how do I know if what I'm feeling is real? What if it's just infatuation?" Sydney persisted.

Agnes tsk-tsked and shook her head. "You think too much, Sydney. Sometimes you just need to follow your heart."

Sydney continued to think about that for several more days before she realized Agnes was right. If she was going to follow her heart, maybe it was time to take the next step. Even if it was scary.

While eating her usual dinner with Agnes that Sunday night, Sydney mentioned that she was planning to go visit Justin.

"I'm so glad," Agnes said, her eyes sparkling. "Talking on the phone will only do so much to further a relationship. You have to be with that lovely man of yours and fall in love with him in person, too."

That clinched it. In the weeks since Justin had left, Sydney had loved their phone conversations, but she missed looking into his thick-lashed green eyes and seeing that heart-stopping smile. She missed the way she felt when he put his arms around her, or when he kissed her with such tenderness that every nerve in her body stood on end.

Her mind made up, Sydney set about making arrangements to fly out to see Justin.

* * *

Justin was typing the final lines of the story Mike had assigned him that day when the phone rang. Still studying his screen, he picked up the phone. "Micklesen."

"Hi, Justin, it's me."

"Sydney!" he exclaimed, a broad smile flashing across his face. He leaned back in his chair, the story forgotten. "How are you?"

"I'm great. I hope I'm not catching you in the middle of anything."

"No, no, it's fine. What's up?"

"Well, I was just wondering if you had any plans next weekend," she asked, her voice hesitant.

"Not that I can think of. Why?"

"How would you feel about a little out-of-town company?"

Justin jerked upright in his seat. "You're coming to visit? Are you serious?"

"If that's okay."

"Yeah, it's okay! It's beyond okay. When would you be coming?"

Sydney told him that she'd checked online and learned that the Friday flights were already booked, but she could get a flight Thursday evening or Saturday morning.

"Go for the Thursday evening one," he said, his heart fluttering at the thought of spending time with her again. "I'm sure I can arrange to take that Friday off. Then we can do some sightseeing and just spend some time together. When will your flight be landing?"

As he wrote the time and flight number down on his notepad, his cheeks felt like they might split from smiling. He couldn't believe it. She was really coming!

"Okay, I got it," he told her, leaning back in his chair. "I can't wait to see you, Sydney. I'm really looking forward to it."

She sounded pleased by his enthusiasm. "I can't wait to see you either. I'll see you at the airport next Thursday then."

"I'll be there. Bye, Sydney." He hung up the phone, feeling happy and dazed.

Just then the sound of a man clearing his throat made Justin turn. To his surprise, Brad stood only a few steps behind him. He was holding a stack of manila folders and, judging from the mischievous expression on his face, he had caught Justin's side of the conversation.

Brad started right in. "Did I hear correctly? Sydney's coming for a visit?"

Justin fixed his friend with a look of mock admonition. "Didn't anyone ever tell you it's rude to eavesdrop?"

"Yeah, I heard that somewhere," Brad said with a wicked grin. "So fill me in. She's flying in to see you? This sounds like a big deal."

Knowing Brad wasn't going to let this go, Justin gave in. "I guess it is. We've been talking on the phone and emailing the past few weeks, and we've gotten pretty close. I was thinking that it was about time I flew out there to see her again, but she beat me to the punch."

"Which is great, because we'll get to meet her," Brad pointed out.

Justin held up a hand. "Now, hold on a second. I haven't seen her for weeks and she's only going to be in town for the weekend. I'm not about to give up any of that time to the likes of you."

Brad let out a snort of laughter. "Are you afraid I might spill all your dark secrets and scare her off? Come on, I want to meet the woman who's made such an impression on you that you have a picture of her sitting on your desk." He gestured at the Chinatown picture of Justin and Sydney sitting prominently next to the computer monitor. "So give me a break, here. I overheard you saying she was flying in next Thursday. Couldn't you bring her by the office on Friday for a few minutes? I'm sure Mike would love to meet her, too."

"Who would I love to meet?"

They both looked up to see Mike stopping beside them, his hands shoved into the pockets of his tan Dockers and his eyes alert with curiosity.

Before Justin could say anything, Brad blurted out the news. "Justin's girlfriend is flying in from San Francisco next Thursday."

Mike raised an eyebrow, and a broad grin slid across his face. "Really? Next Thursday? Well, I agree with Brad—you need to bring her by so we can meet her."

"This is a nightmare," Justin mumbled to himself, shaking his head. Then he gave both his boss and his friend a pleading look. "You two are acting like my parents when I had my first date. I haven't seen Sydney in weeks. Can't I enjoy some time with her without introducing her to every person I know?"

Mike's grin became smug. "Nope. Now bring her by, or you're fired." And with that, he turned on his heel and strode back across the newsroom.

Brad burst out laughing. "Well, that about covers it."

Justin glared at his friend. "Why are you still here?"

"Touchy," Brad said, still grinning. "I was coming by to extend a dinner invitation from Christie. We're having a bunch of friends over next Friday, but it sounds like you might be a little busy."

"Turns out I am. But tell Christie thanks."

After Brad left, Justin let his eyes drift shut, and he shook his head in disbelief. So much for having Sydney to himself.

Even so, a slow rush of excitement began to build inside him. Sydney was coming! He could hardly wait.

# CHAPTER 23

It was early evening in Salt Lake City the next Thursday when Sydney stepped off the airplane. She'd been looking forward to this all week. Her excitement mounted when she finally made it to the baggage-claim area. The airport was busy, and she stood on her tiptoes, trying to spot Justin above the crowd of people surrounding her.

Moments later she heard a familiar voice calling her name. She turned just in time to see Justin descending upon her with a huge grin on his face. She moved readily into his open arms and snuggled up against him, enjoying the sensation of being in his arms once more. When she moved back, he lifted his hands to her face and cupped her cheeks in his palms while he pressed a tender kiss to her lips as if he'd done it a thousand times before. Sydney wished he had, for the rush of happiness it caused.

"It's so good to see you," he breathed when their kiss ended. "How was your flight?"

They talked as they got her luggage, then Justin led her outside to short-term parking, where he had parked his modest four-door sedan. She shivered at the unfamiliar chill in the air and tightened her windbreaker around her.

"I hope you packed a couple of sweaters," Justin said as he put her luggage into the trunk. "It's still relatively mild during the day, but mornings and evenings get chilly this time of year."

She assured him she had, and he put his hand on the small of her back as he guided her to the passenger side and opened her door for her. The skin on her back tingled from the warmth of his touch, and Sydney wondered why on earth she had waited so long to see him again.

As they drove toward the city, Sydney found herself mesmerized by the distant mountains rising against the dusky sky, a touch of white on the tips of the peaks. She remembered the soaring mountains from her visit to the

Salt Lake valley many years ago, but her memories hadn't done them justice. They seemed as majestic a landmark as the Golden Gate Bridge was to San Francisco.

"Are you hungry?" Justin asked, breaking into her thoughts. "I thought maybe we could grab some dinner."

"That sounds great. I'm starving," she admitted.

He picked an Italian restaurant close to his house, and they spent the next couple of hours laughing and talking and enjoying being in each other's company once more. Afterward, Justin drove her to his townhouse, and Sydney was impressed by its neat appearance. She was even more impressed with the spacious interior that was decorated in warm earth tones and overstuffed leather furniture.

"Nice," she said, surprised that a man could have such good taste in décor.

"Thanks. I like it too." He walked with her into the living room, where she stopped to look around. "I should tell you, I've got good news and bad news."

Sydney turned to look at him. "Uh-oh."

"Nothing major," he reassured her. "The good news is, I got you booked into a hotel that's nice but inexpensive just down the street like you wanted."

She flashed him a smile of appreciation. "Thanks. But what's the bad news?"

"Well, the bad news is, I got a phone call from my editor just before I left to pick you up at the airport. Corporate wants to meet with all the staff reporters tomorrow morning, and I can't get out of it."

"How long will the meeting last?"

"A couple of hours at the most." Then he chuckled and shook his head. "To be honest, I wasn't surprised when my editor called. Ever since he and my friend Brad found out you were coming into town, they've been on my case about bringing you in so they could meet you. Knowing Mike, he arranged the meeting as an excuse for me to do just that."

Sydney laughed. "I see. I'm not opposed to going in to work with you. I don't even mind waiting around while you attend your meeting. I brought some new research, hoping we could put our heads together on a few things."

"Oh?" A look of curiosity lit up Justin's eyes. "What new research?"

"Remember how I've been hounding the county investigator, Hyo Park, about getting me a list of cases he suspects the DA has mismanaged?" When Justin nodded, she went on. "Well, I think he got tired of me bugging him, because yesterday he had a list ready for me when I stopped by his office. I thought we could compare it to the list Roger Calloway gave you of the cases Bryce had been working on."

"Sounds like a good idea," he said. "Maybe while I'm in my meeting you could compare both and see if anything jumps out at you."

"I was thinking the same thing."

"Great. Then it's settled." He smiled and leaned in to give her a soft kiss. "Please don't let my editor Mike and my friend Brad scare you off if they suddenly appear, demanding to be introduced. They're good people, just pushy sometimes."

One corner of her mouth quirked into a smile. "I can't blame them for being curious. If you could put up with Agnes's interrogation—and almost being attacked by her ferocious, furry sidekick—then I can take whatever your friends dish out."

Justin laughed at the memory of Princess's teeth almost buried in his ankle. "My friends will be nothing compared to that." He gave her fingers a squeeze. "Thanks for being a good sport."

They spent the rest of the evening together, and then Justin drove Sydney to her hotel. He waited while she checked in, then helped her bring her luggage up to her room.

"You'll be okay?" Justin asked when she and her luggage were safely in her room. When she insisted she would be, he said, "I'll be by for you in the morning so we can go to the *Trib*. Make sure to bring your research so you're not bored while I'm in my meeting. I'd hate for you to have flown all the way here and feel like you've been superseded by my meeting."

She laughed. "I promise I don't feel superseded."

"Good." Justin leaned down to press another gentle kiss to her lips. "Good night, Syd," he said when they pulled apart. "I'll see you in the morning."

Feeling tingly from his kiss, she nodded and Justin gave her one last smile. "Sleep well." And with that, he turned and disappeared down the hall.

Sydney shut her room door and sighed happily. Agnes had been right. This was just what she'd needed.

\* \* \*

Sydney looked herself over in the bathroom mirror the next morning. Excited to be going in to work with Justin, she'd done her hair and makeup, then dressed in nice tan slacks and a semi-dressy blouse. She was just finishing up when she heard Justin knock on her hotel room door. Soon they were on their way to the *Tribune*, and Sydney quizzed him about the stories he was working on.

When they reached the *Tribune*, Justin parked the car, then reached for her hand as they walked into the building. A comfortable feeling of belonging settled over Sydney as she walked into the newsroom. It looked very much like the one at the *Chronicle*, with its myriad of desks set out across the floor and the conference rooms and offices surrounding it. The place was modern and efficient, and the normal hustle and bustle made her feel right at home.

She'd just finished surveying her surroundings when a shorter, stocky man with graying brown hair and kind blue eyes approached, a welcoming smile on his face. He extended his hand and clasped hers tightly.

"You must be Sydney. I'm Mike. Justin's done nothing but talk about you since he got back from San Francisco."

"Nothing bad, I hope," she said, returning his smile.

Mike chuckled warmly. "All good, I assure you. From the way he describes you, you're sure to take my newsroom by storm." He turned to Justin and gave him an apologetic look. "I'm sorry about the last-minute meeting. I know it's supposed to be your day off."

"It's okay. Sydney brought along some research for the Longhurst investigation, and she's going to take the empty desk next to mine and work while I'm in the meeting. That's okay, isn't it?"

"You bet," Mike said with enthusiasm. He looked at Sydney. "Any new leads?"

"A few, but they're slow in coming," she admitted.

"Well, keep at it," he encouraged before turning back to Justin. "The meeting's about to start."

"I'll be right there." When Mike headed for the conference room, Justin retrieved a manila envelope containing a stack of papers from his desk drawer and handed it to Sydney. "This is the information I gathered from Roger Calloway that we wanted to cross-reference." After she took it, he gave her a hesitant look. "You sure you'll be okay out here?"

"Of course." She gave him a confident smile. "I'll just be working on this."

He leaned in to give her a quick kiss. "Have fun," he said before heading off after Mike.

Once he was gone, Sydney sat down at the vacant desk a few feet from Justin's and got to work. She became so engrossed in her research that Justin's hand on her shoulder almost an hour and a half later made her jump. She looked up into Justin's grinning face and her heart fluttered within her chest. She'd forgotten just how much that smile affected her.

"How's it going?" he asked.

"Good. Better than good, actually." She stood up from her chair and started to gather things from several piles, including a couple on Justin's desk.

He chuckled. "One desk wasn't big enough for you?"

She smiled sheepishly. "Sorry. The more I cross-referenced, the more piles I made."

"What did you find?"

"Something very interesting," she said, handing him one of the pages.

Mike suddenly appeared beside them. "Mind if I listen in?"

"Not at all." Sydney turned her attention back to the paper she'd handed Justin. "These are the cases Bryce was involved with in one way or another. And these," she pointed at the sections she'd highlighted, "are the ones that Park told me had been mishandled." She turned to Mike and brought him up to speed. "Park's my source. He's a county investigator at the DA's office."

Mike nodded in understanding. "Mishandled how?" he asked, looking intent.

"Many of the cases were dismissed on technicalities—search warrants with the wrong addresses, evidence going missing, witnesses disappearing—things like that. Park suspects that the DA had a hand in that, but as of yet he can't prove it."

Justin frowned as he studied the list in his hand. "He was involved with a lot of cases that were conveniently dismissed. No wonder Bryce was suspicious."

"Yes, but wait," she told them. "This disturbs me even more."

She handed Justin a small stack of papers and waited while he flipped through and gave them a quick perusal, noting dozens of highlighted cases.

"And these?" he asked.

"Are cases that have been linked to the crime ring I exposed."

Justin's eyebrows rose. "Most of these cases were dismissed."

"Exactly." She nodded. "Disturbing, isn't it? All the work the police and I put into investigating everything related to that crime ring, and most of the cases seem to have been dismissed on technicalities."

"So, whoever's behind this crime ring bought the DA and saw to it that everything related to his venture never went to court," Justin said with a frown.

"Seems that way. So who has the DA in his or her pocket?"

Justin contemplated that as he flipped back through the list of cases. "I'd like to say it was Longhurst, but we don't have any proof of that."

"Do you think your source might know something about that?" Mike asked. "Maybe overheard a conversation, or saw the DA meeting somebody over suspicious circumstances?"

"I'll have to ask him."

Mike leaned against the desk, folding his arms across his chest. "If this guy comes back to you with that kind of information, can you trust him? How solid is he as a source?"

"Solid," she said. "I asked around, made a few calls. I never trust a source until I have him or her thoroughly checked out. Park worked as an investigator in Washington before he came here, with good results. A friend of mine who's a detective at the SFPD knows him and speaks highly of him. This guy's trustworthy. If he thinks something fishy is going on, I believe him."

Mike smiled at her. "Good. I wish all my reporters were as thorough as you. It would save the paper's lawyers a lot of time." He uncrossed his arms and pushed off from the desk. "Well, I've got to catch up on a few things. Sydney, you keep Justin on his toes, you hear? He needs to be yanked out of his comfort zone once in a while, and I think you're just the one to do it."

He headed off, and Sydney smiled at his retreating figure. "I can see why you like working with him. He's great."

"He is. He runs a tight ship, but he really cares for his staff. He's also my parents' bishop. Did I mention that?" At Sydney's look of surprise, he nodded. "He's a good man. He took me under his wing when I first started working here and helped me get going. I owe him a lot."

Sydney started gathering her research, and Justin hurried to help.

"You ready to go have some fun?" he asked with a smile when they were finished. Then he paused. "Oh, but first we need to stop by marketing so I can introduce you to Brad. He'd have my head if he heard you were here and we didn't drop in on him."

Sydney laughed. "Okay, then. Let's go."

Brad turned out to be a likable guy, Sydney decided, charming and funny. She could tell he and Justin had been friends for a long time by how easily the lighthearted verbal jabs flew between them. On the way out of his office and out of the building, they ran into several more people Justin introduced to her. Everybody was so easygoing and friendly, and Sydney felt very welcomed by the people she met.

By the time they made it out of the building it was lunchtime. They stopped for a quick bite to eat, then Justin gave Sydney a personal tour of his city. They walked around Temple Square and saw various sights. Before Sydney was ready, it was dusk, and they were heading home.

Justin's cell phone rang not far from his townhouse, and Sydney could tell from his side of the conversation that something was wrong. When he hung up, he gave her an apologetic look.

"That was Brother Barnes, one of the people I home teach. He just had a virus appear on his computer. It ate part of his master's thesis—which he's supposed to turn in tomorrow. He's desperate, and he knows I know enough about computers to help. I couldn't say no."

"That's fine," she reassured him. "Why don't you drop me off at your place, and I'll hang out there? Maybe I'll even try to make something for dinner."

Justin struggled to contain a grin. "Dinner's not going to be cereal, is it?"

She pretended to be offended. "Hey, I'm learning, right? Agnes has taught me a few different easy meals." When he eyed her skeptically, she rolled her eyes. "Never mind."

He laughed and reached over to squeeze her hand. "I'm just teasing. Dinner's taken care of, though. I put a chicken dish in the Crock-Pot before we left for the meeting this morning. We can eat when I'm finished with Brother Barnes's computer."

When they pulled up in front of his townhouse a few minutes later, he wiggled his house key off his keychain and handed it to her. "I shouldn't be too long."

Sydney leaned over and kissed him lightly. "See you in a bit." Then she got out of the car and walked up the front steps, giving him a wave as he pulled away from the curb.

As she let herself into the house, her mind started to formulate a plan. He had dinner taken care of, but why not impress him with her newly acquired cooking skills by making them some dessert? Something simple, but something that would prove to Justin that she wasn't completely useless in the kitchen anymore.

"Cereal," she grumbled, repeating Justin's taunt as she went into the kitchen and got out a pen and some paper. Then she pulled out her cell phone and dialed Agnes. She would know of a simple dessert recipe she could make. Something that would wipe that teasing grin off Justin's face once and for all.

# CHAPTER 24

Sydney frowned at the white cake sitting on the stovetop in front of her. She'd been so careful to follow Agnes's recipe. She'd been meticulous in her measurements, prepared the pan just as Agnes had said, and cooked it the exact amount of time the recipe called for. She was sure she'd done everything right.

So why did it look so awful?

She poked at the sunken middle of the cake, frowning when it didn't bounce back. Hadn't Agnes said something about it bouncing back? But not only was it sunken, it was gooey in the middle and rock-hard around the edges. She surveyed the ruined dessert with disgust. The way it looked, she wouldn't have been surprised if it slithered out of the pan. She'd been so excited at the thought of surprising Justin when he got home. Instead, she had *this* mess.

Her ringing cell phone was a welcome distraction. She glanced at the caller-ID screen and saw that it was Justin. She wiped her hands off on a dishtowel and answered the phone. "What?" she said grumpily.

His warm laughter reached her ear. "Hello to you, too. I called to tell you I'm on my way home, but it sounds like you're having a crisis. What's wrong?"

She gave the offending dessert one last glare before walking into the living room. "Nothing's wrong. Well, unless you count the inedible dessert I just made. Yuck."

Justin's grin was evident in his voice when he responded. "I had a feeling you were going to try to make something. Dare I ask what you attempted to make?"

"Just a cake recipe that Agnes said was foolproof." She slumped down on the couch. "It turns out it's not. I don't know what I did wrong, but it looks awful."

"Now don't get too discouraged," he scolded gently. "I'll be there in a few minutes, and maybe I can help you figure out what went wrong."

Sydney ended the call and moped on the couch for a few minutes until Justin walked in the door. He was clearly trying not to smile as he followed her into the kitchen, and she wanted to pinch him for thinking this was amusing.

When he caught sight of the offending dessert on the stove, a smile slipped out, and he did his best to wrestle it back. "I can see why you're discouraged."

Sydney smacked his arm, and he started to laugh. "Okay," he said when he managed to compose himself. "Tell me what you did. Every step."

With a sigh, she showed him the paper on which she'd scribbled down the recipe Agnes had given her over the phone. Then she went back through her steps. She was almost done reciting the ingredients she'd used when Justin stopped her.

"Wait a minute, I just thought of something. Did you maybe use baking *powder* instead of baking *soda?*"

"I used exactly what it said on that paper," Sydney grumbled at him, indicating the recipe in his hand.

"Just humor me," he said. "You'd be surprised at the difference baking soda and baking powder can make in a recipe. So show me which one you used."

Sydney let out a heavy sigh and rolled her eyes. Then she strode over to the fridge. Justin's brows furrowed in confusion as he watched her reach into the fridge and pull out a two-liter bottle of 7-Up.

"This was the only soda you had in here," she said, disgruntled. She plopped the bottle of soda pop down on the counter beside him, the contents sloshing around inside from the motion. Then she stopped, her eyes wide with realization. "Should I have used a different flavor? Would that have made a difference?"

That did it. Justin lost it. His laughter rang out loud and long in the room, and tears actually formed in his eyes as he laughed on and on. "The recipe doesn't call for soda *pop,*" he clarified when he was able to choke out a few words. "It calls for *baking* soda. *This.*" He pulled out a box from the cupboard containing a white, flour-like substance.

Sydney wished the floor would open up at her feet and swallow her whole. The recipe just said "one tablespoon soda." She'd been in a hurry when she'd written the information down. Had Agnes said "baking" before soda? She had no idea. She'd never baked anything before, so she doubted she would have known there was an ingredient called baking soda anyway.

The discouragement she felt must have shown on her face, because Justin's laughter finally subsided into softer chuckles as he reached for her and pulled her into a comforting hug.

"I'm sorry for laughing," he said, though he was still grinning as he rocked her gently back and forth. "I think it's great that you tried. And look at it this way. Now that you've made that mistake, you'll never make it again."

She groaned and buried her face in his chest. "I'm hopeless."

"Sydney." He drew the word out, his tone lightly scolding. "You're being too hard on yourself. It just takes practice." He released her a moment later and stepped back. "Now quit moping and let's have dinner. I'm sure you're as hungry as I am."

\* \* \*

Unlike her failed dessert attempt, dinner was fabulous. Sydney had to admit, Justin had this cooking thing down. They both enjoyed the meal, and Justin had her laughing again in no time.

When they finished eating, they lapsed into a comfortable silence, content to sit back and enjoy the quiet. Justin reached for Sydney's hand a few minutes later, giving it a gentle squeeze. Then he lifted it to his lips and pressed a soft kiss to the back of it, smiling at the look of surprise his gesture elicited. He scooted his chair closer and tugged gently on her arm. "Come here."

Sydney didn't need any further prompting. She turned in her chair and leaned into Justin, snuggling up against him. He slid his arm around her and she dropped her head onto his shoulder.

"This is nice," she murmured.

"It is," he agreed. "It makes me wish all over again that we at least lived in the same city, or better yet, worked at the same newspaper. It would be so nice to spend every day with you." He pulled back a moment later, his expression hopeful. "You know, I'd bet you anything that Mike would hire you at the *Tribune*. He liked you, you know. Maybe you should quit your job at the *Chronicle* and come to work here."

Sydney sat up and turned to frown at him. "Or maybe you should quit your job at the *Tribune* and come to work at the *Chronicle*."

Justin's hopeful look faded. "Yeah, I guess it's not that easy, is it."

Sydney shook her head. "No, it's not. You have friends here, and I have friends in San Francisco. And what would I do without Agnes? You know how important she is to me."

"Yeah, I know."

"And I've worked hard to make a name for myself at the *Chronicle*," she went on. "I'm not sure I like the idea of starting from scratch somewhere else."

"I know," Justin repeated. "It just sounded nice."

She sighed. "It does. The long-distance thing is hard, but I don't know what else we could do about it right now."

"I don't know, either. I guess for now we should just enjoy the time we do have together." Justin tightened his arm around her, pulling her back into his side.

Trying to relax once more, Sydney settled back against him, then closed her eyes in contentment as he began running his fingertips lightly up and down her arm. She found herself soothed by the rhythmic motion of Justin's fingertips moving along her forearm, enough so that it almost startled her when his fingers suddenly paused on a spot near her wrist.

"Where did you get these?"

"Hmm?" She lifted her head from his shoulder. With dismay, she realized he was studying the tiny scars around her wrist and the couple further up her forearm. Self-conscious, she pulled her arm away. "Oh, um . . . it's—it's nothing. Just random scars. Everybody has scars from one thing or another."

Deciding she needed some space, she picked up her plate and glass and carried them over to the sink, setting them into the basin with a clatter. Forcing herself to take a deep breath, she stared out the window at the darkness of his backyard beyond the glass. The room seemed suddenly cold. Was it just her?

Preoccupied with her thoughts, she didn't hear Justin approach. She jumped when he put his hands on her shoulders.

"Sydney, what's wrong? I didn't mean to upset you." He turned her around to face him. "I can't help feeling like you're hiding something. It hurts to think you don't trust me enough to tell me."

She averted her gaze. "It's not that I don't trust you. It's just too hard to talk about."

"What is?" He reached for her hands, then frowned. "Syd, you're shaking like a leaf. What is it about your scars that upset you so much?"

Sydney's voice wavered with emotion. "They just bring back bad memories, that's all."

Justin's brow furrowed. "Why do they bring back bad memories?"

Drawing in a shaky breath, she bit her lower lip to stop it from quivering. "I got them in the car accident."

"What car accident?"

Her voice was a mere whisper when she answered, "The one my parents and sister died in."

# CHAPTER 25

Justin's sharp intake of air was the only sound in the room. For several long moments, the announcement weighed heavily on his chest, making it difficult to breathe. She'd told him that her parents and sister had been killed in a car accident, but she'd said nothing about being in the car with them. Why hadn't she told him?

When he managed to pull himself together, he focused on the quivering woman in front of him. "Why didn't you say something? I had no idea . . ." His voice faltered, and he realized that he, himself, was close to tears. "I am so, so sorry."

She nodded without a word, obviously fighting to regain control. His heart went out to her. As if she hadn't had a tough enough time dealing with the loss of her whole family in one fateful accident, she'd been forced to be a part of the horrible experience. Even worse was the fact that the scars served as a constant reminder of what she'd been through.

Without hesitation he reached out and gathered her into his arms. He felt her body shudder as her emotions threatened to overtake her. Pressing a feather-light kiss to the top of her head, he hugged her tightly. "It's okay. Go ahead and cry if you want. I won't think any less of you."

"I don't want to cry," she told him as she started to do just that. He could hardly hear her through her tears because her voice was muffled against his shirt. "I'm sick of crying. I'm sick of wondering why I lived and they didn't. I'm sick of wishing I'd died with them . . ." Her voice broke, and her shoulders started to shake as her crying turned into silent sobbing.

Justin steered her over to the couch and pulled her down beside him, cradling her against him. "Shh, it's okay," he murmured, stroking her hair.

She cried for a long time, and Justin remained silent. When her tears were finally spent, she relaxed against him.

He stroked his fingers along her arm and then softly asked, "So, what happened? Can you tell me about it? If you don't feel like you can, that's okay, but I really want to understand what you went through. I want to be able to help you."

"There's nothing you can do to help," she told him, wiping the stray tears from her cheeks. "There are just times when the memories are too fresh and too painful, even after all these years."

"I'm sorry. I didn't mean to make you remember something so difficult by asking about your scars."

"It's okay," she answered softly. She let out a heavy sigh. "A lot of it's still a blur, to be honest. Everything happened so fast."

After a moment, she continued. "My sister and I were in the back seat, and my parents were in the front, with my dad driving. We were on the highway going home after seeing a play in the city. It was late at night, and it was raining pretty hard."

Sydney shuddered as the memory of that night played through her mind. Her throat grew thick with emotion as she went on, her voice barely a whisper. "The road was slick, and the car in front of us tried to make a lane change too quickly and spun out of control. That car clipped our fender and sent us off the road. We rolled several times down an incline, then slammed into a pole."

She started to shake, and Justin tightened his arms around her protectively.

"I don't know how long it was until the emergency crews arrived. I was in and out of consciousness. The car had crumpled around me, trapping me inside. I was in so much pain that I don't remember much, but I could tell from how urgently the crew worked that it was bad."

She reached down to trace the small scars near her wrist. "There was glass everywhere. I ended up with a lot of stitches, plus a broken leg, a ruptured spleen, and a lot of internal bleeding. The scar you saw on my stomach that night at my apartment was from the surgery when they tried to repair the damage. Ironically, I was the luckiest. The doctors told me my parents died at the scene, and my sister died a short time after arriving at the hospital."

"Oh, Sydney, how awful," Justin responded, his heart wrenching at the details. "How did you cope?"

"For a long time I didn't. I was a mess. I cried all the time, especially when I had to pack up my things and go live with my great aunt." She shook her head at the memory. "My whole world had been turned upside down, and there were days when I honestly didn't feel like I could go on."

She took a deep breath to steady herself. "But then I managed to get into the journalism program at my new high school, and that gave me something to focus on. It was kind of a lifeline, and I soon learned that I loved it. That's why I ended up majoring in journalism. I think journalism is what saved me. It gave me something to take my mind off my life. It was good for me to be able to investigate other people's lives instead of focusing on my own."

"I can understand that." Justin's voice was sincere and full of sympathy. "The fact that you got through it and managed to become the woman you are today is amazing. You're the strongest person I know."

She dropped her gaze from his as her cheeks flushed. "No, I'm not."

"Yes, you are," he insisted. "At least I've had my parents with me all these years to help me through the rough spots. You haven't had anybody. It's inspiring to see how you've managed—and succeeded."

"Thanks." She looked up at him at last. "That means a lot."

Justin lifted a hand to her face and stroked her cheek with the pad of his thumb. "Are you okay?"

She wiped at the remnants of her tears and sniffled. "Yeah, I'm okay. Thanks for listening."

"That's what I'm here for." He studied her for a moment, then said, "Maybe we should get you back to your hotel. You look worn out."

Shaking her head, she stared down at her hands and fidgeted with a chipped fingernail. "I'm not sure I want to be alone right now. Too many painful memories have been drudged up, you know?"

"I understand." Then his eyes flickered with inspiration. "I have an idea. It's a beautiful night. What would you say about a motorcycle ride?"

"Justin . . ." she protested. "Motorcycles really aren't my thing."

"Oh, come on, Syd. You'll love it. Please?"

Sydney looked at him for a long moment, obviously wavering. Then she said, "Fine. But no laughing if I end up clinging to you for dear life."

He chuckled. "I promise."

\* \* \*

Sydney sat behind Justin on the motorcycle, wondering why on earth she'd let him talk her into this. *At least he's safety conscious,* she thought as she fussed with the chin strap of the spare helmet Justin had given her. Before she could talk herself out of this crazy idea, Justin turned the key and the machine roared to life. She held on for dear life as they started to move.

They eased out onto the street, and after a few minutes, Sydney was surprised to find herself relaxing. Riding a motorcycle wasn't as bad as she'd feared. Justin was a skilled driver, and she discovered that she liked the feel of the wind whipping past them. She was so caught up in the exhil-arating experience that she didn't realize they were heading into the canyons until the flat scenery on either side of them gave way to rising mountains.

Their speed finally slowed, and Justin steered them off the road and onto a dirt area to one side. He parked and turned off the ignition, then pulled off his helmet and turned to look at her.

"You okay?" he asked with a smile.

She took off her own helmet and nodded. "Great. You were right. It's pretty amazing."

He laughed, his eyes sparkling at her admission. "I thought you might change your mind." He turned and made a sweeping gesture with his arm toward the horizon behind her. "Take a look at that."

Sydney turned and let out a gasp. The view was spectacular. The city stretched out below them, an array of lights winking in the distance, and the sky was full of gleaming stars she hadn't been able to see from the city.

Justin steadied the motorcycle while she climbed off, then swung his own leg over the seat. When he stood beside her, he held out his hand. "Let's take a walk."

Sydney put her hand in his and followed him closer to the edge of the lookout. He gestured to a long, low boulder, and together they sat down to enjoy the view.

"It's beautiful, isn't it?" Justin asked, slipping an arm around her shoul-ders. "I come up here a lot when I need to think, or when I'm facing a problem. It helps put things into perspective."

After a moment, Justin spoke again. "I got a package in the mail the other day from Bryce's dad. He'd gone through Bryce's things and found a bunch of pictures of us and stuff we'd collected through high school and college. He thought I might want to have them." He was quiet for a minute, the muscles working in his jaw as he tried to keep from getting emotional. "I thought I was over his death and moving on with my life, but looking through those pictures just reopened the wounds. How do you get over it, Syd?" His voice was soft and earnest. "How do you get over losing some-body you loved?"

Sydney blinked back the tears that surfaced at his question. She swal-lowed, then said, "The best thing you can do is let yourself grieve. At least that's what the shrink I was required to see twice a week told me," she quipped with a smile that held no humor. "Bryce was one of your best friends. It's normal to have moments when you miss him more than others. According to the psychologist I talked with, you're supposed to let yourself go through the grieving process. It will help give you closure."

Justin looked at Sydney in the moonlight. "Is that what you did? Let yourself go through the grieving process for your parents and sister?"

Sydney stiffened. "I—I'd rather not make this about what happened with me, okay? The point I'm trying to make is, you need to let yourself grieve for him and move on. It doesn't mean you need to let go of him completely. He'll always be a part of you. But that's the trick, according to my psychologist."

After a long minute, Justin nodded. "Makes sense."

Together they took in the sight of the glowing lights below them until Sydney shivered in the fall breeze.

"I guess we should get going," Justin said.

"Thanks for bringing me up here. You were right. I did like the ride," Sydney replied.

They rode back into the city and were soon pulling up in front of Sydney's hotel. Justin turned off the engine and she climbed off, handing him her helmet. He took it from her, then swung his leg over the motorcycle and stood up next to her.

"You don't have to walk me up," she said, halting his movement. "I'll be fine."

He hesitated, his brow furrowing slightly as he met her gaze. "You sure?"

She nodded, so he lowered himself onto the seat, sitting on it like a chair, still facing her. His position made their faces even, and he smiled into her eyes. "Come here," he said, pulling on her fingers gently.

She closed the distance between them until their knees touched. A swarm of butterflies invaded her belly as Justin reached up to cup her face in his hands. With a tenderness she'd never experienced, he stroked his thumbs along her cheeks as their gazes met and held. Then he pulled her closer, and Sydney felt an explosion of emotion as their lips met.

Their kiss soon deepened, and the world faded around them until all that was left was each other. When they finally pulled apart, they were breathless.

Justin touched his forehead to hers, his hands still warm on her cheeks. "I think I should tell you, Sydney Hallam," he said, his voice husky and deep, "that I'm falling in love with you."

Tears moistened her eyes, and she blinked quickly against the wetness. "Really?" she managed, her voice an emotional whisper. When he nodded, she felt as though her heart would burn right through her chest. She slipped her arms around his neck and kissed him lightly once more, then pressed her cheek to his as she hugged him. "I'm glad to hear that," she said softly in his ear, "because I'm definitely falling in love with *you*."

They held each other for a long moment. Then Justin chuckled, the sound rumbling deep in his chest. "I could enjoy this for hours, but it's getting late. We should probably say good night."

"You're right," she said with a sigh as she moved out of his embrace. "What's the plan for tomorrow?"

"Oh, tomorrow," he said, the word triggering something in his mind. "I meant to ask you. My parents are having a family get-together tomorrow night. How would you feel about going with me?"

Sydney's stomach began to flutter, this time with nerves. Dinner with his family? That was such a big step. But their relationship was moving forward, so she supposed this would happen sooner or later. Taking a deep breath to calm her nerves, she asked, "They won't give me the third degree, will they? Nobody's going to ask where we think our relationship's going, or if we're going to give your parents grandchildren anytime soon?"

He laughed. "Sydney, nobody's going to do anything to make you feel uncomfortable. I told my mom I might be bringing someone, and she was so excited to meet you that she promised to warn my brothers and sister not to give us a hard time. You'll like them, I promise."

"Okay. What time are we supposed to be there?"

"Dinner's at six. We could spend the day together and then head there."

"What should I wear?" She mentally reviewed every item of clothing she had packed. "I want to make a good impression."

He gave her fingers a quick squeeze. "Syd, my parents will love you no matter what you wear, the same as I do. Honestly, don't worry about dressing up. It's a casual dinner."

Reluctantly, they said good night, and Sydney headed up to her hotel room. Once she was inside, she changed into her pajamas and climbed into bed. But sleep wouldn't come. The thought of meeting Justin's family the next day seemed like such a big step. But now that their feelings were out in the open, it seemed like a logical one.

Sydney sighed. Logical or not, she still felt nervous. It was going to be a long night.

# CHAPTER 26

Sydney finished touching up her makeup in her hotel room, her stomach churning. Justin had dropped her off a little over an hour ago to freshen up and change after spending the day together. They'd had a great time, but now that she faced the prospect of meeting Justin's large family, she felt like a basket case.

A knock on her hotel room door made her jump. She gave herself one last look in the mirror then hurried over to open the door. Justin looked as handsome as ever. He wore nice jeans and a green, short-sleeved, button-down shirt that brought out the green and gold in his eyes. She tried to smile, but her face felt stiff.

"Sydney, you look great," he said, his tone sincere.

She glanced down at her tan slacks and nice but casual red sweater and hoped they didn't yell "trying too hard." She looked back up at Justin, taking some comfort in the appreciative look in his eyes. "You don't think I'm too dressed up? Or not enough?"

"You're just right. In fact," he said, "you look more beautiful than ever." And with that, he leaned down to press a kiss to her lips, sending her heart racing. "I promise, you're going to be fine."

The drive to his parents' house took them along a road that wound up through a canyon, and at last they pulled into a neighborhood of beautiful homes set along a hillside. Justin parked along the curb in front of a well-kept, two-story home with stone pillars marking the entryway and colorful flowerbeds near the front door. Sydney stared at the warm, cheery lights emanating from the house and took a deep breath, reminding herself that she wouldn't be going through this alone. Justin was with her.

When they walked inside, Sydney took in the warm, comfortable furnishings in the tastefully decorated living room. A young boy pounded on the piano near the front window, and a toddler in pink overalls and blond pigtails launched herself at Justin's leg.

He laughed as he released Sydney's hand and bent over to pick up the little girl. "This is Makayla," he said, turning the girl to face Sydney. "She's my brother Patrick's daughter." He turned back to the young girl. "Can you say hello, Makayla?"

Makayla gave Sydney a timid smile, then buried her face in Justin's shoulder. He laughed. "She's a little shy around new people." He set her back down, and the little girl took off running.

Justin reached for Sydney's hand and led her toward the commotion in the next room. When they stepped through the arched doorway, Sydney looked around the large kitchen in awe. The waning evening light cast flickering sunlight across the tall, vaulted ceilings with exposed beams and warm, yellow walls, succeeding in making the room feel even larger and brighter than it was.

Several chatting women—two of them holding babies—were sitting at the table or at the barstools around the island in the center of the room, and all of them looked up at Sydney with interest as she and Justin walked in. A woman dressed in a simple yet sophisticated green pantsuit and flattering white blouse stood near the sink. She had sandy blond hair cut short in a trendy style and beautiful green eyes that confirmed Sydney's guess that she was Justin's mother. She turned at their arrival, and Sydney instantly felt herself relax at the warm smile directed her way.

"You two made it," the woman exclaimed, coming over to give Justin a hug.

After Justin returned his mom's hug, he introduced Sydney, and Sydney was surprised when she was given a warm hug as well.

"Sydney, it's so wonderful to meet you. We're glad to have you here."

Sydney felt a blush creep across her cheeks. "Thanks, Sister Micklesen."

"Oh, please, call me Diane." When Sydney nodded, Diane turned to the other women in the room. "Everyone, this is Sydney. Sydney, this is Collette, Sarah, and Brenda." She pointed to the three women at the table in turn. "And over here at the counter is Gaylene."

Justin jumped in to finish the introductions. "Collette, Sarah, and Brenda are my brothers' wives, and Gaylene is my baby sister."

The pretty blond with green eyes very much like her brother's stuck her tongue out at Justin. "Baby sister," she complained to Sydney. "I'm twenty, but he seems to think I'm still two."

They laughed, and Sydney felt the remains of her anxiety vanish.

"The ham needs five more minutes," Diane said, "and by then Tom should be in from the garage." She gave Justin a pointed look. "Your father's out there showing your brothers his new motorcycle."

Justin's eyes widened with excitement. "He bought it? That's great!"

Diane shook her head. "I don't understand this passion for motorcycles you and your father have, but he wanted it so badly I couldn't say no."

Justin grinned. "In other words, he really laid on the guilt trip."

"You got it."

Justin gave Sydney's hand a squeeze. "I'm going to go take a look. I'll be back in a few minutes."

Sydney's eyes widened, and she silently pleaded with him not to leave her alone. But he only smiled and squeezed her hand again, then leaned in to give her a quick kiss. When he pulled back, he mouthed, "You'll be fine," then gave her a wink before hurrying toward the garage.

As the door shut behind him, Sydney glanced over at Diane, who was standing at the table pouring water from a pitcher into several glasses. It was clear from the twitching at the corners of her mouth that the kiss hadn't gone unnoticed.

Feeling uncomfortable, Sydney forced herself to move. She walked to the table and reached for the pitcher. "I'll do that, Diane. I'm sure you have something else you want to check on."

"That'd be great, thanks," Diane replied, relinquishing the pitcher.

"You have a beautiful home," Sydney said by way of conversation. "I love the way you have it decorated."

Diane gave her a warm smile. "Thank you. I decorated it myself. Did Justin mention that I'm an interior designer?"

"Now that you mention it, I think he did. And now it all makes perfect sense."

"What does?"

"Justin's townhouse. I thought it looked too nice for a man to have decorated it himself. You must have had a hand in that."

Diane laughed. "I did, but not as much as you'd think. He has pretty good taste for a man."

Diane pulled the ham out of the oven, and the tantalizing smell filled the kitchen just as Justin and three other men came in from the garage. He hurried over to Sydney and began making more introductions. "Sydney, this is my dad and my brothers Patrick, Woody, and Daniel. Guys, this is Sydney."

Justin's dad was stocky and outdoorsy looking, and he had a wide, friendly smile with brown eyes that crinkled at the corners from behind wire-rimmed glasses.

"Call me Tom," he proclaimed as he reached for her hand. He placed his other hand over their clasped ones and patted Sydney's warmly. "Sydney, it's a pleasure to meet you."

"Thanks for having me." The accepting gesture put Sydney at ease, and she found herself liking him as much as she did Diane.

When it was announced that dinner was ready, there was chaos as children were rounded up and everyone sat at the table. Once the prayer was said, the atmosphere relaxed into that of a friendly family dinner, with much talking and laughter. When dinner was over, Sydney stood up to carry dishes to the counter but Justin's mom shooed her away.

"Why don't you and Justin go out for a walk? We're not going to have many more beautiful fall nights like this one. We can take care of the dishes."

"I think we will," Justin replied. "Only if you're sure you don't need help . . ."

Justin's parents practically shoved them out of the kitchen, and soon they were standing on the back porch. Justin chuckled. "I've never known my mom to pass up help with the dishes."

"She did seem to be in a pretty big hurry to get us out of there, didn't she?"

As they walked down the porch steps, Sydney stared up at the indigo sky pierced with bright pinpoints of light. She took a deep breath, savoring the fresh, cool night air filling her lungs.

"It's so beautiful up here in the canyon," she said, her ears attuned to the songs of the crickets in the darkened yard.

"Yeah, I love it here."

They wandered through the backyard and into the adjoining wooded area for a while, then found themselves back on the porch. The porch swing looked inviting, so Justin picked up the large afghan draped over the back of the swing, wrapped it around his shoulders, then sat down in the corner with one leg stretched out lengthwise on the long swing. He held the afghan open for Sydney invitingly, and she moved to sit on the swing in front of him without hesitation.

Justin wrapped the blanket—and his arms—around her, and pulled her back against his chest.

"This is nice," she breathed, enjoying the comforting rocking motion as Justin moved the swing back and forth with his toe. "Your family is great. I can't believe how welcoming everybody has been."

Justin tightened his arms around her and pressed his cheek against hers. "They like you, you know. Everybody has made a point of telling me so."

She smiled. "That's a relief. I'd hate to be the girlfriend nobody approves of."

The back door opened, and Diane appeared through the doorway. She grinned when she spotted them cuddled up on the swing. "We're serving pie in here if you two are interested," she told them.

"Pie?"

The obvious interest in Justin's voice made Sydney laugh, and she jabbed an elbow into his ribs. He gave a surprised grunt, and his mom laughed and took a step out onto the deck.

"You guys make such a sweet picture, snuggled up on the swing like that." Suddenly, her eyes widened and she held up a hand. "Don't move. I'll be right back."

She hurried into the house and returned a minute later with a camera. Justin groaned and gave Sydney an apologetic look. "Mom's the Micklesen shutterbug. We're all afraid to do anything for fear we'll turn around and see that flash go off in our eyes."

Diane laughed as she ignored Justin's protests and removed the lens cap. Then she took a step back and looked at them through the camera. "You'll all thank me for it someday. Now say cheese."

Sydney and Justin obliged. After Diane hustled back into the house, Sydney laughed. "Your mom is great. You are one lucky man."

"I know. I have you." He pressed a soft kiss to her cheek, then released her and stood up. "Come on," he said, holding out a hand to her. "Let's go have dessert."

At the end of the evening, Sydney and Justin said their good-byes to his family and began making their way back to the city. "Now that wasn't so bad, was it?" Justin asked, glancing over at her with a smile.

"I have to admit, it was nice."

"What time does your flight leave tomorrow?"

"Two. Why?"

"Well, my ward starts at eleven, but I was thinking we could go to my parents' ward, which starts at nine. That way we can go to all three hours, and you can sit with my mom in Relief Society."

"Don't you teach a Sunday School class in your ward? What would you do about that?"

"I've covered for another teacher several times. I can ask him to combine our classes tomorrow to return the favor."

Sydney smiled. "Sounds good to me."

# CHAPTER 27

The next morning Justin picked Sydney up at eight-thirty, and they drove to his parents' ward. The parking lot surrounding the beautiful brick building with its gleaming white steeple was crowded, but they managed to find a spot not far from one of the side entrances. Justin hurried around to Sydney's side of the car to open her door for her, and she smiled her thanks. He reached for her hand, lacing his fingers through hers as he walked with her toward the building.

Cheerful laughter rang out as two different couples hurried their children across the parking lot, and Sydney felt an unexpected stab of longing. One of the families had two teenage girls, both dark haired and slender. Sydney's heart twisted painfully as she noted how much they resembled her and her sister Kate, not only in appearance but in the shared smiles and secretive whispers they exchanged as they walked.

"Are you okay?"

Justin's voice jerked her out of her melancholy memories. She hadn't noticed that they'd stopped walking and were standing in the middle of the parking lot. Justin's face was creased in concern.

Swallowing past the tightness in her throat, she nodded. "I'm fine." But when Justin frowned, she knew he wasn't buying her answer. She sighed as she tried to control the emotion welling up inside of her. "It's just . . . going to church has been hard for me since my parents and Kate died," she admitted. "It's only been recently that I've been going regularly with Agnes again."

Justin's face showed his surprise at her revelation, and his eyes looked suddenly troubled. "You've been inactive?"

She nodded. "For a long time until recently. But even when I wasn't attending church meetings, I'd read my scriptures and Church magazines from home, and watch general conference with Agnes at the stake center. Having a testimony of the gospel has never been an issue, it's just . . ." She lifted her shoulders in a half shrug, looking decidedly vulnerable. "Going to church and sitting by myself, and seeing everyone with their families . . ."

Realization dawned, and a look of sympathy eased the troubled expression in Justin's eyes. "Because it's difficult to be surrounded by families when you've lost yours." His tone was gentle.

She nodded again, not trusting her voice. Justin shook his head, his expression sympathetic, and drew her to him, enfolding her in his arms.

He held her for a long minute. "It's been hard for you," he murmured against her hair. "Harder than you let on."

Feeling comforted by his loving embrace, she relaxed in his arms and pressed her cheek against the lapel of his suit jacket. "Sometimes," she admitted, emotion causing her voice to waver.

"I'm sorry," he whispered, his breath stirring her hair and sending a feeling of comfort through her.

After another moment, she drew a deep, cleansing breath and stepped back, mustering up a tentative smile. "But Agnes has been a lifeline to me. When I moved in and found out she was LDS, I thought, 'what are the odds?' You know . . . moving in next door to another Mormon in a big city. Especially somebody as perfect for me as Agnes. I think there was a little divine intervention in that."

His eyes were kind. "I'm sure there was."

"But I've been going to church with Agnes for the past several weeks, and the bishop even gave me a calling." At Justin's obvious interest, she gave him a smile, this time a genuine one. "Enrichment committee. For the first time in a long time, I feel a part of things. I've also made some friends in the ward who are single too, so that's helped."

"I think that's great, Syd," he said, his tone warm. "Good for you."

Justin let his hands slide down her arms, and he took her hand once more. They walked the rest of the way across the parking lot and were soon inside the spacious chapel, where Justin's parents had saved them seats. Sydney loved seeing his parents again, and she felt a sense of contentment as she sat between Justin and his mom in the chapel.

As the prelude music played, Justin slid his arm around her shoulders and pulled her close. She leaned against him, wondering how she'd gotten so lucky to find somebody as wonderful as him.

Her gaze wandered around the chapel, and when she turned her attention to the stand behind the pulpit, she saw that Mike—or Bishop Kuhn, as she knew she should call him, now that they weren't in the *Tribune*'s newsroom— was staring at her and Justin from his seat on the stand. The knowing smile on his face was a little disconcerting.

She leaned over to whisper to Justin, "Why does Mike—er, Bishop Kuhn—keep staring at us like that?"

Justin chuckled softly in her ear. "Let's just say that my parents haven't been the only ones trying to play matchmaker over the years."

"Great," she mumbled before sitting back upright.

When sacrament meeting was over, Sydney watched with dismay as Mike came down from the stand and headed in their direction. "Uh-oh, here he comes," she whispered from where she stood in the aisle next to their pew.

Mike shook Tom's and Diane's hands, then shook Justin's, and finally hers. "Sydney, I thought you would have flown home by now."

"Not until this afternoon," she explained.

Mike nodded, then leaned around her to say to Justin, "Brother Thompson mentioned that he needs some help setting up more chairs in the cultural hall for his lesson. Would you be able to help him while I talk to Sydney for a few minutes?" He added a wink that made his request seem less formal.

"Sure," Justin answered, then told Sydney, "I'll meet you in Gospel Doctrine in just a few minutes."

Knowing she was stuck, Sydney turned back to Mike, who smiled kindly. "Let's go into the foyer, shall we?"

Sydney followed him out of the chapel and into the foyer, where he gestured to the couch along one wall. As they sat, Sydney twisted her fingers nervously, and Mike caught the gesture.

"I can tell I've made you nervous, but that wasn't my intention, I assure you. I just wanted to tell you how happy you've been making Justin." He gave her a fatherly smile. "I've known him and his family for a long time, and they're good people. And Justin's as good as they come—served an honorable mission, worked hard in college, is good at his job . . . And it seems as if he's finally found a good woman in you."

Sydney felt a flush creep across her cheeks. "Thank you," she responded, touched by this man's approval. "I feel pretty lucky to have him. I just hope he feels the same way."

"Oh, he does, I assure you," Mike said. "He lights up when you're around in a way I've never seen him do before. And you two really work well together. You have a way of bouncing ideas off of each other that's rare." At her look of surprise, he smiled. "I had my eye on you two on Friday. I wish I had a dozen reporters with your and Justin's skills. It would certainly make my job easier."

"Well, thank you," Sydney said again, her appreciation for this man only continuing to grow.

He cocked an eyebrow at her. "I know it's Sunday and this really isn't the place to talk business, but . . . you're not by any chance looking to relocate, are you?"

Sydney hesitated. It was true that she would love to be closer to Justin, but . . . leave San Francisco?

Before she could answer, Mike lifted a hand. "I can tell from your expression that this is a sensitive topic, so don't answer that. Just know that if you ever think about moving here, you have some options with the *Tribune*."

Surprised at his offer, she smiled. "Thank you. I'll keep that in mind."

Just then she saw Justin coming toward them from the end of the hall. Mike brought their conversation to a close with a handshake. "Sydney, it was great to meet you. Have a safe flight home, okay?"

She returned his smile with a grateful one of her own. "Thank you. And thank you for letting me work in your newsroom on Friday. I enjoyed it."

"Anytime. And remember," he said with a meaningful look just as Justin walked up, "that offer is always open." With that, he turned and headed down the hall.

"What offer?" Justin asked, his expression curious.

"Nothing." Sydney shook her head. "Just something we talked about. So, should we go to Gospel Doctrine?"

The rest of the church block went quickly, and before Sydney was ready, she was back at her hotel packing her things. The drive to the airport didn't take long, either, and soon they were standing before the security checkpoints, facing the fact that they were once more being separated.

In an obvious effort to keep the mood light, Justin turned the subject to their investigation. "You'll talk to the county investigator tomorrow, right? Try to pry a little more information out of him?"

"Definitely." Sydney nodded. "I'm also going to call a couple of my other sources in the morning and see if they know anything. I'll let you know what I learn."

Justin glanced at his watch, then sighed. "I guess you'd better get going." He reached for her fingers and drew her close, then lowered his head so their foreheads touched. His face hovered inches from hers, his thick-lashed green eyes staring back into her brown ones.

"I'm going to miss you," he said, his voice husky. "I wish you didn't have to go."

"I wish I didn't either," came her response, and she was surprised at the raw emotion she heard in it.

Lifting a hand to her cheek, he leaned down and gave her a soft, lingering kiss that took her breath away. When they finally moved apart, his voice was soft as he said, "Call me when you get home so I know you arrived safely, okay?"

"I will." Feeling dangerously close to tears, Sydney pulled back and adjusted her bag's strap on her shoulder. "I hope we can see each again before too long."

"I hope so too. Have a safe trip."

\* \* \*

Robert Longhurst dialed, then leaned back in his chair with the phone pressed to his ear, waiting for his colleague to answer. When he did, Robert spoke in a low voice. "It's me. Have you talked to our men in Colombia?"

"Perez says he's overseeing the job himself," his colleague answered. "The goods are in his possession, and everything else has been taken care of. My deal goes down tonight, and then your goods will travel on the same ship as mine. The boat should arrive next Friday."

"You sure you still trust Douglas to get everything through Customs? I lost a lot of money from that raid a few months ago, not to mention some trusted contacts."

"Hallam's investigation cost us both. I've put my best people on this. Douglas is well placed, and he knows what's at stake. I've wanted to acquire these antiquities for a long time."

Longhurst leaned forward and picked up the glossy museum brochure lying open on the desk. He studied the photos for a few moments and shook his head. "I'll never get your obsession with this." He tossed the brochure back onto the desk's uncluttered surface. "You really feel confident our guys can handle this job?"

"They've assured me they have several men who specialize in just this kind of work. They know how much I want those pieces, and I'm paying them well. Nothing will go wrong—with my deal or your goods."

"Let's hope not, because I stand to make a lot of money on this one." A knock sounded on his office door, and Longhurst pushed his chair back and stood up. "I've got to go. Let me know when our boat arrives. The funds from the sale are still set to run through Premiere, right?"

"Just as before. The money should be all neat and clean by tomorrow. You could buy dinner for the head of the FBI with the funds, and no one would be the wiser. Like I said, everything's set."

"Good. Then I'll leave you to your work and I'll get on with mine. I don't want to be late for my press conference." A smile twisted the corners of his mouth. "Apparently, the American taxpayers like to see their politicians on time for public appearances. I'm told it makes us look prompt, considerate, and trustworthy."

The other man's laughter rumbled across the line. "Yes, I know. Those of us in the public eye need to go to great lengths to maintain appearances. Don't worry, I'll be in touch."

# CHAPTER 28

"Please, try to remember," Sydney said, dropping her forehead into her hand and rubbing one throbbing temple gingerly. Her fingers clenched tighter around the phone. "Is there anybody at all that stands out in your mind? There's got to be someone."

Trying to pry information out of an uncooperative Hyo Park wasn't making Sydney's life any easier. As it was, she'd already had a stressful morning. A story she'd been eager to write had been assigned to another reporter in her absence, her computer was giving her fits, two of the sources she'd called to ask for information on the Marengo investigation hadn't returned her calls, and she'd spent the better part of the morning trying to reach Park, who was out on an investigation. She'd finally managed to worm his cell phone number out of his receptionist, who was clearly annoyed about being bothered by Sydney so many times. When she got through to Park, he was distracted and of very little help.

"Griffin sees a lot of people, Ms. Hallam," he said, then covered the mouthpiece to call out some instructions to a colleague.

"Mr. Park!" she said, raising her voice in hopes of regaining his attention.

A second later he responded. "Yes, Ms. Hallam, I'm still here. I'm afraid I can't talk—"

"Please, just answer this one question," she persisted. "I know the DA sees a lot of people, but if he's into something illegal, surely he's met with somebody under suspicious circumstances, or with somebody who looks suspicious. Is there anything that stands out in your mind?"

He was silent for a moment, and she only hoped that meant he was thinking. "There is one thing," he said at last. "I don't know why I didn't think about it before. He's met with one odd character a couple of different times. Once was late one night after everybody had gone home. I stayed late

to finish up some paperwork and was just leaving when I spotted Griffin
and this guy in one of the conference rooms. Griffin called him Doug, I
think. Or something like that." He contemplated that for a minute. "I don't
know, Ms. Hallam, that's all I can remember."

Growing impatient, Sydney asked, "Did you catch a last name? Or can
you describe the guy?"

"I don't remember a last name, but I remember what the guy looked
like. He was about six feet tall, dark hair. He dressed nice, but he looked like
a pretty tough character. Hard, you know? I wouldn't want to meet the guy
in a dark alley."

She heard a couple of shouts in the background, and then Park's voice
came again, sounding harried. "I don't know if that helps, but I've got to
go," he said. "I'll call you if I think of anything else."

"But—" Sydney's protest was silenced by the *click* of her call being
disconnected.

She growled as she set the phone back in its cradle with a frustrated
thud. *Could this day get any worse?* she thought as she dropped her pounding
head into her hands.

"Here," came Jennifer's voice from beside her. "It looks like you could
use these."

Sydney sat up and saw the two ibuprofen tablets in her friend's palm.
"Thank you," she said, taking them and popping them into her mouth. She
downed them with a swallow from the bottled water on her desk.

Jennifer took the chair next to her. "You okay?"

"Yeah, just having a bad morning."

A smile flitted across Jennifer's face. "I bet you're wishing you were still
in Utah."

"You've got that right." She managed to muster a smile. She'd called
Jennifer when she'd gotten back into town the night before to tell her all
about her trip, and her friend had patiently listened as she'd gone on and on
about Justin.

"Anything I can do to help?"

"Thanks, but I don't think so. Unless you can tell me the name of a
dark-haired guy, six feet tall, looks rough."

Jennifer made a face. "Thousands of guys in San Francisco meet that
description."

"I know," Sydney groaned, dropping her head into her hands once
more. "And that's the only lead I've got."

Jennifer put a sympathetic hand on her shoulder and stood up. "Hang
in there. I've got to get back to work."

Sydney closed her eyes, willing her headache away. She was just starting to relax when her phone rang, making her jump. She scrambled to answer it before it could ring again. "Sydney Hallam."

"You called asking for information about the DA," the rough, harried voice of her most valued source said without so much as a hello.

This was the way it worked with this source. No small talk, get to the point. She appreciated it, actually. "Please tell me you have something," she pleaded.

"I don't have anything about Griffin, but it's funny that you called, because I heard an interesting rumor down at the docks over the weekend. It has to do with one of your old persons of interest—Phillip Douglas."

"Douglas?" Sydney sat up straighter in her chair. Phillip Douglas had been the CEO of a company she and the authorities had been investigating for money laundering during her crime-ring investigation. Much of the insurance money for the boat shipments of goods that had been stolen had been processed by his company, creating a suspicious money trail. Douglas had been at the heart of that suspicion. But shortly after his company had merged with another, his job became obsolete and he disappeared. The police had searched for him but had come up empty-handed.

"What did you hear about Douglas?"

"Word is that a big shipment will be arriving at the docks early Friday morning—a shipment Douglas himself is personally overseeing. Rumor is it's even more valuable than the shipment stolen out of the lockup not long ago."

Her heart leaped. "Do you know what it is?"

"No, just that it's valuable. My connections at the dock are scared, so whoever is behind this sounds like somebody you don't want to mess with." He paused for a moment, then warned, "I worry that you're in over your head on this one, Hallam. Be careful, okay?"

A chill ran down her spine at the intensity in his voice. "I'll be careful," she managed. "And thanks."

The line went dead, and she lowered the receiver back into place. For a moment, she let herself dwell on her source's warning. *Was* she in over her head? Trying to shake the unsettling feeling, she picked up the phone once more and punched in Justin's work number. She was glad when he answered on the first ring.

"Hi, Justin, it's me."

"Hey, Syd," he said. "Are you okay? You sound like you're not feeling well."

"Just a headache," she admitted, downplaying as best she could since the ibuprofen hadn't kicked in yet. "I didn't learn much from Park, but I just learned something interesting from one of my sources." She explained what she'd learned, but she was careful to leave out the warning she'd received. There was no need to get Justin worried too.

"What do you think is in that shipment?" he asked.

"I don't know, but I'm going to call Detective Richardson. This is big enough to get the police involved. I just have to warn Richardson to be careful who he tells. If word gets back to the guys behind this shipment, they could reroute it and we'd have nothing."

"I agree."

"I'll make sure to make a deal with Richardson. In exchange for the tip, I want permission to be there and have the exclusive."

Justin's low chuckle sounded in her ear. "I wouldn't expect anything else from you. So do you think he'll give us the exclusive?"

"Us? Justin, you're seven hundred miles away."

"Yes, 'us.' There's no way I'm going to miss this. It could be the big break we've been waiting for. Besides, I'm not going to let you handle something like this alone. It could be dangerous."

There was that word again. *Danger.* Sydney shook her head, refusing to be intimidated. "There's always a risk when you're involved in an investigation like this, but I'm not about to back down. Not now, when everything's heating up."

"I know," Justin said, his voice determined. "That's why I'm coming with you. I'll talk to Mike about when I can leave. I'm sure he'll approve the trip out there when he hears what you learned."

Sydney's stomach quivered with excitement at the thought of seeing Justin again, and even sooner than she'd hoped. "Call me when you know. In the meantime, I'm going to call Richardson and get the ball rolling."

# CHAPTER 29

Sydney lay in bed that night, her mind whirling. Her day had started off badly, but the rest of the day had more than made up for it. Watching Richardson launch an investigation into the mysterious shipment soon to be arriving in the harbor had been exhilarating. He'd even put her to work, asking if she could contact some of her other sources to see if she could learn more. She'd been able to learn a couple more small details from a dock worker who she'd talked with before, and she passed them along to Richardson, who was grateful for anything she could give him.

To make the afternoon even better, Justin had called just before she left work to tell her that Mike had approved the trip to San Francisco. Better yet, he was flying in a day early. He'd tried to get a flight Thursday, but those flights had been sold out, and in the end, Mike had agreed to let him take a Wednesday morning flight. Sydney wasn't complaining. Any extra time she got to spend with Justin was fine by her.

She knew she should be ecstatic with the events of the day, but the one piece of unfinished business refused to leave her alone—the tough-looking man Hyo Park had seen with Griffin. Who was he?

The quiet tick-ticking of the grandfather clock in her living room permeated her thoughts, making her feel restless rather than soothed. With a sigh, she threw back the covers and slid out of bed.

The darkened balcony beckoned her, and she stepped out onto the cool cement in her stocking feet. The air was crisp, and she breathed deeply, trying to clear her head. Crossing to the cushioned lounge chair in the corner, she lay down on it and stared up at the night sky, sprinkled with stars. She always felt comforted by staring up at the never-changing constellations.

Tonight, however, even that comfort proved elusive. What was it about Hyo Park's tale of the tough-looking man talking to Griffin that bothered her? And why did it feel like the answer to that puzzle lurked near the fore-front of her mind, just waiting for her to discover it?

She closed her eyes and breathed slowly and rhythmically, hoping to relax both her body and mind. It was just starting to work when she gasped and bolted upright.

*That's it!*

Park had said he'd overheard Griffin calling the man Doug or some-thing like it. What if it had been Douglas? What if Griffin had been talking to Phillip Douglas?

She got up from the chair and paced across the small balcony, the movement helping her think. Phillip Douglas certainly met the description Park had given her—about six feet tall, dark haired, and a tough, streetwise appearance that made him intimidating. She'd never met the man, but she'd seen the picture of him that Richardson had been showing around during the money laundering investigation.

If Douglas was involved with Griffin, the pieces of the puzzle would certainly fit—all those shipping-inventory court cases being dismissed on technicalities, evidence going missing . . . Griffin was likely being paid off to see that those cases never made it to court.

This was it—the connection she needed to prove that Griffin was corrupt. First thing in the morning, she needed to talk to Richardson and get a photo of Douglas that she could show to Park. If he could ID the guy, she would have enough evidence to go to Richardson with, and then to the state attorney general's office. Proof that the DA had dealings with a man wanted for ques-tioning by the FBI could be enough to launch an official investigation.

Sydney did a little victory dance across the patio. She could hardly wait to tell Justin!

After an almost sleepless night, Sydney rushed to Richardson's office first thing the next morning and explained what she'd learned. He eagerly printed off the photo of Douglas and instructed her to let him know if Park ID'd the man.

And Park did. After calling him on his cell phone and learning he was on his way to his office, Sydney rushed over and managed to catch him in the parking lot just as he arrived. When she showed him the photo, his eyes instantly flashed with recognition. Yes, he told her, Douglas was the man he'd seen with Griffin.

Sydney wanted to cheer. After thanking Park repeatedly, she headed back to the precinct to talk to Richardson about what their next step was going to be. She was so excited that for once she didn't even mind being stuck in the morning rush-hour traffic. It gave her a chance to call Justin from her cell phone to tell him what was going on. He was every bit as excited as she was and promised to take her out for a celebratory dinner the next night when he was in town.

After she hung up, she sat back and marveled at how quickly an investigation could turn. Suddenly leads were panning out, mysterious shipments were arriving at the docks, and Justin was coming to town . . . The next few days were going to be very exciting, indeed.

\* \* \*

"Sorry to interrupt, sir."

Robert Longhurst looked up from the paperwork on his desk to see his assistant standing in his office doorway. "What is it?"

"I have something you might like to see." The man crossed the room and dropped a folder in front of him.

Longhurst gave him a wary glance. The man's anxious expression concerned him. He flipped open the folder to see several 8 x 10 photos inside. He picked up the first glossy sheet and scrutinized the picture. His brow furrowed. "What's this?"

"You wanted her followed these past few weeks. We didn't come across anything worthy of your attention until yesterday. Those pictures were taken by our man outside the San Francisco DA's office yesterday. The men you assigned to follow her have seen her at the police station and the DA's office a few times, but that's not unusual for a reporter. But yesterday was the third time Ms. Hallam has met with Park, the county investigator. When we queried his receptionist, she said Hallam and Park have talked on several occasions. They seem to be working together on something."

Longhurst's mouth drew into a firm line as he studied the photographs. "Do you know what they've been working on?"

"The receptionist overheard them talking about some kind of security footage. We assume they were discussing the footage taken the night Griffin and Douglas retrieved the items from the lockup. Griffin destroyed the footage, but maybe Hallam and this county investigator have information we don't know of."

It was quiet in the room as Longhurst flipped through the rest of the photos. When he looked back up at his assistant, his eyes were cold and hard. "Have Griffin deal with his county investigator. As for Hallam . . ." His fingers tightened on the pictures as a muscle jumped in his jaw. "This woman has already ruined one of my businesses. I can't stand to have her ruin any others. Warn her. Memorably. Tell her to back off or else."

# CHAPTER 30

Sydney was waiting for Justin in the reception area of the *Chronicle* when he walked in. She launched herself at him, throwing herself into his arms with a squeal.

"I can't believe you're here!"

He hugged her back. "I know. I can't believe it either."

"I'm glad you called me to tell me you were on your way over here because I was about to head out," she told him as she stepped back and looked up at him. "The district attorney has called a press conference, and Carl wants me to get over there. I almost missed you."

Justin's grin slipped a bit as his brows narrowed in concern. "Why did Griffin call a press conference?"

"I don't know, but I need to hurry if I'm going to make it." Sydney glanced down at her watch. Then she looked back up at Justin and frowned. "I'm sorry to desert you right after you get here."

"No, don't worry about it." Justin waved off her concern. "It's a workday. I didn't expect you to be able to drop everything to spend time with me. Besides, this is a business trip for me, remember? It's just an added bonus that I get to see you."

When he flashed her that special smile again, Sydney smiled back and stepped closer to give him a tender kiss. "It's a bonus for me too," she agreed.

The ringing of the telephone at the reception desk reminded them they weren't alone, so they reluctantly pulled away.

"So what will you do while I'm dealing with the press conference?" Sydney asked.

"My stuff's still in the rental car out front. I'm staying in Mike's brother's condo again, so I'll just head over there, unpack, and rest up a bit. Do you think you'll be free for lunch?"

"I'd better be," she grumbled. "I'm tired of skipping lunch. How about I call you and give you an update on what time I think I can take a break?"

"Sounds great. I'll talk to you then."

Justin gave her a good-bye kiss that left her flushed. She returned to her desk in a happy daze to gather her things, then headed to the press conference.

Parking was hard to find, so Sydney ended up circling the block twice before she found a space. As she locked her car and started off toward the building, an eerie, tingly feeling crept along her spine. She stiffened, sure that somebody was watching her again.

As inconspicuously as possible, she studied the people along the busy sidewalk and scanned the parked cars nearby for anything out of the ordinary. Nothing. Finally the feeling went away, and she sighed with relief. If there had been someone watching her, whoever it was wasn't watching her anymore.

Sydney joined the dozens of other reporters and news crews on site and managed to find a seat near the front. Griffin approached the podium a few minutes later, surprising everybody by announcing that he was making a change in his staff. His assistant DA had resigned, and his two county investigators were being replaced.

Sydney's heart stopped. She knew what that meant. Hyo Park was being fired.

She was glad she'd turned on her handheld digital recorder to record the press conference, because she didn't hear anything else as she considered the implications. Had Griffin discovered that Park was working with her? And why had the assistant DA resigned? Did it have anything to do with their investigation?

As soon as the press conference finished, she hurried back to the *Chronicle.* She spent the rest of the morning putting her notes together and leaving messages for several sources she thought might be able to give her some additional information. She also tried to reach Hyo Park on his cell phone, but her calls went straight to his voice mail.

Deciding to give Justin a quick call to let him know where things stood, she pulled out her cell and dialed his number. She smiled when her call was answered with Justin's drowsy-sounding hello. "Did I wake you up?"

"Sorry, I dozed off on the couch," he admitted sheepishly. "How'd the press conference go?"

"You won't believe it. Griffin announced that his assistant DA resigned. He's also replacing Park and another investigator."

"What?" Justin sounded very awake now. "Why?"

"All he said was that he and his assistant DA had had too many differences of opinions these past few months, so the guy resigned. He didn't give a reason for replacing the two county investigators." She frowned and shook her head. "What if he somehow found out about Park feeding me information?"

"But that wouldn't explain why the assistant DA's resigning, or why he's letting the other investigator go."

"No, but what if he's planning on replacing them with men that can help him with whatever illegal dealings he's running on the side? That would make sense. The assistant DA has always had a good record. Maybe his ethics have become a problem for Griffin."

"Maybe."

It was quiet for a minute as they mulled this over. Then Sydney changed the subject. "Listen, I still have to write the article, and I'm waiting for a couple of sources to call me back. Do you want to meet me at my apartment for lunch in about an hour?"

"I'd love to," Justin said. "But knowing you, you don't have anything in your kitchen to eat, so I'll pick up some sandwiches on my way there."

Sydney felt a flush creep across her cheeks. "You're probably right. I haven't shopped in a while, and I have no idea what I have on hand."

His deep chuckle came across the line. "How did I guess? Don't worry about it. I'll see you in an hour."

\* \* \*

Sydney spent the next half hour working on her article, but without the extra information from her sources, her story felt a little lean. There wasn't much else she could do until they phoned her back. She leaned back in her chair and tried to decide what to do. She'd told Justin to meet her in an hour, but she was ahead of schedule. Did she wait around for a while to see if her sources would call? Or did she leave a little early for lunch?

The sound of her stomach growling made her decision for her. She decided to head for her apartment even though Justin wouldn't be there yet. She was more than ready for a break.

Gathering her purse and keys, she headed out of the building and crossed the street to the parking garage. Her car was parked in her usual spot, but as she neared it, the hairs stood up on the back of her neck. For the second time that day, the sensation of being watched flooded through her.

She looked around as she approached her car, but nothing seemed to be out of the ordinary. She pushed the button on the key fob to unlock the driver's door, got in, and immediately relocked the door before even starting the car. It wasn't until she had pulled out of the space and was headed down the ramp leading to the ground level, though, that the unnerving feeling finally subsided.

She shivered as she pulled out onto the street. She kept glancing in her rearview mirror as she drove home, but the drive was uneventful. A short while later she pulled into her apartment's underground parking garage, parked, then got into the elevator. As she rode to her floor, she was still having a hard time trying to quell the jittery sensation in her stomach. When she arrived at the fifth floor without incident, she breathed a sigh of relief.

*See, Sydney? There's nothing to worry about. Stop getting so worked up over this,* she scolded as she reached for her keys.

Just as she slipped the key into her apartment's lock, she felt a hand descend upon her shoulder.

# CHAPTER 31

Sydney let out a startled scream and whirled, preparing to let her Shotokan training take over. Instead, she found herself staring into a pair of familiar green eyes.

"Justin!" she gasped, her body slumping with relief. A nervous laugh escaped her lips. "You scared the daylights out of me. Where did you come from?"

"I got here earlier than I expected and decided to wait for you." He looked at her strangely. "You're awfully jumpy. What's going on?"

Just then Agnes's door flew open and she appeared in the doorway, looking startled. "Sydney!" Then she looked at the other figure standing next to her young neighbor. "Oh. Justin. Sydney didn't say anything about you coming for a visit." She turned back to Sydney in confusion. "Is everything okay? I thought I heard somebody scream."

"Sorry, Agnes, that was me," Sydney admitted. "Justin kind of snuck up on me. I didn't know he was here waiting."

Agnes nodded, accepting the explanation. "I'll leave you two now that I know everything's okay." Agnes's eyes twinkled as she turned and winked at Sydney then disappeared back into her apartment.

When they were alone again in the hallway, Sydney laughed. "Sounds like I gave Agnes quite a start." She noticed the bag of sandwiches in Justin's hands as she unlocked and opened her door. She gave him a grateful smile. "Thank you for getting those. I'm starving."

Justin followed her inside, a frown marring his handsome features. "What were you so jumpy about in the hall?"

She set her keys and purse down on the credenza and headed into the kitchen with Justin following close behind. "It seems stupid now—not even worth mentioning." She reached into the cupboard for plates and glasses, then went to the fridge and pulled out a container of juice.

Justin leaned back against the island's countertop and crossed his arms over his broad chest, his expression serious. "Tell me anyway."

"It's nothing, really. I've just had the strangest feeling a couple of times today that I'm being watched. Then you came out of nowhere and scared me, that's all." She laughed a little and shrugged. "It's dumb, I know."

Justin's frown deepened. "It's not dumb. I've learned by now that you have great instincts. And at the moment, that worries me."

"Justin, there's nothing to worry about." She poured herself some juice and took a long drink. "I'm sure I was just being paranoid."

"Paranoia is sometimes what keeps a good reporter alive, Syd. You know that as well as I do. Where were you the times you thought you were being watched?"

Sydney groaned as she carried the plates to the table. "Can't you let this go? I spent the entire morning working on the DA article, and I'm tired and frustrated—and feeling pretty dumb at the moment for worrying you over something that was probably all in my head."

"Sydney." Justin put his hand on her forearm. "You already know I worry about you. If you felt like someone was watching you, somebody probably was." He squeezed her arm. "Promise me you'll be careful? If Griffin or Longhurst or whoever is behind all this somehow found out we're onto them, you could be in danger. We both know that someone already died for knowing too much about this. Don't push the envelope, okay?"

Sydney felt a little defensive at the suggestion. "Justin, I can take care of myself. I've been doing this for a long time, remember? I'm a big girl."

"I know you are," he answered, his voice soft but firm. "And I don't mean to make it sound like you're incompetent. Quite the opposite, actually. You're the most resourceful journalist I know. It's how you sometimes act on that resourcefulness that worries me. I love you, Syd. And I couldn't bear to lose you, especially for the sake of some story."

Sydney softened at his words. "I'm sorry. I know you're not trying to tell me what to do. I'm just not used to having anyone so worried about me. I promise I'll be careful."

The muscles in Justin's face visibly relaxed. "Thank you," he breathed, leaning forward to press a kiss to her forehead. "Now why don't you tell me how Richardson's doing on the shipment that's coming in. Any news on that?"

Sydney brought him up to speed as they ate. All too soon, lunch was over, and Sydney had to get back to work.

She and Justin were just cleaning up when her cell phone rang. When she answered it, Derek's voice came across the line.

"Sydney, a guy named Roger Calloway called the newsroom and said he needed to see you right away, that it was urgent. He wanted me to call you and ask you to go to the police station right now."

Sydney glanced over at Justin, who looked back at her. He apparently read the surprise on her face because he mouthed, "What's up?"

She held up a finger to signal him to wait, then told Derek, "If he calls again, tell him I'm on my way."

As soon as she clicked off her phone, she turned to Justin. "Apparently Roger Calloway needs to see me right away. Derek said it sounded urgent."

"Calloway? As in Bryce's old partner at the precinct?"

She nodded as she hurried to gather her jacket and purse. "I assume you're coming with me?"

"Of course."

They climbed in Sydney's car and drove to the police station. They were shown back to Calloway's small office, where the detective sat looking ill at ease. He seemed surprised to see Justin accompanying Sydney, and brief greetings were exchanged.

Roger made it a point to close the door. After they were all seated, Sydney said, "I was told you had something urgent you wanted to talk to me about."

He nodded, the motion anxious. "I'm glad you're both here, since this involves you too, Justin." He turned to the file cabinet behind him and unlocked the bottom drawer. Then he pulled out a large white envelope and extended it to them.

Sydney reached for it first. "What is it?"

As Sydney started to open the envelope, Roger explained. "This was delivered to me this morning by one of the guys in the forensics lab. He said that Bryce was a friend of his, so when Bryce brought it to him several weeks ago asking for a personal favor, he agreed to help. He didn't know what it was exactly, but Bryce said he needed it cleaned up and the marked section printed off, and that it needed to be kept quiet. The lab tech finished it and was planning to get it back to Bryce, but then Bryce was killed, and he'd forgotten all about it until he was cleaning out his files yesterday. He knew Bryce and I had worked together and been friends, so he decided to bring it to me to see if I would know what to do with it."

Sydney pulled out the contents of the envelope and stared down at them in confusion. There was a computer disc inside a clear jewel case, bearing neither a label nor any writing. She set it on her lap and turned her attention to a set of computer-generated photographs.

Her eyes widened as she looked up at Calloway. "Is this what I think it is?"

He gave her an uneasy nod.

"What is it?" Justin asked, leaning closer to see the photographs in her hands.

Her voice breathless with excitement, she turned to Justin and held up the disc. "If I'm not mistaken, this is the copy Bryce had of the missing security footage from the lockup."

Justin's face registered his shock. "Are you serious?"

"Well, the date stamp shows that these pictures were taken the same night the items were stolen from the lockup." She tilted the pictures toward him and pointed to the bottom right-hand corner, where the security tape information was visible.

"What about the men in the picture?" Justin squinted to study the faces in the photograph. Thanks to the digital enhancements done in the forensics lab, the features of the two men loading a moving-type truck were more apparent, but he didn't recognize either man. "Do you think we can get an ID on them?"

Roger spoke up. "I can tell you who the guy on the right is." When two sets of eyes looked up at him expectantly, he went on. "His name is Mark Thompson. He's the Customs officer that was involved in the investigation of the shipment. He was also in charge of the lockup that night."

Justin and Sydney looked at each other. Sydney was the first to say what they were both thinking. "He's the son of Longhurst's principle advisor." She broke out into a gloating grin and thumped Justin playfully on the shoulder. "Did I call that or what?"

Justin smiled, but his attention was still focused on the photograph. "What about the other guy?"

Roger shook his head. "I don't recognize him."

Sydney looked at the photos again and studied the man. "I do. His name is Phillip Douglas."

Recognition flashed across Roger's face, and Sydney gave Justin a quick explanation about her investigation of Douglas during her crime-ring exposé and how the FBI had been looking for him ever since. She also reminded him that Hyo Park had identified him as the man he'd seen talking with the district attorney, and that he was also rumored to be overseeing the incoming shipment.

"He's wanted by the FBI for a long list of crimes," Roger said. "This footage puts him at the scene of the crime, along with the Customs officer." He looked at Sydney. "I called you because this evidence went missing once.

I didn't know who to give it to. You were the first person who came to mind."

"You can bet I'll see that it gets where it needs to be." Sydney gave him a reassuring nod. "As soon as it's in the proper hands, I'm sure a dozen copies will be made to prevent anything else from happening to it."

Roger looked relieved. "Thank you. I knew I could count on you."

Sydney and Justin thanked him profusely, then headed directly over to see Detective Richardson. The large man was speechless when Sydney explained how they'd come across the missing evidence. He knew as well as Sydney did that this evidence not only incriminated the Customs official, but it strengthened their case against Douglas.

Richardson told Justin and Sydney that his next step would be to contact the FBI and Customs and Border Protection about the footage, but other than that, they needed to keep this under wraps. Going public with the details of the security footage would not only potentially damage the FBI's investigation, but it might drive Douglas even further underground. They would wait and see what happened with the shipment and go from there.

Sydney and Justin agreed, but it was hard not to write about what they knew. Until they could do so, Sydney knew she had other leads to chase. If the Customs official could be linked to Longhurst, maybe Douglas could be too. That opened up several more avenues for them to pursue.

As excited as she was to dive right back into the research, she knew she had to get back to the *Chronicle* to finish her article on the press conference.

"Just drop me off at your apartment so I can get my car, and I'll hang out at the condo while you work," Justin suggested. "You can call me when you're getting close to being finished, and I'll just meet you at your apartment so we can head out for a celebration dinner."

Sydney agreed, and soon she was back at the *Chronicle*. She was cutting her deadline close, but thankfully one of her sources had come through. The woman gave her the names of the attorneys Griffin was considering for replacements for the open assistant DA position, which was something no other news source had, so Sydney was happy that she had something that would make her article stand out.

At quitting time, she turned off her computer and gathered her things. She gave Justin a call to let him know she was on her way to her apartment, and he told her he'd meet her there. As tired as she was from the fast-paced day, she found herself in a heady daze. It was days like this that she was glad she'd become a journalist. It felt great to be making a difference in the world.

Her feet barely touched the ground as she headed to the parking garage across the street and climbed into her car. When she arrived home, she drove into her apartment's underground parking garage. The ominous silence that greeted her as she climbed out of her car immediately set her nerves on edge. She glanced around, her body tense. That's when she felt it.

Eyes. Somebody watching.

The slam of a car door echoed through the parking structure and made her jump. Panic rose in her throat as she spun in a circle, trying desperately to seek out the source of the danger she felt. In a moment of hesitation, she tried to decide—did she get back into her car or make a run for the nearby elevator?

A flash of movement to her left made her whirl. A frightened scream caught in her throat when she saw a man in dark clothes and a gray ski mask barreling down on her.

# CHAPTER 32

Before she even had time to react, the man grabbed her, his arms forming an iron cage around her body. One rough hand clamped over her mouth, suppressing her screams as he dragged her around the cement barrier.

Panic rushed through her as she fought against the man's iron grip. If she didn't get away right now, there was no telling what would happen to her. She started to squirm and kick, trying to land at least one solid blow. Finally her elbow connected, landing solidly in her attacker's gut.

More angry than hurt, the man threw her backward, sending her tumbling into the concrete retaining wall. Her head hit with a sickening crack, and she felt the world dip and spin around her. For a moment she thought she was going to lose consciousness. But then her mind cleared, and she glanced up at her assailant's ski-mask-covered face just as he grabbed her by the throat and hauled her to her feet. The next thing she knew, the hard metal of a gun's barrel was being pressed to her temple.

She struggled for breath and grabbed for the man's hand on her throat, but his grip only tightened more firmly around her windpipe. He shoved her back against the wall once more and loomed closer, his disguised face only inches from hers.

His voice was deep and menacing as he relayed his message. "My boss doesn't appreciate nosy reporters. You're bad for business. So back off your investigation—or else."

His last words sent chills up Sydney's spine, and she knew without a doubt that the threat was serious. She felt the man lower his gun from her temple slightly, and she quickly took advantage of the situation. Letting her self-defense training take over, she brought a knee up forcefully and connected with his groin. When he let out a strangled cry and doubled over, Sydney brought her knee up again hard, this time connecting with his face.

The man grabbed for his nose as red started to appear on his gray ski mask, and Sydney turned to run. But before she could get out of reach, her assailant grabbed her and raised the butt of his gun. In one fast, angry motion, he brought it down hard against the side of her head.

Instantly, the world started to dim, and her vision blurred as she slumped to the ground. Through her foggy haze, she heard her assailant growl, "I'll kill you if you ever do anything like that again, orders or not. And if you tell the cops about our little visit, you won't live to regret it."

Then she heard the sound of retreating footsteps and knew her assailant was gone.

For a few minutes, Sydney lay still, the cold concrete of the parking garage floor pressing against her cheek. Finally her vision began to clear, and the nausea began to dissipate.

She sat up shakily, using her arms to stabilize herself as the garage swayed precariously. Hoping somebody had noticed her attack, she listened for sounds of approaching help but heard nothing. Not even the sound of a passing car.

She half crawled, half pulled herself the few feet to the retaining wall and used it to struggle to her feet. The wooziness returned, and with trembling hands she grasped at the metal railing along the top to steady herself. A wetness on the side of her cheek startled her, and she reached up to touch it. When she drew her hand back, she gasped. Blood. She was bleeding. And heavily, from the looks of it.

She tried not to panic. She reminded herself that head wounds tended to bleed a lot, and that she was probably fine. Deciding she'd better call for help, she reached for her cell phone only to realize she couldn't get a signal in the underground parking garage.

Tears of frustration and pain prickled at the back of her eyes as she pressed her hand to her head to try to stop the bleeding. Deciding Plan B was to get to her apartment and call from there, she let go of the metal bar and took a test step forward. She was surprised to discover that the wooziness was subsiding and she felt more stable. With careful steps, she shuffled toward the elevator.

When she reached it and stepped inside, she punched the button for her floor, and the elevator began to rise. The sudden upward movement caused the nausea and wooziness to return. She grabbed the railing lining the elevator and put a hand to her queasy stomach, praying for the elevator to hurry.

When the doors finally opened, she was relieved to discover that the hall was empty. Explanations for her appearance were the last thing she wanted to give right then. Fumbling with her keys, she found the one to her apartment and let herself in. On unsteady feet, she shut the door behind her and shuffled into the kitchen. She grabbed a hand towel from the island, got several ice cubes from the freezer, and placed them in the towel. She winced as she pressed the roughly constructed ice pack to her temple. The pressure made the room spin around her, and she reached out for the island's countertop to steady herself.

The tears of pain and helplessness she'd managed to keep in check until now began to course down her cheeks and blur her vision. She pulled out her phone and called the only person she wanted to talk to at the moment.

\* \* \*

Justin concentrated on the traffic as he drove toward Sydney's apartment. He'd told her he'd pick her up shortly after six to take her out to dinner, and he was more eager than ever to see her. For some reason, a nagging voice somewhere deep inside of him told him to hurry—told him that something wasn't right.

The conversation he'd had with Sydney during lunch had been unsettling. *Had* somebody been watching her? In the time he'd known her, he'd never seen her so jumpy. She had good instincts; that was inarguable. If she thought somebody had been watching her, chances were that somebody had been.

Trying to quell the uneasy feeling in his stomach, he jumped a little when his cell phone rang. A quick glance at the caller ID told him it was Sydney.

He pressed the TALK button on his phone and put it to his ear. "Hey, beautiful," he answered with a smile. "I was just thinking about you." When he didn't hear a response from her end of the line, he frowned. "Syd? Are you there?"

After a moment he thought he detected a muffled noise. His brow furrowed in concentration. Finally he heard her voice.

"Justin—" she began, and in that instant he could tell she was crying.

His heart leaped in his chest. "Sydney? What's wrong? What happened?"

"I—I need you," she stammered, her voice thick with emotion. "Can you come over? I'm home, but I got hurt . . ."

Justin's heart constricted, and he struggled to contain his panic. "Sydney, don't move. I'll be right there." He ended the call and looked around frantically at the traffic. Praying he'd be able to get there quickly, he steered around the slow-moving car in front of him and punched down on the gas pedal.

It seemed like hours rather than minutes before he arrived at Sydney's apartment, and he rushed up to her floor. He darted out of the elevator and tried to open her door, only to find it locked. He gave a couple quick raps but got no answer. Feeling a sense of urgency, he looked around desperately, trying to find something he could use to jimmy the lock. But there was nothing. Just the elevator, a potted plant, and the doors to the other apartments.

*Agnes!*

Given how close Sydney and Agnes were, he was willing to bet they each had spare keys to the other's apartment. He'd just have to make sure he didn't say anything to worry the kind old woman.

Pasting a calm smile on his face to hide his fear for Sydney, he knocked on Agnes's door. She opened it almost immediately.

"Well, hello, Justin. How are you? Where's Sydney?"

"Actually, I—"

The frenzied yapping of Agnes's little dog cut him off, but Agnes caught the furry rocket before it could attach itself to his ankle.

"Now, Princess," she crooned, stroking the poodle's head, "is that any way to treat Sydney's beau?" Looking up at Justin again, she asked, "Now what is it you need, young man? Have you and Sydney gotten into an argument?"

"Oh, no, it's nothing like that," Justin was quick to reply. "It's just that, well, I was wondering . . . Do you happen to have a spare key to her apartment?"

A broad smile deepened Agnes's wrinkles, and she leaned forward, her eyes sparkling with mischief. "Are you planning a surprise for her? Oh, I know Sydney will love whatever you're planning. Now if I didn't know you were a good Mormon boy I might be worried, but . . . just wait here a second, and I'll go get the key for you."

Justin blew out his breath in relief. For once he was quite appreciative of a woman's ability to come to her own conclusions without allowing him to clarify his intentions. When Agnes came back and handed him the key a moment later, he thanked her, promised to return it soon, and said a quick good-bye. He had Sydney's door open almost before Agnes had shut hers.

"Sydney?" he called out as he tucked the key into his pocket and rushed into the darkened living room. He looked around but didn't detect any movement. "Syd?"

Just then he heard something in the kitchen and followed the sound. Sudden motion near the floor to his left caught his eye. When he turned, he spotted Sydney sitting on the floor with her back up against the fridge. He let out an involuntary gasp when he saw that she was holding a makeshift ice pack to her temple and that rivulets of blood had dried along the side of her face. Her eyes were red and puffy, and he could tell she'd been crying.

"Sydney!" He rushed toward her. "What happened?"

Tears glistened in her eyes as she looked up at him. "There was this guy in the parking garage . . . He grabbed me and shoved me up against the wall and put a gun to my head. He told me to back off the investigation . . . or else."

Justin's jaw clenched in anger as he knelt on the floor in front of her. "We're getting too close," he muttered. He shook his head and reached for the ice pack. "How bad is this? Let me take a look."

She released her grip on the towel, and he lifted the ice pack from her temple. What he saw made him queasy. There was a large gash about two inches long near her temple, and the surrounding skin was already beginning to color. She was going to have an awful bruise. But at least it looked like the bleeding had stopped for the time being.

With gentle fingers, he touched the area around the cut, trying to see how deep it was and determine whether she needed stitches. She flinched at his probing, and he jerked his hand back.

"Sorry," he murmured, his voice gentle and reassuring. In an effort to distract her as he continued to examine the cut, he asked, "So how did this happen? Did you hit your head on the wall when the guy shoved you?"

Sydney shook her head, then stopped quickly and grimaced in pain. "He was choking me, and as soon as he loosened his grip, I kicked him. It must have ticked him off, because he hit me with his gun before he took off running."

"You kicked him?" Justin exclaimed, his gaze shifting to her face.

A tiny smile appeared on Sydney's face. "Twice. I kneed him in the groin, then in the face while he was bent over. I think I broke his nose."

As hard as he tried not to, Justin laughed. What she'd done was stupid and impulsive, but somehow he wasn't surprised. It seemed like a very Sydney thing to do.

He managed to pull himself together and gave her a stern look. "As much as I would have loved to be there to see you take this guy out, what if he had shot you?"

Sydney rolled her eyes and pressed the ice pack Justin had abandoned back to her temple. She winced at the pressure. "He wasn't going to kill me, or he would have done that in the first place," she muttered, closing her eyes in obvious pain. "Whoever hired him just told him to scare me, that's all."

"What about the police? Have you called them yet?"

"No, and I'm not going to. The guy said he'd kill me if I reported this, and I believe him. I'll find out who's behind this myself."

His heart aching for what she'd been through, Justin put his hand on her arm. "This is getting too dangerous, Sydney. Somebody knows we're close, and I don't want to see you hurt again. Maybe you should let *me* get to the bottom of this one."

Sydney's eyes flashed at the suggestion. "Don't tell me to back down from this investigation, Justin. It's *ours.* And the fact that somebody did this to me tells me we *are* getting close. Besides, if we back down, they've won. Is that what you want?"

"No, but I don't want you getting yourself killed either. And even if you don't get yourself killed, you're going to kill me from all the worrying I do about you."

Sydney's anger visibly faded at his tender declaration. When she didn't say anything more, Justin sighed and reached again for her ice pack. He frowned as he looked at the cut again, studying the depth. He knew she wasn't going to like it, but he needed to take her to the hospital. It looked deep enough to warrant stitches.

She suddenly moved under his hand, shifting her position on the hard tile, and he glanced down at her face. He noticed with dismay that she was starting to look a little pale. "Sydney, are you okay? You don't look so good."

"Gee, thanks," she murmured with only a hint of her usual sarcasm, letting her eyelids fall shut. She pressed her arm across her stomach. "I'll be okay. I just feel a little sick to my stomach, that's all."

Justin's frown deepened. "Do you feel dizzy, too?" When she murmured a yes without bothering to open her eyes, he asked, "How long have you felt this way?"

"Since that guy threw me and I hit my head on that concrete barrier."

An invisible hand clenched around Justin's heart. Too many things pointed to the possibility of a concussion, and he knew that concussions weren't anything to mess with.

He put a hand on her arm, hoping his worry for her didn't show so clearly in his eyes. "Sydney, I think we should get you to a hospital. They can take a look at you and see if you have a concussion, and whether or not this gash of yours will need some stitches."

Sydney's response was immediate. Her eyes flew open, and a panicked look crossed her face. "No!" she exclaimed with even more vehemence than he'd expected. "I'm not going to a hospital. I'm okay, really. Besides, you're an Eagle Scout, right? I'm sure you've taken first aid classes. Just put a butterfly bandage on me, and I'll be fine."

Justin's brow furrowed as he considered her reaction. He assumed she'd be stubborn about seeing a doctor, but he hadn't expected her to panic. Shoving the thought aside for the moment, he focused on convincing her, keeping his tone soft yet firm. "But you're dizzy and feeling sick to your stomach. What if you have a concussion?"

She gritted her teeth and shook her head, her expression determined. "Justin, I am not going to a hospital."

Justin studied her for a long moment in silence. He didn't know what this case of hospital phobia was all about, but this was one battle he wasn't going to lose—even if he had to call out the big guns.

"Okay, fine," he said, a quiet note of determination in his voice. "Then I think this calls for a second opinion—a tiebreaker of sorts. Let me go get Agnes. I know she's home."

When he started to rise, Sydney's eyes widened even further, and she grabbed his arm. "No! Agnes will be furious when she finds out what happened. She'll launch into her usual speech about how dangerous it is for a woman in the city, and how I shouldn't have been in the parking garage alone. She's always telling me I'm too stubborn to consider those things."

A muscle twitched in Justin's jaw. "That makes two of us."

Sydney glared at him, but Justin refused to be intimidated. He squatted back down beside her and put his hand on her knee. "Syd, if you don't want both Agnes and me ganging up on you, just say you'll let me take you to the hospital to get checked out. Maybe I'm wrong. Maybe you don't have a concussion. Maybe you don't need stitches. But wouldn't it be better to be safe than sorry?"

He watched Sydney's face intently. She appeared to be silently weighing his argument. Finally, a look of resignation settled across her face. "Fine, let's go. But just so you know, I'm not happy about this."

# CHAPTER 33

Several hours later, Justin walked back into Sydney's apartment, cradling her in his arms. The medication she'd been given had made her groggy and sleepy, and she barely opened her eyes when he carried her into her bedroom and laid her down on her bed.

Concern for the woman he loved threatened to consume him as he stared down at her, studying the pallor of her cheeks in the stream of moonlight filtering in through the curtains. Lifting a hand to her face, he traced his fingertips along her cheek, careful not to touch the large bandage covering her newly acquired stitches. Twelve, to be exact. And his suspicions had been correct. She had a concussion as well.

The doctor had wanted to keep her overnight for observation, but Sydney wouldn't hear of it. The CAT scan results had been clean, so no amount of coaxing on Justin's or the doctor's part had been enough to convince her to stay. The doctor had agreed to let Justin take her home—on the conditions that he wake her every two hours throughout the night and that she get lots of rest over the next couple of days. Justin had accepted, and only then had Sydney relaxed.

He thought back to how she'd reacted as she sat on the ER table when they first arrived, waiting for care. Every small beep from a monitor or message over the intercom had made her jump. She'd seemed even more nauseated sitting there in the ER than she'd been back at her apartment—and he didn't think it had much to do with her injuries. It hadn't been hard to put two and two together and realize she was thinking about the last time she'd been in a hospital. If her obvious hospital phobia was any indication, he was willing to guess that the last time had been the night she'd lost the three most important people in her life.

As he looked down at her now, asleep on her bed, her face pale against the pillowcase, his heart clenched painfully. He slowly lifted his hand from her cheek and reached for the blanket folded at the foot of her bed, spreading it gently over her.

Crossing the darkened room, he tiptoed back out into the living room and settled down onto the couch to stare unseeingly at whatever was on TV. He kept the volume low so he could hear her if she needed him. He hadn't been there to stop her attack from happening, but he was able to be here now. And he would do everything in his power to make sure she got well— and stayed that way.

* * *

Sydney stirred a couple of hours later, her mind foggy and her head throbbing. She tried to open her heavy eyelids, but the grogginess weighed down on her, making even the simplest of tasks seem impossible.

At last she managed to open her eyes, and she glanced around the darkened room. In a flash, the events of that evening came rushing back. Tears filled her eyes as she raised her hand to her head, her fingertips brushing against the thick bandage at her temple. She could still feel the prick of the needle the doctor had used in spite of the numbing medication she'd been given, and each tug of the doctor's thread had brought back the memory of another night she wished she could forget.

The beeping of the machines and the urgent voices of the ER had made her blood run cold, and if she'd felt able, she would have leaped from the table and run out of the cold, sterile room without ever looking back. Justin had no way of knowing, but he had taken her to the very hospital she'd been in after her accident—the accident that had claimed the lives of her parents and sister. She had vowed to never set foot inside those doors again, yet there she was, sitting in the same ER she'd been taken to on that awful night.

She'd kept hoping that the pain medication they'd given her would take effect quickly and numb both her body and mind, but still the images came flooding back. When the medication had at last sent her into a drugged sleep, she had embraced the darkness, knowing that in sleep came peace.

She tried to remember how she'd gotten home, and remnants of images flashed through her mind. She remembered Justin helping her into his car outside of the hospital, and she vaguely remembered him driving her home. After that, she remembered nothing.

She heard the soft, soothing sounds of the television in the front room, and she realized that Justin must be out there keeping watch over her. It gave her comfort, knowing he cared enough to oversee her recovery.

She felt grateful she'd been able to lose herself in a few hours of drugged sleep, but now the pounding and throbbing were back with a vengeance, and she had to swallow hard to force back the nausea that threatened. She rolled over in bed, wincing as even that simple movement sent a stabbing pain through her skull. For what seemed like forever, she lay motionless on her side, forcing back the nausea and praying for the throbbing in her head to subside. But it didn't. It only grew worse.

Realizing she was never going to get back to sleep with the encompassing pain, she struggled to remember if the doctor had prescribed a pain medication, or if he had said to check back in a day or so for that if she needed it. If they had filled a prescription, she assumed Justin would have put it in the medicine cabinet above the bathroom sink. She shifted slightly to eye her bedroom door, which led to the hallway and the bathroom. It seemed miles away. At last she decided that her head hurt enough to go look, so she rolled over and started to sit up.

She immediately regretted the action. Another sharp, stabbing pain shot through her head, sending a flood of unwanted memories rushing to her brain. She'd had a concussion once before—on the night of the accident. But it had been overshadowed by the pain of a rough ambulance ride, surgery, and the news of the loss of her parents and sister. This time, though, the pain in her head was only rivaled by the pain in her heart.

Images began to assault her—her parents' lifeless bodies being pulled from the wreckage and covered by black tarps beside the car, her sister lying so still as they loaded her into a second ambulance, the doctor coming to tell her the next morning after her anesthesia had worn off from surgery that Kate had succumbed to her injuries during the night.

A sob caught in her throat. She hurried to stifle it, aware of Justin stationed in the living room just down the hall. She lifted a shaking hand to cover her mouth but realized she couldn't stop the tears from coming. Moving stiffly to the edge of the bed, she reached out for the nightstand to steady herself as she rose to her feet. As quiet as she tried to be, she heard movement in the living room.

"Sydney?" she heard Justin call.

When she stepped out into the hall, she could make out the look of concern on his face in the flickering lights from the television in the otherwise darkened room.

Making sure she kept her tear-streaked face turned away, she mumbled something about needing a drink of water, then hurried into the bathroom. She shut the door quietly, then flipped on the light. She regretted it as the bright lights sent a thousand stabbing needles into her skull.

The flow of tears increased as she squinted against the light and opened the medicine cabinet. She rummaged through the vitamin jars and miscellaneous over-the-counter pain relievers on the shelves, but she didn't see a prescription pain medication there.

Not caring what kind of pain medication she took at this point, she reached for the jar of ibuprofen and fumbled with the lid. The tears flowed faster as she fought with the safety lid, unable to focus her bleary eyes enough to align the arrows. Finally she gave up, slamming the bottle down in frustration on the sink.

Her shoulders slumped as she started to weep. She sat down on the closed toilet lid beside the sink, dropped her forehead onto her crossed arms resting on the counter, and sobbed quietly.

Moments later there was a quiet knock on the door. Then came Justin's worried voice. "Sydney? Are you okay?"

Sydney swallowed hard, trying to quiet the sob in her throat. She didn't bother to lift her head from her arms, but raised her voice as much as she could without making her head pound even more. "I'm fine," she managed. "Just give me a minute."

There was silence from the other side of the bathroom door, and Sydney wondered if Justin had gone back to the couch. But then she heard the more urgent tone in his voice as he spoke again through the door. "Are you sure you're okay?"

Angered by his persistence during a moment she had intended to keep private, she lifted her head from her arms and glared through her tears at the door. "I'm fine, okay? Just leave me alone." The sob she'd been trying to hold back slipped out, and she dropped her head back onto her arms. "Just leave me alone," she repeated in a whisper as the sobs came once more.

She barely heard Justin's firm declaration of, "I'm coming in," before she felt his hands on her back and arm. Sensing his sympathy through his gentle touch, her shoulders started to shake as her sobs increased, and she felt him kneel beside her and pull her against his chest.

Suddenly grateful for the strong arms around her, she slipped her own arms around his neck and clung to him tightly, afraid that if she let him go she might lose him, too. She sobbed for what felt like hours—for herself and her pain, for the death of her sister, for the death of her parents. For a night that had altered her life so dramatically that she doubted she would ever fully recover.

When her sobs subsided into gentle hiccups, she lifted her cheek from Justin's shoulder and wiped at her tears self-consciously. "I'm sorry," she mumbled, embarrassed. "I can't seem to pull myself together."

"You don't have to," he soothed, slipping his hand beneath her curtain of hair and massaging her neck with his gentle touch. "You've been through a scary experience, and you're hurt. Nobody's going to think any less of you for crying, especially me."

She put a hand to her throbbing forehead. "I feel awful. I came in here to get something for the pain, but I couldn't get the stupid lid off the bottle . . ." She gestured helplessly at the ibuprofen on the counter.

"Then why didn't you ask?" came Justin's gentle rebuke. "That's what I'm here for."

"To open ibuprofen bottles?"

He smiled and wiped the tears from her cheek. "That, too, but mostly just to be here for you." He pressed a loving kiss to her forehead, then reached for the ibuprofen. He shook out a couple of pills, filled a glass of water, and handed them to her.

She chased the pills down with the water, then set the glass back down on the counter. "Come on," he said, putting a hand on her arm. "Let's get you back to bed."

Too worn out to argue, she let Justin help her back to bed. He tucked the blanket more securely around her, then reached up to brush her hair back from her face. Tears pooled in her eyes at his gentle touch.

"This evening has all been too much," she whispered through another set of oncoming tears. "That guy in the garage . . . the hospital . . ."

Her voice broke, and Justin stroked her hair comfortingly. "I understand," he murmured.

And in that moment, Sydney realized he did. She held his hand until sleep finally came, and with it a welcome reprieve from the haunting memories.

# CHAPTER 34

Justin stirred early the next morning as the first morning rays streamed in through the bank of windows in Sydney's living room and roused him from his sleep. He rolled onto his side on the couch and sat up, kicking off the blanket he'd covered up with the night before.

Stretching his arms above his head, he took a minute to wake up more fully. It had been a long night. Following the doctors orders, he'd woken Sydney every two hours to check on her. Other than being tired and grumpy at being woken, she'd seemed fine.

Getting up to check on her once more, he padded down the hall and peeked into her bedroom. His face softened. She looked peaceful, and it gave him an immense sense of relief. He stepped back and pulled the door almost shut so his movements around the apartment wouldn't disturb her. Wandering into the kitchen, he opened the cupboards and frowned at how little was there.

He shook his head. One of these days he'd convince her to shop regularly. And for something besides peanut M&Ms. It hadn't escaped his notice that the large glass canister of peanut M&Ms on the counter seemed to be the only thing she restocked.

Deciding to make a quick run to the small grocery store on the corner, he went into the bathroom to wash his face before heading out to his car. A short time later he was back with two full bags of groceries. He set them on the kitchen counter before hurrying to Sydney's room to make sure she hadn't woken up while he was gone.

When he eased open her door enough to peek in, he saw that Sydney was indeed awake and was easing herself into a sitting position. "Wait, Sydney, let me help you," he said, hurrying in. He moved to her side and propped a couple of pillows behind her back. He noticed that the color had returned to her cheeks and that her strength seemed to be returning. He helped straighten the blanket over her and then sat beside her. "You look like you're feeling better."

"I am," she admitted. "My head still feels a little fuzzy, and the throbbing is starting to come back, but it's not as bad as it was last night."

He gave her a relieved smile. "I'm glad to hear it. Are you hungry? How about some toast and jam and herbal tea?" At her look of surprise, he said, "I just made a quick trip to the grocery store for a few things."

"I'd love some. But maybe just some plain toast? I'm not sure my stomach is up for much else yet."

"You got it." He started to leave but turned back. "Do you need to call your editor to let him know you won't be in to work today?" When she nodded, he retrieved her cell phone from the kitchen and handed it to her. "You make your call, but stay in bed," he ordered. "I want to get some tea and toast in you before you get up and about. I'll be right back."

When Justin reached the kitchen, he made the tea and dropped two slices of bread into the toaster. He could hear Sydney on the phone talking to her boss, and he did his best not to eavesdrop. When her breakfast was ready, he carried it in to her, handing her the plate of toast and setting the tea mug on the nightstand. He was rewarded with a grateful smile.

"I feel guilty about making you go to so much trouble," she said as he settled the plate on her lap.

"It's no trouble," he scolded in a gentle voice. "I stayed so I could take care of you. I love doing it."

As she nibbled on her toast, Justin sat in the stuffed armchair in the corner not far from her bed. "So, what did your boss say?"

"He was worried when I explained what happened, but I assured him I was going to be fine. He insisted that I take a few days off." She was quiet for a minute, then Sydney asked almost hesitantly, "Justin? Do you think you could give me a blessing?"

Justin looked at her in surprise. He knew she was becoming more active and was enjoying her ward, but he hadn't thought she'd ask for a blessing. He felt oddly touched by her request. "I'd be happy to. Is there somebody else I could call to help?"

Sydney suggested calling her home teacher, Brother Hansen, who was retired and lived nearby, to help with the blessing, so Justin called him. He said he'd be right over, so Sydney changed into a pair of comfortable jeans and a T-shirt. Brother Hansen arrived a few minutes later, and Sydney asked Justin to give the blessing. In the blessing, she was promised a swift recovery and encouraged to continue to be active in the Church, as it would bring many blessings into her life. She was told that her Heavenly Father was aware of her and of her struggles in being alone, and she was promised that many blessings awaited her if she remained faithful.

When Justin closed the prayer and stepped back, he gave her a tender smile of understanding and saw tears of appreciation in Sydney's eyes. She stood to shake hands with Brother Hansen and thanked him, then returned to bed under Justin's strict orders.

Justin appeared in her bedroom doorway after seeing Brother Hansen out. He walked over to sit in the chair once more. "Thanks for letting us do that. Did it help?"

"A lot. I'd forgotten how much comfort a blessing gives. Thanks."

"Anytime you feel like you need one, just let me know."

Sydney finished what was left of her toast and tea, and Justin took the plate and mug back to the kitchen. While he was there rinsing out the dishes, a knock sounded on the apartment door. He walked over to answer it and saw Agnes standing there. Her little dog was surprisingly absent from her arms.

"Hi, Agnes. I see you don't have that brute of a dog with you this morning." His eyes were teasing as he opened the door farther and invited her in.

Agnes chuckled. "Yes, well, my 'brute,' as you call her, is sleeping peacefully, and I have no intention of waking her up from her beauty sleep." She glanced around, a look of concern in her eyes. "Is Sydney around? I noticed she didn't leave for work this morning, and I came by to make sure she was okay. And was that Brother Hansen I just saw leaving?"

Justin's eyebrows lifted.

She waved off his questioning look with a quick motion of her hand. "There's very little that goes on around here that I don't know about. But it's not like Sydney to miss work. Is she okay?"

"Hi, Agnes," Sydney said with a somewhat weary smile as she ambled into the living room. "I heard voices out here and came to investigate."

The elderly woman let out a gasp at Sydney's appearance and hurried over to her, surprising Justin with her nimbleness. She took Sydney by the arm and guided her to the couch.

"Sydney, sit down," she mothered. "It doesn't look like you should be up and about. What happened?"

"She's right, Syd. You should be resting," Justin reprimanded before Sydney could answer Agnes's question.

"I'm okay, Justin. I can take a nap in a few minutes." She turned back to Agnes and explained what had happened in the parking garage the night before, but Justin noticed she left out most of the frightening details. He could tell she didn't want to upset her motherly neighbor.

"Anyway, the guy hit me with his gun and then ran off," Sydney finished. "I got some stitches and a concussion, but I'm going to be okay."

Agnes shook her head in apparent frustration. "Sydney, you really need to be more careful. The work you do is too dangerous and makes too many bad people angry with you." She turned to Justin. "Can't you talk her into getting a cushy desk job somewhere? Heaven knows I've tried and am getting nowhere."

Justin grinned. "Somehow I doubt my luck would be any better than yours."

Agnes shook her head, a defeated look in her eyes. She leaned over to clasp Sydney's hands in hers. "Just take it easy the next few days, would you? I'm sure you'll be fine with your young man here to look after you, but let me know if you need anything, you hear?"

"I will." Sydney gave her a grateful smile.

Agnes stood up to leave, but when Sydney got up and started to follow, Agnes put her hand up to stop her. With a stern look, she pointed to the hall leading to the bedroom with a wrinkled, gnarled finger. "Don't you dare walk me to the door, young lady. You need your rest, and I'm not moving from this spot until you get back to bed. Understand?"

Sydney smothered a grin at Agnes's bossy tone. "Yes, ma'am. Thanks for coming by, Agnes. I'll talk to you soon."

Agnes was true to her word and didn't move until Sydney had disappeared down the hall. When her charge had gone, Agnes turned back to Justin with a twinkle in her eye. "That girl needs to be handled with a firm hand."

Justin laughed. "Don't I know it." He followed Agnes to the door and opened it for her.

"Thanks, dear," she told him, patting his arm in an affectionate gesture. Then, to his surprise, a bright sheen of tears appeared in her eyes. "Thank you for taking such good care of her. She's pretty special to me, and I don't think I have to tell you what a rough time she's had. But I can tell by that glow about her that you're making her happy. She deserves a nice young man like you."

Justin felt touched at Agnes's acceptance of him in Sydney's life. "Thanks, Agnes. I promise I'll always do my best to make Sydney happy."

Agnes returned his smile and nodded. "I know you will, dear. You make sure she calls if she needs anything."

"I will."

When she was gone and Justin had shut the door behind her, his heart felt light. He'd learned soon after meeting Sydney that he'd never have to face the challenge of meeting her parents and winning their approval, but earning Agnes's approval meant just as much. And now he had it.

With a warm heart, he headed back to check on Sydney.

# CHAPTER 35

Sydney improved quickly that day, and by evening, Justin knew that she was going to make a full recovery. Though she was tired and achy, her spirits were good.

As they were finishing dinner, Sydney reminded him, "That shipment should be coming in tomorrow morning. I need to call Richardson and find out what time we'll be meeting him at the docks."

"Whoa, hold on," Justin said, holding up a hand. "You've had a concussion. You really should be taking it easy."

"I'll be fine," she assured him. "My head isn't aching like it was, and the stitches will come out in a couple of days. I'm on the mend. Don't worry about me."

He reached out and tucked a stray strand of hair behind her ear. "I'll always worry about you. I can't stop."

Grasping the hand he let slip from her face, she squeezed it and looked at him with pleading in her eyes. "I know that you worry, Justin, but I need to do this."

Justin studied her for a long moment, then sighed. "I know. Just promise me you'll be careful and not overdo it, okay?"

"I promise," she said, giving him a quick kiss before standing to put her plate and silverware in the sink.

They watched a little TV, but when Sydney admitted to feeling a little bored and asked if they could go over some of the research on Longhurst together, Justin knew it was a good sign. Maybe she really was feeling good enough to spend a little time at the docks in the morning.

He found the stack of research on Longhurst that she still had at her apartment, and they spent the next couple of hours going through the information.

"Hey, Justin, look at this," Sydney said, holding out a paper for him to see. "This has information dating back to the time Senator Longhurst's

father passed away. According to Longhurst Sr.'s will, all his corporate holdings were to go to his son."

"We already know that."

"Yes, but it's this next part that's so interesting," she said, her expression
becoming animated. "Apparently, Robert Longhurst Sr.'s longtime attorney
handled the matter and even helped Senator Longhurst with the transition."

"Well, that would make sense." Justin nodded. "If the attorney had
been familiar with all the companies, he would be the ideal person to
oversee the transition."

"Yes, but guess who his attorney was?" She paused for dramatic effect.
"Phillip Douglas."

"What?" The exclamation left Justin's mouth in a rush, and he took the
paper from Sydney to see for himself. "But you investigated this man before.
You didn't know this? That he was a lawyer?"

Sydney shook her head. "I didn't have a clue. I only researched his background a few years back. Not ten. Apparently he resigned from his corporate
attorney position with Longhurst Jr. only months after Longhurst Sr. died,
which was about ten years ago."

"And since then he's been working as CEO of that small company you
investigated?"

"Yes, as well as working in various low-key corporate positions. I never
turned up anything to indicate he'd ever been an attorney. Until now."

Justin was floored. This was huge. It was a direct connection to Senator
Longhurst. The men obviously knew each other—had worked together exten-
sively. This gave them a whole new angle from which to approach their investigation.

It was starting to get late when Justin saw Sydney start to rub her forehead
in a weary gesture. That did it.

"Okay, time to quit for the night," he said, his tone gentle yet firm. He
pulled the research from her hands and set it on the coffee table.

Sydney made a feeble attempt at protesting, but he could tell she was tired
when her halfhearted arguments didn't last long. He shepherded her into her
bedroom and ordered her to change and climb into bed. He asked if she
wanted him to spend another night on her couch, but she assured him she was
feeling much better and would be fine on her own. So he set off for his condo
after securing a promise that she would call him if she needed anything at all.

The next morning he showed up at her apartment and was surprised
when she answered the door fully dressed with her hair styled and makeup
on. Her color had returned, and she seemed raring to go.

"You look great," he said as he leaned in to kiss her.

"I feel so much better." She smiled. "Let's go. I can't wait to see what's on that boat."

* * *

The first rays of sunlight were touching the skyline when Sydney and Justin arrived at the harbor. A thick, dense fog had rolled in during the night, making the air feel heavy and damp. Visibility wasn't great, but in the distance they could make out the shape of a boat moving into the dock, surrounded by an escort of Coast Guard boats.

"Looks like Richardson and his men are here," Sydney said, nodding at a group of men in suits near the dock. Richardson was easy to spot since he towered over the other men. "And I'm sure there are Customs officials on those escort boats."

"Is Richardson still giving us the exclusive in exchange for the tip?"

"Yeah, he's as good as his word. Don't worry."

When Sydney and Justin reached the docks, Richardson lumbered over to greet them. His eyebrows drew together in concern when he spotted the bandage on Sydney's temple. "What happened?"

"I got jumped by a thug in my apartment's parking garage a couple days ago," she said, downplaying the event.

Richardson's tone reflected a fatherly concern when he asked, "You sure you're okay?"

She nodded. "Yeah, I'm fine."

"Did you file a report?"

"Not yet," Sydney hedged. "I've been busy." Then, trying to change the subject, she gestured at the docking boat. "What's the story?"

Richardson followed her gaze. "Don't know yet. Customs boarded the boat, but so far they haven't found anything illegal."

"Do they have any idea what they're looking for?"

"No, we're just working off the tip you gave us. We pulled the shipping manifests, and they look clean. Nothing suspicious."

"Just because the manifests appear aboveboard doesn't mean the entire shipment is."

Richardson nodded in agreement. "True. I'll keep you posted." He gave them a nod before heading back to his men, his broad shoulders hunched against the damp morning air.

Sydney and Justin waited anxiously as the officials performed their search. The fog was finally starting to lift by the time Richardson came back down the ramp, talking with two other officers.

Sydney and Justin hurried over to him. "What did you find?"

"Not a thing," Richardson admitted. "Our search turned up nothing but legitimate goods, all with proper documentation. The manifests gave us several names, though, including Phillip Douglas's."

"Does the crew have anything to say about that?"

"They're being interviewed, but that could take a while. We've put out an APB on Douglas, but it doesn't look like we'll be able to nail him for anything with this shipment. Like I said, all the goods are legit. Other than giving us a lead on Douglas, I think this raid was a bust."

Sydney stared at him in disbelief. "But . . . it can't be!" she exclaimed. "If Douglas is involved, there's something here! I know it."

Richardson's mouth tightened. "I'd love to tell you otherwise, Sydney, but there's nothing here. Our investigation is done."

Sydney's mouth opened and closed a couple of times as she tried to figure out what to say. "Paul," she began carefully. "There's too much evidence of smuggling and illegal activity here for this to be a wild goose chase—"

"Sydney," Richardson interrupted, "you and I both know that without finding hard evidence on that boat right now, no amount of incriminating evidence we thought we had beforehand means anything."

"That's true. I don't deny it," Sydney persisted. "I'm just saying that my source has never been wrong before, and since Justin and I have put in so much work into this—and since you promised to give us the exclusive if your team found anything—I think we deserve a chance to look around ourselves. You've known me long enough to know that I have no other motives beyond making a difference in this world by cleaning up some of the evil in it."

He shook his head and lifted a beefy hand in an effort to ward off her arguments. "My team has already done a thorough search of the entire vessel, and we've gone over the paperwork with a fine-tooth comb. We're even interviewing the crewmembers, but nothing—and I repeat, nothing—shows any evidence of illegal activity. There's no reason for you two to—"

"But what would it hurt?" Sydney broke in, her eyes pleading. "Would it really make any difference to you or the ship's crewmembers if Justin and I took a look around while your team finished up the interviews?"

Justin saw the tightness in Richardson's jaw start to relax, and he knew the man was starting to waver. Sydney must have seen it too, because she moved in for the kill.

"Even if we don't find anything," she went on breathlessly, "at least we'll know we followed our investigation through to the bitter end. You can even watch us look around if you feel like you're responsible for the ship's goods until the crew gets back. Come on, Paul. Really, what could it hurt?"

The detective looked at her for several moments, then let out a slow, resigned sigh. "Okay, fine. I'll walk you down there and you can take a look around. But be quick about it. I really don't want to have to explain to the crew members why I let a couple of reporters on their boat while they were being questioned."

Sydney's face broke out into a huge smile, and she looked as if she were having a hard time refraining from hugging Richardson right then and there. "Thank you, Paul. You're the best. Really, we appreciate it. And you won't regret this. We'll find something—I'm sure of it."

Justin bit back a smile of his own. This woman was the master. If anybody else had tried to win an argument with the burly detective, Justin had no doubt that person would have come out on the losing end. As it was, it was clear that Sydney had the ex-linebacker wrapped around her little finger.

"Yeah, well, we'll see," Richardson said, his tone gruff, but Justin could tell that he'd been touched by Sydney's gushing words of thanks.

When they reached the police officer standing on the deserted docking ramp between the boat and the dock, Richardson motioned Sydney and Justin ahead while he explained their presence. Sydney was more than happy to explore without him and practically ran up the ramp to the boat. Justin caught up with her just as she got to the top of the ramp and headed inside the boat.

As Justin followed Sydney through the under-deck storage areas, he saw that many of the crates had been opened, their contents verified. Sydney gave the open crates a cursory glance and moved on. They continued down to the lower deck, and Sydney once again scanned every nook and cranny. Still nothing.

She turned and glared at Justin, who was leaning back against the doorway, watching her continue her futile search. "Don't just stand there! Help me."

He gave her a one-shouldered shrug. "With what? There's nothing illegal in any of these crates or compartments. Face it. We've been directed to the wrong boat."

She put her hands on her hips stubbornly and glanced around once more. "I refuse to believe this is a wild goose chase! There's got to be something here somewhere."

She looked around the room, her intense gaze searching every inch. Suddenly her eyes widened. "If you were smuggling something in or out of the country, would you leave whatever it was in plain sight for Customs to find?"

The boredom he'd felt began to swing toward interest. "No, I wouldn't."

Without any further discussion, they began to search the passages for anything that would indicate a smuggler's hold.

Sydney's voice drew Justin to her a few minutes later. "Listen," she said, lifting her foot and bringing it down hard on the floor. She glanced around the room, then looked back at him, her eyes wide. "Did you hear that?"

He strained to hear whatever it was that had caught her attention. "I didn't hear anything."

She looked down at her feet, then stomped again. This time Justin heard it too—a faint echoing sound reverberating from beneath them.

Looking smug, Sydney surveyed the room and spotted the largest pile of opened crates, which was in the far corner. She marched over to it and reached for one.

Justin hurried over. "Syd, those are heavy. You still have stitches and a concussion, remember?" He started lifting the crates off the top of the pile for her. "What are you doing, anyway?"

Her eyes sparkled with excitement. "If you were going to hide a door to a smuggler's hold, wouldn't you put the biggest stack of crates over its entrance?"

Justin grinned. "When was the last time I told you you're brilliant?"

She laughed. "I don't know. I think it's been a while. You'd better tell me again."

"I think I will. You're brilliant." He leaned over to give her a soft kiss. "Now let's move these crates and see if you're right."

# CHAPTER 36

Justin helped Sydney move the rest of the crates, and when the spot was clear, Sydney gasped. There was a large door in the floor of the deck. Justin had to fight to keep her from rushing it.

"Sydney, stop," he said, putting a hand on her arm. "There could be somebody armed down there. Let's go get Richardson and have his team check it out."

She crossed her arms and glared at him. "So you want to back down now, before we have any evidence to convince Richardson of anything? You heard him on the dock—as far as he's concerned, this investigation is already over just because the shipping manifests match the goods in the crates Customs opened. We *have* to find out what's down there."

"Okay, okay," Justin said, holding up his hands. "We can take a look. We just need to be careful."

Looking around, Justin picked up a crowbar lying near the wall. *Just in case,* he thought. He lifted the door and listened for a long moment. Then he took a slow, tentative step down the ladder. Sydney grabbed a penlight from her purse, turned it on, and handed it to him. He took it from her and then made his way the rest of the way down the ladder.

At the bottom, Justin shined the flashlight around the smuggler's hold. Other than a dozen or so stacked crates, it was empty.

"All clear," he called up the ladder. Sydney was beside him a moment later. He handed her back her flashlight.

She shined the beam of light around the room as she tried to select a starting point. "Eenie, meenie, minie, moe." Her flashlight stopped on the nearest crate on her right. "I guess we start here." Sydney used the crowbar to try to pry the lid off the crate.

"Sydney, I can do that a lot easier than you can. Why don't you let me do it?"

"Forget it," she said through gritted teeth while continuing to pry with the crowbar. "If I don't get to break and enter at least one time during each investigation, I consider the whole thing a bust."

Justin laughed and stepped back to give her room. When she got the lid loose, he helped her slide it off. She reached in and pushed aside the packing. Her hands met with plastic. With a gasp, she stared down in shock at her discovery.

Bags upon bags of white powder lay just beneath the packing.

"Cocaine," Justin mumbled, eyeing the substance with disdain.

Sydney reached back into the crate and lifted one of the bags. It was heavy. "Justin, if this whole crate is filled with these bags, the street value of this stuff would be incomprehensible."

"Especially if these other crates hold the same thing." Justin picked up the crowbar and pried the lid off the next crate.

Sydney replaced the bag of drugs and dug her hands into the packing inside the second crate. Instead of plastic bags, however, she felt something hard and bumpy. She dug deeper and uncovered what looked like an old, gilded chair covered with beautiful, old, green fabric.

"Wow, this chair is gorgeous." She ran her hand along the back peeking out of the packing. "It looks like it's hundreds of years old. What's in the rest of these crates?"

Justin moved from crate to crate prying off lids while Sydney went along behind him to rummage through the packing. Her efforts revealed another chair, several beautifully bound books that looked to be hundreds of years old, and a painting.

"Hey, I recognize this," Sydney exclaimed when the painting was halfway out of the crate. "This is *Napoléon at Fontainebleau.* It was painted back in the 1800s."

Justin gaped at it. "It's not the original, is it? If it is, it's more than an antique; it's a piece of history. I can't even imagine how much something like this would go for."

"A lot. But then again, I doubt this was bought and paid for." She moved on to the last few crates Justin had opened. Reaching inside one of the last crates, she found a hard box. She lifted it out and managed to work off the lid. When she saw what was inside, she let out another gasp.

The delicate, dark-blue felt hat with the front and back brims folded upright and accessorized with a colorful cockade was familiar . . . She looked from the hat, back to the half-extracted portrait of Napoléon, and then to the other antiquities around her. Her heart began to pound.

"Do you realize what these are?" she whispered, looking at Justin with wide eyes. "These are one-of-a-kind antiquities that once belonged to Napoléon."

"Unbelievable," he murmured, shaking his head in disbelief as he glanced around at the items. "Where did they all come from?"

Sydney didn't say anything for a moment. Then she snapped her fingers. "The *Chronicle's* art section ran an article a few days ago about a traveling exhibition of Napoléon artifacts that made a tour stop in Brazil and had several important pieces stolen the second night they were there. Maybe that's where these came from!"

"You mean somebody stole them and shipped them here? Is there a way to find out who they were intended for?"

"I doubt there's paperwork pointing to anyone. Maybe my source could ask around. Some dock worker has got to know something."

"You'd think." Justin glanced up at the ceiling. "I bet the crew planned on unloading the legitimate goods today in plain sight, throwing off any Customs agents they encountered, then coming back tonight after everybody was gone to unload the smuggled goods."

She nodded, her eyes wide with excitement. "Justin, do you realize what we're onto here? Whoever is behind this whole crime ring is into smuggling anything and everything—the drugs, the Mayan artifacts that got confiscated, the vase that was auctioned off in Europe a few months ago, and now these Napoléon artifacts. This crime organization doesn't seem to care *what* they smuggle, as long as it's profitable. Not to mention supplying some rebel group's government coup with the proceeds."

The muscle in Justin's jaw jumped as he clenched his teeth. "We'll get to the bottom of this, Sydney. I promise. For now, though, I'm going to get the police and Customs down here. This is now officially a crime scene."

\* \* \*

Longhurst ran with long, steady strides through his gated community in the predawn light, passing the still-dark windows of the houses along his route. When he reached the end of the loop, he slowed and began to jog in place. He put his index and middle finger to his neck and consulted his watch as he counted his pulse.

The vibrating motion of the cell phone clipped to his waistband alerted him that he had an incoming call. "It's five o'clock in the morning, for crying out loud," Longhurst grumbled.

He unclipped the phone, hit the TALK button, and put it to his ear. "What?"

"It's me."

Longhurst stopped jogging. "What happened?"

"Why do you assume something happened?"

"It's four o'clock your time," he said, trying to slow his breathing. "You wouldn't be calling me to say hello."

"True. I wanted to tell you what's going on before you read about it in the morning paper. The ship was intercepted yesterday and the goods—both the legitimate goods above deck and our goods below—were taken by Customs."

Longhurst felt his chest constrict. "What!"

"Calm down, Robert, I have it under control. We're getting the goods back. I have dozens of Customs and Border Protection officials in my pocket, and the arrangements have already been made."

"It was that reporter, Hallam, wasn't it? And she was probably working with that new boyfriend of hers from the *Salt Lake Tribune*," Longhurst demanded, his blood pressure rising. "She's already cost us a fortune! Together those two are bad for business. We're going to have to get rid of them."

"I'll deal with them," came the growl from the other end of the line. "You stay out of this, understand? You aren't thinking clearly enough to handle anything. The last thing I need is for you to go off half-cocked and do something stupid because you're panicking."

"I have every right to panic!" the senator bit out. "Hallam has already cost me millions of dollars and given me a year's worth of headaches with all the changes we've had to make to the organization. I won't stand for it any longer!"

"You will let *me* handle this, understand?" the other man demanded, his voice hard and authoritative. "Don't do a thing. Just sit tight and wait for me to contact you with the shipping arrangements. I'll be in touch."

The line went dead, and Longhurst jerked the phone away from his ear to click the END button. His hand shook as he stared at the phone in his palm. How could he be expected to stay out of this? This was becoming a nightmare.

Rage boiled within him, causing his jaw to tighten and his limbs to shake. No, he would take care of this himself. Once and for all.

Punching numbers on the keypad, he put the phone back up to his ear. "It's Robert. Put me through to him now . . . I don't care, wake him up!" After a silence that seemed to drag on forever, a low grumbling voice came on the line, protesting the interruption. "Yeah, I have a job for you. I want Hallam and Micklesen dealt with once and for all. Get Smith to do it. Tell him I want it to make a statement. Pay him whatever he asks through the usual channels."

When the man on the other end promised to take care of the situation, Longhurst ended the call. "There," he said with finality, a touch of sarcasm in his voice, as he refastened the phone to his waistband. "It's already taken care of."

Feeling satisfied that his colleague would thank him in the end, he set off to continue his early-morning run.

# CHAPTER 37

Sydney and Justin went in to the *Chronicle* on Saturday morning, despite the fact that it should have been Sydney's day off. After the thrill of the previous morning, they were more excited than ever to work on their investigation and try to connect the pieces of the puzzle.

After hours of work, they were still on an emotional high but were ready to call it a day. Dusk was falling when they finally left the *Chronicle*, and Justin slipped an arm around Sydney's shoulder as they walked to the car. She looked up to see him smiling at her.

"What?" she asked.

"Nothing. It's just . . . I love working alongside you. I could get used to seeing our names together in a joint byline like the one on the smuggling article this morning."

Sydney's smile grew. "Me too. We make a great team, don't we?"

"The best."

When they climbed into Sydney's car a few minutes later, Sydney's cell phone rang. She fished it out of her purse and pressed it to her ear. "Sydney Hallam."

"Ms. Hallam," a male voice responded. "This is Detective Pascua. I'm one of Richardson's detectives assigned to the case of yesterday's smuggled goods."

"Yes, Detective," she answered, glancing over at Justin. "What can I do for you?"

Justin furrowed his brow. "What?" he mouthed.

She held up a hand, signaling him to wait. "Is there a problem?"

"No, no problem," the detective went on. "In fact, I've been working with Richardson all day, and we think we've found something linking the shipment back to the person behind all this. We'd like to organize a sting operation. I understand that you and your partner have done quite a bit of research into this and may be able to help us make some connections. Can the two of you meet us tonight at nine at the docks by warehouse three? We've set up a temporary base there and are working through the night on this one."

"We'll be there," Sydney told him, then hung up.

Justin looked at her impatiently as she slipped her phone back into her purse. "So?" After Sydney explained what the detective wanted, he asked, "Did he say what they found that links the shipment to the culprit?"

"No, just that they wanted to discuss it with us. I guess Richardson told him about the information we've already given him."

They drove to Sydney's apartment and had a quick bite to eat, then relaxed for a while before it was time to meet with the detective and his team down at the docks. Darkness had settled in by the time they arrived, but finding warehouse three wasn't a problem.

Sydney pulled up outside the building and slipped the car into park, noticing that the surrounding docks were deserted. "I wonder where they left their cars? Maybe I should have asked Detective Pascua where he wanted me to park," she said as she got out of the car.

Justin surveyed the warehouse. "It looks pretty dark in there. Didn't he say they were working all night?"

"Yeah." Sydney stopped in front of the corrugated metal warehouse. "But a sting operation isn't going to want to call a lot of attention to itself, even in the planning stages, right?"

"I guess not."

Sydney reached for the large, metal warehouse door and slid it open with a grind and a rumble. Together she and Justin took a few cautious steps inside and peered into the semidarkness. The light from a couple of fluorescent light ballasts overhead bathed them in a soft glow but did little to brighten the large space. Stacked crates lined the walls and were arranged throughout the center of the warehouse, but there was no sign of anyone amidst the freight.

"Hello?" Sydney called out as she took another step inside. "Is anybody here?"

Justin stopped beside her and put his hand on her arm. "Maybe we should go back to the car and call the police station to see where everybody is." As he said the words, he slid his hand into his pocket for his phone to find it empty. "Shoot. I think I left my phone in your car."

"I've got mine. We can call them right now." Sydney pulled her cell phone out of her purse, hit a button, and put the phone to her ear.

Justin's lips twitched with amusement. "You have the police station on speed dial?"

"I have a lot of contacts there," she said defensively. Her call connected, and a bored-sounding operator answered.

"This is Sydney Hallam, and I've been working with Detective Richardson on the shipment that came in yesterday morning. Somebody from his team called and told us to meet him at the docks at warehouse three, but nobody's here. Do you know—"

An open window on the other side of the warehouse banged in the wind, making them both jump. Sydney stood frozen, her heart pounding and adrenaline rushing through her veins. An unmistakable sense of doom raised gooseflesh on her arms.

"Syd, we need to get out of here," Justin said, his tone urgent. "Now."

Sydney didn't stop to argue. She whirled toward the door.

Just then, there was a distinctive *pop,* and a bullet whizzed past her ear. She screamed as the small window behind them exploded into a thousand pieces of flying glass.

"Sydney!" Justin yelled. There was another horrifying *pop,* and Justin jerked. He cried out in pain and crumpled to the ground.

"Justin!" she screamed in terror. She dropped to the ground beside him as an agonized moan escaped his lips. Struggling to fight off the feeling of desperation, she clenched the fabric of his shirt in her frantic hands. "Justin, can you hear me? Where are you hurt?"

He opened his eyes at her words and reached for the back of his head. He withdrew his hand to find it covered in blood. Sydney's stomach lurched.

Trying to contain the panic she felt bubbling up within her, she looked around frantically, searching for cover. She spotted a stack of large crates to her left and turned back to Justin. "We've got to move! Can you get up?"

"I think so," he answered, his voice forced and unsteady.

With great effort he sat up, and Sydney helped him lurch to his feet. Together they scrambled the few yards to the nearest crate. Another shot rang out just as they dove behind the crate. The bullet clipped the corner of a crate mere inches from Sydney's head and sent wood chips flying. Justin's legs gave out, and Sydney went down with him. She pushed herself up off the cold cement with shaking hands and looked into his agonized gaze.

"Syd . . ." he murmured, his voice sounding thick and slurred.

"Don't talk," she ordered in a muted sob. Terror filled her soul as the realization of what was happening came crashing down around her. Justin could die. This was really happening. Happening all over again.

Swallowing hard to try to keep her panic at bay, she forced herself to think. *Come on, Sydney, you can handle this. Justin's been shot. What's the first thing you should do?*

*Call for help.*

The voice was so direct, so clear, that she didn't stop to question where it had come from. Forcing herself into action, she righted herself on shaking legs and patted her pants pockets, feeling for her cell phone. A new wave of panic shot through her when she realized she didn't have it. She whirled, frantically searching the ground around them. Her eyes followed the path they had taken to their current position until she spotted her phone lying on the ground next to her purse. She must have dropped them when the first shot had been fired.

She hesitated. If she moved out from behind their cover of crates, she'd be exposed. Did she risk leaving their hiding place to get the phone? She sent up a silent prayer. *Please, Heavenly Father, what do I do?*

The voice came again, this time stronger. *Call for help.*

"Okay," she muttered in response to the firm prompting, grateful to have clear direction. Her body trembling, she crawled to the edge of the crates. Then, drawing a deep breath, she poked her head out past the crates and looked in the direction the shots had come from.

*Go.*

Sydney obeyed the silent command and scurried the few feet out into the aisle, grabbed the phone, then whipped around and practically flew back to the protection of the crates. Once there, she flattened herself against the wood and strained to hear anything that would indicate that the shooter was still there.

Nothing. But she wasn't sure she'd be able to hear anything over the sound of her pounding heart anyway. Clutching the cell phone tightly to her chest, she scrambled back to Justin's side.

Putting a hand on his shoulder for comfort, she lifted the phone back to her ear to see if the police operator was still on the line. An anxious, "Hello? Hello?" told her he was. Sydney kept her voice low as she answered the man, giving him an abbreviated account of what had happened and where they were. Her heart fluttered with relief when the man told her help was on the way.

She ended the call and turned back to Justin. "Help's coming," she told him, trying to keep her voice from shaking. Trying to decide what to do now, she felt the cold floor beneath her knees and shivered. Without a second thought, she shrugged out of her jacket and covered Justin's torso with it like a blanket.

At the movement, he blindly reached for her hand. "Syd . . ."

She wrapped her hand around his, grateful it still felt warm against hers. "I'm here. Everything's going to be okay. Just hold on."

Silence fell over them, and Sydney felt desperate for comfort and guidance. Closing her eyes, she offered another brief, silent prayer. *Heavenly Father, thank you for helping me call for help. But what do we do now?*

To her surprise, her mind began to clear, and she found herself able to think. She sat up straighter and assessed their situation. The sound the bullets had made indicated that whoever had been shooting at them must have been using a silencer. A gun with a silencer wasn't the weapon of just any common criminal. This guy had to be a professional.

A chill crept down her spine. A professional . . . hit man? It had to be. Maybe sent by Longhurst or somebody else in the organization as revenge for ruining the smuggling deal?

A sound of metal clanking near the back of the warehouse made her jump. She held her breath and listened. What if it was the shooter? If he *had* been sent to kill them, surely he wouldn't leave until he knew he'd finished the job.

*So what now?* she asked herself. *We can't just sit here and wait for the cavalry. We could be dead long before help gets here.*

Searching the recesses of her mind, she tried to remember her years of self-defense training enough to pull together a plan. She tried to remember the week she'd spent at a shooting range with an instructor when she'd been assigned to do a story on citizens arming themselves. She'd learned about a variety of guns and how to use them, but that didn't do her a lot of good now that she was trying to avoid being shot.

Her natural instinct to survive began to pulse through her veins, and the inklings of a plan filtered into her mind. If they were going to get out of this alive, her best bet was to take the offensive and try to take the shooter by surprise.

Peeking out around the side of the crates, she tried to get a better lay of the land. She spotted a metal catwalk along the far wall—the perfect place for an armed man to pick off his victims as they walked inside.

Berating herself for being so stupid and not recognizing the potential danger of their situation when they'd first arrived, she continued to take in her surroundings. At the far end of the warehouse, the catwalk ended with a narrow set of stairs leading to the ground level. The other end of the catwalk dead-ended into the corrugated-metal side of the building. If the shooter was going to come down after them, he'd have to come down that set of stairs. Then he'd surely be heading for where he'd seen them take cover behind the stack of crates where they now hid.

She moved back and stared down the other side of the long row of crates. About halfway down she saw what appeared to be a gap large enough for a person to walk through between the stacks.

*If you could hide in that gap and wait for the shooter to move past, you could surprise him.*

The thought startled her. Was she really thinking about going after a sniper? She didn't have any special-forces training, and she certainly didn't have a weapon to defend herself with. How could this be smart?

*You can do this.* The same still, small voice from before filled her mind, giving her courage.

Shaking away the cobwebs of doubt, she took a deep breath to steel her nerves and bent over Justin. "Justin, listen to me," she whispered close to his ear, surprised at the strength and determination she heard in her voice. He opened his eyes and met her gaze. She could tell he was listening intently. "Help is coming, but I don't think this guy's going to leave until he finishes the job. I'm going to go down this row and see if I can get a jump on him, or at the very least distract him until help comes."

A new look of fear surfaced in Justin's eyes. "Syd, you can't," he whispered back, fumbling for her hand. "It's too dangerous."

She tightened her fingers around his. "I have to. If we wait for help to come, it could be too late." She leaned down to brush her lips softly against his. "Stay here and use your hand to put some pressure on your head. Try to stop the bleeding." Giving his hand one last squeeze, she pulled her hand from his and pressed the cell phone into his palm. "I love you," she whispered.

"I love you too. Please be careful."

She nodded and got to her feet. As she did, she spotted a stack of tools along a shelf near the wall. A heavy metal crowbar about three feet long caught her eye. *A weapon.* She reached for it without hesitation.

She moved off, forcing herself not to look back at Justin for fear she'd rethink her crazy plan. Knowing that every little sound echoed in a closed warehouse, she walked as silently as she could toward the gap in the crates. When she reached it, she ducked inside, then crept toward the front of the stacks. When she was about a foot from the front, she stopped and flattened herself against the wood. She held her breath, straining to listen. Everything was silent.

Then she heard it. The soft sound of footfalls increasing ever so slightly in volume as they neared.

Her heart pounding, she adjusted her grip on the crowbar. Raising it up like a batter wielding a baseball bat, she inched forward. She closed her eyes and listened, letting instinct tell her what her eyes could not see.

He was almost there.

Drawing a long, deep, silent breath, she felt every muscle in her body tense as she waited for her opportunity. The large, dark form of a man, gun trained in front of him, moved out past her.

It was now or never.

She leaped into action. With one lunging step she was upon him, swinging her makeshift club for all she was worth. Her aim was dead on, and she connected with the man's arm. The cracking of bone accompanied his shrill scream. The gun clattered to the ground, and she moved in, bringing the crowbar down once more and slamming it into the base of her would-be assailant's neck.

He went down with another strangled cry, and Sydney leaped over him to go after his loose gun. His hand shot up and caught the tip of her shoe as she flew over him, throwing her off balance and sending her sprawling onto the hard cement floor. Pain radiated through her chest, but she continued to fight.

She heard the man try to scramble to his feet as she lunged for his pistol, but she knew that if he got to it first it would all be over. With single-minded determination, she half crawled, half slid across the floor even as she heard the man shouting from close behind her. She was only inches from the weapon when a rough, unrelenting hand grabbed the back of her neck and squeezed.

The pressure nearly overwhelmed her, and she cried out in pain. Her eyes never leaving the gun, she gave one last-ditch attempt and lunged forward. Her fingers connected with the hard metal, and miraculously she managed to inch it closer. She gritted her teeth and stretched for all she was worth.

Her fingers closed around the handle. With one quick move she rolled, aimed upward, and fired.

The man jerked and then went still, his face still shrouded in semidarkness. The sound of the bullet firing through the silencer still echoed in Sydney's ears as the man slowly staggered backward, then dropped to his knees. A moment later he tipped to his right and collapsed on the floor.

For a long moment Sydney was unable to move. At last she got to her feet and went to stand over the fallen man. She held the gun out in front of her, training it on him as she studied him. For the first time, she could make out his features in the dim light of the flickering fluorescents above. He appeared to be in his thirties and had dark hair, a deep scar above his left eyebrow, and hard, steel-gray eyes.

The cold eyes of a would-be killer.

She watched in morbid fascination as his eyes glazed over. His head lolled to one side, and his ragged breathing stopped.

A cry escaped Sydney's throat as she lowered the gun to her side. Her shoulders started to shake as silent sobs welled up within her chest.

*Justin.*

The thought came to her with such force that it shook her out of her shock. She made her feet move. Slowly, then faster. Then she was running toward the front of the warehouse, toward Justin. The echoing of her footsteps was soon joined by the distant sound of a wailing siren.

She reached the end of the row and careened around the corner, dropping the gun as she skidded to a halt and dropped to her knees beside Justin's still form. He lay so still that new fear clenched her heart.

"Justin," she breathed, praying harder than she ever had in her life that he was still alive. Her hand went to his shoulder, and she gave him a gentle shake. "Justin!"

A soft moan escaped his lips, and she let out a little cry of relief. He was alive. At least for now.

The wail of sirens grew deafening as several vehicles screeched to a halt outside the open warehouse door. With tears streaming down her cheeks, she clung to his hand. "Hold on, Justin," she told him. "Help is here. Please, hold on."

Then she felt hands on her shoulders, guiding her back from Justin as men rushed in to assess his condition. Memories of one horrible night many years ago came flooding back, making her throat and chest constrict so tightly she could hardly breathe. The sight of paramedics darting about in front of her as they worked on somebody she loved sent a chill rushing down her spine.

She struggled to fight off the feelings of desperation as she looked up at a paramedic who crouched down beside her. She forced herself to pull it together and answer his questions about what had happened and whether she was hurt.

Assuring the man she was physically unharmed, she turned her attention back to Justin as they wheeled in a stretcher and strapped him to it. A blanket was thrown around her shoulders, and she was helped into the back of the ambulance with Justin.

The next two hours were like reliving a nightmare. The wailing siren as they sped through the city cut clear through to her soul, leaving her emotionally beaten and battered. It was all she could do to stand up on shaking legs to climb out of the ambulance once they'd arrived at the hospital. They were taken into the ER in a flurry of activity, and she was questioned and poked and prodded while Justin was assessed in a separate room.

She was diagnosed with a couple of bruised ribs from her fall onto the concrete floor and told that, other than babying her ribs for the next couple of weeks, there was nothing to be done about it. After what seemed like forever, one of the nurses brought back a report on Justin. The bullet hadn't penetrated his skull, but had merely grazed the base of it. He had lost a lot of blood, and the wound would require stitches, but other than being kept overnight for observation and receiving a heavy round of antibiotics, he was going to be fine.

She wanted to sob with relief. Detective Richardson came by to personally take her statement and find out for himself what had happened. She explained about the phone call from one of his detectives and the supposed sting operation. His frown confirmed her new suspicions—he didn't have a man named Pascua on his team, and a sting operation hadn't been planned.

Sydney mentally berated herself for falling for the tactic, but Richardson kept asking questions, forcing her to give him her attention. When she was done giving him her statement, he gave her shoulder a reassuring, fatherly squeeze before he left, promising to talk with her soon.

After an interminable amount of time, she was shown into a private room where Justin lay in a hospital bed, an IV tube threaded into his arm. A nurse making notes on his chart gave Sydney a compassionate smile and gestured for her to have a seat in the chair next to the head of his bed.

"The pain medication put him out, but he's going to be fine," she told her. "You're welcome to stay with him as long as you'd like."

"Thank you." Sydney managed a smile as the nurse finished her notes and headed out of the room.

Alone with Justin, she sat beside him and reached for his hand. It felt strong and warm, the pulse at his wrist reassuring her that he was alive. The realization brought new tears to her eyes, and she lowered her head onto his mattress and let herself cry.

# CHAPTER 38

Sydney drew her knees up to her chest and curled into the corner of the small, upholstered armchair as she watched Justin sleep. He looked peaceful. The contrast was stark as she thought back to how he'd looked on the warehouse floor a few hours before.

She shuddered. The image was one she knew she would never forget. The bullet had come close to ending his life. She'd almost lost him.

A tremor ran through her, and the room suddenly felt chilly. She wrapped her arms around herself in an effort to get warm.

Just then, movement from the bed caught her attention. She looked up to see Justin's head move, and a moment later his eyes fluttered open. They still had a bit of a glassy, drugged look, but the warmth in them was evident when he spotted her sitting in the chair beside his bed.

"Hey," he murmured, his voice groggy. "What time is it?"

"Almost midnight. How are you feeling?"

"Okay, I think."

"You were lucky," she said quietly, though her voice still sounded loud in the silent room. "The doctor said the bullet only grazed your skull. You're going to be fine. You'll be out of here tomorrow."

"Good. How are *you*?" Justin asked, his expression concerned. "Are you okay?"

She attempted a smile, but it felt stiff on her face. "I'm fine. A little scared," she admitted, tightening her arms around herself to quell her trembling. "Richardson was here earlier. I gave him a statement." She looked down at her fingers and said quietly, "The shooter's dead. I killed him."

Justin reached for her hand but caught only her fingertips. "You did what you had to do. And I'm glad you did, or else *we* would have been killed."

"I know," she answered in a mere whisper, a haunted look on her face. "He very nearly killed you."

"But he didn't, thanks to you." Justin smiled at her, but her expression didn't change. "We must have really ticked off the owner of those drugs and antiques if he tried to have us killed."

She looked up and met his gaze, nodding. "I was thinking that, too. What better revenge than to kill the two people who'd cost you millions. It's the only explanation."

"It's scary how close he came to succeeding."

Sydney swallowed. "What if he tries again? Sends another hit man after us?"

"Ask Richardson what he thinks about that," came Justin's weary reply.

She nodded mutely. She felt another shiver rack her body, and this time Justin noticed. His forehead creasing with concern, he managed to put a hand on her arm. His eyes widened as he felt how cold her skin was. "Sydney, you're freezing! Don't you have a jacket or something?"

She shook her head and pressed her quivering lips together. How was she supposed to explain that right now, all she felt was numb? Her body, her senses, her emotions . . . It was all she could do to stay focused on helping Justin get better.

"I'll be fine."

"You're not going to be fine if we don't get you warmed up," he said, the familiar strength and protectiveness he had for her beginning to return. He struggled to reach the button behind him. "I'll call the nurse and see if she can bring in a couple more blankets."

Sydney felt tears spring to her eyes. "Justin, you're the one hurt, okay? Stop pretending that everything's okay with you and treating me like I'm the one who needs to be taken care of. You were shot! How can you dismiss that so easily?"

His head swiveled toward her, and his look of confusion and concern was easy to read. "Sydney, I'm going to be okay," he assured her in soft, measured tones. "I'll be back to my old self in no time, thanks to you."

When she didn't respond, he tried again. "I can't tell you how grateful I am that you were brave enough to go after that guy like that. Or maybe it was stupidity," he said, trying to tease her into a smile. "Regardless, you saved my life."

A couple of tears slid down her cheeks, and she lifted a hand to brush them away. She was aware that Justin was studying her intently, but her fear of what she'd almost lost was too hard to talk about.

She was grateful when they were interrupted by a nurse bustling into the room, announcing she needed to take Justin's blood pressure. Sydney's mind began to drift, and she only half listened as the nurse asked Justin a few questions. An almost overwhelming feeling of exhaustion crept over her. Feeling both physically and emotionally drained, she leaned forward in her chair and rested her head on the edge of Justin's mattress. The smooth, crisp sheets felt heavenly beneath her cheek.

She drew in a long breath, then released it in a deep, cleansing sigh that eased the tightness from her muscles. She shut her eyes and felt herself begin to drift. The sounds of Justin and the nurse conversing grew muted as she slipped into a deeper state of relaxation. A minute later, she was asleep.

\* \* \*

Something touched Sydney's head, startling her awake. She opened her bleary eyes in time to see a hand slip from her hair. Sitting upright, she spotted Justin propped up in his hospital bed, a tender smile on his lips. The color had returned to his cheeks, and the beautiful, soulful glow in his eyes had returned.

"Hi," he murmured quietly when their eyes met.

Sydney wiped at her sleep-filled eyes and glanced around the room, trying to reorient herself to the unexpected surroundings. A tug on her shoulders caused her to look down. She was surprised to see a standard-issue hospital blanket wrapped around her.

"You fell asleep last night when the nurse was here, and we didn't have the heart to wake you," he explained. "I figured it was as comfortable a place for you to sleep as any, so I had the nurse put the blanket around you to keep you warm." His expression grew more serious as he studied her weary face. "How are you this morning? I've been worried about you."

The events of the night before came rushing back, and a heaviness settled in the pit of her stomach. "I'm fine," she answered automatically. A brief glimpse into his eyes told her he didn't think she was being completely honest, but she was grateful he didn't press the issue. She glanced up at the clock on the wall and was surprised to see that it was almost nine.

She sat up a little straighter and stretched, trying to ease the ache from her back and shoulder. She winced as the motion caused pain to shoot through her rib cage, reminding her of her injury. "Does the doctor still expect to release you soon?"

"Yeah, he was in a little while ago and said I'm recovering nicely. They're going to release me by lunchtime."

"That's great," Sydney said, forcing a smile that she hoped looked relaxed and cheerful. She knew she'd failed, however, when a questioning look settled across Justin's face.

For several moments she endured his probing gaze, trying not to squirm under its intensity. When she couldn't stand it any longer, she stood up and walked the short distance to the window under the guise of stretching her legs. She was relieved when a staff member came in carrying a breakfast tray for Justin, effectively cutting off their conversation.

When they were alone again, Justin cocked an eyebrow at her and nodded at the food on his tray. "Hungry?" he offered. "Come share this with me."

Sydney's stomach clenched. Just the smell of food made her queasy. "No, thanks. I'm not hungry."

Justin frowned. "Syd, what's wrong? I'm worried about you."

"Nothing's wrong." When his frown deepened in disbelief, she grasped for something—anything—she could say to get him off her case. "I just didn't sleep well, that's all." Then, turning away, she mumbled, "I need to use the bathroom," before sequestering herself in the small, adjoining room.

With the door shut behind her, she moved to the sink and splashed cold water on her face. She looked up at her reflection in the mirror and noticed the dark circles beneath her eyes and the pained, haunted expression in their depths. *No wonder Justin keeps asking you what's wrong. You look terrible.*

She drew in a long, shaky breath and realized her emotions were still too raw, too close to the surface right now to trust them to anyone else. Even Justin. At the same time, she realized that Justin knew her too well for her to try to fool him with a fake, cheery smile.

No, she was going to have to resort to her mainstay. The trusty walls of her emotional barrier. Nothing got in, nothing got out. She'd made it work for years. She'd make it work now.

Feeling a little stronger, she dried her face and hands and left the bathroom. Over the next hour as she helped Justin get ready to leave, Sydney succeeded in acting cheerful and helpful while maintaining an emotional distance. Even better, she succeeded in stifling all attempts Justin made at getting her to open up about what was bothering her.

When the discharge forms were signed, Sydney arranged for a cab to pick them up and take them back to Justin's condo since her car was still down at the docks. She managed to keep her tender emotions in check during the cab ride as she worked to keep the conversation neutral and away from the events of the last fourteen hours. Still, she couldn't help breathing a sigh of relief when they pulled up in front of Justin's condo.

As Justin climbed out, Sydney paid the driver, and then she helped a weary Justin up the stairs and inside. There she directed him into the bedroom and instructed him to change into something he could sleep in. He insisted he wanted to stay up for a while and talk, but talking was the last thing she wanted to do. She put on her best mothering act and managed to convince him that sleep was what he needed.

She waited in the living room while he changed. He came out a short time later in a pair of shorts and a T-shirt. "Satisfied?" he teased, holding his arms out for inspection.

She nodded and tried to return his smile. "Yes. Now get in bed. You need to rest." She made a shooing motion with her hands as she walked toward him, and he backed up obediently to go back into the bedroom and sat on the bed.

"What are you going to do while I rest?" he asked. "I don't want you to be bored."

"I won't be," she reassured him. "There's a TV and a whole bookcase full of books out there to keep me busy." It was quiet for moment. Then she said, "You're pretty lucky, you know that? You could have died out there last night."

Justin reached for her hand. "But I didn't. I'll be fine, thanks to you." When she didn't respond, he cocked his head at her. "Syd?"

"I'd better let you get some sleep," she hurried to say, effectively cutting off his worrying. "You've had a busy morning. The doctor said you needed rest." When he nodded wordlessly, she offered a tight-lipped smile. "I'll be out on the couch if you need me, okay? I'm going to unwind a bit and watch some TV." With that, she left the room, pulling the bedroom door shut behind her.

With the door as a physical barrier between them, Sydney's emotional barrier started to crumble. She managed to silence the sob before it escaped from her throat, but she was still racked with the ache of what could have been a heartbreaking loss.

The chill she'd felt the night before at the hospital was still with her, and she fought to keep herself from shaking. She grabbed the afghan from the back of the couch, wrapped herself in it, and sank onto the overstuffed leather chair in the corner. She picked up the remote and clicked on the TV—if only so Justin would think she'd been telling him the truth about that.

For what seemed like hours, she stared numbly at the images flickering across the screen, unable to get warm in spite of the thick afghan draped around her shoulders. The cold went clear through to her core, and she couldn't help wondering if she was ever going to feel warm again.

When yet another program ended, she clicked off the television and pulled the blanket more firmly around herself. Even the reassurance that

Justin was going to be fine didn't soothe the stinging pain rising up from deep within her. She felt suffocated by the realization of what she'd almost lost—*had* lost once before.

Quiet sobs rose in her throat once more, and this time she didn't stop them.

# CHAPTER 39

Justin woke some time later with the nagging sense that something was wrong. He sat up a little in bed, propping himself up on his elbows. A dull ache at the base of his skull reminded him of his injury. *Ah. That was it.* He felt his tense muscles relax, and he lay back down. But as the moments passed, the nagging sensation only continued to grow stronger. Something else was wrong.

Rolling onto his side, he listened. He heard the soft ticking of the clock, but there was another subdued sound coming from elsewhere in the apartment. After a few moments, he was able to isolate the noise and discern what it was. It was the sound of someone crying.

*Sydney.*

Getting gingerly to his feet, he walked across the room and opened the bedroom door. His footsteps fell mute on the thick carpet as he moved down the hallway and into the living room. A single lamp was on, but the room otherwise gave no appearance of occupancy.

At last he spotted her. She was curled up in the chair in the far corner of the room, her knees drawn up to her chest and her face buried in them. Her shoulders shook as quiet sobs racked her body.

Surprise and concern propelled him across the living room toward her. "Syd, what's wrong?"

The sound of his voice startled her, and she jerked her head up. Her eyes were red, and tears coursed down her pale cheeks. She sat up straighter and quickly wiped the tears from her face. "Oh, um, Justin. I thought you were asleep."

"I was." He closed the distance between them and sat down on the floor at the foot of her chair. He placed a comforting hand on her knee. "I heard you out here crying. What's wrong?"

Sydney's lower lip trembled, and she looked away. "It's nothing. I'm okay. Sorry I woke you."

"You're not okay." Justin's voice was filled with concern. "You're obviously upset about something. What is it?"

Several more tears escaped and slid down her cheeks despite her valiant efforts to contain them. "When I saw you lying on that warehouse floor, I expected the worst. I kept thinking that here I'd opened up my heart to someone after all these years, only to have that person taken away from me. It was like losing my parents and my sister all over again . . ." She broke off, and sobs overtook her once more.

A heaviness settled over his heart. "Oh, Syd, I'm so sorry. I didn't realize . . ." He reached out to gather her into his embrace. "Come here." She fell forward into his arms and buried her face in his shoulder. He pulled her into his lap and tightened his arms around her, stroking her hair and resorting to the age-old comfort of rocking.

She cried for a long time. When at last she pulled away, her voice was filled with pain as she said, "Justin, I can't do this. I can't go through that all over again."

Justin brushed her hair back from her face. "Can't do what, sweetheart?"

She took a deep, shuddering breath that did nothing to ease the look of fear in her eyes. "Do you realize how terrified I was, thinking I was going to lose you, too? I got lulled into some false sense of security, thinking you couldn't be hurt, couldn't be taken away from me. Maybe that's part of what made me feel like we were so solid. But after seeing you so close to dying . . ."

Justin put a hand on either side of her face and forced her to look at him. "Syd, you're forgetting one all-important thing. I'm still here. I *didn't* die. I'm not going anywhere."

"Yeah, right now. But what about later?" At his look of confusion, she pulled away and got to her feet. She moved a few paces away and wrapped her arms around herself protectively, her back to him.

With a concerned frown, Justin got to his feet and moved to stand behind her. "Syd, I'm lost here. What are you talking about?"

When she spoke, her voice shook. "Justin, I don't know that I can risk losing you again. Maybe this was all just a very bad idea."

"What's a bad idea? What are you saying?"

"Us." Sydney turned and met Justin's alarmed gaze with her frightened one. "I don't think this will work."

His face paled. "Sydney, you can't mean that," he said in a shocked whisper. "Please tell me you don't mean that."

She lifted one shoulder in a vulnerable shrug. "I don't know, Justin. I'm just . . . I'm so scared. I remember how horrible it was to lose not just one person I loved, but three of them in one awful night. It took me years to get back on my feet. I don't ever want to go through that again."

"So, you get scared and immediately turn and run?" Justin's eyes flashed as he stepped closer to her. "That doesn't sound like the Sydney Hallam I know."

"This isn't the Sydney Hallam you know!" she cried, the panic she'd held in check finally bubbling to the surface. "This is the scared, lost little girl who watched her mother, father, and sister all be buried on the same day! I can't pretend she doesn't exist—that none of it happened. It did, Justin! And I'm sorry if it scarred me in ways you can't even begin to imagine, but I don't want to lose another person that I love! I couldn't take it. I just couldn't . . ." Her voice broke, and a quiet sob escaped from her lips.

Justin's heart twisted. He closed the remaining distance between them and gathered her into his arms. With tears in his own eyes, he spoke, his voice soft and gentle. "I lost my best childhood friend not long ago, so I'd like to think I understand something about what you went through. But some people are taken out of our lives and others are brought into them. It's Heavenly Father's way of helping us deal with our grief and helping us along in life."

He paused, searching for just the right words. "Did you ever stop to think that maybe we were brought together for a reason? To help us find our way together? We have something special—something I've never felt with anybody else, and I know you feel the same way. Please don't be so hasty to throw it away. Please."

Sydney stepped back, folding her arms across her chest. Her face was a myriad of conflicting emotions. "I don't know, Justin, I'm so confused. I know I love you and want to be with you, but when I think about how I would feel if I lost you, all those memories of everything I went through after my family died come back to haunt me."

"But Sydney," he said, his tone pleading, "you can't suffer with your memories forever. I can't bear to watch you do it, and I know your parents and sister wouldn't want you to do it. Like you told me that night up in the canyon, you've got to let yourself grieve and find some closure."

Sydney paled. "Don't lecture me, Justin," she bit back in a fierce whisper. "I don't need to be psychoanalyzed about how I manage the death of my family."

Surprised by her angry reaction, Justin studied her, his eyes narrowing. That's when the pieces of the puzzle fell into place. "You've never let yourself grieve, have you?" he accused, taking a step toward her. "Every time we've talked about your parents—or even that night at your apartment after your concussion—you've only allowed yourself brief moments of grief. You told me that night in the canyon that letting yourself go through the grieving process is the only way to get through loss. But you've never let yourself do that, have you?"

One look at her face and he knew he was right. "Sydney, I can't believe you've been such a hypocrite about this! Your family died over ten years ago, but you've never allowed yourself to grieve your loss and move on. How are you ever going to let go of this survivor's guilt if you don't let yourself do that? It was your parents' and sister's time, not yours. They wouldn't want you going on living like this, keeping your grief bottled up inside. Why didn't you grieve and move on all those years ago?"

Sydney's eyes flashed. "I didn't have time to grieve, Justin! I was just trying to survive! I didn't have anyone to pick me up and comfort me. My aunt took me in, but not to love. I was a convenience to her, someone to care for her when she was sick. Nobody loved me. *I* was all that I had. Grieving wasn't a luxury I could afford. So, yes, I buried those feelings deep, so deep that I never fully faced them. It was what I had to do! And you have no idea how hard it was for me. You don't! So don't act all high and mighty and pretend you know what's best for me, because just maybe you don't!"

Justin's heart wrenched at her explanation. "Sydney, I—you're right. I can't say that I know how it was for you." He swallowed hard to get his voice under control, then reached tentatively for her hand. He was relieved when she didn't pull away. "But I do know how it feels to have somebody taken away from you . . . to wonder 'what if.' You can't keep living your life that way. You'll kill yourself with all this bottled-up grief. You need to find some closure and make some peace with your loss and move on, the same way I'll have to from losing Bryce. Maybe together we can do that. Do you think we can do that?"

Sydney looked up to meet Justin's gaze, her eyes shimmering with tears. Justin waited for her response, hardly daring to hope.

At last she whispered, "I don't know, Justin, but I'll try. That's all I can do."

He let out the breath he hadn't realized he'd been holding and closed his eyes, pulling her into his embrace. "That's all I ask," he said as he held her. "That's all I ask."

When they pulled apart, Justin gazed down at the emotionally exhausted woman before him. "I think you need sleep more than I do. Why don't you go lie down in the bedroom and I'll rest out here on the couch. I really think you could use it. When you get up, we'll do something about dinner."

Sydney nodded, and he wrapped his arm around her and pulled her close. With a great sense of relief that she was still here beside him, he led her into the bedroom and helped her climb between the sheets. He was sure everything would look brighter soon—for her as well as for him.

# CHAPTER 40

Sunlight spilled across Sydney's bed the next morning, causing her to stir. She opened her eyes, but they felt sore and gritty. The events of the past day and a half came rushing back, and she groaned and pulled the blankets up over her face. She had slept very little and cried a lot, yet her heart and head were still conflicted. She had spent the night pouring her heart out in prayer, asking for help sorting out her feelings.

After she had woken up from her nap in Justin's apartment the afternoon before, Justin had been concerned, but he hadn't said much. It was as if he worried that he might say something that would push her away. Instead, he'd spent the evening reassuring her with his solid presence that he was still very much there with her. He conveyed his love with his usual touches—a hand on the small of her back as he guided her into the kitchen for a simple meal, his fingers closing momentarily around hers when they brushed over the silverware tray, his gentle hand stroking her hair before giving her a tender kiss good night.

The realization that he loved her so much to want to tread so carefully touched her heart, but at the same time it made her feel incredibly guilty. He was the one who had been shot, but it was clear that his thoughts were only of her. She wouldn't have blamed him if he had taken a good look at the baggage she came with and turned tail and ran, but he hadn't. That spoke volumes as to how committed he was to loving her.

Fresh tears came to her eyes. How could she even think of calling things off when he loved her that much? She remembered how safe and loved she'd felt in his arms when she'd broken down and he'd comforted her. The more she thought about Justin, the more she realized something. He didn't just hold a piece of her heart—he held all of it.

It was horrible to imagine living her life without Justin. But wasn't that what she'd be doing if she decided to cut her losses and stop seeing him in an effort to protect her fragile heart? So, what was the difference, whether he was taken from her or she pushed him away? The bottom line was, she loved him. As much as he loved her. Was it really fair to either of them to end their relationship just because she was scared that one day she might lose him?

A warm feeling began in her heart and spread throughout her body. She recognized it instantly as the whispering of the Holy Ghost. It spoke as an answer to her fervent prayers, telling her what she needed to know.

Justin was meant to be in her life.

Unshed tears blurred her vision. As desperately as she wanted to protect her heart, she knew Justin was right. Nobody could protect their loved ones all the time. If she was afraid to love somebody because she might ultimately lose them, not only would she be letting her fears rule her, but she would be missing out on the happiness Heavenly Father wanted for her. If she was able to love Justin and have his love in return for a year or fifty years, she knew it would be worth it. Each minute would be precious.

She slid out of bed and offered a silent prayer of thanks that she'd finally gotten an answer to her prayers. She also pleaded for help in overcoming her fear of losing another person she loved, so she could have the courage to love Justin as she wanted to.

After closing her prayer, she got up to shower and dress. Justin's plane left in a few hours, and she had told him she'd drive him to the airport. She had just walked into the kitchen to grab a bite to eat when the phone rang.

"Sydney? It's Paul," the detective said when she answered. "Do you and Justin have a minute that you could meet me at my office this morning? I have a couple of updates for you."

Sydney glanced at her watch. "Yeah, I think so. Justin's plane leaves in a couple of hours, but I think we could do that." She told him they'd be there as soon as they could, then hung up. Forgoing breakfast, she grabbed her wallet and keys and headed for her car.

She had taken a taxi to pick her car up from the docks the previous night after leaving Justin's place, and that had been a frightening experience by itself. She had dreaded going, but it hadn't been as bad as she'd feared. The taxi driver had pulled up right beside her car and kindly waited as she got in and started it. Even so, every noise on the docks had made her jump, making her wonder if danger was lurking around every corner. Her underground parking garage hadn't been any better. Every shadow made her start, and every person she saw made her suspicious. She wondered how she was going to go about her daily activities without constantly wondering where the next attempt on her or Justin's lives might come from.

She relaxed in the safety of her car as she drove the short distance to Justin's condo. She was about a block away, however, when new doubts began to creep in. What if Justin had thought about it and decided she wasn't worth this emotional roller coaster? She wouldn't blame him if he had. She wasn't exactly low maintenance these days. Was having a relationship with her still worth it to him?

She agonized over the possibilities the rest of the way to his condo, and it was with a shaking hand that she knocked on his door. Her worries disappeared the second Justin answered, however, when she saw his eyes crinkle with warmth and love.

"Hey, Syd."

The sound of his deep, gentle voice warmed her all the way through. Without hesitation, she threw her arms around him and buried her face in his chest.

He gave a surprised chuckle and hugged her back. "Good morning to you too. What's this all about?"

Feeling timid, she lifted her face to his. "I'm sorry about yesterday."

His eyebrows lifted. "Sorry about what?"

"For my little breakdown," she said, feeling ashamed. "You had just gotten home from the hospital and needed someone to take care of you, but instead you spent the day dealing with me and my insecurities. I was so selfish. I should have been strong enough to put everything aside and take care of you, but I—"

"Shh, Syd, it's okay," he murmured as he cupped her face in his hands and stroked his thumbs along her cheeks. "We're beyond that. You should never apologize for how you feel. It's how you feel. I'm just glad you told me so I knew what you were fighting against. Now that I have a better understanding, I can help you through it."

"But I was supposed to be there for you—"

"You were," he interrupted once more. "You were great to help me so much, and then I helped you. We helped each other through a tough time. I'd like to think that's what we'll always do for each other." He smiled down at her tenderly. "I love you, you know."

Sydney's heart filled with emotion. "I love you too. Thank you for not giving up on me."

He shook his head. "I never will." Then he leaned down, and their lips met in a kiss that made Sydney tingle clear down to her toes.

When Justin released her, she took a step back and remembered what else she was going to tell him. "I got a call from Richardson before I came over. He wanted to know if we could meet him at his office this morning before you left. He said he had some information for us."

"Let me finish packing so we can go straight to the airport if we need to. Have you eaten yet?"

She smiled. He was always thinking of her. "Not yet," she admitted.

He talked her into stopping for a quick bite before meeting with Detective Richardson. Soon afterward they were at the station, with Justin's suitcase and carry-on stowed in Sydney's trunk.

Richardson led them into his office and offered them the chairs in front of his desk. "Here's what we learned," he began. "The shooter was a man named Terrance Smith. We've been after him for a while now, but he's been elusive. I did some looking, though, and your friend Bryce Davies?" He glanced at Justin. "The initial investigation of his break-in didn't turn up much, but we've made a few connections that lead us to believe that Smith was the man who killed Bryce."

Justin's face paled. "Smith killed Bryce?"

"It's looking that way." Richardson looked grim. "I know this isn't easy to hear, but I thought you'd like to know. Give you a little closure."

Sydney slid her hand onto Justin's arm in a silent show of support.

"It does. Thanks," Justin said quietly.

"We also searched Smith's apartment and found bank statements. He'd had a lot of money wired into his account over the past few months, but there was a big deposit yesterday. That seemed a little coincidental, so we traced the wires."

"Did that tell you who paid him to try to kill us?"

Richardson shook his head. "Not yet, but I'm confident we'll know soon."

Sydney shifted in her chair anxiously. "What if whoever paid Smith to do this decides to hire somebody else and try again?"

"I don't think so," he said in a reassuring voice. "A botched attempt brings a lot of attention, and whoever is behind this isn't going to want to draw even more attention by trying again. We were able to trace the payment, which means we're close to tracking down the source. I have every confidence it'll happen in the next few days. We'll have the person running this show behind bars."

Sydney sagged with relief. She knew there was always the possibility they weren't out of danger, but it felt good to hear Richardson say that he thought they would be okay.

"The location where the payment originated is out of our jurisdiction," Richardson went on, "so we had to call in the FBI. The FBI doesn't share information, so I don't know what they did from there. But what I do know is, they raided a PR firm this morning, so they must have found a connection. The FBI is confiscating everything—financial records, work orders, information about who they do business with . . ."

Sydney looked at him in surprise. "Wait a minute. What PR firm? I haven't turned on the TV or read a paper this morning. And nobody called me from the *Chronicle* . . ."

Richardson swiveled in his chair and reached for the morning paper behind him. "Maybe they figure you deserve some time off after everything that's happened." He swiveled back around and tossed a small section of the paper across the desk to her. "The firm is called Premiere Enterprises. They've only been in business a couple of years."

Sydney picked up the newspaper and stared. "Premiere Enterprises? Isn't that—" She turned to Justin, her eyes wide.

Justin nodded. "Yeah, that's the PR firm we learned about, the subsidiary of Sandstone Enterprises." Then his tone grew sarcastic. "Isn't it interesting that this just mysteriously ties back there?"

Frowning, Richardson leaned forward and placed his clasped hands on his desk. He looked from Justin to Sydney. "What aren't you telling me?"

Sydney let out a breath. "We've been investigating what we suspect is an international crime ring. We think Smith was the henchman sent to silence us for interfering with that shipment."

"So you think he was working for Phillip Douglas?" Richardson asked, confused. "If so, we've already got an APB out for him for his involvement in that shipment—the manifests had his signature on the paperwork. If he hired Smith and we can find him, we might be able to make a conviction stick."

Sydney shook her head. "I wouldn't be surprised to find a connection between Smith and Douglas, but we suspect it goes a lot higher than that."

"Who do you think this goes back to?"

Justin and Sydney exchanged glances, then looked back at Richardson. "How long do you have?"

# CHAPTER 41

"I'm sure he's suffering from information overload right now," Sydney said as she and Justin left the police station and walked to the car.

Justin chuckled. "I would be. The sad thing is, there's not a lot he can do with an investigation of this magnitude. He doesn't have the manpower or resources. He said the FBI was already involved. I wonder if they've even tied the PR firm back to Sandstone Enterprises and Longhurst. My uncle works for the FBI in the Salt Lake City field office. We could talk to him, tell him what we've found. Maybe he can tell us a few things off the record, too . . . give us an idea if they have any solid leads on Longhurst's involvement in all this."

"That's a good idea."

As they started across the parking lot, Sydney couldn't help glancing around at their surroundings even after Richardson's reassurances.

"I keep doing that too," Justin said, his voice low and even. When she looked up at him in silent question, he nodded at the parking lot around them. "Looking around, wondering if somebody is just waiting to try again. But Richardson's reassurances made me feel a little better."

"Me too. The possibility still frightens me, though." Sydney moved closer to Justin, and he put an arm around her shoulders. His closeness was comforting.

"It frightens me too," he admitted, "but when people are frightened, they're cautious. If we remain cautious and aware of what's going on around us, and most of all, take precautions, I think we'll be safe until whoever is behind this is caught."

When they reached the car, they got in and Sydney started the engine. She looked over at Justin and watched him lean his head back against the headrest and close his eyes. She reached over to brush her knuckles against his cheek. "I'm sorry about what he had to say about Bryce. That must have been hard to listen to."

"It was, but he's right that at least it gives me some closure."

"Are you okay? You look tired."

"I am tired." He gave her a wry smile. "Getting shot takes a lot out of a guy."

Her breath caught in her chest at the mention of the experience, but she forced the painful emotion away. "You sure you can handle the travel today?"

"Yeah, I'm sure. It's not far—just one airport to another. Besides, as soon as my parents hear what happened, I won't have to lift a finger to do anything."

Sydney looked at him in disbelief. "You haven't told your parents yet? Justin!"

Holding his hands up in a gesture of surrender, he hurried to explain. "I didn't want to worry them! If I'd told them what happened, they would've been on the next plane out here. I love them, but they tend to overreact in situations like this."

"Situations like this?" Sydney cocked an eyebrow and suppressed a smile. "Like when their son is shot by a sniper while investigating a story? They've dealt with that before?"

Justin's face quirked into a smile. "Yeah, okay, maybe they haven't faced situations *exactly* like this, but you know what I mean."

The drive to the airport was uneventful, and it didn't take Justin long to check his luggage. Realizing they still had a few minutes, they sat down near a bank of TVs. Justin relaxed in his seat and entwined his fingers with Sydney's.

"You're not going back to work tomorrow, are you?" she asked. "The doctor did tell you to rest."

Justin chuckled. "You complain about Agnes's mothering, but you're pretty good at it yourself."

"Sorry." She gave him a sheepish grin. "I just worry about you."

He leaned over to give her a light kiss. "Don't worry. I'll be fine. And yes, I'm going to take the day off. A day lounging around my apartment sounds pretty good, actually."

"Especially compared to everything we've been doing lately. It's too bad that—"

"Wait, shh!" Justin cut in, leaning forward to stare intently at the television not far from them. "What's that woman saying?"

Sydney looked up at the TV and saw a CNN reporter standing on the steps of the capitol building in Salt Lake City. A second later, a scroll appeared— "Utah's Senator Longhurst's CFO Implicated in FBI Raid of PR Firm."

Sydney sat up straighter in her chair. What was going on? She stood up with Justin, and together they moved closer to the television.

"The FBI raided Premiere Enterprises, a PR firm in Las Vegas, Nevada, this morning," the reporter updated, "with several people coming under investigation after a suspected hit man was taken down during a botched hit attempt on two reporters in San Francisco, California."

"Hey, we made the news!" Sydney exclaimed, laughing. "Not exactly how I meant to break into the big time—the victim of a botched hit attempt."

Justin laughed and shushed her at the same time. Grinning, she turned her attention back to the TV to hear the rest of the report.

". . . the gunman has been connected to the PR firm. An FBI spokesperson released a statement not long ago stating that James Morrow, the CFO of Sandstone Enterprises—Utah senator Longhurst's biggest conglomerate—was being implicated for laundering money through the PR firm and has been linked to criminal activity. What that criminal activity is, the spokesperson for the FBI refused to comment on, but political backlash has rocked the news. Senator Longhurst has called a press conference. We'll take you there now."

The screen switched to show Senator Longhurst stepping up to a podium and reading a short statement to the gathered press corps, stating that he was shocked by the FBI's findings and was complying fully with their investigation. He went on to deny any wrongdoing and quickly brought the press conference to a close, refusing to take any questions.

The camera cut back to the reporter, who went on. "Senator Robert Longhurst, a known philanthropist, met earlier today with billionaire Stephen Dover in Salt Lake City to break ground on the new science wing that is their latest joint venture. The science wing of Senator Longhurst's research facility will utilize the latest methods to provide research on many life-threatening diseases such as cancer and AIDS. Dover told the press that in light of recent developments, he plans to spend the next few weeks here in Utah to get the project off the ground."

The news channel flashed a segment of the recorded groundbreaking, showing Stephen Dover and Senator Longhurst in suits and hard hats, holding a pair of shovels between them and waving congenially to the gathered crowd.

"I think I'm going to be sick," Sydney grumbled, resisting the urge to throw something at the television screen. "Does everybody really believe this stuff? *Philanthropist* Robert Longhurst. He comes off looking like such a saint, spearheading all these charities and research facilities, but we know better."

With her pent-up energy looking for release, she began to pace in front of Justin. "I just know he's working with Douglas. And I swear, if it's the last thing I do, I'm going to find *something* to nail him with! If that means that I need to go to Salt Lake and help you investigate this day and night until we find some hard evidence that we can use to convict him, that's exactly what I'm going to do."

When her pacing came to a halt and she turned to look at Justin, she saw he was standing there grinning at her.

"What?" she demanded, throwing her arms up in exasperation.

His smile softened into a tender one. "Why don't you?"

"Why don't I what?"

"Come to Salt Lake to help me investigate."

Sydney stared at him in confusion. "For the week?"

"No," he said gently, shaking his head. "Actually, I was thinking a little more long-term."

"How long-term?"

"How does forever sound?"

Sydney's expression softened. "You'd like that, wouldn't you?"

"As a matter of fact, I would," he said, his eyes shining. "Not only do I love the idea of having you with me as we track down Longhurst's involvement in all this and take him down, but I can't tell you how much I love the thought of seeing you every day and working alongside you."

Sydney released a long sigh. "You know as well as I do that I can't stay there forever, Justin."

"Why not?" he asked, his voice pleading. "What's keeping you in San Francisco?"

She let out a humorless laugh. "My job, for one."

"So, get a job at the *Tribune*. Mike already thinks the world of you. You would be an incredible asset to the paper, and he'd be crazy not to hire you."

Sydney looked at him for a long moment, feeling a glimmer of hope. "I have to admit, you make it sound so easy . . ."

"It *is* easy, Syd," he insisted. "Just say the word. Mike would love to have you. And so would I."

Sydney melted at the gentle, loving expression in his eyes. "You would?"

"You know I would. I would love nothing more."

Sydney was surprised when she realized she was actually thinking about what it would be like to be in Salt Lake City with Justin, Mike, and Justin's family. But then the reality of what she was considering hit her.

"I can't just move to Utah." She took a few steps away, as if to distance herself from the irrational thoughts. "I've got obligations to my boss, and to Agnes—"

"But what about your obligation to yourself?" he asked. "What about your obligation to your heart? Doesn't that count for something?"

Emotion welled up inside of her, threatening to confuse her further. "I don't know. I want to. I just . . . I'm confused."

Justin moved forward and gathered her into his arms. "I know. And I know it's unfair of me to even ask you to leave your home. Maybe I should be thinking about leaving *mine* and moving to San Francisco. It just seems like we've reached that point in our relationship where the distance between us has become too great. I want to be with you, Sydney. Every hour of every day. And I know you feel the same way."

"I do feel the same way," she said. "I can't ask you to leave Utah, though. Your friends and family are there, and I know how important they are to you." She shook her head. "No, if anyone is going to move, it should be me. I have the least to leave behind, I guess."

"That's not true. I didn't mean to imply that your life and your friends are any less important than mine. You have Agnes and Jennifer, and they've both been such important people in your life. But moving doesn't mean you have to say good-bye to them forever, you know. Utah isn't *that* far from California."

"I know."

"Besides," he went on, his tone turning teasing as he tried to lighten the moment, "you won't be leaving everybody you know in California behind. Your billionaire wannabe boyfriend is apparently hanging around Utah for a while." He waved his hand at the television, where a reporter was interviewing Dover and Longhurst after they were shown breaking ground on their research facility. "He'll still be nearby if you move to Salt Lake City." Justin paused and made a comical face. "Wait a minute. Should I be worried about that?"

Sydney laughed, grateful to Justin for trying to restore her mood. She stepped closer and slid her arms around his waist. Tipping her face up to his, she declared, "You're the only boyfriend I want." And with that, she stood on her tiptoes and pressed a sweet kiss to Justin's lips.

"Mmm," he murmured against her lips. "Even if I'm not a handsome billionaire?"

She grinned. "Even if."

Justin broke their kiss a moment later and reached up to trail a finger down her cheek. "I'm not saying we have to make a decision right now," he told her. "We can both think about this and talk more about it later. There's no rush, okay?"

She nodded. "Okay."

The loudspeakers announced boarding for Justin's flight, and he glanced at the people moving around them. "I guess I've got to go."

"I guess so," she said, giving him a sad smile.

He reached up and smoothed the frown lines around her mouth with his thumb. "I was wondering . . . I know we've both been spending a lot of money on airfare lately, but Thanksgiving is next week. How would you feel about coming to Salt Lake to spend it with me and my family?"

Sydney was both surprised and touched by his request. "I'd love to."

"That's great!" Justin looked a little relieved. "I was worrying about asking you. I wasn't sure you could handle so much of my family in such a short amount of time."

"Are you kidding? They're wonderful. I love them already."

They walked to the security checkpoint and arrived before Sydney was ready, but it wasn't as hard to say good-bye knowing she'd see him again in less than two weeks.

# CHAPTER 42

The next two days were hectic. With the security footage giving clear evidence to his involvement in the goods stolen from the lockup, Mark Thompson, the Customs official shown on the footage, had been arrested, but Douglas's whereabouts were still unknown. Sydney continued to remain vigilant about taking precautions, as she and Justin had talked about. The feelings of being watched hadn't returned, but still she made sure she was aware of her surroundings at all times.

Then there was the matter of the corruption in the DA's office. Sydney worked tirelessly to gather all her evidence against Griffin in the hopes of contacting the state attorney general's office with enough information to warrant having an investigation launched.

She documented everything she knew, talked to sources, and got written statements from Richardson, Calloway, and many other people within the police department who were willing to go on record with their complaints against the district attorney. She'd even managed to get hold of Hyo Park, who seemed relieved to be out from under the stress of working with Griffin. He gave her a full written statement about everything he'd witnessed and suspected, and he promised to assist the SAG's investigators in any way they needed.

When everything was ready, Sydney contacted the state attorney general's office and presented her evidence. After several lengthy conversations, the investigators at the SAG's office had enough information to launch an investigation against Griffin.

On Wednesday, Sydney presented her editor with the article regarding Griffin coming under investigation by the SAG's office. Carl was ecstatic. His hard-earned words of praise made her glow with pride.

In spite of everything that was going on, the discussion she'd had with Justin at the airport on Monday was never far from her mind. It was true— their relationship had finally reached that point when the distance between them was too great. The decision to move to Utah or stay in San Francisco was going to be one of the hardest she'd ever had to make.

Her editor would hate to lose her, and she had friends in San Francisco who felt like family—Jennifer and Agnes, most notably. But there were people in Salt Lake City that she could also see herself getting close to—Mike, for one, and certainly Justin's family. She'd only been there to see Justin once, but in that short time she'd already felt like she belonged.

So what was she supposed to do? There were pros and cons to each decision. The more she thought about it, the more confused she became.

Knowing this wasn't a decision she could make on her own, Sydney spent a lot of time the next couple of days on her knees. She also had a couple of lengthy conversations with Jennifer. Her friend was upset at the thought of Sydney possibly moving, but she helped her weigh the pros and cons of that decision.

When Sydney got home from work Thursday night, her mind was still occupied with the decision she was trying to make as she stepped out of the elevator. She'd almost reached her apartment door when Agnes appeared beside her in the hall, making her jump.

Sydney gave an embarrassed laugh. "Sorry, Agnes. You startled me."

"Didn't mean to," Agnes said with a repentant smile. "I almost have dinner ready. Why don't you join me and you can tell me what's been going on these last few days?"

The thought of a home-cooked meal and some company was appealing, so Sydney hurried into her apartment to change clothes. She was sitting at her neighbor's table a short time later.

"So tell me about your week," Agnes said over a bubbling dish of lasagna. "You seem so distracted. Did something happen between you and Justin?"

Sydney shook her head. "It's nothing like that. I mean, something *did* happen, but it's not bad. Just hard to decide."

"What happened?"

Sydney released a troubled sigh. "Justin asked me to move to Utah. Our relationship has reached that point where we can't keep going on as we are, living hundreds of miles apart."

Agnes lifted one thin eyebrow. "So what's keeping you here?"

"What do you mean, what's keeping me here?" Sydney's shoulders slumped with dejection at the question. "My job, for one. And you. I don't know how I could leave you."

"Nonsense." Agnes waved a hand at Sydney, dismissing the claim. "I'm just a crotchety old woman who worries too much about you. You should go and be with the man you love."

Sydney felt tears prickle her eyes. "Agnes, I don't think you realize how much you mean to me. Ever since I moved here, you've been like a mother to me. You came into my life when I didn't have anybody. Don't you think that means everything to me? How could I think of leaving without taking you into consideration?"

Agnes's eyes were misty as she reached over to cover Sydney's hand with her own. "You think I don't know that, Sydney, but I do. Like you, I keep a lot of my emotions locked inside. We're two of a kind, you and I. Maybe that's why we've gotten along so well all these years."

Agnes sniffled, then laughed as Sydney sniffled too. She stood and reached for a couple of tissues from the box on a nearby shelf. She handed one to Sydney and kept the other for herself. "Justin is a fine young man," Agnes went on. "You couldn't do any better than him. You should consider yourself lucky to have found him."

"I do," Sydney said truthfully. "And I love every minute I spend with him. But the thought of moving and starting all over somewhere else . . ." She shook her head. "What do you think I should do, Agnes?"

"I can't tell you what you should do, Sydney. The decision must be yours." Agnes leaned back and gave her a sentimental smile. "I do know that I would miss you like crazy if you moved. But I also know that true love doesn't come along every day. I've seen the way Justin looks at you, like he's the luckiest man in the whole world. Some people go their whole lives without finding that special somebody to spend their lives with. It happened to me a long time ago, and I've regretted letting that man go every day of my life."

Sydney's eyes widened. "Agnes! You've never told me about this."

Agnes's eyes took on a sad, faraway look. "John was wonderful. He treated me like a queen. But he was a military man, and I didn't like the idea of his unpredictable lifestyle. He moved around a lot and was often sent overseas during international conflicts. I didn't think I could handle that, not knowing where we would be in ten years, a year, or even six months. Then the day came when he was about to be transferred, and he asked me to marry him and go with him."

"And you said no."

Agnes nodded. "I convinced myself it was for the best, and I let him go." Agnes's eyes dropped to the table, and she traced the pattern in the tablecloth with a wrinkled finger. "It was the hardest thing I've ever done. He'd only been gone a few months when I realized I'd been crazy to let him go. I found out where he was stationed and sent him a letter, telling him how wrong I'd been, and begging him for another chance. I told him that I loved him enough to follow him all the way across the world and back, if that's what it took to be with him."

"And?" Sydney urged.

"He wrote me back a few weeks later, telling me he'd met somebody else and they were getting married." She gave Sydney a sad smile. "That's all water under the bridge now, but my point is, I don't want to see you make the same mistakes I made all those years ago. If you know you've found someone to love, who loves and cherishes you in return, hold onto that and never let go. Don't you dare let trivial things like distance or trials in your relationship keep you apart. If you do, you'll regret it for the rest of your life, just like I have."

Sydney's heart ached for Agnes. What must it have been like to know you had true love and let it go? She realized she didn't want to know.

"Thank you, Agnes," she said, getting up from her chair and going around the table to hug her friend. "I love you."

Agnes hugged her back. "I love you too, dear. And if you do decide to go, just remember to keep in touch, okay? And I'll want an invitation to that temple sealing of yours."

Sydney laughed. "Agnes, Justin hasn't asked me to marry him."

Agnes shook a gnarled finger at her. "When someone asks you to move to a different state for them, they're not just interested in a month-long fling. Justin wants you to work with him, live near him, and be with him. He loves you, and I know you love him. At this point, an engagement ring would only be a formality."

Sydney felt tingles move through her body. Engagement. *Was* it only a formality? Deciding not to think about that right now, she gave Agnes a shrug. "I don't know, Agnes. All I know is that I want to be with him."

"Then go," Agnes said with conviction. "Be with him. He loves you, and you deserve that happiness, sweet girl. You've had too much heartache in your young life."

When Sydney returned to her apartment, she gave Agnes's advice a lot of thought. Agnes was right in that what she and Justin shared was special, something that only came along once in a lifetime. She loved Justin and wanted to be with him more than anything. Suddenly, the decision to alter her life to bring it into step with Justin's didn't seem as hard to make.

As she climbed into bed that night, she realized that for the first time since she'd started considering her options, she was leaning toward the idea of moving. But was that decision the right one?

# CHAPTER 43

When Sydney walked into work the next morning, she felt relieved to have something else to occupy her mind for a while. She had two small stories she needed to finish up, and a few odds and ends to do. She had just sat down at her computer when her phone rang.

"Sydney, it's Paul," the detective said when she answered. "I wanted to give you the news before you heard it from someone else."

Sydney sat up straighter in her chair. "What news?"

"The lockup was raided again last night. Nobody claims to have seen anything, but the shipment of drugs and artifacts is gone."

"Gone!" Sydney's voice rose a few decibels, causing several heads to swivel her way. "Mark Thompson couldn't have had a hand in it this time, since he's in jail. Do you have any clues?"

"Not many," Richardson said, his voice grim. "We're still working on that. But it's of utmost importance that we find out where the drugs and other goods were taken before they get too far away. I was hoping you could think back to the last time this happened and everything you've learned since about this crime ring. Then we could put our heads together to figure this thing out. Getting all my officers up to speed would take too long."

Sydney was always eager to have a hot story to pursue, but this one stirred something even deeper. This one felt personal. "I'll see what I can dig up," she said. "I'll call you as soon as I have anything."

He thanked her and hung up. Absently, Sydney reached for a handful of peanut M&Ms from the jar on her desk and leaned back in her chair. As she munched on the snack, she racked her brain.

From her research, she knew that if Douglas was behind this break-in, as he had been the first one, he'd take the goods and stash them somewhere before shipping them off to a new destination, probably far away. But where would he stash them?

Picking up her phone again, she dialed Justin's number at the *Tribune*. "Justin, it's me," she said when he answered.

"Hey, Syd." The smile in his voice was evident. "It's great to hear from you."

"It's not going to be when you hear what I have to say."

He instantly picked up on her ominous tone. "Uh-oh. What's going on?" When she explained about Detective Richardson's call, he muttered, "Douglas. He has to be behind this. Do you have any ideas where he'd stash the stuff?"

"Not yet. Look, I'm going to spend some time on this today and see what I can find. If you come up with anything brilliant, call me, okay?"

"You bet I will. Keep me posted."

For the next several hours, Sydney pored through her research and contacted sources, but by quitting time she wasn't any closer to finding an answer. She went home and sorted through the research she had there in hopes of finding something. When that also proved futile, she paced and pondered. At midnight, she finally called it quits.

Trying to sleep turned out to be pointless since her mind wouldn't shut off. She had just gotten out of bed and was headed into the kitchen for a late-night snack when it dawned on her.

The old building owned by Longhurst's Sandstone Enterprises. On their research it had claimed to be an art gallery.

She thought back to the time she had driven past the dilapidated building. It would be perfect! It was in a run-down, unfrequented section of the city that would prove isolated and private. A person's comings and goings would go largely unnoticed. What better place to stash stolen goods until Douglas could retrieve them later at his convenience?

A surge of adrenaline shot through her. That had to be it! Her mind started to churn as she considered her next move. She thought about calling Richardson to fill him in on her hunch, but a glance at the clock above her sink reminded her it was after midnight. He was probably home in bed. She didn't want to risk his wrath by having somebody call to wake him up if this turned out to be a wild goose chase.

After some deliberation, she decided that her best course of action was to drive past the warehouse to see if there was any evidence of activity. She'd be safe enough in her car with the doors locked. And if there was any indication that the stolen goods were there, she'd call someone at the station and have them alert Richardson.

She went into her bedroom to change into jeans, a T-shirt, and a hoodie. Then she grabbed her wallet, keys, and cell phone and headed for her car. On her way to the warehouse, she used her cell phone to dial Justin's number. She doubted he'd still be up—it was an hour later in Utah—but she felt compelled to let him know what she was looking into.

Four rings later, his voice mail picked up. "Hey, Justin, it's me," she said. "I think I might have figured out where the stolen goods are. Remember that old building owned by Sandstone Enterprises that was supposedly an art gallery? I think it would be the perfect place. I'm heading there now to check it out. I haven't called Richardson yet because I don't know if there's anything to this hunch, so I thought I'd just drive past and see if there's any activity. Don't worry, I promise to be careful. If there's anything happening, I'll call Richardson. I'll let you know what I find." With that, Sydney ended the call.

Turning her attention to navigating through the dilapidated section of town, she tried to concentrate on remembering how to get to the building. After only a couple of wrong turns and one dead end, she managed to find the right street. As she approached the supposed art gallery, she flicked off her lights and slowed the car to a crawl.

Lights glowed through a small set of windows along the side of the building, but she didn't see any evidence of cars or people around the building or along the street. If it hadn't been for the lights, she would have thought the place was deserted.

She drove on past until she reached the end of the street, then she made a U-turn and drove back, stopping her car near the building and turning off the ignition. She sat in the car for a long minute, trying to decide what to do. Just because the building had some lights on inside didn't mean it was housing drugs and stolen antiquities, did it?

Arguments flew back and forth in her mind as she tried to decide whether or not she should peek in one of the windows. She'd promised Justin she'd be careful, and the memory of last week's sniper attack was still fresh in her mind. On the other hand, she was an investigative reporter. One of the best. Being good at what she did involved some risks. She just had to measure them out in her mind before she took one of them. And in this case, the risk seemed small. Nobody was around, and the side windows of the building were only a dozen yards from her car. If she could just take a quick peek in one of the windows, she would have a better idea of whether or not she was on the right track. If she was, she could justify the call to Richardson in the middle of the night. She could be safely back in her car in one minute, tops.

Giving the area one last glance-over to make sure there wasn't somebody lurking in the shadows, she slipped out of her car. She walked silently to the side of the building, careful to avoid any gravel or debris that would alert somebody to her presence.

The first sound she heard was the low rumble of a truck coming from the back of the building. She crept closer, straining her ears for other signs of activity. That's when she heard it. The sound of men calling out orders. The distinctive beeping of a large piece of equipment dampened by the thick concrete walls of the building.

She tiptoed closer to the nearest window and peeked in. The level of activity inside surprised her. In the large room at least the length and width of a full-size basketball court, she counted at least eight darkly clad men in the cavernous, open space carrying small crates and boxes to the open bay doors at the back. A beeping forklift lifted the larger crates and drove them through the same set of doors. She assumed the men were loading everything into the truck she had heard somewhere behind the building. The crates looked exactly like the ones she had seen in the smuggler's hold on the ship.

Deciding it was time to call in the cavalry, she turned and started to creep back to her car. She hurriedly pulled her cell phone from her pocket and pressed the speed dial button for the police department. A sleepy-sounding clerk answered.

"I need Detective Richardson, *now*," she whispered into the phone.

"He's not on duty tonight, ma'am. Can I help you with something?"

Sydney didn't have time for this. "Yes, you can get me *Richardson*," she said, raising her voice to a rough stage-whisper as she neared her car. "Call him at home. Wake him up. Tell him—and listen very carefully—that this is Sydney Hallam, and that I know where the stolen goods are from the lockup." She gave him the address of the building, praying he'd get it right. Then she added, "You got that? Tell him to hurry. They won't be here long."

She reached her car and opened the driver's side door.

"Could you repeat that address for me, please?" the monotone voice of the officer sounded in her ear.

"Oh, for crying out loud," she hissed into the phone, bristling at this man's refusal to take her seriously.

She slid into the driver's seat and was just about to tell off the good-for-nothing desk clerk when a rough hand clamped down on the back of her neck. Then came the unmistakable pressure of the hard muzzle of a gun being shoved against the back of her skull. Her exclamations died in her throat.

"Get out of the car. *Now*." The low, threatening voice sounded in her ear.

Her body tense, she slowly lifted her hands into the air, her cell phone still clenched in her fingers, and stood up from her seat.

"It's a little late for a pretty little thing like you to be out in a crummy part of town like this, isn't it?" the man snarled. He released his grip on her neck to snatch the cell phone out of her hand. He glanced down at the display. The second he spotted "SFPD" on the screen, he let out a string of curses. Sydney flinched when he threw her phone to the ground. He brought a heavy, booted foot down on it a second later, crushing the screen and keypad. He jabbed her with the muzzle of the gun again as he ordered, "Move!"

Hardly daring to breathe, she did as she was told. The man shoved her roughly ahead of him down the alley and around the back of the building. A large enclosed truck was parked in the loading area, its open doors only feet from the building's bay doors. A man emerged with a stack of boxes to put into the truck and spotted them.

"Who is she?" he barked at Sydney's captor.

"Found her out front. Gotta see what the boss wants me to do with her." With that, he grabbed the hood of Sydney's sweatshirt and jerked her through the open back doors.

Once they were inside, all activity stopped when the crew spotted her. "Somebody get the boss! We have a problem to deal with!" the man with the gun shouted, sending the others scrambling.

Sydney tried to yank her hood free of the man's grip but only succeeding in angering him further. "Where do you think you're going?" he demanded, giving her a rough shove.

The force of his action sent her tumbling to the ground on her hands and knees, and she came face to face with a pair of dark boots that had just come around the corner of a stack of crates.

"Well, well, Ms. Hallam. How nice of you to join us," came a smooth, confident voice from above her.

She looked up and gasped. Standing before her was Phillip Douglas.

# CHAPTER 44

"I found her outside," the man beside her explained. "She had a cell phone and was trying to call the police."

Douglas's cool composure faltered, and anger flickered in his eyes. With a quick movement of his hand, he reached behind him and jerked out the Beretta he had tucked into the waistband of his jeans. Without tearing his gaze from Sydney's, he said to the man beside him, "Go tell everyone to hurry. If the cops are on their way, we need to be packed up and out of here before they arrive."

The man hurried away without protest, and Douglas turned his attention back to Sydney. "Who'd you call on the force?"

Sydney jutted out her jaw and remained silent. Quickly losing patience, he grabbed a handful of her hair and yanked her head back, shoving the muzzle of the gun against the underside of her chin. *"Who did you call!"* he shouted, making her flinch.

She could tell from the twitching muscle in his jaw that he was losing control. Tamping down the fear bubbling up within her, she took a breath and commanded her voice not to waver. "Why? Were you hoping I called one of the cops you and Griffin paid off to look the other way?"

Before she could react, his hand released her hair and flew toward her face, his fist slamming into her jaw. Sydney's head exploded with pain, and lights flashed behind her eyes from the force of the blow. She felt helpless to fight back as Douglas hauled her to her feet, spun her around, and shoved her face-first against the exposed concrete wall.

Her vision began to clear enough that she could see the texture of the wall, but her ears were still ringing when Douglas shoved the gun against her temple.

"You are *not* going to ruin this for me," Douglas hissed in her ear.

He pressed her harder against the wall, and when he did so, she felt something hard and cold jabbing into her thighs. Lowering her gaze, she saw that it was a fire extinguisher on a low, narrow shelf. Realizing it would work as a weapon in a pinch, she decided to stall and wait for her opportunity.

"Ruin this for *you?*" she bit out past the pain in her head. "Or for Longhurst?"

Her bold question caused Douglas to stiffen behind her. Caught off guard, he sounded more surprised than angry. "What do you know about that?"

"I know that you're working for Longhurst," she said, hoping her assumptions were accurate, "and that those crates are the same ones I found on your precious ship. You're not as smart as you think."

The pressure between her shoulder blades eased as Douglas's grip loosened. She twisted slightly against the wall under Douglas's hand so she could look him in the face. Her hands safely out of his line of sight, she tightened her fingers around the neck of the fire extinguisher. "One thing I've always wondered about you," she pressed, "is how a man goes from corporate attorney to henchman. I'm not sure that's an upward career move."

To her surprise, Douglas laughed. "You'd be amazed, sweetheart," he gloated. "Sure, an attorney can make a nice living, but not nearly as nice as this one. Besides, there are perks you couldn't even dream of."

"Really." She hoped to keep him talking until she had the opportunity to make her move. Shifting slightly to get a better grip on the extinguisher near her knees, she quickly surveyed her surroundings. There was a single door near the front of the building that was slightly ajar. And because the crew was loading everything through the back, the front portion of the large room was unoccupied.

Suddenly one of the men shouted, "Douglas, let's go! If she really called the cops, they could be here any minute!"

Douglas nodded but didn't take his eyes off Sydney. "You're gonna wish you'd never come here tonight, princess."

Glancing over his shoulder, Douglas searched among his men, looking for one in particular. He caught the attention of a short, muscular man with a dark goatee. "Hendricks!" he shouted. "Take our guest next door and get rid of her."

Hendricks gave a quick nod and started over. Sydney's heart began to pound. It didn't take a genius to figure out what they intended to do with her.

Seeing that Douglas's attention was momentarily distracted, she decided it was now or never. She tightened her grip on the fire extinguisher and swung it with all her might toward Douglas's head. The metal canister connected with her target, and Douglas went sprawling. His gun skittered under a nearby pallet, and Sydney started to run.

Shouts rang out, and Sydney tried to focus on the door near the front as she sprinted across the cement floor. Her feet barely touched the ground as she ran, praying she could make it before they caught up with her.

She darted around a stack of crates that reached almost to the ceiling, but as she flew around the corner, a sudden flash of movement to her right brought her up short. A forklift was barreling down on her. Too late, she realized she had put herself right in its path.

The startled driver braked and swerved, narrowly missing her. But the abrupt motion was too much for the machine to handle at its current speed, and Sydney watched in horror as the forklift started to overturn beside her. The crates stacked two deep and high on the machine's outstretched metal arms teetered, and in a panic Sydney realized that they were going to come crashing down on top of her.

She turned to run, but it was too late. Crates slammed into the cement floor only feet away from her with an ear-shattering boom, and wood flew everywhere. Reacting instinctively, Sydney hunched over and threw her arms up to try to protect herself. Her efforts proved useless. The heavy lid of one of the crates caught her in the side and spun her around, knocking her to the ground and crashing down onto her outstretched left arm.

She heard the cracking of bone just as the sound of her own scream filled the air. Silence fell in the warehouse for a moment just before chaos broke loose. Men rushed to help their crewman, fearing he might be trapped underneath the overturned forklift.

With the men distracted, Sydney knew this was her chance to run for the door. She raised her head up and shifted, but the movement sent a searing, encompassing pain shooting up her arm. She involuntarily cried out in pain.

The sound of heavy footsteps sounded in her ears, and a moment later the figure of Phillip Douglas hovered over her again. There was a large, bloody gash just in front of his ear from the blow from the fire extinguisher, and anger glinted in his eyes as he stared down at her. He took in her position on the cold cement floor, and his gaze moved slowly along her outstretched arm to where it disappeared beneath the crate's heavy lid. An evil smile spread across his lips.

"That wasn't very smart now, was it?" he said, his voice cold and brusque.

Sydney whimpered as she tried to pull free from the wood crushing her arm, but the motion caught Douglas's attention. Taking two steps closer, he lifted his right leg and stepped down on the wood just above her arm. Her scream of pain reverberated through the room once more.

Just then the sound of sirens punctuated the night air, growing closer and more distinct by the second. One of Douglas's men rushed up to him.

"Come on, Douglas, we gotta get outta here!"

Sydney arched her head and neck against the floor, straining to see the door behind her. She saw a flash of blue and red lights dart across the opening. The cavalry was here.

She turned back to Douglas, and the fury in his eyes was something she knew she would never forget. His jaw clenched, and a muscle jumped in his jaw.

Without even glancing at the man at his side, he stretched out his open hand. "Gun," he ordered.

The man shoved a weapon into his hand, and Douglas's fingers curled around the handle, his gaze never leaving Sydney's. He cocked the gun in an abrupt, angry motion, and the sound reverberated in Sydney's ears.

"You want to know what motto I live by, princess?" he growled. A cold, menacing smile pulled across his face. "Never leave a witness."

Sydney watched in terror as Douglas took aim and his finger tensed on the trigger. She squeezed her eyes shut. It was over.

The sound of the bullet firing shattered the stillness.

Sydney jerked, waiting for the pain. But none came. Her eyes flew open, and she watched in shock as Douglas's face contorted. He staggered and dropped to his knees, then slumped to the floor.

Startled and confused, Sydney jerked her head once more to the door behind her. Detective Richardson stood in the doorway, his gun still pointed at the fallen Douglas.

A sob of relief escaped her lips as members of the SWAT team poured into the building. Detective Richardson ran toward her, shouting for assistance. A moment later the crate lid was carefully lifted off of her, and Richardson was at her side.

"You're okay," he said in gentle tones, putting a reassuring hand on her shoulder.

Sydney bit back another sob and gave Richardson a grateful yet tremulous smile. "Glad to see you got the message. Thanks for coming."

His laughter was a low rumble as he gave her shoulder an affectionate rub. "You're welcome. Now let's take a look at your arm."

\* \* \*

The next two hours passed in a blur. The SWAT team rounded up all the men at the scene and recovered the drugs and other stolen goods— including the entire missing Napoléon collection of antiquities. Detective Richardson had an officer escort Sydney to the hospital, where, thanks to police intervention, she was taken care of quickly. X-rays showed that her arm was broken in two places, and the ER doctor set and cast it.

When she was finished, Sydney realized she had a problem. Her cell phone was destroyed and probably still lying on the ground outside the old building. And her car was there. And her wallet. That meant she didn't even have money for cab fare.

She closed her eyes and groaned. She was going to have to call Agnes.

With a sigh of resignation, she gave Agnes's phone number to a kind nurse, who called and told the elderly woman that Sydney needed a ride home. Twenty minutes later, her haggard-looking and worried neighbor rushed into the ER. The second she spotted Sydney, complete with short-arm cast and bandaged left cheekbone, she stormed over and stood in front of her, her hands on her hips.

"What do you mean, scaring your old neighbor to death like this? Do you have any idea how it feels to get a phone call in the wee hours of the morning from an emergency room nurse, telling me to come down and pick up my young neighbor who has thrown herself in the path of danger yet again?"

"Sorry," Sydney offered, surprised to realize just how much Agnes's motherly tone and fussing meant to her at the moment. "I didn't mean to get myself into trouble."

Agnes let out a melodramatic sigh. "You never do. Come on, let's go."

On the ride home, Sydney explained what had happened and tried to apologize once more. "I'm sorry the call from the ER nurse woke you up. I would have gotten home on my own if I could have."

"Oh, the call from the ER nurse didn't wake me up," Agnes said with a smug smile. "The phone call from Justin an hour earlier did."

# CHAPTER 45

Sydney sat upright in her seat. "Justin called you?"

"Yes, and the poor dear was frantic. How dare you give that nice boy the fright of his life?"

"But . . . how . . . ?" She stared at her neighbor in confusion.

"He apparently got your message a couple of hours ago and was trying to get hold of you. When he couldn't reach you at home or on your cell, he got my number from the directory and called me in a panic. I told him I didn't know anything about where you were, but not long after that the ER called. I called him right away to let him know you were okay and accounted for and that I was leaving to pick you up at the hospital."

Sydney groaned and dropped her head into her good hand. "Oh, great. He's going to be furious with me."

"As well he should be, with you putting yourself in all kinds of danger!" Agnes scolded.

They pulled up to their building a few minutes later, and Agnes put a motherly arm around Sydney as they rode up in the elevator together. When they stopped in front of her door, Sydney fished her keys out of her jeans pocket and let herself in.

The phone was ringing, and Agnes chuckled. "Any bets who that is?"

Sydney grimaced. "Any chance I can get you to talk to him?"

Grinning, Agnes shook her head. "Not on your life. You made your bed, now you have to lie in it." She wiggled her fingers in farewell and retreated out the door.

With a sigh of resignation, Sydney dropped her keys onto the credenza and walked to the phone. "Hello?" she answered halfheartedly.

Justin's voice, anxious and worried, came across the line. "Oh my gosh, Syd . . . You scared the life out of me! What on earth were you thinking, going to that building all by yourself? You should have called the police first instead of rushing over there! And you ended up having to go to the ER? Of all the crazy, impulsive things to do . . ."

She dropped to the couch and rested the heavy cast on her thigh. "I'm okay," she reassured him. "And if you'll stop scolding me for two seconds, I'll tell you what happened."

\* \* \*

It had taken quite a while to convince Justin she was okay, his worry almost tangible through the phone line, and by the time she'd hung up, she was exhausted. She knew she couldn't go to bed yet, though, until she'd covered her bases with Carl.

Knowing she wouldn't feel up to going in to work the next day to work on the story, she left a message on Carl's voice mail briefly explaining what had happened. She then told him she'd type up what she knew about the bust and email it to him before she went to bed so somebody else could follow through with the rest of the story.

She wished she could be the one to write the article, but she knew it would involve a lot of legwork the next day—interviewing the law enforcement involved, gathering quotes, and doing some background work on those arrested. She knew there was no way she would feel up to all that after everything she'd been through. Sadly, she knew she was going to have to sit this one out.

Grateful for the lingering effects of the adrenaline in her system—and the drugs she'd been given in the ER—she managed to peck away at the keyboard with her one good hand, detailing the events that had transpired that evening. By the time she'd finished and sent it to Carl's office email address, she was beyond exhausted.

She barely managed to change her clothes before she fell into bed, asleep almost the instant her head hit the pillow.

\* \* \*

It was afternoon when Sydney finally woke up. She felt rested but very sore. She had a piece of toast to settle her stomach, then took some pain medication. Adjusting to doing everything with a short-arm cast made things difficult, and she wasn't sure she'd ever get used to it.

It didn't take long for the medication to kick in, and when Sydney started feeling better, she called Carl to check in. She was touched by the concern in his voice when he asked how she was doing and if she needed anything. She assured him she was fine, then inquired about the story. He was clearly grateful for her going to all the trouble to type up her notes, and he reassured her that the article was in good hands.

Sydney didn't know whether to feel relieved or disappointed. She knew she shouldn't feel unneeded, but she did. She'd always been in on the action, and this sitting on the sidelines thing wasn't easy to take.

Spending the afternoon lounging around her apartment gave her a lot of time to think, and inevitably her thoughts drifted back to the decision she still had to make regarding Justin. Did she stay in San Francisco? Or did she move to Utah?

One of the things that had been holding her back—the investigation— might not be as big of an issue any longer. Now that Douglas was out of the picture and over a dozen of his men were in custody, it was likely things were coming to a head. The chances one of them knew something and would use that information to plea bargain was high. She could follow through with that information from Utah. Besides, if this all came back to Longhurst, it was likely they could continue the investigation into his involvement in Utah where he actually lived and often worked.

The more she thought about it, and the more she replayed her conversation with Agnes in her mind, she realized Agnes was right. The love she and Justin shared was special, something that didn't come along very often. All those years she'd been searching—for something, for someone. And now that she'd found Justin, her life felt complete. Moving to be near him would be worth the sacrifice.

But there were other things to consider. She'd need a job in Utah. Had Mike been serious about hiring her? She knew there was no sense in considering the move until she knew for sure if she would have a job.

Her stomach started to flutter with nervous anticipation as she realized her next step would be calling Mike. Suddenly this all felt real. Would he hire her?

It was in that moment that she realized just how much she wanted him to. Did that mean she was supposed to move?

Getting down on her knees for what felt like the hundredth time in the last several days, she poured out her heart to her Heavenly Father, telling him that it felt right to move, but asking if that was the right decision. Almost immediately, a warmth settled over her, easing the turmoil in her heart and bringing tears to her eyes. She had her answer. She was supposed to move to Utah.

When she got to her feet, she knew what she had to do next. She needed to call Mike at the *Tribune* and inquire about the possibility of a job. Before she could second-guess herself, she got the number and dialed.

As she waited for the *Tribune* receptionist to transfer her call, she was a bundle of nerves. What if the *Tribune* didn't have any job openings? What if Mike required her to send in an application and go through a waiting and interviewing process like any other applicant? She didn't think she could bear the length of time that would entail.

In the end, she shouldn't have worried. Mike was thrilled to hear why she was calling and immediately made her a job offer with reasonable salary, benefits, and hours. When she accepted the terms, Mike hired her on the spot.

Now that getting a job at the *Tribune* was no longer an issue, it made everything feel more real. She and Justin were going to be in the same city, working together on a daily basis. She was excited to think about what her future held.

But her next task was one of the hardest things she'd ever done. She invited Agnes and Jennifer over for dinner—she even cooked the chicken, which was no easy task with one arm in a cast—to tell them about Mike's job offer. When she announced that she had decided to move, everybody's eyes grew misty—including hers. Agnes and Jennifer were both upset that she was leaving, but they were happy for her as well. Sydney knew she would miss them terribly.

Her emotions swung wildly from one extreme to the other that weekend, from excitement at the prospect of spending every day with Justin, to sadness at the thought of leaving Agnes, Jennifer, and all she knew. It was hard to keep her emotions in check during her daily conversations with Justin. He seemed to sense something was going on, but thankfully he didn't push.

She didn't tell Justin about her job offer—Mike had promised not to say anything, either—or her decision to move because she wanted to surprise him with the news when she flew in to spend Thanksgiving with him and his family in a few days.

As she stepped into the newsroom Monday morning, however, her emotions swung to the other extreme, and her heart felt heavy as she headed for Carl's office. Now that she knew she had a job waiting for her in Salt Lake City, she had no reason not to give her notice. It was something she'd been dreading since making the decision to move.

She knocked on Carl's half-open office door. When she heard him call for her to come in, she stepped inside. He looked up from his paperwork and gave her a smile. "You're back. How are you feeling?"

They exchanged small talk, and then Sydney took a deep breath and explained what she was doing. Carl looked both shocked and saddened.

"I'm happy for you, Sydney, but I have to say, I hate to see you go. You've always livened up this newsroom. I wish I had even one other reporter with your passion and intensity."

"Yeah, well, look where that sometimes gets me." Sydney held up her arm cast.

Carl chuckled. "Even so, you've been a pleasure to work with. You keep in touch, you hear?"

"I will," she told him, feeling a lump rising in her throat. "Thanks for believing in me all these years, Chief."

"It's hard *not* to believe in you. You're the best there is." Carl stood up and reached out to give her a warm handshake. "We'll miss you around here, but I wish you the best."

As Sydney left her editor's office, she felt a little teary eyed, but she was excited as well. She was on her way back to her desk when Jennifer fell into step beside her.

"Hi," Jennifer said, giving her a sympathetic look when she noticed the tears in Sydney's eyes. "I noticed you were in Carl's office. Were you giving your notice?"

She nodded. "As much as Carl yells at me, I'm going to miss him."

"He only acts all tough around you because he's trying to push you. He knows you're the best and expects great things from you."

Sydney stopped and turned to observe her friend. Whenever she'd needed a friend, Jennifer had always been there with a bright smile or attentive ear. She was going to miss everything about Jennifer—the bright, trendy fashions she dressed herself in; the butterfly something-or-other she always wore; the short, spiky, coppery-brown hair that made her look like a pixie. She doubted she'd ever have another friend like her.

She leaned in to give Jennifer a long hug. "Salt Lake City isn't all that far away, you know," she said, her voice wobbly with emotion. "We can still visit—and email and text."

"I know. It just won't be the same," Jennifer said sadly.

Sydney knew she was right.

# CHAPTER 46

Justin stood at the fax machine in the *Tribune* newsroom, waiting for the last of the information Sydney had sent him to print out. It had been several days since Sydney's run-in with Phillip Douglas, and they'd been dealing with the aftermath ever since. Richardson had shared privileged information with Sydney regarding Douglas's ever-growing list of crimes, and together Sydney and Justin hoped the leads would help them trace this all back to Longhurst and whoever else was running this crime ring. That was the information she was faxing him now.

Absently, he lifted his hand to the back of his neck and rubbed the tense muscles there, his fingers brushing against the small bandage at the base of his skull. The headache he'd had that morning had finally subsided, thanks to his pain medication, but the dull, persistent ache continued to remind him of that night at the warehouse. The stitches had finally come out, and his doctor had said the wound was healing nicely. Other than being tired, he was fine. His parents—not so much.

They hadn't handled the news well at all that their son had been shot, but once he'd managed to reassure them that the injury hadn't even needed surgery and that he was on the mend, they'd calmed down. His other prediction about his parents had also proven correct—he hadn't had to do a thing since he'd arrived home. Meals had been brought in by various family members, his mom had seen to any cleaning his townhouse had needed, and the Sunday School president had arranged for a substitute for his class for a couple of weeks.

Everything had been taken care of except the one thing that mattered to him most—Sydney. He was sure Agnes was mothering her in her usual fashion, but he wanted that to be *his* job. *He* wanted to take care of her. And it was hard, talking to her on the phone and hearing how exhausted she sounded. There wasn't anything he could do about it from hundreds of miles away, and he hated that. But he would be picking Sydney up at the airport tonight, and that made everything feel better. He could see for himself that she was indeed alive and well after her encounter with Phillip Douglas, and he planned to spend the entire Thanksgiving holiday seeing to it she was taken care of.

The fax machine printed out the last page, and Justin added it to the small stack on the counter beside it.

"You feeling okay?"

Justin looked up to see Brad approaching, a concerned expression on his face. Justin gave him a reassuring smile. "I'm fine. Just tired."

"And worrying about Sydney, no doubt." Brad lifted one eyebrow in silent question.

Justin had told his friend about everything that had happened, and Brad had done a lot to help him this week. "Yes, and worrying about Sydney," Justin admitted with a sigh. "She's been through so much, but she won't slow down. She didn't even take a day off work. She was right back at it on Monday, running around like a crazy person, trying to connect the dots." He held up the small stack of papers he'd just gotten off the fax machine. "This is her latest attempt."

"Hmm." Brad's tone was noncommittal.

Justin shook his head, his mouth tensing into a firm line. "She's too much of a handful for anybody there to stop her from working herself into the ground. I just wish I was there, you know?"

"So you could slow her down?" Brad gave him a skeptical look. "Are you suggesting she'd slow down for *you*?"

Justin gave a reluctant chuckle. "Yeah, you're right. But at least I could try."

Brad gave him a sympathetic look that told him he understood. He clasped a friendly hand on Justin's shoulder. "I know. Just don't overdo things yourself, okay?"

"I won't." Justin gave Brad a grateful smile, then picked up the faxed pages and headed back to work.

It was almost quitting time. That meant he could go home and relax for a while before going to pick up Sydney from the airport. She had seemed cheerful enough in her texts when she'd told him she was leaving for the airport, then again when she was through security and waiting for her departure. And she'd repeatedly reassured him during their phone calls over the past few days that she was fine, but even so, he doubted he'd be able to stop worrying about her until he saw that for himself.

"Hey, Justin, there's a call for you." The *Tribune*'s newest intern walked up to him and gestured over his shoulder in the direction of Justin's desk. "I had it transferred to your phone."

"Thanks, Tyler," Justin called after the young intern as he hurried off to his next task.

Justin gathered up his papers and headed back to his desk. Easing into his chair, he picked up the phone. "Micklesen."

A guy's raspy voice, indicating years of smoking, came across the line. "Yeah, I have some information for you on a story you've been investigating."

That caught Justin's attention. There was nothing better than a willing source. He leaned forward, picked up a pen, and flipped open his notebook. "I'd love to have it. Which story are you talking about?"

"Robert Longhurst."

Justin's heart rate accelerated. "What information do you have? And can I get your name?"

"The name's Chaz. And I don't want to give any information over the phone," came the gravelly voice. "Can we meet?"

Glancing at his watch, Justin hoped the man's request wouldn't interfere with picking Sydney up from the airport. "What time and where?"

"Tomorrow morning?" Chaz sounded both hesitant and hopeful.

Justin breathed a sigh of relief. That would work. Better yet, Sydney would be here to go with him. "No problem," he said. "Where?"

"I work the early shift at the Highway Café, but I can slip away for a few minutes at seven. I'll meet you near the dumpster at the back of the building."

Justin knew where the Highway Café was. It was in a more run-down part of the city, but it was safe enough. "I'll be there. I've been working with a partner on this and I'd like to bring her along, if that's okay."

"Fine. But don't be late. My break's only ten minutes."

Sensing the man was about to hang up, Justin quickly asked, "How will I know who you are?"

"I'll be wearing a blue shirt and dark jacket. Besides, I'll be the only one hanging around by the dumpster." With that, the man hung up.

Justin replaced the phone in its cradle, excitement and anticipation growing inside him. He and Sydney were so close. All they needed was one solid piece of evidence to bring Longhurst down. Maybe this man, this source, would be the one to do it.

The rest of the evening sped by, and soon he was standing in the baggage claim area at the airport, eagerly searching the faces of the passengers from Sydney's flight who were coming down the escalator to retrieve their luggage.

Finally he spotted her. The second she reached the bottom, he fought his way through the crowd of people and descended upon her in a cloud of relief. He drew her into a crushing hug, savoring the feeling of having her in his arms once more.

"Sydney," he murmured, pressing a gentle kiss into her hair. "I know you told me you were okay, but I couldn't stop worrying until I saw that for myself."

She laughed and slid her arms around his waist. "It's so good to see you, too."

He closed his eyes briefly, breathing in deeply the smell of her shampoo and the scents that were just her. "For a while there, I thought I'd lost you."

She shook her head, and when he released her, she stepped back, smiling and holding her arms out for inspection. "You didn't, and I'm fine. See?"

His scrutinizing gaze took in the short arm cast, then the yellowish, fading bruise along her jaw. "I can't believe what he did to you," he muttered as he lifted a hand to gingerly touch the coloring near her cheek.

"It doesn't matter anymore," she said. "He's dead, so he won't be hurting anybody ever again. Now can we get my luggage and get out of here? I've got something much better to talk to you about." A mysterious smile tugged at the corners of her lips, and Justin relaxed.

"That's right. You told me you had good news." Justin fell into step beside her, his arm draped around her shoulders as they walked. "So, are you going to fill me in?"

"Nope," she teased, her eyes dancing with excitement. "Wait until we get to your place."

Realizing that he wasn't going to be able to drag any information out of her, he changed the subject. "Speaking of news," he began. "You won't believe the phone call I got this afternoon." He went on to tell her about it, and her eyes were wide with anticipation when he finished.

"I can't wait to hear what information he has for us. We're just so close," she said, echoing his thoughts. "Let's hope he's a reliable source."

Their conversation became light and easy for the remainder of the drive to Justin's house, and Justin reveled in the feeling of simply being with her again. He kept up a round of playful protests on the way back to his house about the secret she was harboring, making her laugh. When they neared a small grocery store not far from Justin's townhouse, she instructed Justin to pull into the parking lot, then told him to wait in the car while she ran in.

"Does this have anything to do with your surprise?" he asked, confused.

"Maybe," she responded with a cryptic smile. She got out of the car and shut her door without further explanation. She was back a few minutes later, the contents of her shopping trip concealed in a brown paper grocery bag.

When they arrived at his townhouse, Justin kept trying to peek inside the bag as he unlocked the front door to let them in, making Sydney giggle. He followed her into the kitchen, where she set the bag down on the counter and pulled out the two items.

He grinned at the carton of ice cream and bottle of chocolate syrup. "What's this?"

"This," she explained with a broad grin, "is part of my surprise. It's what I do when I have something to celebrate."

"You eat chocolate ice cream?" He laughed and shook his head. "Why doesn't that surprise me?"

She fished two spoons out of the drawer and pointed them at him. "Be nice, or you're not getting any."

"Okay, I'll stop." He opened another drawer and pulled out the ice cream scoop for her. "What are we celebrating?"

Sydney opened the carton and licked a drop of ice cream from her finger. With a mischievous smile, she asked, "Do you really want to know?"

"Sydney," he said with a playful growl. "You're making me crazy. Yes, I want to know. Are you going to tell me or not?" He reached for the scoop when he saw she was struggling at the task with one arm in a cast. "How many scoops?"

"Two, please."

He put the scoops in her bowl and put the same amount in his. "So?" he asked, picking up his bowl of ice cream and taking a bite.

She flashed him another teasing smile. "Don't you want to guess?"

"Guess. Um, okay." He released a slow breath and tipped his head back to study the ceiling as he pretended to ponder. "You managed to take down this whole crime ring we're investigating."

"I wish," she grumbled, spooning another bite of her ice cream into her mouth.

"You've discovered a cure for the common cold?"

Sydney glared at him. "You're not even trying!"

He laughed. She was clearly enjoying torturing him and was having a hard time stifling her own laughter. "Sydney, I'm awful at this game!" he said in surrender. "Just tell me what's going on."

Finally, she waved her spoon in the air in concession. "Okay, I'll tell you." She set her spoon and bowl down on the table and fumbled in the pocket of her jeans with her good hand. A moment later, she pulled out a single key on a nondescript keychain and tossed it to him.

He looked at it in confusion. "What's this?"

"It's the key to the storage unit in my apartment's parking garage. I thought you might like a little project."

Justin's brow furrowed. "You want me to clean out your storage unit?"

She nodded. "Permanently."

Justin stared at her in confusion for a long moment. Then his eyes widened and he stared at her in disbelief. "Sydney, are you saying . . . ?"

She nodded, and the smile she'd been struggling to contain finally spread across her face. "I've moving to Salt Lake City."

# CHAPTER 47

Justin's mouth fell open and he stood speechless for a long moment. Then he let out a whoop of joy and rushed over to her, sweeping her into his arms and twirling her around, kissing her over and over again. His tears of joy mingled with hers as he held her.

"Sydney, you're really coming?" he asked when he set her down. "But what about your job? What about your apartment?"

"There's a waiting list a mile long for the apartments in my building. Getting out of my lease won't be a problem. As far as my job goes . . ." Her eyes sparkled as she shared her next piece of news. "I called Mike last week, and he offered me a job. I'm your new partner on the city beat."

Justin stared at her, stunned. "I can't believe it," he finally managed. "You arranged this without me even knowing? And Mike knew about this and didn't say a word?"

"I made him promise not to. I wanted it to be a surprise."

"Well, it is." He shook his head again in disbelief. "That would explain the goofy grin Mike's had on his face every day this week whenever we've talked. That man! I'm going to have to get him back for this. Better yet, I should send him the best Christmas present ever."

Sydney's laughter was carefree and happy. "I'll go in on it with you. He's awesome. He even gave me some suggestions for apartment complexes to check out. I called and set up appointments to look at some while I'm in town. Would you come with me? You know the city better than I do, and I'm not sure I can find my way around yet."

"I'd love to," he said, unable to stop smiling. "When do you start work here?"

"Three weeks." A tinge of worry crept across her face. "It seems so fast. I'm not sure I can get everything done in time."

"Don't worry, we'll get it done. I'll take a few days off and fly down to help you. We could rent a U-Haul for your things, and I'll drive back up here with you."

Sydney nodded, looking thoughtful. "That could work. I just hope we can get one on such short notice. I don't know if they're swamped for the holidays or not."

Justin's eyes brightened. "That's right! This means you'll be here for Christmas!" At the realization, he swept her into his arms again, hugging her so tightly she could hardly breathe. When he let her go, he kissed her long and tenderly. "I promise we'll work out all the details," he said. "Everything's going to fall into place. You'll see. I'm just so happy that we're going to be together."

Sydney sighed contentedly and snuggled deeper into his arms. "Me too," she admitted, closing her eyes. "Me too."

\* \* \*

The next morning, Justin picked up Sydney at six-thirty so they'd have plenty of time to drive across town to the Highway Café. He could tell by her constant stream of chatter that she was as excited about meeting this source as he was.

When they pulled into the parking lot and turned off the car, Justin noticed a thin, haggard-looking man with brown shaggy hair and a day-old growth of beard leaning up against the wall near the back of the building. He wore a worn, dark leather jacket over a dingy blue, grease-stained shirt bearing a small Highway Café logo. There were bags under his eyes, indicating it had been a while since he'd had a good night's sleep, and worry lines creased his face, making him appear much older than the mid-thirties Justin judged him to be.

As Justin and Sydney crossed the parking lot, the man pushed off from his place at the wall and moved toward them, his steps wary. Justin suspected one wrong move or word from him could send the guy running.

"Chaz?" he asked when they stopped a couple of feet from each other.

The man nodded. "Yeah." He glanced briefly at Sydney standing silent beside him, then looked apprehensively at their surroundings. When no threat appeared to lurk in the emptiness of the parking lot and the lack of activity on the street, the look in his eye eased.

"Look," he began, shoving his fists deep into the pockets of his jacket and hunching his shoulders against the wind. "I've never been a snitch, but my situation gives me little choice. I've been in hiding the last few months, and I can't keep living like this. I hate looking over my shoulder every time I step out of my place."

"Who are you afraid of?" Sydney asked.

"Longhurst and his associates. I've been in on their operation for years, overseeing the arrival and distribution of shipments from the Utah warehouses. Everything ran like clockwork until Longhurst discovered how profitable dealing in black market ancient artifacts could be. Longhurst hooked up with his man, Carlos Rojas, in Colombia two years ago and started funding various archaeological digs in Central and South America through a South American rebel group posing as a charity organization."

"Let me guess," Justin interjected. "The Colombian New Council."

Chaz's eyebrows crept up his forehead in surprise. "How'd you know?"

Justin exchanged a glance with Sydney. "Because we've done a lot of research into all this. What did the group have to do with the artifacts?"

"They're basically a large, extended group of thugs for hire. They have men who specialize in all areas—drug running, high-tech thefts, smuggling, black marketeering . . . you name it, these men do it. In this particular case, their connections to the Colombian government safeguard Longhurst's artifact smuggling operation. The senator's donations pay off the officials to look the other way. Then his shipping man takes charge and sees his drugs and goods safely to a boat and then to San Francisco, where they're stored before being shipped to Longhurst's warehouses here in Utah to be delivered to their buyers."

"The shipping man must have been Phillip Douglas," Sydney drawled, her voice laced with disdain. At Chaz's questioning look, she lifted her arm cast. "Let's just say we've met."

"You're that reporter from the *San Francisco Chronicle*." A satisfied smile twisted the corners of Chaz's lips. "The one he tried to kill in his storage building."

Sydney dropped her arm back to her side. "Apparently I'm harder to kill than he expected."

"We both are," Justin ground out. "Longhurst hired a hit man to get rid of us in San Francisco, but that didn't work, either. We want nothing more than to see Longhurst behind bars."

Chaz's expression sobered and his voice grew determined. "That makes three of us. After what happened with my wife, revenge is all I've been able to think about. That's why I'm talking to you."

"What happened to your wife?" Justin asked.

Chaz clenched his teeth together and a tense muscle jumped in his jaw. "They killed her."

"Who did?"

"Don't know who exactly did the deed, but it was one of Longhurst's men. Longhurst ordered the hit. Tried to make it look like an accident. She was driving home one night and she went off the road. The police said the brakes were shot and that's why she'd lost control, but I'd just had the brakes done the week before. They were in perfect working order. It was a warning, plain and simple."

"A warning about what?"

Chaz cleared his throat, then swallowed, working to contain the emotion showing plainly on his face. "Like I said, I'd worked for Longhurst for a few years and everything ran like clockwork until he started smuggling and shipping the artifacts. We knew he was making money hand over fist, what with the addition of the artifacts sales added to our regular smuggling and black market operations. Quite often me and my men would work double shifts without extra compensation, and my crew started feeling disgruntled. We told Longhurst's man that we wanted a bigger cut, but he just laughed us off. So the crew and I took matters into our own hands."

"Wait a minute," Justin cut in, sudden realization flooding through him. "The string of warehouse break-ins I was investigating this summer . . ."

"Me and my crew." Chaz nodded, his expression grim.

"One of the security guards I interviewed said he thought he'd recognized one of the men in the security footage," Justin said. "I asked him if I could show him the footage from the other break-ins to see if he recognized anyone from those, but when I tried to get in touch with him a week later, he was gone. Nobody knew where."

"Must have been Frank." Chaz scrubbed a hand across his face. "Poor guy never knew what he was getting into. He was as honest as the day was long, and as soon as he learned that the goods in the warehouses he was watching were hot, he got scared and hightailed it out of there. I was gone by that point, so I don't know where he went. My wife had been killed a week earlier as an example of what happened when you messed with Longhurst and his associates. After that, the other guys in my crew backed off. They got the message. They were too scared to complain or protest.

"The one thing Longhurst hadn't counted on was me running," Chaz went on. "They knew I was a threat because of everything I know. I've been on the run ever since, working at dives like this," he jammed his thumb over his shoulder at the Highway Café behind him, "and moving from one hole-in-the-wall apartment to another. I'm tired of it. I haven't lived a perfect life.

Far from it. But I want to move on, do something aboveboard for once in my life. I've seen firsthand what working for men like this can do to someone, and I don't want anything else to do with it. That's why I'm talking to you. I'm tired of constantly looking over my shoulder and living in fear."

Justin nodded. He understood what the man meant about being afraid of where the next danger was going to come from. He knew Sydney understood too.

"We'd love to help, and take down Longhurst in the process," Sydney spoke up, her tone sympathetic. "But we need something solid to nail him with. Can you help us with that?"

"As a matter of fact I can." Chaz glanced around the parking lot once more, then pulled a crumpled piece of paper out of his jacket pocket and handed it to Sydney. "From what I heard, you had your run-in with Douglas shortly after the bigger portion of the drugs left the San Francisco storage building. This is a list of the dealers the shipment is going to, and when and where the deal's going down."

Sydney's eyes widened as she read the scribbling on the paper in her hand. "Tomorrow night? The deal's going down the night of Thanksgiving?"

Chaz shrugged. "When better? Everybody's focusing on the holiday, and these guys are hoping to fly under the radar. With the heat coming from the sting operation in San Francisco, the deal got delayed. But now that everything's back on track, the drugs, as well as several new artifacts being shipped here by Rojas's men, are on their way here now. But you'll have to move fast. Longhurst has stepped up his timetable and wants everything handled quickly and quietly."

Justin looked at Sydney, and a current of excited energy passed between them. He turned back to Chaz. "How'd you learn this information?"

"I still have a couple of friends on the inside, but they're scared. They know what these guys are capable of. Longhurst proved it with what he did to my wife."

"You realize that I'm going to have to go to the authorities with this information," Justin said. "My partner and I have been investigating Longhurst for months, and this information could finally put him behind bars."

Chaz nodded. "I know. That's why I'm telling you. I'm tired of being afraid."

"But why didn't you just go to the authorities with this yourself?" Sydney asked, curious.

Chaz's expression turned grim once more. "I was involved, remember? If I go to the police, they're going to arrest me on the spot."

"But what about making a deal?" Justin said. "You could plea bargain. You may end up only spending a short time in jail."

Chaz shoved his hands into his pockets and scuffed at the loose gravel of the parking lot with the toe of his shoe as he contemplated that. "Yeah, maybe. And then I'd have served my time and I could finally put all this behind me. But in the meantime . . ." He nodded down at the paper Sydney still clenched in her hand.

"We'll take care of it," Justin reassured him. "I have a friend at the DEA's office. I'll call him, and we'll make sure we don't let this opportunity slip away." Then, understanding just how much this man had stuck his neck out to get this information to them, Justin said, "Thank you. Really."

Chaz seemed uncomfortable with the thanks, shrugging as he said, "Just see to it that Longhurst is put away for good. That's all I ask." Then he nodded at them and turned and walked back inside the building.

As soon as they were alone again in the parking lot, Sydney waved the paper Chaz had given her in the air. "Can you believe this? This could be the piece of evidence that we've been looking for that finally puts the nail in Longhurst's coffin!"

"Let's not get too excited yet," Justin cautioned. "First we need to check out Chaz, see if we can verify the things he told us. And we need to talk to my friend Agent Ramus at the DEA's office. The authorities need to hear this and get involved."

"Then what are we waiting for?" Sydney looked at him impatiently. "Let's go!"

# CHAPTER 48

"We only need five minutes," Sydney pleaded.

The receptionist manning the DEA office's front desk shook her head. "I'm sorry, but Agent Ramus is about to head into a meeting."

"Please." Justin stepped in. "It's urgent. We're investigative reporters, and we just learned of a big drug deal going down tomorrow night." When the receptionist's eyes widened, Justin rushed on. "And we don't want to give these details to anybody else. I've talked with Agent Ramus about our investigation before, so we won't have to waste time bringing somebody else up to speed."

The receptionist paused. A moment later, she reached for the phone and pressed the intercom button.

Justin and Sydney released collective breaths and exchanged relieved smiles when the receptionist stood and gestured down the hallway to her left. "This way," she said.

Moments later they were shown into Agent Ramus's office. Ramus looked up from his paperwork through his glasses and motioned them to the two chairs in front of his desk. He smiled at Justin and then Sydney as Justin introduced them to each other.

"Now what's this urgent matter?" Ramus asked, tipping back in his chair and pushing his glasses farther up the bridge of his nose with a slender finger.

Knowing the man was in a hurry, Justin filled him in on what he and Sydney had learned. They also showed him the information Chaz had given them.

Agent Ramus took the paper and studied it, his brows furrowing as he read. When he was done, he looked back up at them. "And this guy Chaz . . . you don't think he's feeding you false information?"

Justin shook his head. "I don't think so. What would he stand to gain? But just in case, I called one of my researchers right after meeting with Chaz and had his story checked out. Everything fits, down to the details of his wife's death. I think he's telling us the truth. And if we don't act now, we're going to miss our opportunity to get these guys once and for all."

Agent Ramus studied the crumpled piece of paper in his hand for another moment, then picked up his phone. "Tell the director I need to see him right away," he told the person on the other end. "And cancel my meeting."

* * *

"I still wish we could be there," Sydney said as she and Justin left the DEA's office some three hours later.

Justin unlocked his car and held her door open for her to climb in. "I know you do, but it's just not possible, so get it out of your mind. It's a sting operation, Syd. That means no reporters allowed."

"I know, I know." Sydney got in the car and buckled her seat belt while Justin went around and got in the driver's side. As soon as he was settled behind the wheel, she went on. "But why can't we wait outside in the car, like a block away?"

Justin looked over at her and lifted one sandy eyebrow. "You *have* watched movies and TV, right? Read the news? You know what can happen in a sting operation, especially one with drugs involved. Drug dealers are armed. Agent Ramus's SWAT team will be armed. It's a very real possibility there will be gunfire. We're not going anywhere near that warehouse."

"But then how will we know when everything is said and done?" she protested. "Ramus said that in exchange for the information, he'd give us the exclusive before the DEA issues the press release. We'll be the first reporters with the story—unless we're not first on the scene."

"Syd, Ramus said that if the sting operation does indeed go down, their agency won't even issue a press release until late tomorrow morning, and even then it will be sketchy with details, at best," he said, distracted, as he turned to watch behind him while backing out of their parking space. "If we get there around dawn, we'll still get the exclusive, and it won't be dangerous." When he reached to put the car in drive, he shot her a look while the corners of his lips twitched in amusement. "Man, you're like a dog with a bone. You just can't let it go."

"And that's a bad thing?" she challenged, a half smile playing across her face. "You don't get where I am in this business by letting things go."

"Well, I'm afraid you're going to have to this time." Justin placed a hand on her knee and gave it an affectionate squeeze before returning his hand to the steering wheel. "We're not getting in their way."

"I know. And I didn't mean we should be. I understand that it's dangerous, and after all we've been through these past few weeks, I don't want to court danger. I just want us to be the ones to break the story."

"We will be," Justin reassured her. "We'll go at dawn."

\* \* \*

The insistent ringing of Justin's phone on the nightstand dragged him out of a deep sleep. Cracking one eyelid, he glanced at the luminescent red numbers on his alarm clock. Four a.m. Who could possibly be calling at this hour?

With a groan of protest, he rolled over and fumbled for the cell phone on his nightstand. Clenching the offending piece of technology in his hand, he silenced the ring tone by pressing the TALK button. He took a moment to relish the silence before putting the phone to his ear.

"Hullo?" he mumbled.

"Justin, it's me. You weren't still sleeping, were you?"

The familiarity of the voice ripped away at the cobwebs of sleep criss-crossing his mind. He pushed himself up on one elbow. "Sydney? Is that you?"

"Who else would be calling you at four in the morning?"

He pushed a hand through his rumpled hair. "Why would *you* call me at four in the morning?"

"It's dawn."

Her voice was so matter-of-fact that he was certain he must know what that meant. But for the life of him he didn't.

"Yeah, in New York," he agreed halfheartedly. "What's going on?"

"The sting operation!" Her impatient exclamation was so loud that he grimaced and jerked the phone away from his ear. After a moment, he cautiously put the phone back to his ear. "Don't you remember?" she went on. "It's dawn! Wake up, let's go!"

Justin groaned and let himself fall back onto his pillow. She couldn't possibly be serious. "Syd, four o'clock is not dawn. There's still a good two or three hours of sleep before dawn."

"Yeah, well, obviously your idea of dawn and mine aren't the same," she informed him, her tone insistent. "Get dressed. If you're not over here in fifteen minutes, I'm going to call a cab and go to the warehouse by myself."

Justin groaned again. Unfortunately, he knew she meant it. "I'll get dressed," he mumbled into the phone, then hung up.

He reached over to flip on the lamp on his nightstand, cringing against the sudden brightness. When he felt able, he slid his legs over the side of the bed and got to his feet.

*Four o'clock in the morning the day after Thanksgiving,* he thought, disgruntled, as he reached for his clothes. *The woman gives a whole new meaning to the word* tenacious. *This had better be worth it.*

Half an hour later, Justin and Sydney were driving up to the chain-link gates separating the warehouse's parking lot from the street. The pre-dawn stillness had been shattered by a level of activity that surprised even Justin. The parking lot was lit up by the red and blue lights sitting atop more than a dozen police cars. Men and women—some in police uniforms, others in plain clothes—swarmed the place. The warehouse lights were on and spilled out through the myriad of open doors.

A uniformed officer stepped in front of Justin's car as they pulled up to the gates. He held up a hand and shook his head as he moved to the driver's side window. Justin rolled it down.

"You can't stop here," the officer said. "Police business only."

"Agent Ramus of the DEA is expecting us," Justin told him.

The man pulled out his radio to confirm this, then waved them through the gate. Justin steered through the parked vehicles as they approached the warehouse.

"Will you calm down?" Justin said, the slightest of smiles playing at the corners of his mouth as Sydney fidgeted in the passenger seat just as she'd done the entire drive there. "You're making *me* nervous."

"Sorry," she offered, sounding only half sincere, leaning forward to try to make out the faces of the agents in the darkness. A moment later she spotted one she recognized. "There's Ramus."

Justin looked to see where she was pointing and saw his colleague emerging from the warehouse's front loading-bay doors. They stopped the car and got out, meeting Ramus a few yards from the building.

"So?" Sydney asked breathlessly. "What happened?"

Agent Ramus gave them a tired smile. "Your informant was right. Everything was as he'd said it would be. We seized almost a thousand packages of heroin and cocaine and arrested sixteen people. We suspect we'll arrest dozens more by the time we're done with our investigation. Two of the men we arrested were ones we'd been after for a long time, so I suppose an exclusive is the least we can do to thank you."

Sydney's face creased into a broad smile. "Sounds fair to me. What about Longhurst?"

Ramus's expression grew taut. "We're still searching the warehouse and going through records, but so far we haven't found anything to tie him to the drugs other than the fact that he owns the warehouse."

"There's got to be something to prove his involvement," Justin persisted, a feeling of dread rising within him. "He can't possibly walk away from all this."

A new voice entered into the conversation. "He's not going to."

# CHAPTER 49

Justin and Sydney turned to see the silhouette of a man approaching. Even though Justin was unable to see the man's features in the darkness, something about his stocky build, broad shoulders, and confident swagger was familiar to him. When the man was close enough for Justin to make out his face, Justin broke out in a smile. "Uncle Kevin. I didn't expect to see you here."

"Hey, Justin." Kevin gave him an affectionate thump on his shoulder, his lean face creasing into a smile that reached a set of warm brown eyes. He then looked at Sydney. "This must be the woman I've been hearing so much about from your dad."

"Yes, it is." Justin slipped an arm around her shoulders and pulled her close. "Sydney, this is my uncle, Kevin Micklesen, who works for the FBI in the Salt Lake City field division. He's my dad's brother."

Sydney returned the man's smile and grasped his outstretched hand. "It's nice to meet you."

"It's great to finally meet the woman who's keeping Justin here on his toes." He flashed Justin a teasing smile. "He needs somebody to keep him in line."

Just then one of the plainclothes agents inside the warehouse called for Agent Ramus, who excused himself and told them he'd be back in a minute.

They watched Ramus walk away, and when Justin turned back to his uncle, he noted his expression had sobered. "When I saw you over here talking to Ramus, I thought I'd come talk to you. Since you two are involved in this, I wanted you to know what was going on." He paused to gather his thoughts. "The DEA may not have anything yet to charge Robert Longhurst with, but as of about an hour ago, the FBI does."

Justin stared at his uncle in surprise. "What did you find?"

"I'm going to tell you a few things," Kevin told them, his voice low, "but this is off the record. You can't go public with this until after Longhurst's arrest. Even then, there are some aspects of this investigation we don't want to be made public."

"We understand," Sydney reassured him.

Kevin nodded. "Our Salt Lake City field division has been working with the agents in Nevada who raided Premiere Enterprises, and I'd been assigned to the case. But when I found out you and Sydney were connected with all this, it made me even more determined to get to the bottom of things."

Sydney's expression became hopeful. "And you have?"

Kevin sighed and shook his head. "Not to the bottom of it, no. Not by any means. It's beginning to look like Longhurst has been involved in so much criminal activity it could take months before we can formally charge him with everything. But thanks to you guys, we knew where to start."

As he looked at Justin and Sydney, there was pride in his eyes. "I can't tell you two how impressed I am at all the legwork you did to investigate all this. I talked with Detective Richardson in San Francisco several times to gather information, and he filled me in about everything you guys had been able to turn up—especially you, Sydney." He gave her a broad smile. "Sounds like you're a top-notch investigator."

"She's the best," Justin said proudly, exchanging a warm look with her.

"Well, it sounds like you two make a great team," Kevin agreed with a nod. "We've had our suspicions about Longhurst's involvement in things that have blown across our radar, in the past year especially, but we were never able to nail down anything to formally charge him with. Until now."

"What did you find?" Sydney asked, impatient to know the details.

"When we raided Premiere Enterprises in Nevada a couple of weeks ago, one of the first things we did was go through their financial records. Our guys turned up enough evidence to prove that the PR firm was being used to launder money."

"That was something we suspected," Justin said, listening intently.

"But that's not all. We found hundreds of suspicious money wires to and from the PR firm over the past couple of years. And remember when we arrested James Morrow, the CFO of Sandstone Enterprises, Longhurst's biggest conglomerate?"

Justin nodded.

"Well, Morrow was also the CFO for Premiere Enterprises. Since the PR firm was small, something like that wouldn't have been too unusual. But when all this went down, the FBI had enough evidence from the financial records of the PR firm to charge Morrow with money laundering. Morrow is denying any involvement in this, saying that Longhurst had always taken a special interest in managing the financial affairs of that particular company and saw to a lot of its accounts personally. But a large sum of money was wired into Terrence Smith's bank account through Premiere the same day Smith tried to gun you two down in the warehouse."

Justin flinched at the memory. Without thinking about it, he lifted a hand to rub the base of his skull where the bullet had nicked him, nearly taking his life. He knew that his uncle was aware of what had happened because he had called to check up on him a couple of times that first week he'd gotten back in town.

Sydney jumped in. "So somebody paid for the job through Premiere?"

Kevin inclined his head. "The authorities originally thought it was Morrow, but when they questioned Morrow about it, he said that Longhurst had personally approved that transfer into Smith's account, and that he didn't even realize that's what the money had been for. He'd just signed the paper-work, thinking it was a legitimate transaction."

Sydney's expression became grim. "So now we have proof. Longhurst was behind it."

Kevin's expression was equally as sober. "Yes. That's one of the things we're going to charge him with this morning when we arrest him."

"What else will you charge him with?" Justin asked.

"We also tracked large payments in Longhurst's name disguised as charity contributions to a man named Carlos Rojas, a known black-market art dealer in Colombia with connections to the Colombian New Council. We've been going through the records in the warehouse and we found names of buyers, along with shipment dates that correspond to an investiga-tion we've been handling over the past two years dealing with artifacts being smuggled out of South America. The information we've gathered indicates Longhurst has been stealing and smuggling those artifacts, mostly Mayan in nature, from the archaeological dig sites he's been funding the past two years."

"And making a fortune selling them on the black market," Justin chimed in. "Our source told us that."

Kevin nodded. "We'd suspected as much for the past couple of years, but we didn't have the proof we needed to confirm our suspicions. It was the list of buyers' names and the shipment dates we found this morning in the warehouse records that put the final nail in his coffin. We're waiting for a judge to sign the search warrants as we speak. We'll arrest Longhurst as soon as we have the warrants. Now that we have him, we want to make sure we play this by the books. We don't want him slipping through our fingers."

"Did you get search warrants for Longhurst's home as well as his office?"

"We did. Longhurst's wife is known to have an extensive collection of ancient civilization artifacts—Mayan and otherwise. She's an ancient civilizations professor, remember, and pre-Colombian life is a fascination of hers. We're bringing in some experts in the field to try to identify the pieces in her collection to determine if any of them were the ones reported as stolen from the digs."

"Yes, and it would have been easy for Longhurst to feign an interest in his wife's obsession, all the while gathering information about where to fund digs to acquire the artifacts to sell on the black market."

Sydney cringed. "If his wife is really innocent in all this, I'm sure she's going to be feeling awfully used."

"I'm sure she will," Kevin said solemnly.

It was quiet for a minute as they let the information sink in. "Thanks for letting us know what's going on," Justin told his uncle. "I think I'm still in shock. I mean, we suspected Longhurst was involved, but to finally have proof . . ." Sydney nodded in agreement.

"Just remember that a lot of that information is for your ears only," Kevin said. "We don't want certain aspects going public until we confirm some things, like what we learn from the searches of Longhurst's home and offices. The investigation will be ongoing for awhile, I suspect."

"We'll be careful what we write," Sydney assured him.

"Well, I need to be getting back to my team." Kevin nodded to a handful of men just inside the warehouse. "I'll probably talk to you two later today if I can hurry and wrap things up here."

"Oh, that's right. You guys are going to my parents' house for dessert." Justin turned to Sydney. "Since Kevin and his family were at his wife's parents' house for Thanksgiving, they're coming over to my folks' house for dessert tonight." Then his voice grew teasing. "Just think—more names for you to try to memorize."

Kevin laughed at Sydney's stricken expression and gave her arm a squeeze. "Don't worry, we're a forgiving bunch. I look forward to getting to know you a little better, Sydney. Maybe it'll help me figure out how you put up with this clown." He clapped Justin on the shoulder. "Good work, you two. It's because of all your hard work that Longhurst will be going to jail. Thank you." With that, he gave them a grateful wave and headed back to work.

After a moment, Sydney turned back to Justin and a grin started to spread across her face. "We did it!" she said with a squeal. "Can you believe it? Because of us, Longhurst is being *arrested*!"

Justin let out a celebratory yell of his own that caused several nearby heads to turn. Ignoring their onlookers, he grabbed Sydney in a bear hug and spun her around until they were both dizzy. Then he put her back on her feet and kissed her senseless.

When they finally pulled apart, breathless and laughing, Sydney's eyes sparkled with excitement as she smiled up at him. "Now are you sorry I woke you up at four o'clock this morning?"

Justin threw his head back and laughed. "Syd, if these are the kinds of stories we break when you wake me up at four in the morning, you can do it every day of the week. Now, let's find Agent Ramus and get our exclusive on the drug bust. Then we should get out of here. We have one heck of a story to write."

# CHAPTER 50

"I'll need it by the fifteenth at the latest," Longhurst grumped at his intern, watching as the young man nodded and scribbled the information on his notepad. "Now is there anything else? I've got some urgent business to attend to this morning." *Like trying to do damage control from the drug bust that went down several hours ago.*

His intern shook his head. "I have nothing else, Senator."

"Good."

As he picked up the stack of papers on his desk and thumped them into order, his jaw clenched at the reality of what he was facing this morning. He had to find something to tell his network of dealers who'd been expecting their shipments this morning. He still didn't know what he was going to say. At least there was nothing that would link him, personally, to the drugs.

"Take this proposal over to Gene's office and put it directly into his hands. If you leave it with his infernal assistant, he'll never get it. By the way, where is everybody? Doesn't anyone realize it's a work day?"

"A lot of the staff took today off since it's the day after Thanksgiving," the intern reported.

"A long weekend? That's ridiculous." Longhurst shook his head in disgust. "One day off wasn't enough for everyone?"

He handed the stack of papers to the well-dressed young man when a commotion sounded outside in the hall. His eyebrows drew together. *What in the world . . . ?*

The sound of arguing voices grew closer, and a moment later his office door was thrown open. Two uniformed police officers and a handful of men in conservative suits stood in the doorway. His receptionist and two of his staffers hovered behind the men in the hall, making continued sounds of protest at the intrusion.

Longhurst rose from his chair. "What's going on here?" he demanded. "You can't just barge in here and—"

"Senator Longhurst, you're under arrest," a man in a navy suit said as he crossed the room to stand in front of the desk. "You have the right to remain silent . . ."

Longhurst paled as the man continued to recite his Miranda rights. But then he rallied, his surging anger fueling his next words. "This is preposterous! I demand to know what's going on!"

"I'm Agent Ramus of the DEA, and this is Agent Micklesen with the FBI." Agent Ramus nodded toward a man in a black suit standing near the doorway. Then Agent Ramus gave a signal to one of the police officers, who stepped forward and walked around the corner of the desk.

Longhurst took one look at the handcuffs in the approaching officer's hands and took a hasty step back. "Now wait just a minute!" He shot a deadly glare at Agent Ramus. "What are you talking about? You can't be serious!" A glance around the room revealed several staffers gathered in his doorway next to his shaken intern, gawking at the scene unfolding before them. Nobody said another word as the officer stopped beside him and tried to reach for his hand. Longhurst jerked it away.

"Oh, I assure you, I'm very serious," Agent Ramus drawled, making another signal to the officer, who grabbed the senator by the upper arm with a firm hand and spun him toward the desk. The snap of the first cuff closing around his wrist was alarmingly loud in the silent room.

"This is ridiculous!" Longhurst blustered, indignant that such a scene was taking place in front of so many witnesses. "What are the charges?"

"Possession of narcotics with the intent to distribute," Ramus began, stepping closer. "Possession of stolen artifacts from archaeological dig sites with intent to sell them on the black market. And," he went on, stopping before the senator and fixing him with an unrelenting stare, "attempted murder. You ordered a hit on two reporters in San Francisco, did you not?"

Several sets of eyes widened as his staff stared at him in shock. *Deny everything,* came the thought.

"You have no proof of any of this!" he hollered as the officer clamped the second cuff around his other wrist.

"I have enough," Ramus ground out, giving him a cold stare. "And I'm about to find more." He lifted a folded document in his hand for Longhurst to see. "I have search warrants for your office and home—"

A brief flash of fear darted across Longhurst's face before he was able to compose it back into an indignant mask. "I didn't do anything! There must be some mistake . . ." he protested as the officer behind him grabbed his arm and gave him a little shove to get him moving.

"That's for a court to decide."

Longhurst struggled against the officer's unyielding grip as he was manhandled around the expensive Italian furniture in his office. "I'm a United States senator!" he yelled at the agents as they neared the doorway, where the staffers parted like the Red Sea before the entourage. "I'll have your jobs for this!"

Several other men were waiting in the hall, watching as the events unfolded. When Agent Ramus was satisfied Longhurst was under control, he turned to the man standing nearest him, who looked at Ramus expectantly.

"Take everything. We'll go through it later." Ramus turned to observe the staff members who were still standing in the hallway, looking more than a little shell-shocked and starting to whisper amongst themselves. "And have your team interview the staff thoroughly. Tell them not to overlook a single detail."

# CHAPTER 51

"Stop the presses!"

Sydney's exclamation brought Mike's head up from his paperwork with a jerk. But when he saw her standing dramatically in the doorway—stance wide, arms out, expression intense but with barely restrained mischief in her eyes—his face creased into a smile. "Sydney!"

Before Mike could say anything else, Justin rolled his eyes at Sydney's dramatic entrance and drawled, "Syd, you know as well as I do that nobody actually says that. It's just in the movies."

"Yeah, I know," she said, giving them both a sheepish smile and straightening up from her stance. "But it felt good to say."

Justin chuckled, Sydney's enthusiasm contagious. Apparently Mike thought so, too, because he laughed as he got to his feet and came around the corner of his desk. He greeted her with a fatherly hug. "Justin said you were flying in to spend Thanksgiving with him. But what are you two doing here?" He shot Justin a confused look. "Didn't you arrange for today off?"

"I did, but as Sydney decided to dramatize"—he rolled his eyes once more in Sydney's direction—"that was before the story of the year hit. Take a look."

Mike took the several typed pages Justin handed him. When he read the headline, his eyes widened in shock. "What's this?"

Sydney's eyes glowed with excitement. "Follow us. There's something you've got to see."

Mike hurried out of his office after them. They walked over to the area of the newsroom where a bank of televisions played the top stories on various news channels. They pointed to the one broadcasting CNN.

Mike's jaw dropped as the footage showed Longhurst, surrounded by several plainclothes agents and uniformed officers, being led out of an office building in handcuffs. The reporter on site didn't have many details, saying only that they would be forthcoming.

"Okay, what's going on?" Mike turned to Sydney and Justin and held up the papers in his hand. "And how do you have an article already written when CNN only has sketchy details?"

Justin beamed. "Sydney and I have the exclusive. My uncle, who's with the FBI's Salt Lake City field office, was in on certain aspects of the investigation. Because Sydney and I were directly involved, he filled us in on what was happening with the understanding that we can't print everything he told us because parts of the investigation are still ongoing. Even so, we have exclusive information from several other branches involved in the investigation, such as the DEA, so our story will be much more complete than any other paper, local or national, even after the press conferences are held by the agencies."

"Which means circulation is going to go through the roof. I love that." Mike grinned. "So how did all this happen?"

Unable to contain their excitement, Sydney and Justin rushed to tell Mike everything, their sentences tumbling together. They told him about meeting with Chaz on Wednesday morning, then going to see Agent Ramus. Then they filled him in on the sting operation, the seized drugs and arrests at the bust, and the things Justin's uncle had told them.

"That's incredible," Mike said, stunned, when they finished. "And what about this company you two were originally investigating? Marengo, was it? How does that all fit in?"

Sydney sighed. "We don't know for sure how it ties in. Longhurst's lists of corporate holdings stretches on forever. It could take a while to determine how everything is linked."

"The important thing," Justin chimed in, "is that Longhurst is in jail. We no longer have to look over our shoulders every time we step outside. It's over."

Sydney's face softened into a smile. "Yes, it is."

"Well, I'd better hurry and go through this," Mike said, holding up their article. "I want to make sure to get it in the next edition." He cocked an eyebrow at them and smiled. "I'm assuming you want joint bylines?"

Sydney laughed. "Of course."

"Speaking of that . . ." Justin gave Mike a look of mock accusation. "I can't believe you didn't tell me you'd hired Sydney. All those secretive smiles every time we talked about an article or something—you knew. How could you keep that from me?"

Mike let out a rumbling laugh. "I'll tell you, it wasn't easy." He clapped Justin on the shoulder and gave Sydney another wink. "Sydney, you're already an asset to this paper. Welcome to the *Tribune*."

"Thanks." Sydney smiled. "And thanks for keeping it a secret until I could tell Justin."

"You two just be happy, you hear?"

Justin nodded and pulled Sydney into a hug. "I think we can handle that."

# CHAPTER 52

Sydney reached into the back of the moving truck for one of the boxes, struggled with it for a moment, then staggered up the curb toward her new apartment building.

She couldn't believe she was finally here. The past couple of weeks had been chaotic. She'd spent her weekdays finishing up her pending stories at work and her nights and weekends packing. She'd been concerned at first about finding an apartment in Utah that she liked, but she needn't have worried. She and Justin had found the perfect place. The apartment was in a nice complex not far from Justin's townhouse and an easy drive to the *Tribune*. She loved the open floor plan and the larger-than-expected bedroom and bathroom.

Knowing everything was sorted out didn't make bidding farewell to her friends and colleagues in San Francisco any easier. A lump still formed in her throat whenever she thought of saying good-bye to Agnes.

*"Oh, Agnes, I'm going to miss you," she said as she hugged her neighbor. "I'm going to miss your fussing and your dinners, and even your silly little dog."*

*Agnes laughed. "I'm sure she'll miss you as much as I will."*

They'd made promises to stay in touch and said their last good-byes, and soon Sydney was on her way to Utah with Justin in their rented U-Haul, towing her car behind. Now they were here, and they had a full U-Haul to unpack.

With the large box in her arms mostly blocking her view, it threatened to tumble out of Sydney's hands when she stumbled on a crack in the sidewalk and collided with something solid.

A laugh let her know that the "something" was a person. The sound of Justin's voice filled her heart with warmth. "Sydney, you're deadly with that thing," he teased as he reached for the box. "Here, let me get that."

"I can get it," she protested.

"No, you can't," he insisted, taking the box from her and carrying it effortlessly. "You have your arm in a cast and shouldn't be doing this kind of thing. Besides, we have a lot of help."

Sydney glanced around, her heart full of gratitude, as she watched the many ward members bustling around who had shown up to welcome her to the ward and help her unload the truck. When she caught up with Justin on the stairs, he let go of the box with one arm so he could put his free hand on the small of her back to guide her up.

She smiled and rolled her eyes at his show of strength. "Show-off."

Justin laughed again. It was something he did a lot of these days.

They walked together to her second-floor apartment and into the living room crowded with unpacked boxes.

"Why don't you start unpacking the boxes in the kitchen, and I'll go finish helping the guys," Justin offered. "I'd be faster than you out there, and you're the only one who knows where you want your kitchen stuff."

"I can't argue with that." She walked over and lifted one of the smaller boxes marked KITCHEN from the top of the stack. "Besides, this won't take me very long. It's not like I ever bought a lot of pots and pans and utensils, since I never cooked."

Justin laughed. "Well, now that we're in the same city, I plan to remedy that."

"Oh, great." Sydney groaned. "That means more cooking lessons, doesn't it?"

"You bet it does."

Justin left the apartment to get another box from the truck, and Sydney rolled her eyes. "Maybe if I blow something up, he'll give up on me," she muttered.

"I heard that!" Justin called out to her from down the hall.

Sydney laughed and shook her head. Living near Justin was going to be more wonderful than she could have ever hoped for.

She was almost done unpacking the few dishes and pans she owned— and putting the glass canister for her peanut M&Ms on the counter—when Justin came bustling back through the door with an armload of boxes, a huge smile on his face.

"What?" she asked curiously.

He set the boxes down, hurried over to grab her hand, and dragged her toward the door. "Come with me. There's something I've got to show you."

Giggling at his childlike enthusiasm, she followed him into the hall, playfully demanding to know where they were going. Her questions were met only by a mischievous grin. He pulled her into the back stairwell and up the remaining few flights of stairs. Finally, they burst through the door and emerged onto the roof.

With a grand, sweeping motion of his outstretched arms, he gestured to their surroundings and the horizon. "Take a look at this, would you?"

Sydney let out a gasp. She'd always heard people complain about city life—smog, tall buildings, congested traffic. But clearly there was beauty to be found if only one knew where to look. And Justin had found just such a place.

The early evening sunlight glinted off the windows of the tall buildings in the distance, turning the cityscape into a wall of mirrors reflecting the beautiful pinks, yellows, and reds of the sunset. This sunset wasn't any less beautiful than the ones she had witnessed from her own balcony reflecting off the ocean's surf.

"Justin, it's wonderful," she whispered in awe. She walked to the edge of the roof and crossed her arms along the chest-high brick wall surrounding the space. Justin followed and stopped beside her, wrapping an arm around her.

For several long minutes, they stood together, gazing out at the sunset and savoring its beauty as the sun slipped lower and lower in the sky, leaving smudges of pastel colors in its wake. Soon the pastels deepened in hue, becoming oranges and reds and purples, until finally the sun sank beneath the horizon and the sky dimmed in color to a more even, inky blue.

As they watched the last of the colors fade, Justin drew her closer. "I can't tell you how great this feels to be standing here with you, knowing you're still going to be here tomorrow."

"I feel the same way." Sydney snuggled into his side. "It was hard to leave San Francisco, but I know this move was the right thing for me."

A breeze picked up, causing Sydney to shiver. Snow was predicted that night—the city's first of the season. She was surprised to discover that she was actually looking forward to it. It would be her first snowstorm.

She smiled. There were a lot of firsts in her life lately. And she was loving every minute.

Justin nudged her, rousing her from her contented state. "Come on. I have one more thing to show you."

Sydney laughed at his continuing enthusiasm as he pulled her back toward the stairs. "You're just full of surprises today, aren't you?"

"Of course." He grinned back at her over his shoulder. "You're in a new city. I couldn't let you be bored, could I?"

They went down the flights of stairs and reached the apartment just in time to meet up with one of the guys from the ward setting the very last box in Sydney's living room. They chatted with him for a few minutes, then he let them know everybody was heading out. They thanked him profusely as he left, and then they were alone.

Justin's eyes held a mischievous gleam as he took her hand and led her down the hall. For the first time that afternoon, Sydney noticed that her bedroom door had been conspicuously shut. Her curiosity mounting, she watched as Justin twisted the doorknob and pushed the door open. When he did, Sydney's mouth fell open.

The wild array of unassembled furniture that had cluttered the bedroom that morning was gone. Her bed had been set up and made, and her furniture had been arranged the way she'd told Justin days ago she'd wanted.

"Ta-dah!" he sang, opening his arms and gesturing at the room the same way he'd done on the roof a short time before.

"Justin, when did you do all this?" she asked, stunned, as she gazed around the immaculate room in wonder.

"This afternoon when you and my mom ran to get curtains and things. My dad and brothers all helped, so we were able to whip this room into shape pretty quickly."

She shook her head and turned to step into his arms. "Justin, you are amazing. Thank you."

"You're welcome," he murmured against her hair. "I know the rest of your apartment is still in a state of chaos, but I wanted you to have at least your room finished so you could sleep well tonight and enjoy some order."

She smiled and tipped her face up to his. "I think you are the most thoughtful man alive."

Justin beamed. "Oh, by the way," he said, his gaze falling on her dresser in the corner. "I took the liberty of unpacking a couple of things into your dresser. I hoped it might make you a little less homesick."

Curious about the twinkle in his eyes, she crossed the room to her dresser and opened the top drawer. Inside were two large, hardcover scrapbook albums, one on top of the other. Surprised, she lifted out the first one and opened the cover.

A gasp escaped her lips when she saw the pictures inside. There was one of Carl Langley and Jennifer and her other coworkers standing in the *Chronicle* newsroom, holding a banner in front of them that said, "We love you, Sydney! We'll miss you!"

Tears sprang unbidden to her eyes as she noticed that Justin had tucked that same banner into the front sleeve of the album. She pulled it out and saw that everyone had signed it, saying nice things about the time they'd spent working with her and wishing her well.

"How did you do this?" she whispered, her voice choked with emotion.

Justin took a step closer, peering over her shoulder with her at the photograph. The look on his face told her how touched he was by her reaction. "I told Carl what a tough time you were having with the thought of leaving everybody, and we came up with this. You talk about him being hard-nosed, but it's obvious he has a soft spot for you."

She smiled. "I know he does. That's one of the things that made it so hard to leave."

Justin squeezed her shoulder. "I know." After a moment, he urged, "Turn the page."

She did, and this time she saw a series of pictures taken of her old apartment, Jennifer, Agnes, and even Princess. Sydney's heart ached as she realized just how much she missed her friends and the familiar places of her old home.

Turning the page, she let out another gasp. The next dozen or so pages were filled with pictures she'd collected over the years of her parents and Kate, as well as the friends she'd had growing up.

"Agnes tipped me off that you stored a bunch of pictures in a box on the shelf in your hall closet. She helped me sort through them, and we put in the ones we thought might mean the most to you."

Sydney's tears finally spilled over as the happy memories from her early youth stared up at her from the pages. "It's perfect," she whispered.

She turned the last page, then closed the album. With tears streaming down her face, she turned and threw her arms around Justin. "Thank you," she said, her voice thick with emotion. "For understanding how important this last chapter of my life has been to me."

"You're welcome." His arms tightened around her as he hugged her back. "I know what a big decision this was for you to make, and it means all the more to me, knowing the sacrifice you made."

"It wasn't so much a sacrifice, really," she said, pulling back to wipe the tears from her cheeks. "I just knew this was the next step I needed to take in my life. And as much as I'll miss what I've left behind, I know I'm going to love what I have right here even more."

"I'm glad you said that," he said with a grin, stepping back with purpose, "because you haven't opened the other album yet."

"There's more?"

He nodded, his eyes twinkling. "There is."

She stepped back to the dresser and reached again into the top drawer for the other hardbound album. Setting it on top of the dresser, she opened it and smiled with delight. The picture Justin's mother had taken of her and

Justin not long ago as they'd cuddled together on the porch swing stared back at her. Justin had blown it up and inserted it into the sleeve on the first page.

She traced a finger along Justin's smiling face in the photograph. "Your mom was right. We really did look cute all cuddled up like that on the swing, didn't we? I guess I can see why she darted back in for that camera of hers."

"Yeah, well, thanks to Mom, my photo album is jam-packed, while I'm sure yours has always been a little lacking. I wanted to make up for that."

She smiled in appreciation and turned the page, seeing pictures of Diane and Tom, Justin's brothers and sisters and their kids at a family get-together, and even a picture taken of Brad and Mike inside the newsroom, working.

"The other album is of your past," he explained. "This one is of your future—one that I hope you'll always let me be a part of."

"Oh, Justin, of course you will be," she told him, leaning over to give him a kiss. Then she turned back to the album and turned the next page. When she did, she froze.

Taped to the next page, which was devoid of pictures, was a large, glittering diamond solitaire ring.

Her exclamation died in her throat. For several long moments she felt unable to move, unable to breathe. Her heart hammered so loudly in her chest she was sure Justin could hear it. When she was finally able to regain control of her emotions, she turned to Justin and found herself staring into his soulful green eyes with her own tear-filled ones.

"Justin . . . ?"

With trembling hands, Justin reached for hers and got down on one knee in front of her. "Sydney, my life changed dramatically the day I met you. I knew instantly that there was something special about you, and every second I spend with you confirms that's true. You are the person I thought I'd never find. And now that I've found you, I never want to spend another day without you, without knowing you'll be mine forever. Sydney, will you marry me?"

Tears began to stream down her cheeks once more as she stared down at the man kneeling before her. "Oh, Justin," she managed to whisper past the lump in her throat. She opened her mouth to say more but found herself at a loss for words. Finally, she dropped to her knees before him and threw her arms around his neck.

"So, is that a yes?" Justin asked, his smile curving against her cheek.

Her shoulders started to shake, and he pulled back to look into her face.

Instead of crying, she was laughing. She nodded vigorously, a large smile splitting her face. "Yes, that's a yes."

Justin's face lit up with a look of pure joy, and a sheen of tears misted his eyes. Sydney's heart felt as though it would burst as Justin cradled her face in his hands and leaned down to kiss her tenderly. It was a kiss full of love and promise—a promise of many wonderful tomorrows with him.

When he finally released her, he drew her to her feet. With one arm still securely around her waist, he reached for the ring taped to the page of the album and pulled it off carefully. He turned back to her, his eyes shining. His hands still shaking, he reached for her left hand and slipped the ring onto her finger.

Sydney giggled with delight when he released her fingers, and she stretched her hand out in front of her to better admire the shimmering diamond. Justin held her against him, his cheek pressed against hers, as they both enjoyed the sight of his ring on her finger.

"Oh, Justin, I'm so happy," Sydney breathed, tears glistening on her cheeks. "Agnes told me she thought it was only a matter of time before we got engaged, but I wasn't sure I wanted to believe her. I mean, I figured it was going to happen eventually, but . . ." She broke off. "It just makes me feel like everything has fallen into place."

"It has." He turned her toward him and smiled. "And I want you to think of this move here as a new beginning . . . the beginning of our life together."

Sydney tipped her head back to look up into the familiar warm, green eyes she'd grown to love so much in such a short amount of time.

*A new beginning,* Justin had said.

She thought about that. Once upon a time, beginnings had scared her. There had been too many of them in her life, and not necessarily good ones. But this time . . . this time she knew things were going to be different. She had no doubt that her life here with Justin was going to be wonderful.

"A new beginning," she repeated in a contemplative whisper. Then she met Justin's tender gaze, and a slow smile spread across her face. "I can hardly wait."

# About the Author

Erin Klingler grew up in northern California and graduated from Ricks College with an associate's degree in preschool education. When she's not shuttling her kids to their activities or working part-time from home as a medical transcriptionist, she loves to indulge in her two favorite pastimes—reading and writing. She never goes anywhere without a book in her purse and her trusty eBook reader that she uses to download her current works and edit them while sitting through kids' soccer practices or at red lights. Her passion for writing romantic suspense comes from a penchant for television shows that mix romance with criminal investigation. She loves writing bad guys almost as much as she loves writing romance. In her spare time, she loves to decorate homes, sew, design Web sites, and run errands in her classic yellow 1979 Volkswagen Beetle convertible, affectionately named "Tweety."